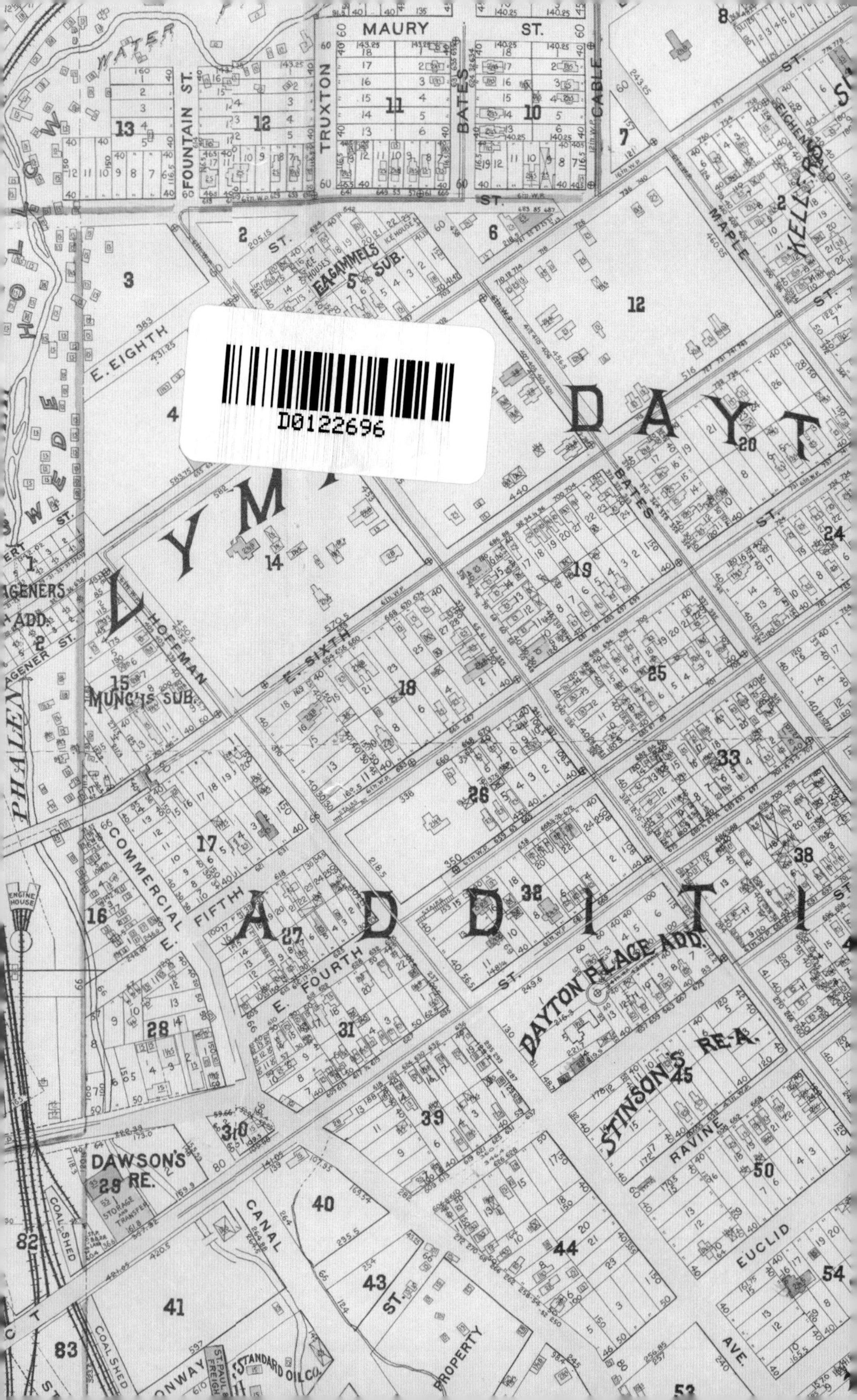

LYMAN DAYTON ADDITION
MAURY ST.
TRUXTON
BATES
CABLE
FOUNTAIN ST.
WATER
E. EIGHTH
E. SIXTH
E. FIFTH
E. FOURTH
HOFFMAN
COMMERCIAL
MAPLE
EICHENWALD
KELLY RD.
PHALEN
WAGENER ST.
WAGENERS ADD.
MUNCH'S SUB.
E.A. GAMMELS SUB.
ICE HOUSES
ICE HOUSE
DAYTON PLACE ADD.
STINSON'S RE-A.
RAVINE
EUCLID
AVE.
DAWSON'S RE.
STORAGE AND TRANSFER
COAL SHED
ENGINE HOUSE
CANAL ST.
PROPERTY
STANDARD OIL CO.
ST. PAUL FREIGHT
D0122696

# SWEDE HOLLOW

# SWEDE HOLLOW

A Novel

Ola Larsmo

Translated by Tiina Nunnally

*University of Minnesota Press*
*Minneapolis*

Endpapers: From *Donnelley's Atlas of the City of St. Paul, Minnesota, Volume 1* (1892). Swede Hollow, along Phalen Creek, is near the center of this map. Map drawn by Roger H. Pidgeon. Courtesy of the John R. Borchert Map Library, University of Minnesota.

Frontispiece: Swede Hollow, circa 1910. Photograph by Albert Charles Munson. Courtesy of the Minnesota Historical Society.

The University of Minnesota Press gratefully acknowledges financial support from the Swedish Arts Council for the translation of this book.

The University of Minnesota Press gratefully acknowledges the generous assistance provided for the publication of this book by the Hognander Family Foundation.

*Swede Hollow* was first published in Swedish by Albert Bonniers Förlag, Sweden. English translation published by arrangement with Nordin Agency AB, Sweden.



Published by the University of Minnesota Press
111 Third Avenue South, Suite 290
Minneapolis, MN 55401-2520
http://www.upress.umn.edu

ISBN 978-1-5179-0451-7 (hc) — ISBN 978-1-5179-0452-4 (pb)

A Cataloging-in-Publication record for this book is available from the Library of Congress.

Printed in the United States of America on acid-free paper



25 24 23 22 21 20 19 10 9 8 7 6 5 4 3 2 1

For Rita

As I went walking I saw a sign there
And on the sign it said "No Trespassing."
But on the other side it didn't say nothing,
That side was made for you and me.
—WOODY GUTHRIE, "This Land Is Your Land"

## EMIGRANT CONTRACT

Between C. W. Hällström, authorized emigrant agent in Göteborg, and the emigrants listed below.

I, C. W. Hällström, do bind myself herewith, in the manner detailed below, to convey from Göteborg to New York in North America the Klar family, consisting of five persons, in return for an already fully paid and received fee of 118 Swedish kronor, which includes, upon arrival in America, the usual disembarkation fees.

# I

*Queenstown, Cork*
June 1897

ANNA KLAR FOUND IT STRANGE that the fog lay so thick over the sea and land even though the sun was already up and clearly visible in the sky. She hadn't seen anything like it since she was a child. And she recalled, right then and there, a morning when she was very young and had gone out before getting properly dressed. At that moment she'd imagined that she could gather up the heavy fog like an armful of wool she might hold close and carry back to show her mother. Even though she was freezing, she had gone all the way out to the ditch, which was a good distance beyond the fence. In the fog she saw a couple of long-legged silhouettes, and she took several steps forward with her arms spread wide but didn't manage to clasp anything at all. In the winter-hardened field stood two birds, tall as men, with slender necks that slowly, as if in a dream, swiveled in her direction. Their eyes were shiny black buttons. She looked at them and then turned and silently ran back to the house. She had never seen such big birds before. Later she found out they were cranes.

Now, inside the white fog, Anna could hear the shriek of gulls. She and the others sat in silence along the rail of the vessel's foredeck, where they had gained free access after the seamen had opened the hatch and rolled away the sailcloth that otherwise covered the opening. Although it was early June, the morning was unexpectedly chilly. She was already hungry and would soon return below deck to wake the others, who seemed to have settled into the sort of clammy sleep that can come over people in stuffy, cramped spaces with not enough air. The panic she had initially felt when she opened her eyes in the stifling darkness had slowly dissipated out here under the white vault of the sky.

She was sitting with three of the older women whose names she hadn't yet learned and whose language she didn't speak. She thought they might be from England. Or maybe Germany. They didn't say a word as they looked toward land, their eyes focused on something she couldn't see. One of them was smoking a pipe. All three had dark shawls draped over their shoulders. They had looked up and nodded, neither friendly nor unfriendly, before turning their gaze once more toward the invisible coastline.

A blast from the big steam whistle high overhead shattered the silence. And as if the sound had somehow set the air moving, a very tall and pointed church tower took shape out of nothing.

This was her time alone. Soon she would clamber down the worn wooden ladder, blackened from thousands of hands, to the steerage deck and make sure the others were awake for the morning porridge. The seagulls glided out of the fog on rigid outspread wings, looking exactly like the gulls back home. So far nothing had happened. This was the first morning after they had left England behind.

"There should be five cups," said Gustaf. "We bought five."

He peered at Anna from under the lock of hair falling into his face. Elisabet and Ellen stood behind her, each of them clinging to the waistband of her apron, as she'd taught them to do when onboard ship. Carl lay motionless on the mattress, but he was awake now, looking at them expectantly, waiting to see what would happen next.

Again she searched the jute sack at the foot of the mattress, running one hand along the outside, the other rummaging through bundles of clothing all the way down to where Gustaf's concertina lay hidden. Nothing. She felt his gaze on her back, unwavering and, it seemed to her, more and more stern, while out of the corner of her eye she saw the line growing longer at the foot of the ladder. They were going to be the very last in line. Then she noticed part of the straw mattress sticking up next to Carl's head. She turned away, without meeting Gustaf's eyes, and reached down. Her fingertips touched metal.

"Here it is," Anna said, keeping her tone even. Gustaf nodded curtly and headed for the line of people. The girls stayed where they were, holding on to her apron. She picked up Carl in her arms and handed him his cup. He must have been the one to hide it there. He'd grown so big, it seemed almost as if he'd done nothing but grow since they'd left Göteborg. The boy took the cup, then turned to look over her shoulder, searching for his father. They all went to join him in line.

Behind her stood one of the older women she recognized from the crossing to England. Mrs. Lundgren was a widow traveling with her son, a dark-haired young man named David. Anna didn't know Mrs. Lundgren's first name. She seemed a retiring sort of person.

"You should tie them together," Mrs. Lundgren said now. "Ask the steward for one of those leather straps. There's already a hole for them in the handle, but they don't give out the straps because they want you to pay for them. Tie the cups together so they won't get lost again. The same goes for the bowls and spoons."

Anna felt herself blushing. She didn't know how the old woman had discerned their problem, although of course the door to "1A—married quarters," as their section was called, had stood open. She mutely nodded her thanks and then pushed forward in line behind Gustaf as she wondered what to say to the steward and what "strap" might be called in English. She felt the girls' hands holding tight to her apron and tugging in opposite directions, like a pair of weights that kept her balanced and steady on the slightly sloping deck.

Breakfast, which was served out on the foredeck, consisted of porridge and bread, still quite fresh and presumably brought from shore. Weak coffee was also served with the food. In a few days there probably won't be much of either, Anna thought, trying to get the girls to drink their coffee, even though it wasn't something they were used to. Elisabet made faces at the taste.

Gustaf had sat down on a bench and was holding Carl on his lap, putting his own big cap on the boy's head. It slid down over Carl's eyes, making him laugh. Anna wrapped her shawl tighter around her shoulders and went over to the rail. The fog had gone. The church on shore was now clear to see, and what she'd earlier taken for an unusually pointed tower was actually just the beginning of one. The slender spire was still encased in scaffolding. In front of the church's gray façade stood a row of small buildings, alternately brown and gray and almost impossible to distinguish from the rock face behind. And on their way out to the *Majestic* were two small, overloaded boats in which black-clad passengers were crowded all the way forward into the bow. They looked like insects, and everywhere she could see their big rucksacks, which some people were actually holding over the side, probably because every last inch of space had already been taken.

Anna wasn't happy about their reaching the ship. Only now did she realize why there were a few empty bunks in their section of the married quarters; she had thought they were simply lucky. She felt herself breathing faster, and even though it was getting colder, beads of sweat formed along her hairline.

"There certainly are a lot of them. It's going to get crowded."

She glanced over at Inga, who was from the west coast of Sweden. She'd talked to her during the train ride from Hull. Inga had dark hair and brown eyes and was no doubt a few years younger than she was. Inga had explained that she was traveling alone, headed for St. Paul in

Minnesota to "find a place." It wasn't clear whether this meant a job she hoped to land or a need for greater space. She was short and plump and always wore a black apron with a floral pattern.

"And we probably won't be able to talk to them," said Inga. "I've heard the Irish sometimes speak English, but more often they rely on their own language, which is impossible to understand. Do you speak any English?"

Anna shook her head, a bit unsettled by the young woman's talkative nature. "A few words," she said then. "But where we're headed, I think we can manage fine with Swedish."

"Maybe so," said Inga. "Where is it you're headed?"

"Gustaf has several different places in mind," she replied. "I suppose we'll probably go to Minnesota. But he also says there's a shoe factory in New York, so maybe we'll stay there for a while until we make enough money to move on."

Inga shook her head.

"Everything is more expensive in New York," she said. "You'll see. Some people get stuck there because they think they'll be able to earn enough wages to save up for traveling farther. But if you go just a little farther inland, it's easier to find work and things aren't so costly."

"How do you know all this?" Anna asked, hoping she didn't sound too nosy.

"My cousin has lived in both New York and Minnesota," said Inga. "She sent letters home and told us about everything. But now she's back in Sweden, and she helped pay part of my ticket."

The sound of voices and boat motors was getting closer, and Anna saw that both ferries had begun to slow as they came alongside the hull of the *Majestic.*

"It's probably best if we go below," said Inga. "Bring your children and husband and sit on your bunks. When the newcomers see how many you are, maybe they won't spread out so much."

Inga nodded and then headed for the far hatch, which led down to the quarters for unmarried women. The younger woman seemed to take everything in stride, while Anna couldn't get herself to budge. She swayed back and forth on the balls of her feet as she tried to keep her balance on the unsteady deck. Yet the ship still lay at anchor, and the inlet was calm, the surface of the water merely rippled by a light wind from shore. A week, she thought, eight days. It will go fast. She repeated these words to herself several times, like a litany, and the cadence finally got her moving. Behind her Anna heard the thudding of boat motors, and the sharp clang of a church bell. Voices speaking unfamiliar languages glided across the water, answered by the sailors on deck who began lowering the gangplank.

The family who took the unoccupied bunks had eight members, and their name was Gavin. That much she understood. Five of them—the parents and three little girls—were quartered in the married section, while the two older sons and a daughter were housed in the sections for bachelors and single women fore and aft. They protested when the steward said they had to be separated, and that led to a heated exchange. Anna and her family merely sat on their bunks the whole time, pretending not to pay attention. She saw Gustaf's jaw tense as he clenched his teeth without saying a word.

The steward led away the three youths, still protesting, and then the father of the family, a short, pale man with a mustache and unruly brown hair, turned to Gustaf and said something in English. It sounded like a jocular remark, but Gustaf merely shook his head. The man gave a brief nod and turned back to his own family, which now occupied a large portion of the long and narrow space. Anna felt as if it were her family that was now quartered with the Gavin clan instead of the other way around.

There were no portholes, which made the space stuffy and sweltering. Onboard were eight hundred people traveling in steerage class. Inga had told her that. Down here below the foredeck, they numbered close to three hundred, while there were many more in the other third-class section in the stern, even though the space was about the same size. Anna refused to think about what that must be like; it wasn't something she could even investigate, because the section for cabin passengers was located in between, with locked gates on either side.

There were people everywhere, but before they docked at Queenstown she had thought they would have part of the between-deck to themselves. That was no longer the case. In their section of the quarters for married people, there were now thirty adults, and she awoke every morning with a pounding headache and a growing sense of panic. The girls, who slept with her in the same bunk, were restless too, constantly kicking and wriggling. Later she would ask herself whether she'd slept at all during the crossing. Some of the Finns at the far end had hung up an old, tattered sheet on the other side of the doorway that led to the ladder, partitioning off the space and creating a semblance of privacy. But that left her family on the other side and alone with the Gavins, who talked far into the night. It was mostly the mother who talked. She was a small, thin woman who always wore a black shawl as she carried the youngest daughter in her arms. She would subject her husband to endless torrents of words. Eventually he would snarl a retort and then try to escape by going up on deck or turning over in his bunk. Anna had no idea what they were saying. And even if she had understood English, she didn't think that was the language the woman was speaking. Her harangues were filled with hissing sounds, rising and falling in tone. It sounded a bit like Finnish, but it wasn't. She was able to recognize spoken Finnish and English, but that was the extent of her knowledge. The Gavin little girls seemed to be always hungry, and they would complain long after night had fallen. Only the youngest would remain quiet when the mother nursed the child in her bunk. Then a certain calm would settle over the space.

Anna would lie in bed with her daughters next to her and listen to the Finnish voices on the other side of the stained sheet. And she would count the days.

The food onboard was not as bad as she'd heard it would be, but it was unspeakably dreary. Always potatoes and carrots, boiled too long, and tough pieces of meat that had been cut up and simmered. All of it was served along with the same bread and coffee they had for breakfast, with the previous day's meat and potatoes mixed together in a big pot. None of it tasted of much, but at least it was a hot meal. Inga said it was called Irish stew, and the Irish passengers onboard ate it with gusto. But as they sat at the long, rough table mid-ship eating their food, Anna was already dreading having to wash the dishes. That and using the toilet were the worst moments of the day for her. The girls always ate slowly, and she often held Carl on her lap, feeding him pieces of potato, so they were usually the last to finish. By then the hot dish water in the trough on deck would have gone cold, and it was transformed into a glistening greenish soup of potato peels and gristly scraps of meat with bits of fat floating on the surface. She would stick their plates into the water, one after the other, barely dipping them in for a moment, and then wipe them off with her hand. Ellen tried to be helpful and follow her example, peering up at her mother to see if she was doing it properly. Then they would set the plates against the side of the bunk to air dry, but the dishes tipped over whenever the ship rolled.

Gustaf was usually among the first to get up after eating. He would try to disappear as much as was possible in the limited space allotted to the steerage passengers. They could go halfway mid-ship before coming to the locked gates that led to the section for cabin passengers. They could also go forward to the bow, where the men gathered to smoke whenever the wind wasn't blowing from that direction. Gustaf was getting increasingly restless. Sometimes he tried to start up a conversation with crew members if they had a few minutes to spare. He did his best to learn some English words from them, and occasionally Anna saw him sharing a laugh with one of the deckhands or the steward. After one visit midship, Gustaf came back with some leather straps, which he'd managed to talk someone into giving him without charging a fee. Then he sat on the bunk and deftly tied their plates and cutlery together in an ingenious way so that they could be taken apart without undoing the knots. She'd seen this trick before, which involved tying various big knots that could be twined together. It took Gustaf fifteen minutes to get the task done. Then his restlessness returned.

They were sitting on the foredeck. A cold wind had started blowing, but no one wanted to go below as long as there was still some daylight. All the people around Anna were crowded together, sitting on whatever they could find, like hens in a chicken coop. In the gathering dusk she could see what looked like a mist of body heat rising up from those seated across from her with their backs to the west. The girls were quietly playing a game that involved hopping on one leg around each other while counting to themselves; when they reached a certain number they would grab each other's hands. Some of the Irish children stood nearby, watching, though not wanting to appear overly interested. Carl was sitting on Gustaf's lap, but now he'd started to squirm. When Gustaf set him down, the boy clung to his father's leg and wanted to be lifted up again. His whole face contorted into a plaintive mask. He was growing tired, and any moment now he would start to whine. Anna got ready to stand up and take him below. But not yet. She was still sitting there when Inga came over and sat down beside her.

"It's getting really cold," the younger woman said.

She merely nodded.

"We're headed far to the north. I've read that at this time of year we might actually see icebergs."

At first Anna didn't reply, simply wondered where Inga got all her information.

"Where did you read about that?" she asked at last, just for something to say.

"I got a book for emigrants from the agent. Didn't you get one?"

"Maybe Gustaf has it somewhere."

For a moment Inga sat in silence, but then she said in a more serious tone, "Have the two of you given more thought to where you'll go?" She pushed back a lock of hair that had escaped from under the shawl draped over her head.

"We haven't had a chance to talk about it yet. There's been so much to do." When Anna said that, she felt her stomach lurch. The stench from the women's privy gusted toward them on the wind. And yet, she thought, so far I haven't felt the slightest bit seasick.

"Well, you should," said Inga. "I mean, you have a few days to think about it. But maybe we should talk to some of the others. Together, I mean. Because you have to decide where you're going before we dock. You have to say where you're headed."

The smell was getting worse. Anna was keeping half an eye on Carl, who was squirming more and more on his father's lap. But part of her wanted to stay and listen to what Inga had to say.

"Who do you think we should talk to?" she asked now.

"I was thinking of starting with Mrs. Lundgren and her son David. They're going to St. Paul in Minnesota. David's brother is already there. He has a job with the railroad."

Anna wondered what Inga's real intentions were. The young woman had deliberately sought her out and seemed to have some purpose in mind. But right now it was so nice merely to sit and listen to her talking. Inga clearly had goals and plans. It felt somehow liberating to listen to her, almost as if listening to music.

"That's where you're going too, isn't it?"

Inga nodded.

"So are you suggesting that we should go there? Gustaf has talked about both Minnesota and New York. But he has mostly worked in shoe factories, so . . ."

Inga quietly waited for Anna to go on.

She ended up saying something different from what she'd planned. "Until he was let go, that is." Then she fell silent. Yet Inga didn't seem to pay much attention to what she'd just said.

"I think you should talk to the Lundgrens. They know a lot about St. Paul, because of the letters they've received from David's older brother. He's told them about places to live and where to find work. If there's a shoe factory, they might know about that too."

*Minnesota. New York.* They were nothing but words in Anna's head, words without pictures. She'd seen a sketch of the Statue of Liberty in a newspaper, and the same drawing on a poster at the harbor area in Göteborg. Otherwise the names conjured up no images in her mind. *St. Paul.* Carl wriggled out of Gustaf's grip and fell to the deck, though he didn't land particularly hard. Even so, he scrunched up his eyes and opened his mouth to what was certain to be an angry howl.

"Let's talk more later," Anna said as she quickly got to her feet.

Then she swept up the boy and headed for the ladder to go below, holding against her shoulder his warm and hard little body, now trembling with sobs. The sea was a leaden black beneath an equally dark gray cloud cover. It was their second night.

About the crossing on the *Majestic,* Carl would remember only this: how he'd fallen and landed hard on the rough, gray planks of the deck where the varnish was completely worn away except in the cracks. Gray and brown and a sudden white pain. That would be his first memory. Along with being carried beneath the high, dark vault of the railway tunnel and out into a heavy snowfall. Both memories seemed to follow closely upon each other, with no distance from one to the other. Strangely enough, he remembered nothing at all of the big fire that took place in between.

Anna never understood where they'd gotten hold of the liquor. As far as she knew, none could be purchased onboard unless you were a cabin passenger. But the next evening the steerage deck was crowded with shouting people, and a brawl broke out in the forward section reserved for bachelors, on the other side of the central passageway's endlessly long "dining table" made of unpainted boards. Raucous voices yelled in Finnish and other languages, followed by loud thuds as men were repeatedly shoved against the wooden wall, along with the sound of bottles shattering and glass skittering across the deck. Then someone came running into their section, screaming shrilly. It was one of the Gavin girls. She was crying and calling for her mother. The woman, whose name Anna hadn't yet learned, simply handed over her youngest child before hitching up her skirts and following her daughter out to the central passageway where a man's voice bellowed nonstop, with equal parts anger and pure terror.

There Anna sat, holding on her lap a stranger's child, who stared up at her without fear in her alert green eyes. The little girl was wrapped in a gray woolen shawl, and on her head she wore a white crocheted cap.

With a great deal of noise Mr. Gavin abruptly came in, half carrying and half dragging his son, who was draped over his back. Behind them came Mrs. Gavin and the eldest daughter, who had placed a supportive hand on her brother's shoulder. She was crying soundlessly, openmouthed.

The young man's shirt was dark across the chest, and he held one hand pressed against his shoulder. The blood was coming from his arm.

They laid him down on the lower bunk. Mr. Gavin took a clay jug from under the bed and poured something on his son's outstretched arm, making the boy swear and try to get away, but his mother and sister held him in place. Before the women's backs blocked her view, Anna caught a glimpse of a long, ragged wound reaching up to the crook in his arm. Dark blood was still gushing out. The mother ripped a pillowcase in strips and wrapped them around his arm. The sister squatted down and spoke to her brother in a soothing tone, the way she might talk to a family pet. Then the father held up his son's arm. Blood was already seeping through the improvised bandage. Anna turned away and closed her eyes tight. She didn't want to see any more blood.

She opened her eyes when she felt someone sit down on the mattress next to her. It was Gustaf. She hadn't noticed him come in.

"What a damn ruckus out there," he said quietly. "The steward arrived and brought a couple of sailors to help him. They've seized one of the Finnish boys. I don't know what's going to happen to him, but he's just as drunk as that boy over there."

He motioned toward the pale and sweaty young Gavin boy, who was now peering up at his bandaged arm, which his father held pressed against the head of the bunk.

The youngest Gavin daughter squirmed a bit as she lay on Anna's lap, so she looked down at the child. The girl reached up a hand to grab her hair, seemingly unaffected by all the nearby commotion. Things were settling down. Mrs. Gavin stood with her forehead pressed against the edge of the upper bunk, muttering to herself words that sounded like a prayer: *sé do bheatha a Mhuire atá lán de ghrásta tá an Tiarna leat.*

If not for the bloody bandage visible inside the bunk, it might have been an idyllic tableau. No one said a word. And Anna breathed a sigh of relief as the child grabbed hold of her thumb with her strong little fingers. She was ashamed to admit that her sense of relief came from knowing that Gustaf clearly hadn't been involved in the brawl.

That was the only incident to occur during the crossing. That night the wind picked up, and the *Majestic* changed course so as to sail more directly into the wind, which might delay their arrival by as much as a day, or so the steward had said to someone. Yet it did little to ease the seasickness many were suffering. Anna noted with surprise that she remained largely unaffected.

The stench of vomit spread over the entire between-deck, and there was the constant sound of people moaning in incomprehensible languages. Sometimes there were no words at all. Gustaf was able to stay on his feet, but he was even less vocal than usual. They took turns sitting with the children, who lay on the bunks, pale and whimpering. Anna went to get water from the big tank mid-ship and immediately fell into a wordless argument with the steward, who didn't want to let her use her own cup. Everyone was supposed to use the cup hanging on a string from the tank. Without knowing exactly how she did it, Anna managed to convince him the water was for her children. He then allowed her to fill her enameled metal cup and take the water back, carefully holding the cup in both hands. She concentrated on keeping steady in order to counterbalance the rolling motion of the ship and avoid spilling any water. Before Anna reached their quarters she began feeling a little dizzy. I wonder if this is what it feels like to be seasick, she thought. But the feeling subsided as soon as she looked up and no longer kept her eyes fixed on the rippling water in the cup. The children would take only a sip, and Carl vomited as soon as he swallowed the water, which rose up in his throat and ran down his chin. Gustaf waved her away, signaling that she shouldn't worry about them. She should go out on deck. Mostly to get out of the way, she did as he wished.

The passageway was filled with people listlessly lying on the floor. Some of them had vomited as they lay there, too lethargic to get cleaned up. Anna wondered if the situation was the same on the cabin deck. In her mind she pictured women wearing elegant clothing spattered with vomit lying next to each other on red carpets, but she quickly dismissed the thought. Holding her breath, she climbed up the ladder and pushed aside the sailcloth covering the hatch.

The sky was a dark gray swiftly turning black. The sea was surging and heaving in every direction. The foredeck, normally teeming with people, was pleasantly deserted and rinsed clean, gleaming in the nebulous dim light. She saw only one other person on deck, wearing a dark shawl over her head and shoulders. At first she thought it was one of the Irish women, but then she recognized Inga. The young woman was sitting in a nook that offered the only shelter, beneath the wall of the bridge and the door to the women's privy, which thank goodness had been properly latched from the outside. Otherwise the door had a tendency to fly open whenever the ship rolled. Holding on to the rope that acted as a handrail, she made her way over to Inga, who looked as if she was feeling the effects of seasickness but had nevertheless ventured outside to get some fresh air.

At first Anna didn't speak, merely held on to the rope and stared out at the sea. This was nothing like looking at the ceaselessly rolling waves from shore. Here there was no specific direction. The water seemed to pour in from all sides. The ship rose up on one wave and then turned slightly on the next, which came from a different point of the compass.

"Breakers," said Inga dully. "That's what those waves are called."

Alone on the foredeck, the two women tried to make sense of the unpredictable motion of the sea. For all Anna knew, the ship might have turned around and be headed back to Ireland. There were no directional markers or fixed points on which to focus. She couldn't tell whether they were moving forward or in circles. The knot in her stomach was not from nausea but pure fear. She wasn't scared they might sink, because the ship was upright and smoke was streaming from the three smokestacks, but she was frightened by this vast, new world that offered no discernible sense of direction. She'd never seen anything like it before. And that was how things would be for the rest of her life.

Someone placed a hand on her shoulder, as if seeking support. She gave a start and then looked up to see Mrs. Gavin's narrow, pallid face under her shawl. The woman's colorless lips managed a thin smile as she clung to her while the ship once again made what felt like a quarter-turn. Anna kept a tight grip on the rope. If I close my eyes now, she thought, I'm going to be sick. I have to keep looking at the sea, even if it pulls my soul from me. The other woman held on to her shoulder, her grip firm yet gentle. Inga held out a hand to help them sit down beside her. Then the three of them silently looked out at the sea, which lacked any horizon.

The next day the weather was calmer and a little warmer, so it was a good time to talk. The deck was once again crowded with people, some of whom could not settle down but instead insisted on walking restlessly from the rail on one side of the ship to the other and then back again. Yet it was still much too soon to be dreaming of land. Others marked off a space for themselves in the morning and then guarded it for the rest of the day, or at least until the next meal was served. A man wearing a waistcoat and brimless cap had brought out a fiddle. He sat down on a coil of rope and every once in a while squeaked forth little dance tunes. Some of the Irish youths tried a few dance steps, but they were constantly scolded by the deck passengers after colliding with them. Finally they simply gave up.

Inga was the youngest of the group of women, yet she was always at the center whenever they gathered. Today she'd seen to it that Mrs. Lundgren and her taciturn son David had joined them. Occasionally Gustaf would appear at the edge of the group, holding Carl by the hand.

He and his son would disappear in the space between the privies and the bridge over by the rail on the port side, but soon they'd be back again. In addition to the Lundgrens, the group was joined by the slightly older Mr. Nilsson, a carpenter, and his wife and two teenage daughters who never said a word. One of them always smelled faintly of urine. Elisabet and Ellen sat beside their mother, whispering as they played with a paper fortune teller they'd made from a sheet of newsprint they'd found somewhere. At the moment, Mrs. Lundgren was the one doing the talking, though she spoke so quietly it was hard to catch what she was saying. She had brought along some letters, which she smoothed out and then read aloud. They were from her son Jonathan in St. Paul, and she had underlined certain sections. Like the part about how winters were colder than back home in Sweden. And how you needed good shoes and boots. It was possible to find a place to live, her son wrote, at least in Minnesota. When he'd first arrived several years ago, he'd stopped in New York, but things had been much more difficult there. He hadn't been able to find a place to sleep so he could get to work on time, so he'd spent the last of his money to head west. There were jobs available both in New York and in St. Paul, where he'd started out as a day laborer for the railroad and then found work in the forests to the north. Now he was back in the city. There were several big mills there because of the river rapids, and they were building the railroad north to Canada. The work in the forests was much harder than back home, especially in the wintertime, so he'd decided to stay in the city.

"He doesn't write anything about the need for maids," said Inga. She smiled, so no doubt she meant it as a joke. But the widow Lundgren looked uneasy and fixed her eyes on the letters again. David sat behind her, reading over her shoulder. Or at least it looked as if he were reading. His unshaven face was motionless, shadowed by the visor of his cap. There was something about David that made Anna nervous. He was quiet and calm and friendly whenever anyone spoke to him, yet he seemed filled with a great tension, as if he had something very important to divulge. But he never mentioned a word about it as far as anyone could tell. When he looked out at the sea, his eyes were as black as a bird's.

The widow Lundgren licked her fingertips as she leafed through the letters, the corners of which were already dark with smudges. The stamps on the creased envelopes were red and green and looked quite strange. She kept on smoothing down the paper with her hand, which explained why the letters were so worn looking, as if they were very old. But the latest one had actually arrived only a few weeks before Mrs. Lundgren and her son had set out from their home in Västergötland.

"Gustaf worked in the shoe factory back home in Örebro," Anna heard herself explaining. Then she looked over her shoulder to see if he'd heard. But her husband and son were now standing with other passengers at the rail, right in front of the locked wrought iron gate leading to the section for second- and first-class passengers.

"Does he write anything about shoe factories?" she asked, a bit more confidently. To her surprise, the older woman looked up and smiled.

"He does, in fact," she said. "Jonathan says they make a lot of shoes in St. Paul. And everywhere in Minnesota."

Mrs. Lundgren's words made Anna's heart skip a beat. Then she heaved a big sigh of relief, as she could now set some of her worries aside for a while.

"I'll tell Gustaf," she said, hoping no one would notice the quaver in her voice. She stuck her trembling hands under her apron.

Silence settled over them. Gusts of wind from the stern whirled the smoke from the smokestack high above; a glimpse of sunlight between the clouds sketched strange, long shadows across the white-painted façade of the bridge. There for a moment, then gone. Shadows of smoke. Shadows of a dream. *This is me. Anna. Right here.* Everyone else was heading toward something new, while she was heading away from something old and familiar that had shattered. But then it occurred to her that she couldn't be sure about the others. She didn't actually know why they were now sitting here around her.

The widow's son David sat quietly on a coil of rope, staring steadily at the sea, as if he wanted to be the first to catch sight of the new coastline. Yet Anna could tell he wasn't looking at anything specific but, rather, at something he carried inside him.

"How many of you are thinking of going on to St. Paul?" asked Inga, sounding as if she were asking if anyone wanted a cup of coffee. One by one everybody in the group raised their hands. And, much to her surprise, Anna found herself raising her hand too, without even a trace of hesitation. Later, looking back on that moment, she would recall that David Lundgren was the first to raise his hand, and she remembered how his insolent expression changed to an almost embarrassed smile of pleasure when he saw that everyone was in agreement.

This was a moment that stayed in Ellen's memory as well. The sight of her mother's thin, pale hand raised in the air against a billowy, acrid cloud of coal smoke. She knew they were on their way to America on the world's biggest ship and that things would be better when they got there. There was something about her mother's face, the way her mouth twitched, the way she let out a deep sigh. The way the lines at the corners of her eyes seemed to smooth out from inside, for just a moment. The way she then looked down at them, smiling. And the way Ellen herself wiggled a loose tooth with her tongue, and how important this all was.

The next day they saw land for the first time. One by one they all went up on deck and pushed their way forward until they could look over the shoulders of the other passengers and see a strip of gray beneath the bank of clouds. The steward told them to keep their shoes and socks on, meaning they shouldn't get too excited, because the storm had carried the ship off course. What they were seeing was Cape Cod. It was still a good distance to New York, where they would dock sometime the following morning. But now they would be traveling along the coast until they reached their destination. No more open waters.

"Cape Cod," said Inga. "That translates as *Torskholmen* in Swedish. We have a place called the same thing back home."

There Anna and Inga stood, after finally jostling their way forward to the rail. They looked at each other and laughed without really knowing why.

"That's not something you can just decide on your own," Gustaf persisted, without looking his wife in the eye.

"But you weren't there."

"I was minding the boy. It was impossible to follow the conversation. I couldn't hear everything that was said."

Anna felt her words and decisiveness seeping away as she looked down at her hands. Then she straightened up and said, "We had to decide *something.* And it'll be good to have some folks with us that we know. We can't speak the language, after all. And we have to say where we're going when we show our papers. Inga told me that."

Gustaf sat on the bunk, soundlessly tapping his foot on the deck, as if he were on his way somewhere else. His jaw muscles tightened, then relaxed, then tightened again.

"I don't think we should bind ourselves to anything. There may be opportunities we don't yet know about when we get to New York. There are Swedes living there, too. And probably jobs. It's a big city."

"You may see it as 'binding ourselves,'" she said, noticing how shrill her voice sounded, yet there was nothing she could do about it. "But the others are going to continue west. There are more Swedes where they're going. And shoe factories too. Inga says—"

"Inga, Inga. . . . Can't you talk about anything but that damn Inga? Is she the one making all the decisions?"

Anna didn't know what to say, so she kept quiet.

Finally Gustaf said, "I don't want to decide anything until we get ashore. I want to see how things go and make some inquiries. Is that too much to ask?"

He got up without waiting for an answer and headed for the door. Then he was gone. She stayed where she was, feeling that everything was once again wide open and drifting, like when the ice broke up during the spring thaw. Nothing was solid enough to stand on.

At first the shoreline was merely a darker shadow against the gray of the sea; gradually long sandy beaches emerged from the haze. After a while individual buildings could be distinguished, both ordinary houses and grand estates along the coast. Several ships appeared in the morning, all of them heading for the inlet to the large bay.

All the steerage passengers had already gathered on deck. It was crowded, and everyone was feeling irritable. Anna kept close to Gustaf, who was letting the children take turns sitting on his shoulders so they could see above the heads of the grown-ups. Inga stood on the other side of Anna, holding her well-thumbed book in her hands. She had opened it to a page with a small map and was trying to make out where they were whenever they caught sight of some landmark. Perched on a hill was what looked like a fortress. When they drew closer, Inga said it was a lighthouse, but with a long wall encircling the top. Then they glided past it.

The *Majestic* issued two blasts on its steam whistle and received a brief reply from somewhere farther away, out of sight. Like cattle lowing in a field, Anna thought. Then she wondered aloud where the tall buildings were that she'd heard so much about. "You'll see them later," said Inga. "But I expect we'll soon be seeing the statue—the Statue of Liberty, you know." Then she slipped away around the corner, looking suddenly excited.

One of the Irish women abruptly left her place at the rail, and Anna took a step forward, but the space was quickly taken by others, so she caught only a glimpse of a castle-like structure made of red brick. This time there really were cannons sticking out over the parapets. Holding up the hem of her skirts, Inga came rushing back to Anna.

"She's on the other side," she shouted. "Come quick!" Then she turned on her heel and again disappeared through the narrow doorway leading to the row of privies. Anna grabbed her daughters' hands and told them,

"Come on," before following the younger woman. She held her breath as they passed the white-painted doors of the toilets.

Inga had wriggled her way in between some of the stout women wearing gray aprons who were standing at the rail. When Anna pushed the two little girls forward, the women grudgingly made room for them. Their narrowed lips and disapproving expressions showed they weren't happy about it, but they moved aside. The children pressed their faces between the rust-colored posts of the rail to stare at the island with the high stone foundation. Anna worried that the rust might fleck off onto their skin. Then she looked up.

She had thought the statue would be white, but Lady Liberty was a green hue that reminded her of an old two-öre coin, the way it might look when emerging from the melting ice on the street in the springtime. The ship was now on its way toward the dock, so they could no longer see the statue's face, only the arm holding the stone tablet and, on the other side, the torch that rose straight up into the gray sky.

"They light it up at night," said Inga. "That's what it says in my book."

The ship made a half-turn in the water and issued yet another muffled blast. Anna was suddenly afraid they might collide with some other vessel. There were ships' masts everywhere, and because she was standing behind Inga, her view was obstructed. The coastline slowly swung forward, along with buildings on a hillside. But what she at first took for a natural slope turned out to have rows of windows, shining faintly in the gray light.

"Buildings that tall can't possibly exist," she said, placing her hands on her daughters' backs, as if to protect them.

"It's probably only rich people who live in them," said Inga, trying to sound knowledgeable. "At least on the top floors."

"But surely they would collapse," said Anna. "They must be far too heavy to stay up."

Inga's lips moved silently, as if she were murmuring something to herself.

"Fifteen," she said then. "I count fifteen stories."

The ship continued turning in the water, as if it couldn't decide in which direction to go. Then it began moving forward once again with a strong vibration that spread across the deck and made the privy doors rattle. Anna heard from a distance folks cheering up on the cabin deck, so she leaned forward to peer over her daughters' heads.

As the ship turned, a new island slid into view. It seemed to consist of nothing but buildings, with no shore areas at all. On one side stood a huge chimney of yellow brick, billowing gray smoke. There were rows of black windows in what looked like a warehouse, the walls of which stretched right down to the water. On the other side was a long wooden building with towers and pinnacles. The black slate roof shone faintly in the hazy light.

"That looks like the open-air baths in Strömstad," said Inga with a laugh. "Although much bigger, of course." After glancing at her book, she added, with a trace of awe, "It must be Ellis Island."

Suddenly the engines of the *Majestic* fell silent for the first time in a week, and everything was quiet. The ship continued to glide more and more slowly past the island, which rested on its own dark reflection in the water. They were heading for the rows of harbor storehouses, where people were waiting on the dock. The cheering on the upper decks was now much louder. But below on the between-deck, everyone stood mutely as they watched the dock approach at an infinitely slow pace.

They waited in line for more than an hour while the cabin passengers disembarked. One by one or in groups they disappeared through the big door to the harbor terminal of the White Star Line, accompanied by porters wearing blue uniforms. Slowly the dock cleared of people. A couple of watchmen emerged and closed the wrought iron gates to the terminal building. Then they coiled away the ropes blocking the gangplanks and allowed the first passengers from the between-deck to move forward on unsteady legs and step ashore.

Soon the line began moving. Anna held Elisabet's hand while Ellen held on to Carl. Gustaf carried the big suitcase with the number 3304 chalked on the side, and he had their seaman's sack slung over his shoulder. The vein at his temple was visibly pulsing, but he didn't say a word. Anna carried the shapeless bundle, wrapped in sailcloth and tied with a string, that contained their bed linens and other belongings. She could hardly see where she was going.

"Watch your step," Gustaf muttered in a stifled voice in front of her. Suddenly her foot struck a metal threshold and she was out on the sloping gangplank. The people behind her surged forward, but she regained her balance in midstride.

Then they set foot on solid ground. *America.* Anna still held the bundle under one arm, undecided whether to set it down on the cobblestones. Between her feet she saw that the cracks between the stones were filled with dried horse manure, so she decided not to. Gustaf set down the suitcase, sat down on it, and pulled Carl onto his lap. Anna leaned the bundle against her husband's back, and he offered no objection. Over the top of the bundle she found herself staring straight into the morning light. At the other end of the bay the Statue of Liberty was still visible like a shadow in the haze. Behind her she heard the city, the sounds echoing through the stone vault on the other side of the double gates, now locked. Shouting voices, wagon wheels, horse hooves against pavement, as well as what sounded like the clang of bells some distance away. Later she would realize it was the streetcars she had heard. Here she noticed the same smell of coal smoke as she'd known in Göteborg. And all around them more and more passengers continued to stream down from the ship's double gangplanks to form a dark mass of humanity.

The dock was soon teeming with people because they had nowhere else to go. Elisabet fretted and said she was hungry. Anna tried to get her to look at the Statue of Liberty, but the child merely buried her face in her mother's apron. The air felt hot and damp, even though the sky was overcast and threatened rain. Not the sort of weather she was familiar with in Sweden. She saw Inga sitting on her suitcase a short distance away, holding a parcel on her lap, and with her shawl knotted firmly under her chin, in spite of the heat. Anna waved, and Inga waved back but otherwise didn't move. Anna called to her over the heads of the other passengers, "What now?"

"Now we wait," Inga replied. "A ferryboat will come to pick us up."

"That's right," said Gustaf, taking off his cap. "We have to go back over there."

Anna shaded her eyes with her hand and looked where he was pointing. Over there. Toward the island with the building with all the towers and pinnacles made of wood.

"Do you think we could find some water for the children?" she asked.

"I don't think so. Not until we get over there," replied Gustaf. After that he fell silent. When she looked at him again, he had dozed off, leaning against the bundle of linens and clothing. Carl was asleep on his lap, both of them sleeping with their mouths open. Tiny beads of sweat covered the boy's forehead.

They waited for more than an hour. Then a side-wheeler painted a uniform gray arrived and docked next to the *Majestic,* on the right side of the stern. Gangplanks were slammed into place. Anna shook Gustaf's shoulder, surprised the noise hadn't roused him. Then Carl began fidgeting on his lap, and Gustaf abruptly sat up straight.

"Time to go," Anna told him as quietly as she could. The crowd on the dock was already in motion. She saw Inga heading for the ferry with tall David Lundgren right behind her.

They started gathering up their belongings. The girls moved slowly, as if not yet fully awake. When they reached the ferry, a mustachioed crewman suddenly appeared in front of them, holding out his hand to block their way. "Full," he merely said, and Anna understood. The people onboard occupied every inch of space, with suitcases clutched in their arms or parked at their feet. She saw row upon row of faces, both familiar and unfamiliar. She thought she caught a glimpse of the Gavin family. She couldn't see Inga or the Lundgrens anywhere.

"Next," said the man as he held up a finger in front of Gustaf's face. "One hour." He said the words as if speaking to a deaf-mute. Anna noticed how Gustaf squared his shoulders. The suitcase landed with a thud on the cobblestones, and she worried half-heartedly about the fate of the few coffee cups they had left. Gustaf sat down.

The ferry slowly started to move in a cloud of coal smoke, backing away from the dock with water dripping off the big paddle wheel. Then it disappeared behind the *Majestic*'s dark hull.

"Water," said Anna. "We need to find water to drink." Gustaf didn't budge, his back turned to her as he gazed out at the harbor.

"I'm staying here," he said. "I have no intention of missing any more boats. You go and look for something to drink, if you like."

Anna had no idea where to go. She looked around at all the other people and suitcases. Everyone was sitting in silence, as if dumbfounded that the ferry had left the dock without them. The noise from the city beyond the gates grew louder. She suddenly realized how thirsty she was.

She took Elisabet with her. Hand in hand they walked toward the closest and biggest of the wrought iron gates. A guard wearing a blue uniform watched them approach. Holding her daughter's hand, Anna dared to go over to him. He looked down at them without saying a word. She raised her hand and pretended to lift an invisible cup to her lips and then pointed at Elisabet. At first the guard didn't react. Then he gave a nearly imperceptible nod to his left before once again staring straight ahead. Anna curtsied, and she and Elisabet followed the wall of the building past rows of windows covered with iron bars. After passing three more gates they saw a group of boys wearing rugged shirts huddled next to the wall. They had dark hair, and Anna thought she recognized them from among the Irish passengers onboard. She saw water spraying over the boys' bare feet. When she got closer, they stood still. Next to the wall was a simple black faucet. Traces of rust colored the wall's cracked plaster, and thick, green moss grew along the pavement. She heard the sudden shriek of seagulls, then silence. Her head began throbbing.

The smallest boy made as if to block their way, but a bigger boy pulled him aside so they could step forward. Anna went over and touched the faucet. The metal was still warm from the boys' hands. When she turned the faucet, a trickle of dark water spurted out and ran over her feet. She leaned down, careful to hold her shawl away, and tried to catch the stream of water in her mouth.

The water was unexpectedly cold and tasted strongly of iron. Anna watched as Elisabet repeatedly caught the water in her cupped hands and slowly drank it, the pooled water reflecting the sky. Then she found herself thanking the boys, as if the faucet belonged to them. They gave her an anxious smile and stayed where they were. Anna took Elisabet's hand, and they walked back along the dock. A ray of sunshine appeared out in the bay, glided over the waves toward the far shore and then was gone. For a moment she experienced such a sense of calm at being where she was. *This is me. Right here.* It passed through her like a change in the weather.

She and Gustaf took turns accompanying the children to the water faucet. She thought Gustaf and Carl were gone a long time, and she started to worry. Others had now discovered there was water to drink, and from where she was sitting Anna could see a short line had formed. But her husband and son were back well before the ferry arrived, moving just as slowly as the first one, a dark shape against the gray water beneath a long plume of black smoke. This time they were among the first to go onboard, and they kept having to move farther back as the deck filled with more people and baggage. There was nowhere to sit, just a large open space on the afterdeck. The children sat on the suitcase, dangling their feet. When the boat started moving, Anna gazed at the city skyline where the tallest buildings now came into view. In the opposite direction she saw a big bridge spanning the water, though half of it was shrouded in fog.

"So, we're off again," said Gustaf, having to repeat his words to be heard above the din of the big paddle wheel. As Anna stood there, she felt herself smiling.

They were the second to the last family to come ashore and join the line moving through one of the three doors in the big wooden building. It was still hot and humid, and Carl had a bad cough that she thought had been brought on by the weather. "It's not good that the boy is coughing," said Gustaf. "They might think he's sick, and that could mean trouble for us. Get him to stop coughing." Brusquely he handed his son over to Anna.

She pressed the little boy against her shoulder and patted him hard on the back. His arms hung limply down her back, but he was quiet now. She could feel rather than hear every breath rattling in his airways.

The line was slowly moving forward. "Later," Gustaf kept telling the girls. "Later we'll have something to eat." It became a constant refrain. On the small ferry boat that had brought them from the harbor to this island, they'd been surrounded by people Anna presumed were German and Italian. Now in front of them stood a family that must have come from Italy—a short, wizened woman with a gloomy expression, and a tall, silent man wearing a waistcoat and striped shirt. Anna tried several times to catch the woman's eye to say hello, but she seemed to look straight through her. Or maybe she was merely looking inward, at some distant landscape, now lost.

Finally they stepped through the doorway into a vast hall. When Anna's eyes grew accustomed to the dim light, she noticed, with a pang of despair, that the whole place consisted of people standing in lines that wound their way between wooden posts toward a row of desks at the far end of the hall. A man stood just inside the doorway writing something on a pad of paper. He pointed to the mountain of suitcases and other personal belongings neatly stacked along the wall. Hesitantly they set down what they were carrying. The man, who still hadn't uttered a word, tore off a receipt, which he handed to Gustaf. Behind him stood another man, this one wearing a white coat and holding a lit cigarette in his hand. His eyes narrowed, his expression seemingly indifferent as he looked at all the new arrivals slowly passing by him.

The stifling air smelled of dust and barnyards and sweat. Entering at a slant as in a biblical painting, light streamed through a row of windows high up near the ceiling. Under the windows hung a row of American flags, motionless. There had to be several hundred people in the hall. Hovering above the crowds was a muted murmur of voices, words spoken in so many different languages that they seemed to dissolve until they lost all meaning.

Outside in the daylight, yet another ferry had arrived with engines thudding and the sound of water falling from the big paddle wheel. Then came the scraping of the gangplanks and more voices. Soon the line was surging behind them.

Anna had lapsed into silence as they waited. Elisabet pressed her face against Anna's apron. She placed one hand on her daughter's head. They took only a few steps forward at a time. Now and then Anna would look around for a familiar face from their own group, but she saw no one she recognized. The line wound its way back and forth between the posts.

When they got closer to the far end of the hall, she was able to study the row of desks. Men sweating in their shirtsleeves and waistcoats, with uniform caps on their heads, sat behind the desks and accepted the emigrants' papers. Without looking up, they asked brief questions, speaking curtly with hoarse voices. Carl squirmed in his mother's arms, but he was no longer coughing.

Anna grew tense as their turn approached. She kept swallowing out of nervousness, and she asked Gustaf so many times whether all their papers were in order that he got annoyed and shut his mouth tight, as if he had no intention of ever saying another word.

A man wearing what looked like a police uniform and helmet ushered the Italian family ahead in line, and Anna saw the woman curtsy, almost ceremonially, before the man seated at the desk. Another policeman appeared at Gustaf's side and pointed them toward a desk farther down the row. Anna shooed the girls forward as she heard Gustaf say "Sweden" to the policeman, who then waved across the room to another tall man wearing a similar uniform with shiny badges on his chest. The man made his way over to where they were standing. "I speak Swedish," he said, and Gustaf looked relieved. As they talked to the man at the desk, Anna saw the guard at the next desk pick up a piece of chalk and write a big *X* on the jackets of two of the Italian children who had been standing ahead of them in line. The children were led away, followed by their mother.

The tall man in uniform stood next to Gustaf as he placed their papers on the desk. Anna saw that his hand was shaking. The man behind the desk looked up only briefly, as if to count how many they were, and then stamped the papers. He handed another packet of papers to Gustaf, who exchanged a few words with the Swedish-speaking policeman, and then turned to his family.

"We have to split up," he said, handing Anna several cardboard tags on strings. "And we have to wear these."

She handed Carl to her husband, then squatted down to hang the number tags around the girls' necks. When she stood up, she cast a glance at the door where they'd entered. The line was just as long as before. Hundreds of faces were looking in her direction.

"Why do we have to split up?" she asked, holding the girls by the hand.

"There are doctors who want to look at us. To see if we've brought any diseases. They say it goes fast, but they look at males and females separately."

The tall man in uniform placed a hand on Gustaf's back and firmly pushed him and Carl toward one of the doors behind the desk. With his other gloved hand he pointed to another door for Anna and the girls. Behind them a new family had already taken their place in front of the desk.

Reluctantly Anna and her daughters joined the line of women wearing dark dresses who stood in front of them in the smaller room next door. They spoke quietly to one another in what she assumed was Italian. No one paid any attention to her or the girls. A doctor in a white coat and a nurse wearing a blue blouse and starched apron stood at a low table. A basin filled with a pungent, brown liquid was on the table in front of them. They dipped several long, shiny steel pegs in the liquid. She knew what this was; she'd heard others talking about it onboard. Using the steel peg, they would turn the person's eyelids inside out, looking for parasites. She tried to think about something else and found herself worrying about Carl's cough, thinking the strong smell might make it start up again. As they moved forward, Elisabet began crying harder and harder the closer they got to the doctor and nurse. She tried to pull free of her mother's grasp, but Anna held on tight. There was nowhere else to go. The doctor raised the steel peg.

Only after they'd passed inspection did they get anything to eat. In a huge dining hall with long tables they showed their number tags and each received a bowl of vegetable soup and a couple of slices of bread. Then they headed for the table with the same number.

Gustaf was already sitting there, holding Carl on his lap and letting him dip pieces of bread in the soup. Anna wanted to say something about how unpleasant, and difficult, it had been to undress in front of strangers. But now that the girls finally had something to eat, they seemed content, as if they'd forgotten all about how they had struggled and cried.

"How did it go with his cough?" That was the first thing Anna said as she sat down.

"It was fine. But if they'd found anything wrong with us, we might have had to return home, even as soon as today. That's what a few Norwegians were told. I think they took them to a separate room because I didn't see them again."

"Can they really do that?"

Gustaf merely nodded.

"What happens now?" she asked.

"They said we'll sleep here tonight. There are bunks for everyone, although we'll have to split up again. It's getting late, but we'll see each other in the morning."

At last Anna saw a familiar face. Inga was sitting alone at a table near the window, calmly eating her soup. “I need to talk to her,” said Anna, getting up before Gustaf could object.

Inga looked up and smiled. “There you are,” she said. “I hope everything went well.”

Anna nodded and sat down next to her friend.

“Where are the other Swedes?” she asked.

“They’re here somewhere. I was the first one through, and I’ve been here a while. Do you know where you and your family are going to sleep? You’ll get your baggage back when you leave in the morning.”

Inga regaled her with so much information that Anna had a hard time asking the one question that was on her mind. When Inga paused for a moment, she seized her chance.

“Do you know when we’ll be able to continue on?” she asked. “What happens when we’re done here?”

Inga looked at her for a few seconds without answering.

“It says in your papers,” she then replied. “It says where you’re going. Everyone had to say where they’re headed when they talked to the man at the desk.”

Inga looked at Anna’s blank expression and then went on, as if to fill in the silence: “I’m sleeping here tonight with the others in the group. Early in the morning we’re taking a ferry to Hoboken on the other side of the river. From there we’ll catch a train to Minnesota. Here. See this?” she said, placing her papers on the table. She pulled out a piece of brown paper printed with big letters:

**SPECIAL EMIGRANT TICKET**

*Valid for ONE PASSAGE New York—Minneapolis.*

*(In emigrant cars only)*

The names of the cities had been handwritten in ink, in a slanting style, and the rest of the text wasn’t easy to decipher, but Anna understood enough of it.

“So you were given this paper with the other ones?” she asked quietly, looking down at her lap. Inga didn’t reply. No answer was necessary.

“You’ll have to ask your husband,” Inga said at last.

Anna nodded. She was ashamed that she hadn’t understood before now.

“I assume you’ll stay here overnight too,” said Inga. “I think the last ferry of the night has already left.”

“Yes, I suppose we will,” Anna said in a toneless voice. “Maybe I’ll see you again before you leave.”

She got up and returned to her own table without looking back. The children saw her coming and already looked anxious about what she might tell them. From across the room Gustaf had watched her talking to Inga. Now he had his eyes fixed on the table, and he didn't say a word as she came back. In silence they sat there opposite each other as the room filled with hungry people who were still filled with anticipation.

The dormitory was situated on the far side of the island, the side facing the tall buildings on shore. Again they had to split up, with Gustaf and Carl ending up on the ground floor. Anna and her husband had barely said a word to each other. Even the children were quiet. She felt exhaustion overtake her like a snowfall that gradually grew thicker, making it harder and harder to see anything except what was close at hand.

She wished they'd had access to their baggage and their own blankets and clothes. But they wouldn't get their belongings back until morning on the ferry that would take them to a place called Battery Park. It left at 8 a.m. That much Gustaf had told her.

In the women's dormitory she saw mostly dark-clad Italian women sitting on the beds in twos and threes, talking in low voices. One woman wore a light nightgown and had unfastened her hair. Anna wondered what they were talking about so quietly and intimately, until she realized that many of them had their eyes closed. Then it occurred to her that they were saying their bedtime prayers. Some of them held in their hands the same sort of beads that she'd seen Mrs. Gavin hold onboard the *Majestic*. But she didn't see any of the Irish women anywhere. She thought she caught a glimpse of Inga and the widow Lundgren in the inner room, but she didn't feel like talking to anyone else today.

She had to share a bunk with the girls. Unlike the Italian women, they had no nightgowns to wear, so she told her daughters to take off all but their shifts and get under the covers. There was no sheet, but the gray blankets seemed clean enough. The girls were happy to have the top bunk. They sat side by side, whispering to each other. That was the last thing Anna heard before falling into a dark, heavy slumber that was indistinguishable from sorrow.

She was aware of voices and footsteps on the stairs even before she was fully awake. Someone grabbed her by the shoulder and began shaking her as a calm but insistent voice spoke in her ear, telling her she had to *Get up, get up.*

Anna opened her eyes and saw a strange light that made her think it must be dawn. But something was wrong. The person tugging at her shift was none other than Inga, fully dressed and with her eyes oddly glittering.

"Listen carefully, Anna," she said, still speaking quietly. "Tell the girls to put on all their clothes because we have to get out of here. I think there's a fire. Don't frighten them, but you have to hurry."

Her friend's forced calm had an instant effect on Anna. She got out of bed, still half-asleep, and reached up to shake the girls awake as they slept with their arms around each other on the horsehair mattress. "Come along, girls," she said. "Get dressed now, or we'll miss the boat. You don't need to tie your shoelaces." Anna wasn't sure why she said that, except she wanted them to hurry.

Inga was already standing by the door when they heard men's voices downstairs shouting in English. Mrs. Lundgren appeared, followed close behind by Mrs. Nilsson and her teenage daughters. Unlike Inga, they all looked terrified, yet they hadn't lost their composure. Anna realized that Inga was the person they had turned to with their fear, putting all their trust in her. The flickering yellow light on the wall grew brighter, and she couldn't think why she'd thought it was the sun. Now she also smelled smoke.

"Everybody needs to stay calm," said Inga, keeping her voice level, "or things will turn out badly. If you have all your belongings, then let's go. It's this way."

She kept up a steady stream of words, as if it were pitch dark and she wanted them to follow the sound of her voice. But the light from outside kept getting brighter, and the bunk beds cast sharp shadows across the dormitory floor. They heard men shouting and the echo of hurried footsteps, as from a great distance, even though they had to be very close. They also heard boat engines and big paddle wheels approaching across the water.

The Italian women were all on their feet, having quickly gathered up their possessions. The nightgown-clad woman that Anna had seen praying was now fully dressed. The woman exchanged a quick glance with Inga, who nodded. Without saying anything more, the whole group headed for the stairwell.

When they came out to the gravel-covered yard, the smoke and the hot wind from the fire struck them with sudden force. The other end of the island was in flames. The huge hall where they had entered and received their papers was ablaze, with flames shooting out from what was left of the roof beams. Anna drew her daughters close so that they were practically one body as they quickly made their way through the smoky haze toward the dock. They passed policemen, their uniforms unbuttoned, who were urging everyone to keep moving toward the gangplank of the paddle wheeler. Anna looked around, searching through the smoke for Gustaf and Carl. With panic in her eyes, she turned to Inga but didn't manage to say a word before her friend, still displaying great composure, said, "They're probably already onboard. The men's dormitory was on the ground floor, so they got out first." Then Inga urged Anna up the gangplank and onto the boat. The engine was running, and the deck shuddered with the force of the idling engine.

Everyone seemed to lose their self-possession as soon as they came onboard. Growing more and more agitated, people began shouting at each other as they were jostled this way and that by the crowds that continued to push their way up the gangplank. Anna yelled for Carl and Gustaf, but her words were drowned out in the chorus of other voices yelling frantically for missing family members, names and words that meant nothing to her. The big paddle wheeler slowly began to move, and the roar of the engine grew so loud that Anna could no longer hear her own voice. Yet she kept on shouting. Inga stood next to her, motionless, her eyes fixed on the island and the glow from the fire playing over her round face. Anna turned to see what she was looking at and saw men struggling with fire pumps on the dock. A dog raced along the shoreline to the place where the dock turned and then ran just as fast in the opposite direction, as if in a fever.

Then a warning shout came from the island as one of the towers on the building suddenly collapsed in a shower of sparks that flew out across the water. The men swiftly scattered, long shadows stretching out behind them. Inga leaned closer to Anna and yelled over the engine noise, "It looks like everyone escaped."

The boat slowly turned in the water, and the island slipped out of sight. The Statue of Liberty came into view, one side illuminated by the flickering firelight, with dark shadows in all the folds of the copper cloak. Then the ferry set course for the opposite shore and the white and yellow lights that looked like a string of pearls. Anna realized she needed to sit down. She felt faint with worry, and her legs were about to give out. But there was no room to sit or even kneel on the planks of the deck, so she stayed on her feet with her arms around the girls. They didn't say a word as they stared at the burning island. For a moment, in between two heartbeats, she wondered distractedly what had become of the dog.

* * *

They went ashore half an hour later, arriving at a dock some distance away from the one where they'd spent the morning. Here too there was a great commotion. Several wagons with fire pumps stood lined up along the edge while curious onlookers thronged outside the partially open wrought iron gates that were being guarded by policemen.

Anna recognized the family's belongings even before she caught sight of Gustaf and Carl. They sat huddled together, turned away so they could look at the island, where flames were still shooting into the air, with the smoke from the fire lit up from below like a distant thunderstorm. She called their names, again and again, and Gustaf jumped to his feet. The girls ran to their father and grabbed hold of his legs. Anna took Carl from Gustaf and burrowed her nose in his white-blond hair. Both of them reeked of smoke.

Gustaf was still nervous about looking her in the eye. He said gruffly, "They wouldn't let me go upstairs to find you. I did try."

Then he turned around and pointed. "But at least I was able to collect most of our things."

Anna didn't know what to say. She looked at their bags again and burst out laughing.

The early morning hours were chilly, but now they were greeted with great kindness from everyone. An old woman wearing a Salvation Army uniform handed out blankets. Eventually a steam cart was rolled in, and they were all served weak coffee or hot milk in tin cups. A boy carried around a big basket of fragrant bread, freshly baked. They took two and then sat down on their bags once again to watch the sunlight break through from behind the tall buildings that looked like a row of teeth farther along the dock. Gray smoke rose up from the island out in the river and drifted over the lower houses on the opposite shore. Everything out there was black; nothing moved.

The wrought iron gates now stood wide open, and the police had disappeared. The city was starting to awaken. Anna saw a man she thought must be Chinese slowly dragging down the street a loaded cart, which back in Sweden would have required a horse to move. He took short, quick steps, and the cart was a lovely red color. She saw all sorts of people wearing different types of clothing, staring, pointing, on their way somewhere. Most seemed to be smiling, as if almost elated by the nighttime calamity. And she was surprised by her own thoughts: I could simply stand up and walk straight into the city and no one would ever find me again.

She dozed for a while, leaning against Gustaf's shoulder. When she awoke, she found someone staring at her. The sun was high overhead, and Inga was standing next to them. Her suitcase was at her feet, and her lovely shawl was neatly knotted under her chin.

"We're leaving now, Anna," said Inga. "The ferries have started up again, and they'll take us across the water."

Anna didn't know what to say. She squinted at the water.

"And you're going to be staying here?" said Inga.

"Yes," said Gustaf. "We are. At least for a time."

For a moment no one spoke.

"They say that nobody died last night," Inga then told them. "In the fire, I mean. Everyone managed to escape. Probably because we all stayed calm."

Anna still had no idea what to say. She thought about the dog and how it had run back and forth, and it occurred to her that maybe it had been looking for a means of escape. Without success.

"I've written down the address," said Inga. "To where we're going, although I don't know how long we'll stay in the same place." She handed over a piece of paper, neatly folded in half.

When Anna opened it she read:

*Inga Norström, Swede Hollow, St. Paul, Minnesota*

Anna merely nodded her thanks. Then she stood up to hug her friend. Gustaf stood up too. Inga gave them a quick smile and then went over to join her group waiting farther along the dock. Anna saw streaks of smoke from the fire in the clear morning air. And she recalled the dream she'd been having as she slept with her head on her husband's shoulder. Maybe it wasn't so much a dream as an insight. Still dozing, she'd realized why Gustaf wanted to stay here, in the big city. It reminded her of her own thoughts when she'd seen the Chinese man pulling his wagon. In this place you could disappear and spend your entire lifetime without being found. Even if somebody should decide to come looking for you.

This was the morning of their first day in their new country. Anna stood with her back to the city and watched the other Swedes—dark figures among so many others—heading for the ferry boats that were lined up at the dock, waiting to carry them away.

*Mulberry Street, New York*
October—November 1897

AT THIS EARLY HOUR of the morning the street was a tunnel of stone, the sky as gray as coal smoke above the surrounding buildings. Gustaf walked quickly, stooping forward as his fingers dug into the rough seams at the bottom of the pockets of his blue workman's jacket. He kept his eyes on the uneven cobblestones, barely visible in the dim light. All around him were the shadows of other men, most of them equally silent at this hour, although a few muttered words in languages that he hadn't yet learned to recognize.

At the intersection he caught a glimpse of the pale glow of street lamps from Delancey Street—an entirely different world with curtains behind the windowpanes. Farther away and in the opposite direction was the Chinese district, but that was not somewhere he'd ever gone. Gustaf cast a hasty glance at the narrow alley between the brick walls when he passed Silberstein's little cubbyhole of a shop that sold tin goods. The Norwegian, a man who usually sat in the alley behind the shop, wasn't there, although the stool where he always sat was. Apparently no one felt tempted to steal it.

Far too many of the men Gustaf saw seemed to be headed in the same direction. That worried him more and more the farther they went, especially after passing Canal Street. A tension grew among those walking shoulder to shoulder, so close they might touch, though no one spoke to one another. The nearer they came to the waterfront, the greater the distance between the men, even as they all pushed forward. When they finally stood side by side at the gate to the Pike Slip, everyone tried to jostle their way to the front.

Gustaf looked around. Most of the men were older than he was. They wore brown or dark jackets, with their caps pulled down over their foreheads and their hands stuffed in their pockets. But there were some youths among them. When he heard the sound of wagon wheels and horses' hooves against wooden planks, he stood up straight and fixed his gaze on some vague spot in front of him.

The man in the first wagon was named Mulligan, and Gustaf had had dealings with him before. Mulligan was one of the worst. Thickset and dark complexioned, he was always smoking a crooked, old pipe. But his was not the only wagon today. Two more now appeared, each pulled by a pair of horses. Gustaf recognized the man in the farthest wagon, which was much bigger. His name was Nielsen, and he was Danish. The Norwegian had spoken well of the man, saying he might turn up here. Trying to draw as little attention as possible, Gustaf edged toward the other side of the brick gate so that Mulligan would not be between him and Nielsen. He avoided looking the Irishman in the eye, even as he tried to stand taller. Mulligan was on his feet, sucking on his pipe, as he pointed the shaft of his horsewhip at various men in the crowd. He had no need to say anything. Whoever he pointed at would immediately move to the back of his wagon and stand there.

Nielsen's wagon was bigger, and he didn't seem to be in much of a hurry. He lit a cigar and then scanned the closest group of men. He called out in a soft, rolling English, "How many of you have children?" All the men raised their hands. Nielsen peered at them, his gaze unwavering, as he said with an amused smile, "And how many have more than two?" Some were honest enough to lower their hands, but most kept their hands raised. Nielsen laughed and pointed with the cigar he was holding: "You and you and you. And you." The glowing tip of the cigar pointed briefly at Gustaf. He was the last one to clamber up onto the flatbed of the wagon, which was already nearly full of workers. The horses slowly set off. At first Gustaf thought the weight of the wagon would be too much for them. Then the wagon wheels began turning with a plaintive creaking sound. He was crouched down with his back to a big man he didn't know. He watched as the men who had been left behind reluctantly turned on their heel and walked back the same way they had come. In the narrow opening between the buildings down by the river, a steely gray morning light began filtering through. He ventured a few words in English to his neighbor. "What will it be today?" The man looked up, his expression already weary, and replied briefly, "Sandbags. A barge." Trying to keep his balance as the wagon swayed, Gustaf tied his scarf tighter around his neck and then stuck his free hand under his jacket and tucked it in his armpit. Yet another day of hard labor. The aroma of fresh coffee suddenly wafted toward him from one of the roasting houses down at the harbor, making his stomach clench.

It was dark by the time Gustaf made his way back. This time he took a different route without as many landmarks. The barge had been moored under the bridge construction on the east side. It was a rusty old vessel sitting in the water at a tilt, which determined how they loaded the cargo. If they did it wrong, the barge leaned even more, and the work took longer than it was supposed to take. That, in turn, prompted angry shouts from an invisible foreman up on the dock, standing at a spot hidden by the rusty railing. When the men finished the job and received their wages, there was no wagon waiting for them, so Gustaf began walking, feeling a weariness deep in his bones. It was the sort of fatigue he hadn't felt since he was a boy and worked as a farmhand in Hammar. He told himself he would walk for fifteen minutes at a time and then pause to rest. He wasn't hungry. In fact, he felt slightly nauseated. For a while he had no idea where he was. He saw one tall stone building after another and doorways everywhere, along with men wearing fine-looking dark suits. Then he glimpsed the gas street lamps from Delancey Street. Only half-awake he headed in that direction. If he followed Delancey, he would sooner or later come to the Bowery, and from there he could find his way even in the dark.

There were so many people out and about although it was probably close to eight in the evening. Carried on the wind was the sound of horns playing music that seemed as unfamiliar and toneless as the braying of a donkey. Gustaf stopped to lean against a wall to gather enough strength to keep going. He felt as if he'd been walking for an eternity. When he looked up again he suddenly became alert. He knew where he was. Across the street he recognized Silberstein's shop. Now he could breathe easier.

The Norwegian was sitting outside in his usual place on the stool with his hands in his pockets and a cigarette hanging from his lips. The tip glowed every time he inhaled. He wore a heavy gray jacket and didn't seem to be cold. Straw stuck up from the tops of his boots, giving him the look of a scarecrow.

"Good evening, Swede," he said quietly when he caught sight of Gustaf. "How'd it go today?"

"I got hired on by Nielsen," he replied, leaning against the wall and closing his eyes for a moment. "We loaded sand for the bridge construction. Nielsen had moved to the Pike location, just like you told me yesterday," he added, nodding his thanks to the man sitting on the stool.

"So what was that worth?" said the Norwegian, meeting his eye. Gustaf dug a ten cent coin out of his pocket and placed it in the rough palm of the man's hand. Others had told him that the Norwegian had been involved in an accident down at the harbor and could no longer work. That was years ago, yet the man's hand was still calloused. Gustaf wondered again how the Norwegian managed to get here every morning, since it was said he had trouble walking. And how did he always know what was on for the day? But exhaustion burned in Gustaf's head and prevented him from asking any questions. Besides, he probably wouldn't get an answer.

"Did Nielsen say anything about tomorrow?" the Norwegian asked him now after sticking the coin in his pocket. Gustaf shook his head.

"He didn't mention anything at all?"

"No. He just dropped us off at the work site, as usual."

"Then you can go back to the same place near Pike tomorrow," said the Norwegian, pinching the end of his cigarette to put it out. "He'll be back. And at the same time. Was fat Mulligan there?"

Gustaf nodded.

"Watch out for him. He's been getting stingy and that has riled the Italians. They're not the sort you want to play around with. Mulligan's been in a surly mood, and he takes out his anger on whoever is dumb enough to climb into his wagon. It wouldn't surprise me if he disappears one day."

The Norwegian picked up his flask of whiskey and filled the capsule lid, offering it to Gustaf. He never allowed anyone to drink from the bottle, which was probably wise. But Gustaf shook his head, so the Norwegian silently poured the liquor back in the flask.

"See you tomorrow then," he said.

Gustaf gave him a brief nod and, with a tug on his cap, repeated, "Tomorrow."

He'd seen how some young boys managed to get inside the building late in the evening. They simply jumped up, grabbed hold of the lowest rung of the fire escape ladder, and pulled themselves up. On a night like this, trying to copy that ploy seemed as possible as reaching for the moon. Gustaf leaned against the front door, hoping to find it unlocked. It wasn't. He rattled the door handle, not so much in an attempt to unbolt the door as to get someone to hear him.

He was in luck. After a minute the door opened a crack, and in the opening he glimpsed the frizzy hair of the old Russian woman.

Gustaf pushed open the door as he searched for the right words, starting off with "Many—" but she merely waved her hand dismissively and shuffled back toward her own place without even looking at him. She spoke no English at all. And for the most part, neither did he.

His hand found the banister in the dark, and he began climbing the stairs. It was nearly impossible to see anything, but from the surrounding rooms came the sound of footsteps and voices and children crying, even though it was already late. A dim light issued from the little window above the Italians' door on the second floor, making it easier for him to find his way through all the rubbish they'd left on the landing.

His family's room was at the very top of the building, on the sixth floor, which he'd initially tried to describe as an advantage, because they would get more daylight through the window facing the street. On the other hand, there was always a lot of noise from the surrounding rooftops. Gustaf knocked quietly, using their agreed signal: four raps with his knuckles, a pause, and then four more. Anna unlatched the door to let him in. She was still dressed. She sat down on a chair at the kitchen table without saying a word. He went over to the stove, holding out his hands to assess the heat in the dark. The stove was still lukewarm, and he saw a saucepan on the single burner. He picked it up and took it over to the table, sitting down across from his wife. He took a spoon from the shelf drawer and started eating. Potatoes with butter, and at the bottom of the pan he found tiny pieces of bacon.

"Was she here again?" he asked. "The Salvation Army lady?"

Anna nodded. He couldn't see her face, only her silhouette against the lighter rectangle of the window.

"She brought us a piece of bacon," Anna said. "For the children's sake. But there was a little bit left over for you."

Gustaf was about to say something but held his tongue. Now that he'd come home, his appetite had returned. He tried to eat slowly.

"So what was on her mind today?" he ventured.

"She says she thinks we ought to move. We'd be better off with other Swedes. And more of them live on the other side of the river. Up in Harlem."

"I worked down by the river today," he said. "At the bridge construction. When the bridge is finished, it'll be easier to get over there."

He didn't know why he said that. It was his fatigue talking.

"But that'll take years," she said.

"You know it's more expensive on the other side of the river," he replied. "Not to mention in Harlem."

"I thought we could go to the Swedish church some Sunday," she said. He could hear the worry and urgency in her voice, the way the words seemed to tumble out, as if she'd been carrying them around for a long time before he came home. He didn't feel angry.

"But it's so far to go," he said. "How would the children manage?"

"It would be nice to talk to people who speak Swedish," she said.

He let the subject drop.

"How is Carl?" he asked instead. "Was he coughing today?"

She nodded in the dark.

"We were up on the roof for a while," she told him. "Just Carl and me. That's when she came. Lieutenant Gustafsson."

He chuckled quietly. He couldn't help himself, even though Anna would be annoyed. He thought it sounded so funny. *Lieutenant Gustafsson.*

"She visits us because of the children," Anna said.

And there it came, spoken in the brusque voice she used only occasionally. "She thinks we should try to find a different place to live. For the children's sake."

Fatigue wrapped itself tighter around Gustaf. Harsh and yet enticingly gentle, Anna's voice reached him as if from the other side of a curtain. Maybe it grew darker outside at the same time, he wasn't sure. Only a dim light entered the room. And she kept on talking.

Reluctantly he took the coins from his pocket and placed them next to her hand on the table.

"Here," he said. "I took only ten cents from my wages."

She fell silent but didn't touch the money.

"I have to get some sleep," Gustaf said. "We'll talk in the morning." Then he undressed and placed his clothes neatly on the chair next to the window, which was open slightly, in spite of the cold night air. He tiptoed over to the bed, pulled on his nightshirt, and cautiously slipped under the covers next to the children, feeling the warmth of their small bodies. For a moment he rested his hand on Carl's forehead. It was neither cold nor hot to the touch. The boy stirred, rolling closer to the wall. The children snuggled together, still sound asleep as they settled as best they could into the cramped space beside their father. Anna remained sitting on the chair in the corner, not moving, her face turned in their direction. Then Gustaf closed his eyes and was gone.

For several weeks he was able to find temporary work each day. With the Norwegian's help, he managed to follow Nielsen around to various hiring spots. If he got there on time, the Dane would choose him almost every morning. He kept away from Mulligan, and sure enough, the man soon stopped showing up at the harbor. No one knew where he'd gone, but many said the Italians had taken him, which meant no trace of the man would ever be seen again. He wasn't missed.

Gustaf and a hundred other men spent a couple of warm Indian summer days digging up the streets around Grand Central Station. He had to teeter along wooden planks placed above ditches six or seven feet deep, pushing a wheelbarrow filled with stones and sand. No dawdling was permitted. But the weather was good, and the men were given beer to drink. Gustaf had never found work this far north in the city before, and he was worried about how he'd get home. But Nielsen came back with the wagon at the end of each workday. The men were told they were making way for new railway tunnels. Other men who spoke other languages came after them to construct scaffolding in the places where the dirt had been dug out to a depth equivalent to the height of several men below the street. But farther ahead they had hit bedrock. The work stopped as the supervisors calculated what it would cost to use dynamite and whether it would even be feasible to use explosives in the middle of the city. Gustaf had hoped the job would last longer. Yet it made him nervous to be so far from any familiar neighborhoods, so he wasn't sorry when Nielsen announced one morning that the excavation work had been put on hold indefinitely. Instead they would be going to the west side of the harbor to load rags. From there Gustaf could find his way home even if they were left behind without transport in the evening.

But the work was harder than he'd expected. It involved handling big bales of fabric, with chaff flying through the air in the stifling cargo hold and making it hard to see. After a while it was also hard to breathe, even with a handkerchief tied over his mouth. And the whole time the autumn sun poured through the open cargo hatch, like a solid pillar of light in the midst of the shimmering dust of fibers. He coughed all the way home, and when Anna grew worried, he said that when he had time, he'd cough up an entire new mattress for them. But she didn't laugh. It had been a long time since he'd been able to make her laugh.

Lieutenant Gustafsson apparently continued to visit, crossing from one rooftop to another. Anna never mentioned her, but the children sometimes asked whether "that lady" would be coming over again. Her visits left clear traces behind: a couple of small, wizened apples, one of which Anna had put aside for Gustaf; another bit of bacon in his supper. One day he found a magazine called *The War Cry* lying on the kitchen table, although it was in English. Anna didn't seem to pay it any mind, and the next day it was lying in the exact same spot.

Gustaf mentioned the magazine only in passing, but Anna would get upset every time he joked about the "lady soldier."

Occasionally, while he was at work, he would imagine the scene as if in a waking dream: how Lieutenant Gustafsson would come to see them, solemnly striding across the gaps between the buildings like Jesus in an illustration from the Bible, dressed in her violet uniform and old-fashioned bonnet. He pictured her as an older woman, but he had no real idea what she looked like since he'd never seen her in person. She probably looked nothing like the Salvation Army soldier named Belle on the theater posters that had been plastered all over town.

One Sunday afternoon Gustaf returned home after a somewhat shorter workday, hired on as a stevedore at the East Harbor. He was astonished to find a strange woman sitting at the kitchen table. She wore the Salvation Army uniform and beribboned hat, so he surmised this must be Lieutenant Gustafsson. But she was younger than both he and Anna were. The children sat on the edge of the bed eating pieces of wheat bread that she must have brought for them. Anna stood in the background with a closed expression, clasping her hands under her apron. He knew this was a clear sign of how nervous she felt. The lieutenant stood up and curtsied when she saw Gustaf come in. He was unprepared for visitors, covered with sweat and dust as he was, and he didn't know what to do with himself, even though he was standing in his own kitchen. So he merely nodded and drank a ladleful of water from the bucket before sitting down across from the woman.

"You must be wondering what I'm doing here on a Sunday afternoon, Mr. Klar," she said in Swedish, looking him in the eye. Gustaf stared at her without saying a word. After a moment she looked away but then went on. "Anna and I have been talking during the past few weeks. It's not easy to come here to a new country and find your way."

"We're doing all right," he said, surprised at how muffled his voice sounded. His nose and throat must still be filled with dust. He looked down at his hands lying on the rough, grained surface of the wooden table.

"Anna has told me how hard you work to make ends meet, Mr. Klar," said the lieutenant. "But there's a lot to consider for a family like yours."

Gustaf felt a rising anger at the impudence of this young woman, who came here to their lodgings and spoke to him as if they were the same age. A fancy uniform could not disguise her youth. At the same time, he sensed Anna's nervousness growing as his own expression darkened. The situation felt suddenly painfully familiar.

"What is it the lieutenant is thinking of in particular?" he managed to say as he blinked and swallowed hard, trying to suppress his anger as best he could. For Anna's sake.

The lieutenant continued. "It's about the weather," she told him. They'd had a warm autumn this year, but winter was on its way, and they wouldn't believe how cold it could get here in New York. "It's worse than back home in Sweden," she said. "Every morning people are found frozen to death on the streets. You have to keep a fire going around the clock, especially in buildings like this one," she added, casting a glance at the stove in the corner. "And then there are the summers."

"We came here in the summer," Gustaf interjected. "And we've managed fine."

The lieutenant nodded and then lowered her head so the upper part of her face was hidden by the brim of her bonnet. But he could still see her lips moving.

"We had a good summer this year," she said, "without any bad heat waves. But the summer of '96 was so hot that the tar melted on the rooftops. Old people and children suffer in that kind of heat. And you have only one window here."

Even though Gustaf couldn't see her eyes, he could tell that she was glancing at Carl, who was still sitting quietly on the bed.

Then she raised her head to look him in the eye. Her face was very pale, framed and shadowed as it was by her bonnet, which made her features seem to hover in the dim light.

"You can't stay here," she said. "It may be all right at the moment, but winter is coming. And even if you make it through the winter, the summer could be worse. You need to find a different place to live. They've already started tearing down buildings in this neighborhood."

She fell silent, her gaze unwavering.

"I have to work," was all he said.

"Anna says you don't know anyone else here in the city," the lieutenant persisted. "But there's a Swedish community up in Harlem. And another one in Brooklyn."

"Those places are too expensive," he said. "And there's no work there. Not unless you know someone. Don't think I haven't tried."

Those last words stung on his tongue, and again he felt anger surge inside him. She was here to take them to task, to take *him* to task, with God on her side. He clasped his hands tightly under the table.

"Is there nowhere else you could go?" she asked. Her brown eyes were fixed on him. The whole situation was becoming unbearable. His family could sense it too. No one said a word or moved a muscle as Gustaf and the lieutenant sat across from each other at the table.

"Not here," he said finally. "Not here in the city."

Anna was the one who dispelled the tension in the air by abruptly turning to the window and shoving it open with a bang. The smell of coal smoke drifted in on a cool breeze. She stood with her back to the room, and Gustaf realized she wanted to hide her face from him and the children.

The lieutenant also sensed that the moment had passed. Slowly she stood up and then pushed her chair under the table.

"I must be on my way," she said. "I enjoyed our conversation, Mr. Klar."

She gave a quick curtsy and then moved past him to the door. Anna turned briefly to give the woman a nod. Then she went over to the cupboard and without a word began taking out the plates for supper.

Gustaf stayed where he was, listening to the lieutenant's retreating footsteps until they were swallowed up by the building's noisy stairwell. Then he stood up and went over to the window, mostly to get out of Anna's way. A few minutes later he caught sight of the lieutenant's violet cape below. Without pausing to look around, she quickly crossed Mulberry Street and disappeared into the crowds of people around the street stalls on the opposite pavement before she continued down the street.

Winter arrived suddenly, catching Gustaf completely off guard. One day they could go outdoors without wearing a scarf or cap, walking beneath a pale autumn sun that still gave off a faint warmth when it was at its zenith above the buildings. The next morning an icy wind blew through the long valleys of the streets, whirling chaff and papers into the air. Then came the snow, the flakes as sharp as hail. He'd never seen anything like it. And the month of November had only just started. On his way to the hiring spot at the harbor, Gustaf wrapped his scarf over his nose and mouth, even though that meant the cold seeped under the collar of his jacket because a button had come off. The wind from the river was so fierce that it dredged up dust from the many layers of horseshit that had long ago dried and been trampled on the streets. The dust stung his eyes and clogged his airways. He didn't glance around, wrapped in his own thoughts as he was, trying to keep warm.

When he arrived at Pike, he found the street corner deserted. He was the only one there, and he felt panic seize hold of him. Something had changed. Everyone else had gone somewhere else, but he had no idea where that might be. And last night the Norwegian had not been sitting on his stool in the alley, though at the time he hadn't given it much thought.

For a moment Gustaf stood in the shelter of a brick wall, black with soot, not knowing what to do next. No one else showed up. Several men on their way out onto the piers glowered at him, clearly wondering what he was doing there. Then they fixed their eyes on the ground again to avoid getting the full blast of the wind in their faces. Gustaf made up his mind. He counted the coins in his pocket without taking them out and then headed toward town.

If he walked halfway there, he'd be able to afford to take the train most of the way back. On the other hand, it would be good to arrive rested and looking as alert as possible. He walked as fast as he could down to the ferry dock at Castle Garden. There he joined a line of equally silent passengers, all of them shivering in the icy cold as they waited to go onboard the ferry. The wind and sleet whipped at the smoke issuing from the double smokestacks, shredding it to pieces before it managed to rise into the air. But the ferry floated steadily in the choppy water.

Gustaf stayed as long as he could in the smoking lounge on the ferry's forward deck until the cigar smoke and crowded space began inducing a panic in him that he hadn't felt since the ocean crossing onboard the *Majestic.* There was nowhere to sit. He stood closest to the door amid a group of men until he could no longer breathe. Then he slipped outside into the drifting snow on the forward deck. The ferry lurched as it headed into the wind, and one of the horses on the wagon deck whinnied repeatedly, sounding more and more shrill each time the blasts of wind struck the boat.

Gustaf hadn't seen the city from the water since they'd docked on that first day. When they'd been taken away from the burning wooden castle on Ellis Island, he'd been frantic with worry as he'd stared across the water at the fire. The buildings along the shoreline still looked just as unbelievably tall through the whirling snow, but they now reminded him of an old man's broken teeth. The windows mutely reflected the dove-gray snowy sky above the river. Then he was forced to close his eyes and turn away, raising one hand to hold on to his cap, as a new gust of wind blew the snow, sharp as salt, against his face.

When the boat docked, he was carried along by the throng of people through the warehouse-sized ferry terminal and beneath the railway station's high vault, made of cast iron and grimy glass. Finally freed from the crowds, he found himself standing next to a pillar covered with signs and lists of distant destinations, printed in small type. He read through the lists as best he could, then looked around to find someone to ask for help as he turned over like stones in his mouth the few appropriate English words he knew. The names of the towns said very little to him until he finally found the one he was looking for on one of the timetables, as tall as a man, posted on the wall. *Newark.*

He handed over his little gray third-class ticket at the right gate and then made his way to the platform where a short train was already waiting under a plume of gray smoke. He found a seat next to the window in an overcrowded car. He ended up across from a black-clad woman who seemed to be suffering from chronic hiccups. As regular as clockwork, her body would spasm as she sat in silence, her lips pressed tight and her eyes closed. He turned away to look out the window, feeling dizzy as the train car lurched dangerously. They seemed to be flying through thin air above the rooftops and the bare trees down below, traveling along a slender bridge he could hardly even see except for the track flickering past. His heart pounded under his blue workman's jacket.

Gustaf got out at what he hoped was the right station. It had stopped snowing. The Norwegian had given him the address long ago, jotted down on a scrap of paper he'd put in his wallet and then almost forgotten. *29 Magazine Street.* He hunched forward, seeing no one else around as he walked along the muddy edge of the street, as yet unpaved. The wind was still blowing, but the needlelike snowflakes had diminished, evident now only in sudden gusts when the wind turned across the river and came back from a different direction.

On one side of the street stood a row of wooden buildings. On the other was a low series of brick structures, looking like one long connected building. Some had windows, some did not. He couldn't see any street numbers, and there was no one around to ask. The wind blew through the telephone wires above his head, issuing a monotonous whining sound.

A tall man, a Negro, came out of the opening in a board fence, which was more than five feet high. He too hunched his shoulders against the wind. Gustaf hurried forward, holding in his hand the scribbled note that read *Mueller and Sons Boot Company, 29 Magazine Street, Newark.*

The man looked up in surprise when Gustaf stammered his question, and at first he seemed uncomprehending. Gustaf repeated the question as best he could, feeling as if his words were disappearing into the wind. The man had already put up his hands, an apologetic smile on his face, when Gustaf held out the note. The man scanned the words and then nodded. He rubbed his chin and then pointed farther along the brick building. Then the man shut the gate in the fence and took off before Gustaf had time to thank him.

He had expected to see more people around, yet the area did not have the air of an entirely abandoned site. He thought he could sense through the brick walls the presence of people diligently working.

Above a gate to a large inner courtyard hung a sign that looked brand new, with words printed in bright colors: MÜLLER & SONS BOOTS & FINE LEATHER. He was just about to step beneath the vault, which offered shelter from the wind, when a door opened in a small shed that was probably meant to be a sentry's box. A large man with a dark, full beard and wearing spectacles looked Gustaf up and down without uttering a word.

Gustaf went over and removed his cap, even though the wind was still cold and managed to say "How do you do?" in a voice a bit too loud.

The man nodded curtly but didn't budge from the doorway. Inside the courtyard behind him a gentle yellow glow issued from the windows. Someone had turned on the electric lights. Gustaf saw men wearing shirts and waistcoats seated in rows at cutting tables, all of them focused on whatever it was their hands were working with. He felt his eyes drawn in that direction, toward the warm light and the bowed heads of the workers.

The guard with the full beard said something, and Gustaf leaned forward to catch the words, but he didn't understand. The man repeated what he'd said. Now Gustaf realized he was not speaking English. He shook his head, smiled, and said "Swede" as he pointed at himself.

The guard stared but didn't speak, so Gustaf tried to explain what he wanted. "I do work. Like this. In Sweden." He waved his hands in the air, mimicking how he would hold on to a piece of tanned leather with one hand while cutting it with the other.

The man again said a few words Gustaf didn't understand. He stood still, his arms hanging at his sides, waiting for more. The guard then repeated what he'd said, this time in equally broken English: "Here all speak German." Then he went inside, shutting the door behind him.

For a moment Gustaf stood still, staring at the illuminated window on the other side of the vaulted courtyard. He watched the rhythmic movements of the men as they, one by one, leaned forward to pull cord through the cut leather. It looked as if they were trying to mimic one another's gestures in some sort of slow-moving dance. From their posture and the bend of their shoulders he could tell what part of the job they were doing. They worked quickly and without casting a single glance out the window. Silence had settled around Gustaf, not a sound except for the blowing of the wind through the tangle of telephone wires high overhead. His feet were freezing. Then he began walking back the same way he'd come.

He had just enough money for the train and the ferry ride back. The wind had died down. It was late, so there were no wagons on deck, and he could sit inside the smoking lounge without feeling suffocated. Half the benches were empty, and he saw mostly elderly men reading their newspapers or dozing.

He had no words, none he could resort to, even in his own mind. The trip had cost him two days' wages, and he had nothing to show for it. He was hungry and tired, and he slowly headed for home, empty of all thoughts and feelings.

After a while he realized where he was in the gathering dusk. Behind shuttered doors, closed for the night, he saw the tin goods shop that belonged to Silberstein, the Jew. Gustaf walked around the corner and peered into the alleyway, even though he knew it was late. The Norwegian must have left his usual spot outdoors long ago. The narrow passageway was deserted, as he'd known it would be. But there was something else Gustaf noticed, something so blatant that it took him a moment to fully comprehend what he was seeing.

The tall stool where the Norwegian always sat was gone.

He stood there with his hand pressed against the cold brick wall, wondering whether he might be in the wrong alleyway. But he knew he wouldn't have made such a simple mistake. Something was fundamentally different, which he'd already sensed early in the morning, though he had refused to acknowledge what it might be. Now the ground seemed to give way beneath his feet.

The front door was unlocked and the smell of various cooked root vegetables still hung in the dark stairwell. Gustaf was so tired that he had to pause on each landing to catch his breath. The walls seemed to press in on him whenever he closed his eyes.

There was nothing he could do. Now he opened his eyes. At first he could see nothing at all. He was floating in the dark, picturing in his mind's eye how he was a man who had lost both his arms and legs and was incapable of doing anything at all even though he was still young and strong. The stifling darkness was closing around all of them until there would be no air left to breathe.

Anna was awake. She was sitting on a chair in the dim light, and she raised her head when he came in. Although he couldn't see her face, he knew she'd been crying.

"Where have you been?" she asked quietly. The children were asleep, three small heads lined up on their side of the bed.

"Let me sit down and I'll tell you," he said as he sank onto a chair. In silence he took several deep breaths, but what he then said was not what he had planned. "Forgive me."

She didn't reply.

Stumbling over his words, Gustaf told her about his attempt to find the sort of work he'd always been seeking, a job that would make it possible for them to start over. But now that door seemed to have been definitively closed to him.

"So there was no work," she said at last, sounding strangely relieved.

"No," he said, without adding the obvious, *Not here either.* He sat quietly, listening to the beating of his own heart.

"The lieutenant was here today," said Anna after a moment.

"What did she want?" he asked, feeling too empty inside to muster even a trace of anger. It could gain no foothold.

"She brought us this," she said, pushing a piece of cloth across the table toward him.

It was a big, embroidered handkerchief, clean and pressed but folded into a little package. It rustled when Gustaf picked it up. He untied the simple knot. Anna struck a match. Over in the bed Ellen stirred as the light flickered over her closed eyelids.

Lying on the cloth on the table were several wrinkled bills that someone had tried to smooth out. Uncomprehending, Gustaf peered at the money.

"But we're not beggars," he said then, about to place his hand over the bills, but Anna seized hold of his arm in a painful grip. She moved his hand away from the little bundle of banknotes on the table.

"They took up a collection," she told him. "At the Salvation Army in Brooklyn. So that we could move away from here."

She spoke through clenched teeth, each syllable little more than a hiss. He couldn't decide whether she was angry or glad, or maybe both emotions were coursing through her at once, so that even she couldn't tell. He hardly recognized his wife.

"They prayed over the money," she said in that same unfamiliar voice. "They *prayed* over it. Do you understand? That means the money can be used for only one purpose. Anything else would lead to misfortune."

The match she was holding in her other hand burned out. She was still gripping his arm.

"And what purpose might that be?" he asked in a subdued voice, trying to keep her calm, this stranger sitting across from him who had such a feverish and unshakable hold on his arm.

"To move away from here," said Anna with surprise in her voice, as if she couldn't understand why he hadn't realized that at once. Her hand loosened its grip on his arm. "To follow the others. That's the only thing we can use this money for, if you don't want to bring disaster upon us."

*But that's what I've already done,* Gustaf thought without uttering the words out loud. *That's what I've already done.*

"Light another match," he said, trying to keep his voice steady, though he could hear he was not successful. "Light another." She let go of his arm and struck another match.

Before the flame burned out, he counted the bills. Forty-two dollars. That was more than he'd earned in two whole months. It should be enough, he thought, even after they paid the back rent they owed. But it would be tight.

His heart was still pounding in his chest. He was neither calm nor happy. What he felt could not be put into words. But he was no longer freezing.

With his hand he kept smoothing out the handkerchief on the table, trying to read with his fingertips the embroidered text in the dim light. Eventually he gave up and reached for the matchbox, noting that it was one of the last they'd brought with them from Sweden. Waxed safety matches, patented by the Jönköping match factory.

The words on the handkerchief had been embroidered in red, in an ornate style. He spelled out the words: *He maketh me to lie down in green pastures.* But he had no idea what they meant. And he tried to recall whether he'd ever before held in his hand so much money in cash.

## *Hoboken–St. Paul*
## November–December 1897

AT FIRST IT WAS HORRID, because neither I nor Ellen wanted to go past that island again. I thought we were going to burn up the last time. When Mother said we had to take the ferryboat past the same place, it made my stomach hurt. I didn't want to go onboard a boat again either, but I had to. There were lots of people, and we had to stand in line outside the fence and wait while Father bought the tickets. Mother said it would be only a short boat ride, and then we would travel by train for a long time. She could see how scared I was, so as soon as we stepped onboard the ferry, she told me to take Carl inside. Then I wouldn't have to stay outside on the deck. We sat down on a bench, and Carl kept coughing until I told him to stop. Mother had said it was mostly a bad habit he'd acquired. Ellen was just as scared as I was, and she said that if I caught sight of the Statue of Liberty, then I'd be safe. She was sitting on the other side of me, and the boat was supposed to go between the islands.

Except that it didn't. I was holding Carl on my lap, keeping my eyes fixed on the wooden floorboards until he got restless and wanted to climb up and look out the window. Then I was forced to look out too. The island seemed to slide toward us from the side, and there was nothing I could do to stop it. I tried to look down at the water until Ellen tugged at my arm and said, "It's all right to look out." And so I did. There was a lot of black, charred wood piled up on one side of the island. But on the other side I saw that they had started to rebuild. I saw tall frameworks made of new wood, and workmen everywhere. We came very close. A faint burnt smell slipped inside to where we were sitting, and my stomach started hurting again. But over the roar of the boat engine I mostly heard the sound of pounding hammers and men shouting, and I thought to myself that it was actually going to be good when they finished their work. On the dock stood a big black horse harnessed to a wagon loaded with boards. And the horse was so hot that steam rose off him even though it was winter. I could see it clearly in the sunlight. The horse watched as the ferry passed by, twitching his ears several times. Then he too was gone.

I'd been on a train before. Both in Sweden and England. But this time it was different, because we were going to travel much farther. It would take almost two whole days, Mother told us, and then we'd meet the others again. I didn't really know who she meant, but it wasn't Granny, at any rate. Then Ellen said Mother was talking about the other people from the ship. There was supposed to be more snow where we were going, in St. Paul, not like here where the snow turned black almost at once. White snow like back home in Sweden.

We had to wait a really long time before we could get on the train. Mother and Father carried the big suitcases, so we took turns carrying Carl when he refused to walk on his own. He would purposely make himself heavy and grin at us. Then we sat down with Mother and waited some more next to an iron gate, but at least it was indoors. Lots of people were running around in all directions and talking loudly, and it smelled awful and people got mad because they thought we were in their way. Then Father came back with tickets for all of us. I was allowed to hold mine for a while, but then Mother got worried and said it was best if Father kept all of the tickets. Our train car was painted red, and it had benches made of dark wood and it smelled like horses, but Father said there was no space on the train for animals, it was probably just some stable boy who had been sitting there before we came. We got a corner all to ourselves where Mother and Father could set down our suitcases and other things so they almost formed a little hut for us. Carl was allowed to sit on Mother's lap and look out the window, and that kept him calm for a while. Our car was crowded with people, and when the train began to move and we left the station behind, I looked up and saw that a man sitting on the next bench was Chinese. He was wearing some sort of dress, but with trousers underneath, and big boots. I thought it looked so strange. Maybe he was the one who smelled of horses. I was scared to look at him, but I couldn't help it, and he noticed me staring. I was embarrassed and looked down at the floor, but when I glanced up again, he was looking right at me and laughing. Then he did something funny. He held up his hands in front of his face and curled his fingers so it looked like he was wearing spectacles. I laughed and he did too. Then I closed my eyes and pretended to sleep, but I must have really fallen asleep because when I opened my eyes again it was dark outside and the Chinese man was gone. Instead I saw the train conductor walking past, holding a long stick that he used to light the only lamp in the car. I thought the lamp looked like it was swaying, and that made me worried, so I pointed it out to Mother. She said she didn't think there was any danger, and it was probably meant to sway like that, but she'd keep an eye on it for me and I could go back to sleep. So that's what I did, and I didn't wake up until morning, and the sun was shining in the window and I felt sticky with sweat. But we weren't there yet. Outside the window I saw snow and forests.

It snowed harder and the train made the snow whirl up so you could hardly see anything at all, and then it got dark again. It happened fast. We could see lights far away, through the woods, and then we went across a bridge and a river. It was awful to travel across a bridge in the dark. Mother had brought bread and herring, and I was a little worried about spilling food on my clothes when the train car shook. After a while I tried to go to sleep again, but it was hard because the railroad tracks made so much noise. So I mostly sat and stared out the window. Ellen had brought an arithmetic book and was trying to write her numbers, but she got mad because of all the swaying from side to side, and she said it made her head hurt. She dropped her pencil stub and it rolled away under the seats and disappeared. I thought I would try to find it for her, but it kept rolling in different directions because the car was shaking so much, and I had to get down on all fours to look for it. The pencil ended up between the feet of a man with a long black beard who was wearing a big hat. He was sleeping with his mouth open, so I thought I would crawl over there and get the pencil, which I did. But his wife, who was sitting next to him and crocheting, hissed something I didn't understand and kicked her foot at me, as if I was in her way. But I got the pencil. When I went back, Mother was mad at me because my dress was dirty from crawling around on the floor. She said I never thought about things like that, and she tried to brush away the dirt, but some of it wouldn't come off. I should try and take care of my dress because it's the only one I have.

I sat and looked out the window, thinking about nothing at all, and after a while I could see what things looked like again because it started to get light, even though the sun hadn't come up yet. Everything out there was gray. All the others were asleep. It was a little scary to be the only one awake but also a little exciting. I couldn't stop looking out the window, because all the houses looked so strange. They stood in long rows out there, looking almost exactly the same, low gray houses with black roofs, and it seemed like nobody lived there. They went on and on, row after row, and some had tall smokestacks, but there were no people in sight. The houses kept on going, and the sky gradually grew light. The only sound was the train moving slowly and the people snoring and breathing loudly. It was as if there was no color left in the world, and I thought maybe this was what it looked like if you traveled far enough. Then I must have fallen asleep too. I remember nothing more about the trip until we arrived.

*St. Paul Union Railway Depot*
December 1897

When they arrived it was night once again. The train was going to continue on, so they had to hurry to gather their belongings while the conductor held up his lantern. Then he stepped up from the platform and waved the lantern to the engine driver. With a hissing sound the whole train began to move. Anna looked down and closed her eyes as she held tightly to her daughters' hands until the train had gone beyond earshot. Then she raised her head and opened her eyes again.

It had started to snow, blowing in on gusts of wind that found their way under the simple wooden roof above the platform. For a short time it was deceptively silent. They were the only ones who had gotten off the train except for three others—a man and a woman with their half-grown daughter, all dressed in black and speaking quietly in a language that was not Swedish. They walked away, moving with a confidence that indicated they knew precisely where they were going.

In the meantime Anna and the children stood beneath the snow-covered roof next to the train station, which at least offered some shelter from the weather, while Gustaf went to ask for directions. The whole station was dark. She saw only a couple of men farther down the track, carrying sledgehammers and lanterns as they walked along. A single lamppost glowed from the open space in front of the palace-like train station. The girls were clinging to her skirt, and Carl slept as she held him against her shoulder. For a few moments everything was quiet.

Gustaf came back, walking slowly with slumped shoulders, and Anna already knew what he would say.

"Nothing's open. There was nobody to ask. There's a sign that says the station will open at five in the morning."

She had no idea what time it was, though it had to be past midnight. Which meant five more hours until they could go inside to get warm, and they didn't even know where they were. Neither of them spoke as they watched the slanting snow suddenly gust through the circle of light from the lamppost. Beyond was nothing but darkness.

Leaving her family, Anna went out to the area of windswept snow in front of the station, thinking she might find a clock high up on what looked like a church tower on the building's façade. What she first took to be a clock turned out to be a circular window at the top of the spire, but it was just as dark as all the other windows. When she turned around, she again caught sight of the two workmen, who were both still carrying sledgehammers in one hand and lanterns, no longer lit, in the other. They were about to disappear into the darkness beyond the gaslight. Without thinking, Anna raised her hand and shouted.

The men stopped. They turned around and looked at her across the open space covered with snow that was still unmarred by any footprints. Slowly they began heading toward her. Gustaf came over to stand behind his wife, as if to offer protection.

The men wore identical gray jackets and caps made of sturdy cotton, with bandannas tied around their necks. In spite of the cold, they wore no gloves. And with a shock of surprise, Anna realized she recognized the shorter man. He was the younger son of the Gavin family, with whom they'd shared a cabin, the one who had been knifed onboard the *Majestic*. And she saw from his searching expression that he recognized her too. He gave a brief nod, without saying a word. They had never spoken to each other onboard ship, and she didn't know what to say. If she'd known any words in his language, or in English, she would have first asked after his mother. But now they simply stood there, staring at each other.

Gustaf was the first to say anything. He took off his cap, as a clumsy gesture of courtesy, and nodded. Then he asked in Swedish, exaggerating the pronunciation of every syllable: "Where is Swede Hollow?"

At the same time he threw out his hand, inquiringly. The men standing in the glow of the lamppost regarded him solemnly. Gustaf repeated his question, though now uncertainty was evident in his voice. The two men looked at each other and muttered something that Anna assumed must be Irish. Then they looked at Gustaf and Anna and shook their heads. But the Gavin boy gave them a friendly grin.

Gustaf leaned forward and used his index finger to write the Swedish words in the snow: SVENSKA DALEN.

They looked down and laughed quietly, again shaking their heads. They seemed to find the situation comical. Anna was freezing and cast an uneasy glance at her children, who were barely visible over by the corner of the station, waiting beneath the wooden roof. Gustaf straightened up and tried again, this time in English: "Swedish. Swede."

The men exchanged a few words. It sounded as if they were repeating the word *Swedish,* though in their own dialect.

Then the Gavin boy looked up and smiled, saying only, "Come." Both men turned and disappeared into the dark. Gustaf called to the children, who hesitantly emerged from the shadow of the train station. The family gathered up their belongings, and then they all began following in the footsteps of the two Irishmen, who were ten feet ahead, walking along the snowy street. No one spoke. The men merely glanced back a few times to see if the family was still following. The wind had subsided, but it had started snowing again with big flakes falling straight down from the dark sky.

Later Anna would become very familiar with the route from the train station to the Hollow, simply because many people went there to work every morning. But on that night the distance seemed endless—a tunnel of darkness and falling snow. Both men eventually veered off the street, which had become a well-trampled and frozen path, and headed down a narrow stairway to the river that was almost completely covered with ice. Off in the distance, on the opposite bank, which seemed impossibly far away, she could see occasional yellow lights flickering through the cold mist above open spaces in the wide river current. They walked past a row of barges, some of them apparently abandoned while others were covered with sailcloth and barely visible in the swirling white darkness. Then both men climbed back up the steep slope, and Anna had to help the girls to the top, holding them by the hand, before she went back down to help Gustaf carry all their bags. Elisabet whimpered quietly to herself. Anna still didn't know where they were. They seemed to be standing in the middle of nowhere, and the snow was still falling.

The two Irishmen walked slowly along the edge of the bluff and then stopped. One of them hefted his sledgehammer, holding it by the middle of the shaft, and cautiously struck it against the ground. The sound of a small farm bell suddenly rang from under the snow, a dreamlike sound that oddly seemed to slice right through Anna's weariness.

When she drew closer, she saw they were standing on a railroad embankment. Both young men began tapping here and there on the snow-covered track, prompting a dull ringing sound. It seemed as if they'd forgotten all about the family who'd come with them. Then the older boy straightened up and pointed the shaft of his sledgehammer toward what looked like a rock face. "Swede," he said and began walking.

What Anna took for a bare hill turned out to be a railroad tunnel made of stone. As they drew closer, she saw there were in fact two tunnel openings, side by side. Both Irishmen walked quickly into one of the wide tunnels and disappeared into the dark. Gustaf, who was carrying Carl, followed without hesitation.

She could hear the boys' footsteps and their voices as they calmly chatted in the soft tones of their own language. She took Ellen's hand. All of them, except for Carl, had to carry some of their belongings. Elisabet was still whimpering tiredly, but she didn't lag behind.

It was so dark that at first Anna didn't realize when they'd come out the other side of the tunnel, but then she noticed the snowflakes brushing her face and the echo of their footsteps diminishing. The boys had stopped and were saying something to Gustaf, repeating words that he didn't seem to understand. Then one of them struck a match, and their faces appeared in the tiny light issuing from his cupped hand. She looked away. When her eyes had again grown accustomed to the dark, she saw that the ravine below the railroad embankment was not filled with shrubs, as she first thought, but with the roofs of low, dark sheds.

The Gavin boy came over to Anna and placed his hand on her arm to get her to turn around. He pointed into the darkness, trying to make her see something that wasn't visible. "There," he said. "Swede." He gave her a friendly nod, and she understood that this was where their ways parted. She said loudly, "Thank you," in English. He touched his finger to his cap and turned on his heel, as if he'd already forgotten her. Then both boys climbed down the embankment, slipped in among the wooden shacks, and were gone.

"It must be over there," said Gustaf, his voice now sounding stronger. They picked up their bags and continued along the track. She tried to set her feet firmly on the railroad ties in the dark as she thought over and over, *Surely there are no trains at this time of night.*

A candle was burning in a candlestick in the upstairs window of a house made of bare boards. Gustaf went over to the little door and knocked. Once. Then again. They stood in silence at the bottom of the steps, waiting. Anna's head felt as if it were reverberating with exhaustion. Then she heard the sound of a wooden hasp being thrown back. The door opened a crack, and a gray head appeared.

"Yes?" said a voice in pure Swedish. "What is it?"

It took a moment for Anna to realize the voice was familiar. Then memories came rushing back to her. It was the widow Lundgren, whom she hadn't seen since they said goodbye in Battery Park.

"Oh. I thought it was David or Jonathan coming home from the night shift," the woman said, speaking in the same kindly tone of voice that Anna remembered from the ship. "But it's not yet time. So. The

Klar family. And you're here now. Well, Inga said you might well turn up one day."

Mrs. Lundgren raised the candlestick as if she could light up the entire hollow for them and then pointed at a dark wall of wood on the other side of the path.

"Inga lives over there in what used to be the Olssons' house. It's a bit drafty, but I'm sure she'll have enough room for you to stay the night. If it gets too crowded, you can send the little girls back over here to me. It'll be fine."

They went over to the house across the way while the widow stood in her doorway, holding the candle. Anna knocked. It took a while, but then the door slid open, and Inga came into view, tousled dark hair framing her round face.

"Oh, how nice to see you!" she said cheerfully, as if she'd been waiting up for them to arrive. "Come in, dear Anna."

She opened the door wide, and the whole family stumbled into a room that smelled of wood smoke and tar. Inga lit a candle stump that had been stuck in a bottle on the table. Anna saw a tiny kitchen with a sofa bed in one corner and in the other a small potbellied woodstove. A plain wooden table and a few chairs. That was all.

"I'm afraid I don't have much I can offer you in the middle of the night," said Inga apologetically, "but I assume you must be tired. Did you just arrive?"

Anna didn't have the energy to reply. All she wanted was to stretch out full length on the floor and go to sleep.

"Yes," she heard Gustaf say. "About an hour ago. We had a hard time finding our way here. I'm sorry about putting you to so much trouble, but we didn't know where else to turn."

"Nonsense," said Inga. "Things will be better in the morning. There's room enough, but I don't have many beds. The children can sleep on the kitchen sofa, and maybe the Lundgrens have a few extra blankets we can borrow. I sleep up in the loft."

Inga kept on talking in the same calm tone as usual, asking the girls what they'd thought of the trip. They answered in monosyllables, already half-asleep. Anna sank down on a chair, suddenly noticing how wet her shoes and stockings were. She wanted to lean forward, place her arms on the table, and rest her head so she could fall asleep right there, but at the moment she couldn't take her eyes off Inga. She was walking around wearing only a white shift and what looked like heavy socks big enough for a man. She showed no sign of embarrassment.

"It'll probably warm up soon," said Inga, "now that there are so many of us here, but maybe we should light the stove all the same. For the children's sake."

She bent down to open the stove door, then poked at the ashes to see if there were any embers still burning. She touched a wood shaving to the candle flame and then added a couple of pieces of kindling. When she leaned forward and blew on the wood, her dark hair shone red in the glow of the fire. Then she straightened up and smiled. "Welcome to Swede Hollow," she said.

IN THE MORNING everything looked different. Anna sat with Inga on the front stoop, wrapped in a borrowed blanket, and gazed out across the Hollow. Inga and the widow Lundgren with her two sons had managed to find these two small houses—she would have used the Swedish word *torp,* or *cottage,* to describe them, but apparently that's not what people called them here in America. They stood high on a hill with a view of the lower part of the Hollow, toward the railroad viaduct the family had walked along in the night. Today several trains passed every hour. The rail traffic had started up in the middle of the night, and Anna couldn't believe they'd dared come that way with the children and all their bags. But Inga said the Irish regularly took that route, and the Swedes did too when they headed for their jobs with the railroad. It wasn't dangerous if you knew the schedule of the Duluth train.

Anna glanced at her friend sitting beside her and wondered if Inga ever thought anything was dangerous. An alternate route was via the Drewry Tunnel a bit farther up the hill, and then along the street. But there they had to watch out for the brewery's dray horses, which could gallop past at a perilous speed, and then there was the wooden stairway up to Seventh Street, which was difficult for children.

It was above freezing now, and the eaves were dripping. The snow on the Hollow's hillside gleamed yellow in the sunlight, which off and on shone through the wispy clouds. Across the way Anna caught a glimpse of tiled roofs and a tower beyond the treetops. Inga turned to see what she was looking at, as eager as ever to point out things and explain.

"That's the Hamm mansion," she said. "Mr. Hamm owns the brewery on the hill. They only hire German workers. Tell the children to stay away from his house, because he's mean and he has dogs."

Below stretched the Hollow, rooftop next to rooftop, set at all different angles, with the dilapidated houses wedged into whatever space could be found, like a patchwork quilt in various hues of brown, white, and black. Anna had never seen a neighborhood like this before, where no order seemed to exist. But Inga had said that she knew nearly all the houses down there. The Irish mostly kept to themselves on either side of the railroad bridge. A couple of Italian families had also moved in farther up, and they were nice enough.

"Every once in a while there's an empty house, whenever a family is able to get a real house up on the street," Inga said. "Then they simply move out. I think there are two or three empty places a little farther down the slope. You'll have to see what you can find."

An hour earlier Gustaf and the girls had left, with David Lundgren as their guide and interpreter. They were going to see if they could find a roof over their heads for the coming nights. They'd gone down into the ravine while she and Inga stayed behind with Carl, who was asleep on Inga's kitchen sofa. He'd been restless and whiny almost all night, but now he was sleeping soundly. Anna was waiting for the right moment to bring up the topic she wanted to discuss before the others came back.

Inga had been living alone in the house for about a month, ever since the Olsson family had found a place to live on Railroad Island, which was closer to work and school. At first she'd stayed with the Lundgrens, but it was too crowded there with both boys at home. The Olssons had offered their place to her first, since they wanted a Swede to have the house before any Italians took it. Inga had agreed, even though in spots the roof was about to give way. "It's just a matter of moving in when you find an empty house," Inga said. If you wanted to establish proof of where you lived, you had to fill in the paperwork at city hall, but not many bothered to do that. Sheriff Waggoner's man came once a month to collect two dollars, and as long as you could come up with the payment, nobody asked any questions.

The Olsson house was one of the oldest in the Hollow. No one knew its age for certain, but it had undoubtedly been built before any Swedes arrived. The house had a good foundation, and it was in a nice, high position for when the spring floods came. Apparently the creek could get quite wild in March and April.

"Right now everything's covered in snow," said Inga. "And that's a blessing because you can't see all the trash people have thrown everywhere. And it doesn't smell of all the shit and dead animals."

She saw that Anna was surprised by what she'd said, so she pointed down at the creek, where the brown water could be glimpsed through the bare alderwood thickets.

"Just after we arrived in the summer, we saw the body of a calf down there. Somebody must have stolen it up on the street, taken what could be eaten, and then left the rest there. The corpse lay there, stinking, until I got some of the boys to bury it up on the slope. I don't even dare think about how it would have smelled if it was still there when the weather turned hot.

"Winters are hard here," Inga went on. "Worse than back home. But so far it hasn't been too bad. Pretty much like today. The summers are very hot."

"But they can't be as hot as in New York," Anna interjected.

"We'll have to wait and see," said Inga. "It's a long time until summer."

She told Anna how she'd "taken on cleaning" for some Swedish ladies up on Seventh Street, which meant long hours, but decent pay, although one of the ladies who paid best had now gone away for an indefinite length of time to nurse her sister in Wisconsin. She'd have to see if there would be more work when the woman came home.

"But I'm sure we'll find something," said Inga, not sounding worried at all. "There are always the laundries, and if you're in luck, you can get a job working up on Payne, in one of the Swedish shops. But you mustn't say that you're from the Hollow."

Anna listened to her friend's voice, which sounded like music to her ears. She understood only half of what Inga was talking about, but it was soothing merely to hear her speak.

Then Inga fell silent, as if she'd realized she'd been gabbing for a long time.

Anna was cold sitting there on the stoop. She wrapped the blanket more tightly around her. "There's a reason why we decided to leave Sweden," she said at last.

Inga didn't say a word.

"We were forced to leave." Her voice felt unsteady, so she paused for a moment and swallowed hard.

Inga stared down at the long valley, her hair frizzy under her blue kerchief. The sound of running water could now be heard clearly. Anna felt the tears spill down her face, but her voice didn't falter as she again spoke.

"Gustaf stabbed a man with a knife. A foreman at the shoe factory. Gustaf was paid the lowest wages of anybody, even though he had children to feed. And he was just as skilled as all the other workers. That man was always after him. And finally Gustaf stabbed him in the throat."

Inga still said nothing.

Anna didn't look at her as she went on, speaking as if to no one in particular.

"Things went badly, and the man bled a lot. He wasn't dead before we left, but I don't know what happened later. Everyone saw what happened."

She wiped her eyes and rubbed her face. She sighed heavily and then said in a stronger voice, "It was hard to wash away all that blood on his shirt, all the blood that wasn't his.

"The police came, asking for Gustaf, but we left before they could come back. We'd already been thinking about leaving, though at the time it seemed more like a game we were playing. But our papers were all in order. Gustaf's paternal grandfather paid for the tickets when we had to leave in a hurry. And then we just left. Now I don't know whether I even dare write home. The family doesn't know where we are."

"Wait for a while," said Inga firmly. "Wait until you know a little more."

"Gustaf is not a bad man. He doesn't drink anymore. And he hardly drank much before either."

"I know he's not a bad man," said her friend.

"I wanted to tell you about this, Inga. In case someone should come here asking questions."

Inga gave Anna a searching look, a little smile tugging at her lips.

"You should know that lots of people have brought one sort of baggage or another from back home. And then they end up here. What's important," she went on, "is to leave all that behind in Sweden. Then everything will be fine. If you carry your worries with you, things might turn out badly. And there are others here in the Hollow who worry me more than Gustaf Klar. People who can't leave things behind. Like David Lundgren, for instance."

Inga said no more, merely nodding at the path that Gustaf and the girls had taken, as if it were down there that her worry lay. And Anna remembered from their time on the ship how she'd thought that David Lundgren seemed to be bursting with something that was pressing on him from inside, something that might explode if it found no release. Yet he was always calm and friendly, though somewhat preoccupied, no matter what he said or did. She hadn't been able to make him out back then, but she'd had so many other things to worry about and ponder.

Anna now sat here, taking deep breaths and blinking away the last of her tears. She felt as if she'd emerged from a long and feverish illness. Soon Carl would wake up, and he'd be hungry. She longed for some coffee but didn't dare ask Inga if she had any.

The sun broke through a small gap in the low-lying clouds above the Hollow. For a moment light played over the roofs and bare treetops. In the sunshine she saw Gustaf and David with the girls in tow as they calmly walked up the path, chatting as if they didn't have a care in the world. Then the light moved on and everything looked the same as before.

*Swede Hollow, St. Paul*
February 1898

EVERYTHING BEGAN with one of the world's largest lakes, which long after it disappeared was given the name Lake Agassiz. The melt water from the glaciers collected until the rushing current broke through the remaining layers of earth and, during a single dramatic week that was witnessed by no one, it formed the enormous body of water that now flowed through the channels carved into the landscape by the ice. The Ojibwe named it *Misi-ziibi,* meaning "the great river." When the ice retreated farther north and the waters diminished, these channels remained in the land. One of them stretched south from what would eventually be called Lake Phalen.

Born in Derry, Ireland, Edward Phelan was a soldier from the military outpost of Fort Snelling who had settled in that long valley. In 1839, he was discharged from the U.S. Army in the middle of what would someday be called Minnesota. There he built himself a house with a proper stone foundation. Phelan left few traces behind, other than the suspicion that he'd been involved in the killing of another settler, as well as in some sleazy land dealings, which had forced him to flee to California. On his way there, he was murdered. His sole remaining legacy was a misspelled name on the first maps, as his name was assigned to the current that ran through the old glacial ravine. It became known as Phalen Creek. He also left behind the plot of land on which he'd built the wooden house, perched high up in the middle of the ravine, which one day in 1897 would become the dwelling place of Inga Norström from Dalsland, Sweden.

A wind from the north is gathering speed over Lake Phalen, driving snow flurries through the morning, gusting through forests and then falling as whirling bits of ice onto the smokestacks and wheat silos along the banks of the Mississippi, where work has been going on nonstop all night, then making its way between the vertical, tall dark, brick façades in the warehouse district. Almost meditatively the wind wanders back across the river and follows the narrow glacial channel, circling down upon the rooftops that have otherwise been sheltered through the night.

Ellen steps out onto the front stoop of the one-room house she has called home for the past two months and brushes off the fresh snow from the railing of the as-yet-unfinished porch. The steps up to the house had rotted through, and in order to get her mother to agree to move in, her father had to promise to build a new railing and stairs. They had turned out nice and solid, almost more solid than the rest of the house, which is already tilting a bit toward the bank of the creek, but the work has stopped for lack of boards and nails. Then more snow fell, and now they'll have to wait until spring to finish building. But the wood under the snow is still fresh and bright, and Ellen likes the feeling of the wood grain under her fingertips. None of the other small houses farther down toward the creek has new-built steps. And none of them has a porch.

A man starts singing hoarsely on the other side of the alderwood thicket next to the path. In the dim morning light she can't yet see anyone, but she knows who it is. Then he comes into view, a tall and stooped elderly man, dressed all in black. He walks along, looking straight ahead without a glance to either side, as he sings loudly "A Mighty Fortress Is Our God." It's old Jonsson, the father of Horrible Hans, who has once again been overcome by the urge to sing. Whenever that happens, the old man sings nearly all day long without stopping, as he switches between hymns and comic ballads while he goes about his tasks as usual. Ellen sometimes wonders whether he even notices that he's singing. But he does no harm to anyone, except for the fact that he often sings off-key. Right now he's headed to his long, narrow, and dark house farther down in the Hollow—the house he shares with his nasty son Hans; the son's thin, fair-haired, and silent wife, Agnes Karin; and the couple's two equally thin and silent little girls. Now Jonsson disappears behind the empty herring barrels that are stacked against the end of the house, continuing to sing off-key, although now his voice is more muted.

*And though this world, with devils filled,*
*Should threaten to undo us,*
*We will not fear, for God hath willed*
*His truth to triumph through us.*

Ellen is waiting for Elisabet. Even though her hands are freezing, she can't resist running her fingers through the pillow of loosely packed new snow on the partially finished porch railing. It looks so soft, and each time the feeling of scorching cold is just as surprising, making her a little more alert.

It's still barely light outside, and the Lincoln School is only three blocks away, but they can't be late. Elisabet always takes such a long time to get ready. Their teacher, Miss Swanson, speaks passable Swedish, but she has made it clear to her students that coming from Sweden gives them no advantage, and they are not allowed to speak their own language in the classroom. If they arrive late, Ellen will once again have to apologize to the entire class in English, and that's something she can't yet manage. For her and her little sister, the schoolwork is like long gray tunnels of incomprehension. Trying hard to concentrate and looking straight ahead, she has to make it through hour after hour of words that mean nothing to her. But it's better to go to school than to sit home and not be allowed out at all, the way it was in New York.

Mother pushes Elisabet out the door and Ellen wraps the yellow kerchief around her sister's head as a scarf, knotting it under her chin. Ellen knows Elisabet will take it off as soon as they're out of sight, but she does it anyway. Then they go down the three steps to the ice-covered path and head for the footbridge across the creek. Ellen worries that her little sister, stubborn as she is, will want to take the route through the tunnel instead of the stairs up to Seventh Street. She takes a tight hold on Elisabet's arm, prompting an angry squeak in reply. But neither of them speaks. They're both too sleepy to resort to words.

The wooden stairs up to Seventh Street are steep and slippery. In places the railing is missing, but it's still better than the Drewry Tunnel, where Mr. Lambine was run over by a brewery wagon while on his way to work. He died on the spot. That was four years ago now, long before they came here, but everybody still talks about it. Lambine's widow received compensation from the brewer, Mr. Hamm, which enabled her to move out. Since then she has not set foot in the Hollow. But you can still see the mark where the wagon scraped against the tunnel wall and where Lambine died, crushed between a wagon wheel and the cement wall. That's what the older children say.

Ellen clutches her sister's hand all the way up to the street, and neither of them glances around because then they might get scared and fall. Several of the steps have split apart and come loose, and the girls know they have to tread lightly on the third step from the top before they can reach the street. The steps are almost hidden underneath brushwood that no one has bothered to clear away, yet everybody knows the steps are there—like so much else, when it comes to the Hollow.

They turn onto Bradley Street and hurry past Larson's grocery store, its windows still covered with steel shutters for the night. Then they round the corner onto Collins Street, where the school looms, three stories high. A single window, belonging to the principal's office, shines with a cold electric light from the top floor under the school's clock, its dial also lit from within. Sometimes the principal's silhouette can be seen in the window as he keeps watch to make sure all the pupils arrive on time. Ellen has never seen him close up, and she wouldn't recognize him, although she knows his name is Mr. Watkins. The ice-covered schoolyard is now dark with children who are all heading for the stairs, so the two sisters wait until there is less of a crowd.

Then everyone lines up outside the classroom doors, with the girls on the left, the boys on the right. Above them, from the white-plastered ceiling, hangs the only lit kerosene lamp beneath its bloom of soot. Suddenly the air is hot and so filled with the smell of wet clothing and kerosene fumes that Ellen finds it hard to breathe. All she wants is to go inside the classroom so this incomprehensible day can begin. Everyone is quiet except for a few of the Flaherty boys, who also live in the Hollow. As usual, they are whispering and jostling each other at the back of the line. She feels their sharp eyes looking at her and takes a firmer grip on Elisabet's hand.

By the time they emerge from the school again, the sky is covered with dark snow clouds. A faint glow comes from the city far away on the other side of the river. She is hungry. Her sister quietly intones a chant they learned in class to practice their numbers: "One little, two little, three little Indians, four little, five little, six little Indians." Ellen doesn't like the song. She doesn't like the fact that her sister can't carry a tune, and she hates the words. Elisabet pays her no mind, continuing her mumbled song as she walks. Ten little Indian boys.

They pass Larson's again, and now the store is open. They slow their pace. Ellen is dawdling as she peers through the window at the rows of wheat bread and, farther inside, the more or less forbidden glass jars of peppermint sticks. She squints her eyes to quell her hunger, which is again making her stomach churn. Today Mr. Larson is the one standing behind the counter, allowing a customer to scoop snuff from a cask. He refuses to touch tobacco himself, being a member of the Baptist congregation and not a snuff user, but he lets people buy it if they serve themselves. Inga says Larson lived in the Hollow when he first came to the city, but he pretends that never happened whenever anyone goes in to buy groceries.

A snowball strikes Ellen's temple, and for a moment the world goes dark. When she opens her eyes again she sees tiny stars against the gray sky and shadows coming along the street, jumping over the snow drifts. The shadows take shape, turning into the Flaherty boys, all four of them, along with two of their pals whose names she doesn't know, but they also live in the houses on the other side of the railroad tunnel. Ellen pushes Elisabet behind her, between her back and the wall of the building, and stands with her head bowed, hoping the boys will simply go past. But not today. The next snowball hits her right in the stomach, but it doesn't hurt as much. Then the boys crouch behind the snow drift left by the plow and begin pelting the sisters with a barrage of hurriedly made snowballs mixed with gravel, but they do little damage because they aren't made of ice. Ellen closes her eyes and waits for it to be over, as Elisabet wraps her arms around her sister's waist. Today the boys have apparently decided that one onslaught is not enough, and she hears them shouting in unison, "Norskies! Norskies! Norskies!" It was when she had tried to explain that they were Swedes and not Norwegians that they had become enemies, and ever since the Flaherty boys have yelled "Norskie" after them.

Ellen is standing there with her head bowed and arms crossed when she hears a cracking sound followed by a sharp cry, like the yelp of a little dog being kicked. When she opens her eyes, she sees Micheál, the oldest Flaherty boy, lying in the snow drift with his hand over his mouth. She hears with surprise that he's crying loudly. The other boys are holding ready-made snowballs in their hands, but they're glancing around uncertainly, as if they'd woken from a dream. And bending over Micheál Flaherty is a big shadow.

The man—or boy, he's somewhere in between—straightens up and aims a kick at the boy lying in the snow, who cringes with fright. But the kick was only a threat, a "watch out or there'll be more." The big boy casts a quick glance in the girls' direction and then turns back to watch the boys grab Micheál under the armpits and haul him to his feet. He is still holding his hand to his cheek and crying, but more quietly now.

The big boy turns toward Ellen and Elisabet, and Ellen recognizes him at once. It's Leonard Hammerberg, the only son of the widow who lives at the very bottom of the Hollow, among those who have lived there the longest. He left school in the spring. He's wearing the gray jacket and cap of a railroad worker, along with a pair of real boots with steel-tipped toes. He looks like a grown man, but when he comes closer, Ellen can see his plump face and the brown fringe of his hair under the visor of his cap. She doesn't know what to say so she lowers her eyes.

"Damn micks," says Leonard, and then a little louder, as if he thought they might not have heard. "Damn micks!"

The little bell jingles as the door of Larson's grocery store opens behind them. Larson himself comes out onto the steps, wearing a waistcoat and shop apron. He peers down at them as they stand there in the rectangle of light cast by the bare bulb from the store.

"I don't want any trouble here, Hammerberg," the man says. "You need to settle any scores down in the Hollow."

Ellen stands up straight and opens her mouth to protest that it was the Irish boys' fault, but Leonard merely touches a finger to the visor of his cap and replies, "Sure thing, Mr. Larson." The door closes. Ellen sees that Elisabet has now stepped forward to take the big boy's hand. Ellen raises her own hand, as if to pull her sister back, but she doesn't know what to say. He did help them, after all.

"Thanks, Leonard," she says then. The girls start walking, with Leonard between them, and she notices that he's heading for the Drewry Tunnel. She wants to refuse to take that route, but he's going with them, and he's practically grown up, so maybe it will be all right.

"What cowards," Leonard says, "attacking a couple of girls." Ellen merely nods.

"You're the Klar sisters, right?" he says as he gives her a sidelong look. She nods. He asks how long they've been here.

"Since before Christmas," she says, adding without knowing why, "It's hard to figure out English."

"It'll come," he says. "It'll come." Elisabet is still holding his hand.

"Do you work for the railroad?" she asks, mostly just for something to say.

"The Great Northern," he tells her, seeming to savor the words, as if wanting them to go on and on. "Started after Christmas." Then he smiles with embarrassment and adds, "Though I mostly do odd jobs here and there. Waiting for an opening, as they say."

They enter the tunnel's lower vault, and their footsteps echo in the dark. Elisabet shouts at the top of her lungs, "AHHhhhhhh!!!" She does it partly so people will know they're there, but mostly to make the echo as loud as possible. They walk through the dark, and Ellen thinks everything is fine, even though her temple still hurts. Everything turned out as it should, and they're together and helping one another, as Inga always says they should. But when Ellen closes her eyes, she pictures Leonard bending over Micheál Flaherty, twice as big as the boy lying on the ground, and she recalls how he kicked at the air and how his face then broke into a big smile when he saw the other boy's fear. She opens her eyes. It's still dark all around them, with the sound of their footsteps on the gravel and ice echoing off the tunnel walls.

* * *

WHAT ANNA REMEMBERED from those first weeks was how cold she was. A draft seeped in from every corner of the house they'd found, especially from around the only window. It made no difference how much they stoked the stove. She would lie awake at night, listening to the children breathing, especially Carl, as her uneasiness grew with every wheeze or gasp. Soon some form of sickness, all that was wrong in life, would overtake them; it always found its way forward. The boy still slept between his parents, and sometimes, as Anna hovered between sleeping and waking, she thought that would protect him from all invisible threats that tried to reach them the way the gusts of wind reached through the gaps in the wallboards.

In late February a snowstorm raged for several days in a row, and the wind blew so hard it seemed to sweep right across the kitchen floor. The school was closed. From the window Anna could see nothing but white for as long as the daylight lasted, and she made the children stay in bed. When Gustaf went out to tend to an errand, he disappeared from view after taking only a few steps into the whiteness. Even the train stopped running for a day, and silence descended over the Hollow.

Then the real cold set in. Overnight the snow was transformed into armor. The spring on the hill froze. She tapped at icicles to melt them for drinking water, and they broke off with a sharp ringing sound, as if they were made of metal. They would stick to her hand if she wasn't careful. All sounds seemed louder than usual: the steam whistles from the boats far away on the river could be heard in the morning as clearly as the voices up on Bradley Street. All sounds seemed as close as the barking of the Irish families' dogs. They barked ceaselessly down by the vaulted railroad tunnels, echoing so it was impossible to tell how far away they were. The train up on the embankment, which remained her constant fear, could now be heard over great distances. It was true that the engineer would always blow the whistle as the train neared the Hollow, but now the tracks started clacking only a minute before the locomotive appeared, practically hidden behind a plume of loose snow and smoke.

Inga came over, bringing warm loaves of bread she'd baked directly on the stove from cornmeal, which was something she'd learned from the Italians. The bread was crumbly and dry, but it tasted good while it was warm. Anna wished she had a little dab of butter to melt on top of the warm loaf, but no one had butter. The children ate the bread so fast that she was afraid they'd develop intestinal blockage.

"That was fun," said Inga as she swept up the crumbs on the table. "The snow was crusted so hard that I could walk on top of it almost the whole way. And I'm not a small person."

That was so typical of Inga. In her mind, so many things were fun.

Gustaf hadn't yet found steady work. Since New Year's he'd gone out to shovel snow, and occasionally he was hired to break ice off the railroad tracks and switches. He had wanted to go across the river to seek work at the big mills, but everyone told him that wouldn't be a good idea until spring. At this time of year so many men had been let go, even if they had a family to support. And it made no difference what language a person spoke. Yet up at the Hamm brewery, they required the workers to speak German.

Gustaf would leave the house every morning, and sometimes he was lucky enough to have earned a few coins by the time he returned. Now and then Anna wondered if he stayed away out of sheer shame on those days when he could find no work. Right now she was so cold that she pulled the knitted shawl closer around her shoulders. Then she licked her fingertip to gather up the crumbs left on the table. The crumbs of cornbread shone yellow on the grained, gray surface of the table.

"Things will be easier in the spring," said Inga. That sounded comforting, but Anna reminded herself that Inga herself had not yet spent a spring in the Hollow. Yet she seemed to know more about everything in the area than those who had lived there ten years. She knew who was sick and who was well. Who was trustworthy and who was a liar. Where jobs were to be had whenever there were any at all. Every morning Inga would climb the stairs from the Hollow, just like the workmen on their way to the engine sheds and then proceed along the street, where she'd once again found work cleaning the homes of a number of elderly Swedish ladies, such as the widow Ingesson up on Seventh Street. Sometimes she also worked at the home of the pastor's wife on Burr Street, though Inga didn't care for the woman. Occasionally Inga would bring home small food packets that she would share with the Klar children.

"I can tell that you think things are hard here," said Inga as they sat at the table. "But it's still better here than in New York. And no doubt it's better that all of you came here instead of staying back home in Sweden. I suppose it's small comfort that other people have it worse. But this is where we live and not somewhere else. Keep that in mind."

Inga's remark came a bit brusquely, and at first Anna thought it sounded like a reprimand, even though she had never complained. At least not out loud. Maybe she should have been cross with Inga for voicing what seemed to be a criticism, but she didn't feel angry or offended. Instead her curiosity was piqued. So she asked her friend, "What did you mean when you said that other people have it worse?"

Inga paused before answering, as if pondering how much to reveal. Then she said, "Surely you know, Anna, that there's been talk here in the Hollow."

She shook her head. Talk about what?

Inga smiled.

"You've been here a while, and yet you don't seem to notice anything happening around you. Like the fact that the Lindgren girls left a week ago, on their way to the clinic out in the prairie to be cured of the pox. Unless they die first. I think one of them was very badly off."

Anna could hardly make sense of what she was saying. She must have looked bewildered, so Inga explained.

"The pox, the French disease, that they picked up when they worked as 'seamstresses.' Didn't you have that back in Örebro? There was a lot of coming and going down there for a while. But now the house is empty, and that's just as well."

The younger woman could tell that Anna either had no idea what she meant, or else she didn't want to talk about it. For a moment Inga sat in silence. Then she went on, "But there's another matter that is worrying me, and it might end badly. Haven't you noticed anything? Even though you see Mrs. Lundgren all the time? Hasn't she said anything to you?"

Anna shook her head.

"It's about David," said Inga. "He was so quiet during the whole crossing, and I thought he was a good son who had agreed to accompany his mother on the voyage. But now I think it was the other way around, and she was the one accompanying him, maybe for the sole purpose of keeping an eye on him. He seemed to lack all gumption, and he was so quiet that it seemed his very sanity might be in question, the way he kept mostly to himself. Until we arrived here, that is. Then some of us realized that he had his own reason for leaving Sweden. And he wanted to lure all of us to this place, as if we were attached by a string to him and his mother. It was here he was headed, traveling with a single-mindedness that made everyone else in the group follow along without giving the matter proper thought. After a while it turned out that his brother was not the only one who's settled here in Swede Hollow."

Anna listened with interest, almost against her will. She couldn't recall the last time she'd talked like this with someone. Gossiping.

"So who else came here?" she asked.

Inga hesitated before replying, "Everybody knows. It was Agnes Karin." When she saw that Anna didn't understand, she added, "Agnes. Horrible Hans's wife. David came here to look for her. They're from the same district in Västergötland, and they've known each other for ages. And by *known* I mean in the most intimate sense, and that's why Horrible Hans finally took his whole family and left Sweden. Then David followed them here. It was his brother Jonathan who wrote home to say they were here. Maybe he shouldn't have done that. Ever since, everybody has been waiting for the big confrontation. Everybody except you, apparently."

There was nothing the least bit amusing about the situation, yet Anna couldn't help smiling. Here they sat, talking about other people's misfortunes. As if the cold, the snow, and this hovel of a house were suddenly all part of something so familiar, something she recognized, and no longer a foreign country.

## ST. PAUL DAILY GLOBE

**The Squatter's Home**

**A Foreign Settlement in the Midst of the City of St. Paul—The Foreign Residents Thereof.**

**"Swede Hollow," Its Quaint Appearance.**

**How the Little Hamlet of Shanties and Huts Appears on a Winter's Day—A Quiet Scene.**

**Something of the Legal Status of the Holdings and the Extent of the Flaxen-Haired Population.**

Nestled in a little valley between Dayton's Bluff and St. Paul proper, right in the midst of the bustling and growing capital city of Minnesota, is "Swede Hollow." Nature made it the center of an amphitheater of hills. Man improved thereon and by filling up East Seventh Street to the grade, divided the lowlands and still more protected it from the wintry winds and the summer's sun. A railroad track, cut out from the side hills, skirts along the squatter settlement. Down through the little hamlet of huts, contributing not a little to the foreign picturesqueness of the scene, flows a clear and transparent brook. On either side of the tiny stream, which originates in a bubbling spring in the foot-hills, are ranged in pleasing disorder weather-beaten shanties. No street mars the foreign appearance of "Swede Hollow." The tracks of wagon wheels and the imprints of horses' hoofs are visible in the bottom of the pellucid little brook and along its snow-girted banks, showing that the few who desire to bring or carry away such bulky articles as require a wagon must follow up the stream. The sun shines brightly on the

HOME OF THE SQUATTER.

Its rays illuminate the quiet little scene at the bottom of the hills, and bring into prominence the many characteristic features of the foreign gathering of unpretentious and humble homes. The sloping hills that rise up all about the settlement are coated with deep snow. The valley itself is covered with the same white mantle. The blue, flowing brook forms a striking contrast to the general whiteness of the winter picture. The general impression, created in the mind of the thoughtful observer of the scene, is that "Swede Hollow" seeks no notoriety but would prefer to go along just as it has been for years without any public notice or alteration. "Swede Hollow" is not deserted on this bright, beautiful winter day, for evidences of its foreign population are visible on every hand.

Leading away from the bottom of the long flight of stairs that descend from Seventh Street is a well-beaten footpath. It goes directly to the nearest shanty and then divides, one branch leading across a primitive footbridge that spans the running brook, the other leading up the hollow to the next shanty. These divisions take place at every shanty. At some places the brook is crossed by boulders placed at convenient distances for those desiring to reach the opposite shore by stepping from stone to stone.

SMOKE CIRCLES UP

from the stove pipe and brick chimneys of many of the shanties. It does not issue out into the keen, frosty air in any volume but rather floats up in scanty quantity, as if from a well-guarded fire where the fuel was limited and the requirements great. It comes up very much as though it was compelled to steal away from some careful housewife, who knew the value of wood and was determined to get all the heat possible out of each stick and splinter.

Yards there are none in "Swede Hollow." Fences do not disfigure the quiet little hamlet. Cows and goats and sheep and horses are unknown possessions in that locality. Ducks and geese and dogs and pigeons are visible. Down on the brook the ducks and geese while away their time, occasionally forming into line and waddling over the snow to a convenient shelter. Dogs doze away on the sunny side of the little shanties. Pigeons, in rudely-constructed houses and cotes, fly out and in at pleasure.

CHILDREN ARE AT PLAY.

Little tow-headed girls and boys are in sight throughout the settlement. They are dressed in ill-fitting garments of different colors. No child has a suit throughout of the same color or texture. They are at play with the dogs on the sunny side of their shanty homes. One side of the dividing brook is quite a hill. Down its back the children of "Swede Hollow" are coasting. They have a board. This serves as a sled. Five or six of them pile on, as they have dragged or carried it up to the top, and down they go. They make no noise about it, however. Even the children seem to appreciate that they must not attract outside attention, and their squatter homes depend on being left alone. They slide in silence; save that now and then they prattle to each other in a foreign language. Even the dogs are not disposed to bark in "Swede Hollow." If things do not please these canine inhabitants, they will bite. Barking would excite outside attention: they respect their owners' wishes and follow their example. The ducks are less pronounced in their manifestation of pleasure at reaching the water than is ordinarily the case. The quietness of the scene affects every living being within its surrounding hills.

DOWN IN THE VALLEY

you go, prompted by a desire to learn something more of the strange settlement. Far below the surface of the street it rests, a perfect type of a Swedish hamlet. You start down the long flight of steps that lead from Seventh Street to the Hollow. The eyes of the infantile and canine portions of its population are upon you. The children stop their play and watch your descent. The dogs, with heads on paws, take in your coming. Not a sound is heard in "Swede Hollow." Presently womanly faces are seen peering out windows and doors. They have discovered you. Visitors, especially men who wear a stiff hat and overcoat and gloves, are rare.

You stop on one of the landings down the long flight of steps and gaze about the great scene. The immense stone archway, that forms part of the foundation for the Seventh Street fill, and through which the St. Paul & Duluth railroad tunnel is constructed, appears in sight. It is covered with huge icicles that have formed from the water trickling down from the surface of the street. The sight has no attraction for the residents of the Hollow. As you stop to view it, several flaxen-haired men and boys pass you on their way down to the settlement. They look at you intently, but give not the ice display on the stone arch a passing glance.

ONCE IN THE HOLLOW

you are met by the oldest squatter. He has on a cardigan jacket, with a dirty worsted scarf about his neck. On his head he has a worsted cap. "Is it going fur to sell?" he queries. "Ve pays too much for shanty. A dollar, a half for month. Don't want to buy, eh? Vaggoner, he owns Svede Holler; pay him rent. Ve be here sex, seben yers—all time de same, dollar, a half for month."

He, as well as the other residents of the Hollow, is very deferential to you, although they mistrust you and entertain the belief that you have come to look over the property with a view of purchasing it. While down in the Hollow you observe that the shanties are of the simplest pattern. None of them is over a story and a half high. The majority are but a single story. The shanties are weatherbeaten. Paint is a scarce article. A few of the doors are treated to a coat of paint. The brightest colors are used, and the contrast between the weather-beaten boards over the flaming-colored door is very striking. When the shanty is over a single story, the stairs leading to the loft are constructed on the outside. The interiors of these huts is simple from the uneven floors, without a carpet, through the few absolutely essential articles of furniture to the tissue paper curtains at the windows and hanging from the shelves, where the rude chinaware is kept. The tissue paper is cut in points and half circles, and is of many different colors. The occupants of these shanties are many; the rooms are few.

THE OWNER OF THE HOLLOW

is J. Waggoner, whose office is on Seventh Street, directly over his landed possessions. "Swede Hollow" includes ten acres, and is an open, fan-shaped valley that begins in a narrow strip at Fourth Street, west of Kittson Street and the railroad viaducts, and follows up between the immense hills to the north, widening as it goes until at North Street, its northern boundary, when the hills circle around and join one another. It derived its name years ago, before the city reached out that far, from the fact that the Swede laborers occupied it with their shanties. The squatters increased and soon the shanties grew in numbers and a little settlement was formed. The lower portion of it is known as "Connemara," and is occupied by natives of the Emerald Isle, who emigrated from the County Connemara. The upper portion of it, north of the Seventh Street fill, is "Swede Hollow" proper, although a few Swedes exist on the southern side of that artificial divide. Each shanty owner pays $1.50 per month for the privilege of occupying 20x40 feet of the Hollow with his shanty. This he puts up himself at an expense varying from $15 to $75. He is simply a squatter and has no rights that a new purchaser of the Hollow is bound to respect. There are no stores, a single saloon being the only public place within the valley. The saloon occupies the front room of a little shanty and is kept by a woman.

Crime is not common among the occupants of the little shanties. They are a rude, simple people and their wants are few. They live quietly and are not given to drunkenness, although beer is drunk as a great luxury on Sundays and holidays. But one murder has taken place in the hollow, and that was the work of the inhabitants of "Connemara." The health of the denizens of the lowlands is a mooted question. Many contend that the surface drainage is productive of disease. Others maintain that statistics, which have been returned to the health department, show that it is one of the healthiest districts in St. Paul.

Little care the white-haired men and women and children, far down in the valley, away from the noise and confusion of the city; little do they care for such discussions. They know that the sun's rays, even in the wintertime, warm the little valley. They know that wood is hard to get. They are content to sit in the little room, where the sunshine comes streaming through the window, and, thus warmed, to smoke their pipes and indulge in day dreams. Their greatest fear is that they will be routed out of their shanties. Their greatest desire is that they may be let alone.

The sun sets and "Swede Hollow" is at rest. It is silent and at peace for the night. No one will disturb the squatters or their possessions until daylight. Its occupants are happy.

*—GRUNDY*

## *The Tragic Story of Agnes Karin, David, and Horrible Hans, As Reported in the Court Records of the Blue Earth County Courthouse, Mankato, Minnesota*
## 1898–99

DAVID LUNDGREN was considered a tall man. When he was consigned to the Minnesota State Prison in Stillwater, where he would spend the next thirty years of his life, his height was listed as five foot eight. Otherwise there doesn't seem to have been anything remarkable about him. A quiet man who kept to the background but was not afraid to lend a hand. He had worked on his father's small farm outside Kinna, in Västergötland, Sweden, until he turned twenty. He then went to Göteborg where he found work as a tobacco roller. After that, things happened in rapid succession. His father died and his older brother left for America, paying for his passage with his share of the inheritance money. When David returned home to the family farm, everything had changed. Agnes Karin, the girl whom he had viewed as his fiancée, had become engaged and was soon married to the nastiest man in the whole district. No one could explain to David how this had happened. He'd been away, that was all, and life simply goes on if you turn your back.

His father's farm gradually declined, and it no longer seemed possible to keep it going. As soon as one thing was repaired, something else would fall apart. All the buildings were rickety and ramshackle and on the verge of collapse. And soon all of David's peers and acquaintances had gone to America.

He found that he could no longer stay away from Agnes Karin. In the evenings he would find some reason to walk past her house, and if he couldn't come up with an excuse, he'd simply go over there and stand outside. Agnes Karin would take time to chat with him if Horrible Hans wasn't around. As David's mother said on one of the few occasions when she discussed the matter with her son, Agnes Karin seemed happy only when she had the opportunity to talk with him. Otherwise she had become quite solemn and taciturn after marrying.

So one day when Agnes Karin was pregnant with her second child, it became known that Horrible Hans intended to emigrate. He didn't share his plan with anyone, but it became widely known nevertheless because he had to go to the county sheriff to get the proper documents. Two weeks later the whole family was gone, and their home was left empty. Rumor had it that Horrible Hans wasn't sure whether this second child was actually his or not, and so he chose to leave rather than live with the shame.

That's where the story might have ended if not for a letter that arrived one day from David's brother, Jonathan, who sent his greetings and wrote that he was living in St. Paul, where he'd found a job with the railroad. There was also something else he wanted to report.

Six months later the widow Lundgren and her younger son David arrived in the Hollow. Now things reverted to the way they were before, as if nothing had changed. Horrible Hans, Agnes Karin, and their two daughters lived in a little, unpainted house farther down in the Hollow, near the stairs leading up to Seventh Street and surrounded by the Italian and Irish families who lived on both sides of the viaduct and railroad tunnels. Horrible Hans had also brought over his old father, who wasn't quite right in the head. The man was harmless enough, although he would startle people on those days when he broke into song, singing loudly and off-key.

Eventually, with the help of his brother, David managed to find various odd jobs working for the Great Northern or Northern Pacific, although the work was temporary and seasonal. But every morning, on his way to the freight depot on Fourth Street or to the coal heap on Third, he headed along a route that took him past Agnes Karin's house. And he would often stop for a moment, whether anyone was around or not.

Agnes Karin was a short, thin woman. She didn't look like someone who was thirty, nor like someone who'd had two children. She was a couple of years older than David, and a good twenty years younger than Horrible Hans. She had fine, light brown hair and a wide mouth. But her smile was lovely, and she had all her teeth. Everyone who knew her wished her well, even though no one ever felt particularly close to her. They blamed that mostly on her husband and his dreadful temper.

Horrible Hans had no friends, nor did he want any, as evidenced by his surly manner. For that reason no one really knew how he made a living to support himself and his family. All anyone knew was that when the family first arrived in the Hollow, he'd actually had a good job as some sort of clerk at Hackett's hardware store—a job that partially involved dealing with the accounts of the Swedish customers. But people said he'd lost the job because of his foul disposition. Everybody also knew that he periodically beat his wife and children, sometimes quite badly, although

Agnes Karin never complained. But he didn't drink. After being fired from his office job, he'd go into town on certain days and come back late at night, leaving Agnes Karin and the children in peace for a while. Some people said that he went around to the Swedish bars and begged.

Things were bound to go badly, starting in the Hollow. Horrible Hans was a small man but hot tempered and violent. One morning when David Lundgren again walked past their house, Horrible Hans came rushing out in his shirtsleeves, clutching a hammer in one hand. He seemed to hesitate for a moment, as if seeing Lundgren eye to eye made him realize how much taller the man was. The next instant he threw the hammer right at Lundgren's head, just barely missing his mark.

David Lundgren said nothing. He leaned down, pulled the hammer out of the snow, and brushed it off. Then he slowly walked over to the fence. Horrible Hans may have taken a step back, but he kept his eyes fixed on Lundgren as he stood there with his suspenders hanging and one hand holding up the waistband of his pants. Lundgren raised the hammer and then flung it down with all his might at the gatepost. The hammer plowed into the rotting wood until only the shaft remained visible. Then he turned around and left.

One day Horrible Hans and his family were gone. The Klar girls heard about it from their classmates. Agnes Karin's daughters did not go to school, but Elisabet came home and said that their house, at the very bottom of the Hollow, stood empty, and maybe this time some Italians would move in. When Anna told Inga about this, she went over to have a look. She came walking back up the hill with the hem of her skirt muddied and told them it was true. Horrible Hans's house was empty. She'd even gone inside to see if there might be a letter or a note that would say where they'd gone, but she'd found nothing like that. The family had left behind the furniture, though it was of little value. But all the household items, bed linens, and curtains were gone.

David Lundgren was beside himself. The move had taken place while he was at work, and when he heard about it he reacted the way he usually did whenever he was upset: he fell silent. He didn't talk to anyone about the matter. Not even his brother. He was even quieter than before, with a stony expression on his face, but he was extremely restless. Several times a night he would go over to see if the house was truly empty. It remained that way until a man by the name of Pascella, whose older brother already lived in the Hollow, moved in with his young wife. The elder Pascella came in person to tell Jonathan Lundgren, asking that he speak to the other Swedes so that no one would take offense.

Several weeks passed before anyone heard anything more about the matter. Then rumors began to fly. Someone had seen Horrible Hans from the train. This report did not come from any of David Lundgren's workmates on the Great Northern. Instead it originated with a day laborer who knew Jonathan and who sometimes stopped by the Hollow to visit Lame Lotta's saloon farther down the slope. The man had been working as a brakeman on a Northwestern freight train that traveled between Mankato and Le Sueur. When the train slowed down around a curve, he'd been in his place up on the roof of the train car, and from there he'd caught sight of a solitary man plodding along the road, leaning into the wind. He was carrying a bundle, moving unsteadily, and looking generally miserable. The tracks followed the road for a short distance so the brakeman had time to study the man, and he saw his face when he raised his head to look at the train. That was when he recognized the man, although it took a few minutes for him to recall where he'd seen him. Several more weeks went by before the brakeman again ran into the elder Lundgren brother. More or less in passing he happened to mention the strange-looking man he'd seen struggling against the snow and wind out on the prairie. He said he was fairly certain it was that Horrible Hans character who was always at loggerheads with Jonathan's younger brother. But what was he doing in the middle of nowhere? It had been such a strange sight: a short, gaunt man dressed all in black, hunched forward and all alone in the wind blowing across the snow-covered prairie, where everything was white and even the crows didn't venture out.

When the rumor reached David Lundgren, it had an odd effect on him. He became utterly calm. For weeks he'd been walking around in dogged silence, but now this intense detachment eased and he became more like himself, although that didn't make him any more communicative. But he worked hard all spring. He took any job he could get, coming home only to sleep, unless he overnighted in a freight car up at the switch yard. It was only after he disappeared that people realized why he'd been working so hard. He needed to save up enough money to leave. One day he too was gone. It took close to a year before it was possible to piece together the whole story of what had happened, and by then it was all over.

On a rainy day in April, the widow Lundgren came over to the Klars' house and sat down at the kitchen table. Inga was already there. At that point no one had heard from David for several weeks.

"No, I have no idea where he is," said Mrs. Lundgren, smiling. She always sucked in her lips to hide the fact that she was missing a few lower teeth, but she looked calm and cheerful even though her words sounded sad. “I think he’s out there on the prairie somewhere, and I know what he’s after.”

And she said further, “Back home in Sweden he was silent and withdrawn all the time. When we came here, it was if he’d suddenly woken up. But when Agnes and her husband and children disappeared, it was as if he withdrew again even though he was still here. Of course I knew why he wanted to come to the Hollow. I knew from the very beginning. But why should we have stayed in Sweden? There was nothing left for him or for me. Now we’re here, and I have Jonathan back. David is out there somewhere, in some place he has always wanted to go. But Jonathan will stay here with me.”

And when the old woman again sucked in her lips to smile, Anna pictured the older brother, Jonathan—big and tall with strong shoulders, his hands hanging at his sides, always ready to help out. And she thought Mrs. Lundgren was right. Jonathan would no longer be the one who set off impulsively into the world, in search of what he so earnestly wanted. And for the first time she found Mrs. Lundgren slightly frightening as the big and stout woman sat there at her own kitchen table.

*Swede Hollow*
March 1898

THE MORNINGS HERE were different from how they were in New York. In some ways they reminded Gustaf of back home. He would eat his corn mush, which was certainly a bit sweeter, drink his coffee if there was any, and then put on his jacket and a dark yellow scarf, winding it around his neck and ears, since he had no cap. Then he went out the door, usually while everyone else was still asleep. It was pitch-dark. There were no street lights in the Hollow, but in some of the houses farther down the slope lights shone from the loft windows. And above the viaduct, to the south toward Seventh Street, he could see the lights of the city, faint but clear. But down here everything was quiet. Before he climbed the stairs, it was like being out in the country.

Yet one thing here was the same as back in Sweden and in New York, during those months they'd lived there: more and more men joined him as he walked along the path toward the stairs, until he was just one of many barely visible gray figures in the dark. They greeted each other briefly as they exhaled, trying to save their breath and moving cautiously so as to hold on to the warmth from their beds, which still clung to their skin under their shirts. The snow creaked beneath their wooden soles. Some had been able to afford real boots with steel-tipped toes, but only those who'd already managed to find steady work. If Gustaf could get hold of the right type of leather and glue, he'd be able to make himself a pair of boots. He thought about that a lot, but it cost more money than he could spare.

Some of the men who had found permanent jobs might soon move away. Then they'd start off on their morning route somewhere else in the city, way up there on Railroad Island or even farther away. Occasionally there was a line at the bottom of the stairs; then the others had to stop and wait as the cold set in and annoyance took the form of a cloud hovering above their heads. When Gustaf reached Seventh Street he would merely follow along with everyone else heading to a spot where work might be found. Usually this meant the railway repair shops and freight depots. He followed the other men across the viaduct, sometimes passing right through the billowing smoke from the locomotive that now and then passed below them. Then they proceeded down to Fourth Street where the long brick buildings of the railroad companies began. From that direction the railroad depot itself looked almost like a church, with tall, arched windows designed to let in as much light as possible. Only those men who already had permanent positions headed over there. Gustaf joined the others, which meant most of the men, as they walked toward the long and narrow barracks, also built of soot-covered brick. If he was in luck, he'd get hired as a freight loader and could spend parts of the day indoors. It varied from day to day how many men were needed. Even if the man wearing a waistcoat on the loading dock didn't choose Gustaf, it was still worth waiting for a bit, since workers were needed to clear the tracks of snow or knock ice off the switches. Like everyone else, he had slipped the Irish foreman a bigger bribe than he could really afford—a dollar a month—but the man didn't always seem to remember that fact.

If it turned out that all the shovels and pickaxes were taken on any specific day, he could always head across the switchyard's tangle of tracks to the warehouse belonging to the Great Northern on the other side. Maybe more workers were needed over there, although the Northern Pacific paid a little better.

Today Gustaf and Jonathan Lundgren were the only ones left from the Hollow. They were standing with some other men who also hadn't been chosen when the doors to the warehouse were closed. Without a word Lundgren began walking toward the tracks, and Gustaf followed. For a while Lundgren had had a permanent job with the Northern Pacific, but he'd been let go a few years back and then worked in the forests. Now he was here again, doing various odd jobs. But he knew how everything functioned, so Gustaf thought it was wise to stick close.

He stuffed his hands in his pockets and paid careful attention to where he set his feet, stepping over the ties and rails, now and then raising his head to see if any train might be on its way into the track area. Slowly the sky turned gray in the east. There was no wind. In the middle of the tracks, Lundgren suddenly stopped. At first Gustaf thought he was thinking of taking a pinch of snuff, but he merely stood there in silence, without sticking his hand in his pocket. Gustaf got restless, wanting to move on to see if there might be any odd jobs left for them. The other man glanced over his shoulder and said something. Gustaf had to lean forward to catch what he was saying. At first he thought he'd misheard. Here they stood in the middle of all the tracks, beneath a leaden gray sky, and they would have to hurry if they hoped to find work. Yet the big man had said quite simply, "It's a long way home." For a brief, heartbreaking moment Gustaf thought Lundgren was about to start crying. Then they both began walking toward the low warehouse buildings on the other side.

He hadn't been over to the Great Northern very often. Today it was just the two of them and some Irishmen who huddled together a short distance away from the loading dock. The door to the warehouse stood open a few feet or so. A man wearing a long military coat and boots stood with his back turned, talking angrily to someone inside. Then he turned around, came out onto the ramp, and looked down at them. The Irishmen stepped forward but still kept their distance by several yards. The man in the coat turned first to the two Swedes. "Swedes?" he asked. "Any English?"

They both nodded. Jonathan Lundgren, who had been here the longest, could understand quite a lot.

"You two," said the man, pointing at them. Then he fired off a long stream of words that Gustaf couldn't follow. Lundgren listened intently, nodded, and then turned to go. The Irishmen stayed where they were, still waiting.

"What did he say?" asked Gustaf as they went around the side of the warehouse. "What are we supposed to do?"

"Here's what he said: 'I know you're good workers as long as you understand what we say to you.' That was mostly a test to see if we understood what he said. When I told him we did, he said we should walk along the tracks toward town and de-ice the switches. Have you ever done that before?"

Gustaf shook his head.

"It's not hard. First we need to get some tools from the foreman."

They reported to a little cubbyhole at the corner, where they were given ropes, a blowtorch, a snow shovel, a bucket of grease, and a hammer for each of them. In a ledger they had to both print and sign their names. Then the foreman rattled off a long series of words, and Lundgren nodded and said, "Okay," several times. Gustaf stood there trying to look as if he understood every word. Then they went back out into the winter.

They followed the tangle of tracks leading away from the train station and headed down toward the river. It was very quiet. The branches of slender deciduous trees, bowed beneath the weight of the snow, formed a vault over the embankment. Down at the river a couple of tugboats moved upstream toward the falls, and on the other side white smoke rose up from the huge steam mills. Gustaf hadn't yet been over to the opposite shore. They walked in silence, their breath coming out in clouds.

The day had begun. It had been given a direction, and suddenly it held a place for him.

"You should wear gloves instead of mittens," said Jonathan. That was one of the few things he said all morning. They chopped ice off the levers and pinions and then melted away whatever frost was left. Gustaf worked as hard as he could, thinking he was moving quite fast. But he had to keep taking breaks to warm up his hands by sticking them in his armpits, and that made him lose time. Then Lundgren had to wait, holding his hammer, until the feeling returned to Gustaf's fingertips.

"I'd still have to take them off so I can feel what I'm doing," Gustaf said curtly as he raised the numb palms of his hands and with all his might brought the sledgehammer down on the jammed lever—which gave way and slammed into the exact spot where his left hand had been only moments ago. The bang was swallowed up by the sound of a switch engine approaching on the side track, but he felt the blood drain from his head, leaving him dizzy. If his hand had still been lying there, it would have been chopped off at the wrist.

Lundgren looked at him.

"You should wear gloves," he said after a moment.

"I can't afford them," replied Gustaf, looking down. "Real gloves made from soft leather cost money. But I suppose I could make some myself." He knew the other man couldn't hear him. The hissing from the pistons of the approaching locomotive was getting louder, and the smoke was already casting a shadow on the snow, still white. He looked up.

The switch engine, bearing the colors of the Great Northern, was as shiny as a plaything. Clinging to the side was a man holding one arm out, as if performing some sort of odd circus trick. It was the boy named Hammerberg, who often prowled around their house in the evening. He was holding on tight with one hand as he stood on the bottom rung of the ladder and flailed his other hand in the air, his fingers splayed as if to catch the wind. The boy caught sight of them and waved, his face lit up with an expression of delight. Then the locomotive drew even with them, a crashing wall of metal and smoke and a deafening hissing sound. Leonard Hammerberg slid past above them, like one of the Lord's angels, and then disappeared into the coal smoke that settled behind the engine. They saw him again down at the bend, still hanging on with one hand and with the other stretched out as the locomotive went around the last curve before the bridge. Then he was gone. Only the smoke remained, hovering among the tree branches like an ever-diminishing spiderweb.

"That one's not right in the head," said Lundgren, bending down again to inspect the switch to see if any part of the mechanism had broken when it was released. Gustaf looked down at his own hand, as if to make sure it was still there. He was hungry, and his sense of relief suddenly faded, giving way to an encroaching headache. As he watched Lundgren struggling with the jammed and frozen hinges, he thought that maybe the young boy they'd just seen was not the one who lacked all common sense.

IT WAS WHEN THEY WERE SETTING THE TABLE for supper that the darkness took shape again. That was how Ellen always thought of it: *the darkness,* a shadow just at the edge of her vision, refusing to disappear, always there as a reminder of something awful to come. She could have also called it *the bitterness,* like a bad taste at the back of her mouth. It had been there for as long as she could remember. At times it would grow, at times it would shrink. Now it reappeared when her mother once again was cross with Elisabet, who had carelessly set the tin plates down on the kitchen table with a great clatter. They were the same plates they'd had onboard ship, but they were still usable. Elisabet never paid attention to what she was doing; she always made too much noise and flitted about no matter what she did. She hadn't yet learned to restrain her movements, and she chattered to herself as she set the table. Ellen followed behind her little sister, correcting the placement of everything so the table would look nice. Their mother glanced at them over her shoulder from where she stood at the stove. Then she blurted out something so suddenly that at first Ellen couldn't decide who she was talking to. She heard her mother ask, "What did you say?"

Both girls froze. All at once everything seemed uncertain and shaky.

"What do you mean, Mother?" Ellen asked.

"I was talking to Elisabet. What did you just say?"

Elisabet peered up at her through the strands of her straight, blond hair hanging in her face. She looked puzzled, as if unaware of the approaching storm.

"I just said what a lot of work there is to do."

Their mother had now turned away from the stove to face them. Behind her the brisket and potatoes were bubbling in the family's only copper cook pot.

"No, that's not what you said. Say it again."

"I said, 'Musha, musha,' what a lot of work there is to do."

Their mother took two steps forward and gave Elisabet a swift box on the ear. Then she went back to the stove and began stirring the pot as if nothing had happened. Elisabet stood like a statue in the middle of the room with her arms hanging at her sides as she blinked hard to keep from crying.

"That's not how we talk," said their mother in a matter-of-fact tone. Elisabet's voice quavered as she replied, but she was defiant.

"All I said was . . ."

*And Ellen thought as she stood there, still holding one of the dull, scratched plates in her hand: don't make it any worse than it already is.*

"All I said was that Father will be home soon."

"No, you didn't. You're not to use words like that."

"All I said was—"

Speaking in a harsh voice, her face turned away as she stirred the pot, their mother said, "You sound like an Irishman. You sound like a *mick*. I don't want to hear that sort of language in this house."

*And Ellen thought, They're so alike. The same straight hair, although Mother's is darker; the same thin face that gets even sharper with stubbornness. I'm nothing like them.*

From far away she heard their mother go on: "I don't want you talking like them. I don't want you talking *to* them. You've been hanging around those ramshackle houses of theirs and those children way down in the Hollow. They need to keep to themselves, and we'll keep to ourselves up here."

*Ellen wondered whether she ought to say that, on the contrary, it was the Irish children who kept to themselves and who didn't want to have anything to do with them in school, but she also knew that no matter what she said, she risked getting in hot water. So she didn't say a word.*

Silently Elisabet headed for the door. She could no longer hold back the tears, and her face was red and contorted. She took her shawl from its hook and went out. Ellen took two steps toward the door to call her sister back, but her mother waved her hand abruptly, a gesture that meant *Leave her be.*

"She'll go over to Inga's place," she said from the stove. "She'll come back when she gets hungry. You stay here. I want to have a talk with you before your father comes home."

Ellen stood still, as if frozen midstride, waiting for what would come next. She was still holding the plate in her hand. And the darkness was growing from the corners of the room.

Her mother took the cook pot off the stove and put on the lid. Ellen had been feeling hungry, but the smell of brisket and cabbage now made her stomach churn. All of a sudden she was terribly thirsty and wanted to go over to the bucket of water, but she didn't dare move. Her mother stood at the stove. Ellen could feel her looking at her, but she didn't dare look up. Her mother said something. She heard the words as if from far away, but at first they made no sense. "What is he doing here every evening?"

She didn't know who her mother was talking about. For a long moment neither of them spoke. Finally it seemed more dangerous to remain silent, so she asked, "Who? Who do you mean, Mother?"

She expected to be slapped. But instead her mother said calmly from where she stood at the stove, "You know very well who I mean. That Hammerberg boy. Leonard. He keeps running around the house as if he's looking for something. Don't think I haven't seen him."

Ellen looked up. "So that's what you meant," she said.

Her mother gave her a stern look with her black-pepper eyes.

"It's not like you think, Mother," said Ellen after a moment. "I'm not the one he wants to talk to. He talks to Elisabet a lot."

Now her mother didn't look mad. Instead she seemed mostly surprised. Then she turned around, picked up the ladle, and took the lid off the pot. From over by the sideboard she said in a husky voice, "What could he want with Elisabet? He's practically a grown man."

Ellen mulled over these words in her mind. They felt like shards of pottery with sharp edges, and she had to scrape past them so as not to make matters worse. She had only one chance before the darkness once again closed in around them.

"He walks us home from school," she said. "When he has time after work, that is. So the Flaherty boys won't bother us. Those boys who live down by the tunnels."

"You and Elisabet need to stay away from them," her mother automatically said as she stood there, holding her hands in front of her.

"They're scared of Leonard. When he's with us, they don't dare do anything. Besides, he thinks it's fun to talk to Elisabet, because she says such silly things."

And Ellen pictured the two of them in her mind, the broad-shouldered Leonard wearing his sailcloth jacket and her skinny little sister in a much-washed, checked dress walking five steps ahead of her, on their way through the Drewry Tunnel. Elisabet would say something she couldn't hear, but it made the boy with the big hands snort with laughter. She pictured the way his face would first light up with surprise that a little girl could say something so funny. Ellen almost never heard what they said to each other, but if she did, she didn't find it funny. She merely walked along, feeling safe, in their wake. The fact that her mother might be worried about Elisabet had never even occurred to Ellen. She knew that Leonard was unpredictable and that some people were wary of him. But Elisabet was the last person her mother needed to worry about.

Her mother straightened up. Ellen couldn't see her face, but she could hear that her breathing was now calmer. Then she blew her nose on the corner of her apron and said in a perfectly ordinary voice, "It's best you go and fetch Elisabet and Carl at Inga's place. We'll be eating soon."

That was all she said. In the silence Ellen slowly slipped out the door, closing it behind her. She didn't stop to put on a coat because she didn't want to risk upsetting the calm that had now been restored. She stood on the half-finished porch, shivering in the chill of the evening as she looked out over the Hollow. She paused for a moment before setting off up the hill to Inga's house. The lights in the ravine down below were like tiny autumn leaves on the surface of a deep well. She felt as if she were seeing everything for the first time. In the blue dusk along the creek the windows, set apart, glowed yellow, one after the other. Smoke rose up through the dark behind a wall of shimmering lights. She breathed in through her nostrils, which closed up with a sharp smell of iron. Down where the Irish lived, a dog barked, obstinately and unceasingly.

Then came the whistle from the Duluth train, which always gave two blasts before entering the tunnel and one blast inside to warn everybody who lived next to the track. Soon the train would appear behind a cloud of coal smoke, gliding along the embankment that cut them off from the street above. Ellen suddenly felt so cold that it frightened her, and she ran as fast as she could up the path to Inga's slanting house, which looked like a silhouette cut out of paper against the last of the daylight above the slope to the west.

*Swede Hollow*
April 1898

EVERY SUNDAY some of the people who lived in the Hollow went to the Swedish Lutheran Church up on the hill. That was expected of those who were about to marry or if a child had been born, and at least that much was the same as back home. Others went to the First Swedish Baptist Church, which was in the opposite direction, up on Payne Avenue. There had been much discussion about whether it was obligatory to join the Lutheran church even if a person attended the Baptist church; this was the opinion of many of those who had lived the longest in the Hollow. But those who were part of the Baptist congregation would get quite cross if anyone voiced such an idea. They would usually declare that since they were now in the United States, the pastor had nothing to say about the matter, at least not in the same way as he had back in Sweden. But most people living in the Hollow went to no church at all, except when it became necessary.

Nilsson, the carpenter, and his family were among those who had joined the Baptists. Mr. Nilsson didn't always attend the services, but every Sunday his wife could be seen, with her two daughters in tow, heading for the Drewry Tunnel and continuing up to Beaumont Street. The girls, who were nearly grown, would walk along holding hands, which presented a comical picture. In general there was something odd about them, though it had nothing to do with the fact that they attended the Baptist church instead of the usual Lutheran church. Nilsson was a taciturn man who could usually find work on some construction project in the area, and no doubt his work situation would improve even more when spring arrived. His wife and daughters were even quieter than he was, if that could be possible. Ellen had heard her mother and Inga talking about them, lowering their voices in such a way that made her automatically prick up her ears. Mrs. Nilsson was not unpleasant, but she seemed bowed beneath some invisible burden. After a while Ellen understood what that burden was, even though the grown-ups avoided discussing the topic. Apparently one of the daughters was not quite right in the head. This wasn't something you could tell just by looking at her, but she had trouble taking care of herself, and that's why she often smelled faintly of urine. Since the whole family said so little, no one was fully aware of the situation at first. The Nilssons mostly kept to themselves, living in a small white-painted house that the carpenter had built from scraps of lumber he'd hauled home from one of his construction jobs. Inga thought it must have been because of the daughter that the Nilssons had left Sweden. The work opportunities for the father probably fluctuated in the same way back home, sometimes good and sometimes bad, so she wondered what they had thought would be different in another country. Ellen could have explained, if anyone had asked her. She thought it was the simple fact that nobody knew the family here, so they were allowed to suffer their invisible burden in peace. And they probably wouldn't leave the Hollow anytime soon.

Inga continued to do various odd jobs for the "ladies," who wanted her to clean house and help with all sorts of chores. Ellen could understand why they hired her. Inga was always good-natured, and she didn't get mad if anyone bossed her around. She might not be a particularly fast worker, but everything got done properly. Inga said that it had become popular to hire Swedish servants; they were acquiring a good reputation, especially those who could speak some English. Yet most of Inga's ladies had actually come from Sweden themselves.

One Sunday Inga came over to the Klar house, as she usually did after work. But this time it was Ellen she wanted to see. She came right to the point and asked Ellen whether she'd be willing to help out with a big cleaning job at the home of Mrs. Gustafson up on Seventh Street. She wanted to do a spring cleaning of her entire apartment. They would have to beat the rugs, change the curtains, and scrub the floors. Ellen would be paid a dollar, as would the Nilsson girl, who would also be helping out. The other Nilsson daughter couldn't work away from home, so they needed one more person. That's why Inga wanted to know if Ellen would come. It was only for one day.

"I have to go to school," she said, but out of the corner of her eye she saw her mother's back stiffen as she stood at the window.

"Missing one day of school won't matter," Anna said. "We need the money."

Ellen was about to say something about Elisabet, who shouldn't be walking alone, yet she knew that for the time being her mother had accepted the fact that Leonard would make sure Elisabet got home from school safely. So she didn't say anything, although she could already feel how a hole was growing inside her where that school day should have been. Somebody was always missing from the classroom because they were needed to help out with some job or other, and she could picture how Miss Swanson's face, already strained, would seem to tighten from the inside when Ellen's absence was noted during the morning roll call. She imagined the scene on Thursday when her name was called and no one answered. Miss Swanson would press her thin, bloodless lips together even harder but refrain from saying a word about the matter.

"It's only for one day," said Ellen's mother without looking at her. She nodded and lowered her eyes, feeling Inga's warmth from the other side of the table radiating through the room and making the situation a little easier to bear. Inga would be there too, after all, and not just that Lisbet Nilsson, with whom Ellen had hardly spoken.

It was still dark when Inga came to get her. Before dawn, a cold fog hovered over the creek down in the Hollow, but most people were already awake. For the past half-hour the lights had been on in almost all the loft windows farther down the slope, and many of the men were already on their way to work. Ellen wrapped her shawl around her shoulders and followed Inga down the slushy and slippery path to carpenter Nilsson's house. Inga didn't say a word as she led the way while chewing on something. She too was only half-awake. As they got closer to the house, Ellen saw Lisbet waiting on the front steps, standing quite still with her arms hanging at her sides. She must be freezing, thought Ellen. Then all three of them walked down through the Hollow, following the beaten path made by the men who had passed that way a half-hour earlier. In the semi-darkness, the stairs looked steeper and higher than in daylight, and Ellen was reminded how only a week ago she'd gathered her courage and asked Leonard if he knew who had built the stairs and how long they'd been there. He'd merely laughed soundlessly, the way he always did, and then said, "It was Ola Värmlänning who built them a long time ago." That was what most people said, and it meant that he didn't really know. He said no more about the topic. Ellen didn't think the stairs looked like the work of one man, but she didn't ask any more questions. Right now she followed Lisbet Nilsson up the icy steps, holding tight to the railing, which she noticed got more and more wobbly on each day that passed.

Up on Seventh Street the world began. On the other side she caught a glimpse of the river with barges towing lumber and an old paddle wheeler off in the distance, fighting its way against the current. From far away came sounds from the engine sheds. And she could see the steam mills beneath their hovering plumes of smoke. Inga began walking into the wind, which always seemed to be blowing at the top of the stairs. She and Lisbet followed, heading toward town.

Ellen had never been this far from home since they'd arrived here, and Seventh Street was longer than she'd previously imagined. She'd pictured Mrs. Gustafson living right across from the stairs, or at least nearby. But Inga kept going, leaning into the wind, which swept along the wide street. It felt as if they'd been walking for an eternity under the swaying telephone wires. The buildings on either side of the street began to change, getting bigger the closer they came to the city; soon the buildings were three or four stories high and made of stone. Lisbet Nilsson didn't say a word as she walked along, swinging her arms. Ellen thought maybe that's how a person would get if she had a sister like Lisbet had; if there was no one to talk to, she might simply stop talking and keep to herself.

Mrs. Gustafson lived on the third floor in a block of buildings with various businesses on the ground floor. Next door was a shop with big glass windows and a gilded sign with the words EKHOLM FURS. Across the street a red-and-white barber pole slowly spun in the wind. There was hardly anyone around, and none of the businesses were open yet.

"This is it," said Inga, holding open the door to the stairwell. In the dim light inside Ellen could make out a steep staircase. For a moment she thought she was back in New York, and her stomach lurched. But the smell here was completely different, mostly wood fires and dust and a whiff of coffee from somewhere.

Mrs. Gustafson seemed to have been waiting for them just inside the big double doors of her apartment. She was in her sixties, a short woman wearing a dark dress with ruffles at the neck, and at first she seemed taller than she was. Her gray hair was pinned up and gathered under a net. She didn't say "Good morning" but merely turned to Inga, whom she'd known for a long time, and said, "The cleaning things are in the kitchen cupboard." She didn't even glance at the young girls standing in the hall, their cheeks still flushed from the wind outside. Inga simply nodded and led the way to the kitchen.

The apartment consisted of three rooms and a kitchen, and there was running water from a tap above the sink. In the dining room an electric lamp hung from a chain in the ceiling, but it was turned off. The kitchen had a wooden floor, but the floors in the other rooms were covered with linoleum in dull colors.

"Linoleum is good," Inga whispered to them as she issued instructions. "It's easier to scrub clean than an ordinary wood floor, and you don't need to use as much water."

Inga had said this would be a spring cleaning, and that's exactly what it was. They began by wetting the adhesive tape around the windows.

"Start at the top and work downward," Inga said. The whole time Mrs. Gustafson remained somewhere in the apartment. She didn't say anything, so it was possible to imagine that she'd gone out without telling them. But then her shadow would sweep past the open double doors. She was like a dark and vigilant bird who would suddenly glide in front of the light, casting her shadow over their work.

Lisbet now spoke once in a while. The warmer they got, the more she seemed to thaw out. She said that one day she too wanted to have linoleum on their wood floors at home. And Ellen could only agree.

The tall windows in the big parlor faced the street, which was now teeming with people. The street vendors had set up their stalls, and the wind seemed to have subsided a bit. Muted sounds seeped in through the double panes and heavy drapes, which yielded an entire avalanche of dust when shaken. They had to carry the drapes downstairs and outside in order to beat the dust out of them.

Toward afternoon they were each given a glass of weak coffee and some bread and butter; otherwise they had been working without a break.

Then Mrs. Gustafson glided soundlessly in the door and told Inga that she had to leave to tend to an errand, but she would be back before they finished for the day. As Ellen polished the door handle with a chamois, she watched Mrs. Gustafson get ready to go out. The woman opened an upper cupboard and took out a big black hat adorned with a ribbon and a bunch of dyed cloth flowers in front. Then she leaned close to the hall mirror and carefully put on the hat, fastening it with a couple of long hat pins. Ellen kept on staring as her hand automatically rubbed the brass knob of the door handle. But then she met Mrs. Gustafson's eye in the mirror and she lowered her gaze until she heard the apartment door close. It was the most beautiful hat she'd ever seen.

They didn't stop working just because Mrs. Gustafson had left, but they did slow their pace. Afternoon fatigue had set in, and they dragged their feet as they moved through the big rooms where a peaceful silence now reigned in the owner's absence. The big clock ticked steadily. The sound of voices came from the street below.

Lisbet Nilsson stood for a long time in front of a chiffonier that had a small crocheted cloth on top of the glass surface. The shelves above were crowded with small porcelain figurines. Swans swimming on a mirror, girls and boys dressed as shepherds, and a leaping deer. It was Lisbet's job to dust all of them. For a long time she held a miniature blue porcelain basket in her hand. It was filled with the most perfect tiny porcelain roses, and she was reluctant to put it back where it belonged. Inga went to stand behind Lisbet and said calmly, without a trace of reproach in her voice, "It's lovely, but she would notice it was missing the minute we went out the door." Lisbet carefully set the little basket down and began polishing the dining table, even though she'd already done that. She kept her back turned, but Ellen could see that she was crying.

Just as they were wondering whether there was anything else for them to do, Mrs. Gustafson returned. They put all the cleaning supplies back in the kitchen cupboard in the big pantry. Lisbet was no longer crying, but she was once again just as silent and withdrawn as she had been in the morning. The two girls listened as Mrs. Gustafson counted out the coins into Inga's hand. When that was done, they curtsied to her and put on their coats and shawls. Then they went down the stairs and stepped outside into the wind.

It had begun to snow. Sharp little flakes blew slantwise across the street, but above the rooftops the sky was the dove-blue dusk of spring. Feeling both light-hearted and tired, they made their way past the street vendors who were taking down their stalls and chatting to one another in various languages, none of them Swedish.

As they approached the bridge and stairs, Ellen quietly said to Lisbet so that Inga wouldn't hear, "One day I'm going to have a hat like that."

Lisbet merely nodded, as if not paying particular attention. But suddenly, as if speaking from the very depths of her own thoughts, she said, "It doesn't seem right to be working for someone who speaks Swedish to us."

That hadn't occurred to Ellen, but when she heard the words spoken out loud, she understood exactly what Lisbet meant. Inga heard too, but she didn't offer any comment. She simply walked faster, making it hard for the girls to keep up with her even though they were younger.

None of them said another word as they headed for home.

## *ST. PAUL DAILY GLOBE*

### THEY HAD A FREE FIGHT

**Row at Swede Hollow Led to Several Arrests.**

Algot Sundstrom, 575 Bradley; Charles Lindgren, 575 Bradley; Albert Swanson, No. 10, Swede Hollow; and Coleman McDonough, 81 Tennessee Street, are all at their respective homes, suffering from cuts, bruises and injuries received in a free-for-all fight in Swede Hollow shortly before 6 o'clock yesterday afternoon.

Coleman McDonough got the worst of the deal and has a number of small cuts on his body, one of which is under the heart and is quite severe. He was attended by Dr. Hall. The other men suffered mostly from cuts about the eyes and bruises on the face.

John Metz and Albert Metz were arrested in connection with the case shortly afterwards on the charge of assault with a dangerous weapon, and are at the Margaret Street police station. Patrick O'Tierney and John McDaley were arrested on the charge of disorderly conduct.

It seems that Swanson and Lindgren were coming down the Hollow, when they met John and Albert Metz, Patrick O'Tierney, and Coleman McDonough, with some others, "rushing the can." Swanson and Lindgren claim that the men insulted them and they ordered them to get out of Swede Hollow, as it was not the place for them.

This started words between them, and before anyone really knew what had happened, the entire gang, with several more denizens of the Hollow, were throwing stones and taking clubs at each other whenever they got a chance.

Albert Swanson, who lives at No. 10 Swede Hollow, was bruised about the face and head and claims his jaw is broken.

Albert Metz, however, did not seem to relish his cell as a bedroom and made an attempt to break jail by breaking off a leg of the bunk and using it as a bore to make a hole in the floor. He had succeeded in making a hole about eight inches wide when Sergeant Flanigan heard a suspicious noise. He immediately had Jailor Hoefer investigate and the hole was discovered.

## *Swede Hollow*
## April 1898

HALFWAY DOWN THE SLOPE in the Hollow stood a long and narrow gray building with a sagging roof beam. It was one of the older houses, and no one really knew who had lived there in the beginning. It was set at an angle, as if there had been no other nearby houses to consider when it was first built, and it was downstream from the row of outhouses set on stilts out over Phalen Creek. No one lived in the house anymore, but on a number of evenings each week the widow Larson would serve beer in the long and narrow space furnished with only a couple of chairs and a rickety table. There were two small windows in the room, which was always dimly lit and smelled of spilled beer. Outside, the corners of the building stank of urine. Children were not allowed to go anywhere near the place, yet they would occasionally venture over there in the daytime when no one was around. They would climb onto each other's shoulders to peer in the windows, even though there was nothing to see. Before becoming a saloon, the house had had an entirely different sort of history, which was still remembered by those grown-ups who had lived the longest in the Hollow. The Lindgren sisters, who were the last two occupants of what had once been a household of a dozen women, had finally wasted away in a sanatorium far out on the prairie, succumbing to the effects of an advanced case of syphilis. Now the serving of strong drink was all that remained of those previous activities in the house, and some people thought that was bad enough. But now, just as in the past, the house lured customers from far up the street.

The widow Larson lived upstream in a small house that had once been painted white. Nobody knew or cared what her first name actually was, though she was always called Lame Lotta. She bought the beer by the bucket from workers at the Hamm brewery at the top of the slope. The beer they sold her was the sort that would have otherwise been poured out into the creek. Whenever there was beer to be bought behind Mr. Hamm's back, Lame Lotta's place would be open for business, but not at other times. The beer was served in smaller buckets called "growlers." Two or three men would buy a growler, which they would pass around. If the weather was good, the customers would stand outside, drinking and smoking. The following day the widow Larson could be seen rooting through the bushes along the creek and taking the stairs up to Seventh Street to collect all the discarded growlers, which she would need the next time her place was open. If there was trouble, she would always blame the Hamm workers, saying they had sold her beer that was too strong or in some other way defective and should have been poured out. If anyone contradicted her, she claimed that it was not the alcohol itself that caused bad tempers but everything else that was found in bad beer. And if anyone wanted something better to drink, all they had to do was go up to the street and pay three times the price for a Hamm pilsner. On a good day, the beer was the same in both places.

It wasn't so much the taste as the low price that prompted many customers to go down to the Hollow to seek out Lame Lotta's place. Late at night a virtual migration of men could be seen heading over from the Irish sector and also coming down from the street. They all wanted to find out whether she had any beer left when the other pubs were about to close.

That was the situation on one night in April. Gustaf was on his way home after a late work shift, having been given a few extra hours raking cinders out of the big coal-burning smokestack over by the Northern Pacific's engine shed. In the gathering dusk, beneath the crackling light of a single electric arc lamp, he and ten other men had wielded big scrapers to rake up what was still usable coal so that none would go to waste. Finally the faint light and the clouds of coal dust made it impossible to keep working. The foreman blew his whistle and handed out their wages. Gustaf was tired, coughing, and shivering in the early spring night, and he wanted to go home. Yet he decided not to head through the Irish Connemara sector next to the tunnel and instead went to Seventh Street to go down the stairs.

Halfway there he heard men shouting drunkenly in several different languages. For a moment he hesitated, but then he continued on. He was anxious to get home.

Suddenly a man came flying out of the dark at the bottom of the stairs and rammed into Gustaf, knocking him off-balance. He put up his hands, as much to protect himself as to fend off the man, and he instantly felt something warm running over his fingers. In the faint light his hands looked black, and he wiped them on his pants, without giving it much thought. The man bent over the stair railing and stuck his hand under his jacket for a moment. When he pulled it back out, he looked in surprise at the blood on his palm. Then he said something incomprehensible in Irish and sank down onto the bottom step, where he sat motionless, looking as if he might never get up again.

Other men appeared in the dim light issuing from the one gas lamppost up on Seventh Street. Words in broken English, Swedish, and what sounded like German whirled through the air. Gustaf peered into the darkness, recognizing one man. It was Albert Swanson, who lived a little farther down in the Hollow and sometimes worked on the railroad. He wore a waistcoat and a shirt that had once been white but was now covered with big dark patches. When Swanson came closer, Gustaf saw blood dripping from his mouth. His gray hair stood on end, and he had a wild look in his eyes. "Get those bastards out of here!" he said over and over. "Get those bastards out of here!" He was having trouble talking, and he kept wiping his mouth on his wrist, but the bleeding didn't stop.

More people emerged in the semi-darkness, until there was an entire crowd at the bottom of the stairs. Gustaf saw men in their shirtsleeves and women who had hurriedly draped shawls over their heads and were now silently tugging at their husbands' arms, trying to get them to leave. Three men had pushed their way over to the foot of the stairs and now stood next to the seated Irishman, but Gustaf recognized only one of them, O'Tierney, from the houses on the other side of the tunnel, a man he'd also noticed working at the switchyard. The other two, whom he'd never seen before, were trying to pull the man sitting on the step to his feet, but he kept falling out of their grasp as he clutched at his chest. Then O'Tierney made another lunge at the bystanders, wildly swinging his fists like windmills and yelling something incomprehensible. His eyes were wide, like a horse racing at top speed, and he landed a punch on someone in the crowd who fell down with a shriek of pain. "Fucking hell!" Swanson now shouted in a thick voice, wielding a piece of wood as he launched himself at O'Tierney. The wood struck the Irishman's skull with a dry-sounding smack and promptly broke in half, but O'Tierney was so enraged that at first he didn't seem to notice he'd been hit. Finally four men grabbed hold of him, and then he seemed to collapse, hanging limply in their arms. Two of these men were the Gavin boys from the ship, and Gustaf murmured to them in the best English he could muster, "Get him away before they kill him." The Gavin brothers nodded and began dragging the semiconscious man toward the tunnel entrance. The crowd parted before them like the Red Sea. There were mostly women present now, both Swedish and Irish.

Suddenly a woman shouted in perfectly clear Swedish, "Stop! This man is dying!" Out of the corner of his eye, Gustaf saw someone leading away Albert, who was still bleeding. But that was not who she meant.

He realized it was Inga who had shouted. When he made his way through the crowd, he saw her squatting down next to the bleeding Irishman, who was now practically lying on the step, his face ghastly pale. His eyes were still open wide, but his breathing was rapid and shallow. Inga glanced up and recognized Gustaf. "Help us carry this man," she said. He grabbed the Irishman's legs while the two Germans stood on one side and lifted his torso. Inga helped lift on the other side. It was strange how heavy such a thin young man could be when his body was so limp. They nearly dropped him several times, and all the while he kept gasping for breath. Carefully they carried him up the stairs to Seventh Street, where they laid him on the ground in the glow of the streetlamp.

They heard footsteps racing toward them over the cobblestones. When Gustaf looked up, he saw police constables come running along the street, holding their billy clubs. Two of them seized hold of the Germans and the third slammed Gustaf so hard against the cold iron of the lamppost that his whole back shuddered. The policeman was breathing heavily, and the smell of old beer fumes hovered around his lips.

Then Inga came over and said calmly in a clear voice, "That's quite unnecessary, Constable. He was just trying to help."

The policeman apparently spoke Swedish, but he was reluctant to let Gustaf go.

"That man lying on the ground is the one who needs help," Inga went on, pointing to the Irishman stretched out on the cobblestones. Then she grabbed Gustaf by the arm and said curtly, "Let's go."

They headed down the stairs without looking back. A few people were still standing at the bottom, but most had already left now that the police had shown up.

Together Inga and Gustaf walked along the creek. Gustaf kept on wiping his hands on his pants legs. Neither of them said a word until they had to go their separate ways.

Then Inga said, "So what were you doing there?" There was a trace of reproach in her voice. He couldn't see her face in the dark but he felt her eyes fixed on him.

"I was on my way home from work," he said indignantly. She merely nodded. That much he could see.

"That policeman could have arrested me," he said, sounding calmer now. "They thought I was the one who did it."

"Not him," said Inga calmly. "His name is Olsson. He used to live in the Hollow. They'll probably send him down here tomorrow to find out what happened, and I'll tell him exactly what I saw. I think they'll send both a Swede and an Irishman."

She nodded again and then headed for her own house up on the slope.

Gustaf paused before going on. He crouched down to rub his hands over a remaining patch of snow, feeling the cold practically burn his skin. In the dark he couldn't tell whether he'd managed to get rid of all the blood between his fingers and under his nails, so he kept scraping the palms of his hands over the hard ice crystals until he worried that he too might bleed. It felt as if he'd never get clean. There was nothing he could do about the bloodstains that had now dried on his pants legs, but he didn't want to even think about coming home once again with blood-ied hands.

*Swede Hollow*
April 1898

THE ENTIRE RAVINE was surrounded by railroad tracks. No matter in what direction you went, there were trains. To the south, on the other side of the tunnels and the Irish sector, the landscape was a virtual wasteland of tracks, with a railroad yard that no one was allowed to cross unless specifically authorized. Passing through the Hollow itself were the two tracks leading to Duluth and farther north past Hinckley, with side lines to Center City and Taylors Falls. Inga had said that a lot of Swedes lived up that way, but nobody she knew from back home had settled there, so she knew very little about those people. Running along the river, before the tracks reached the Hollow, was a double track that disappeared across the water over its own narrow bridge, heading for the big granary on the opposite bank. Farther up, toward Bradley Street and the school, the railroad tracks divided and continued on in separate directions into the distance, toward places out on the prairie, toward the West Coast, and toward Canada. Few people had ever gone far enough from the Hollow to see the tangle of tracks unravel and stretch out in different directions, with one end even heading into an underground tunnel. But the men who worked on the railroad and sometimes caught a ride on the trains knew that it was so.

Many of the men in the Hollow, Swedes and Irishmen alike, made their living by working for the railroad. At dawn they would head out, a flood of gray figures walking up the stairs or through the tunnels, on their way to the engine sheds and workshops operating under the auspices of companies like the Great Northern, the Soo Line, the Chicago, St. Paul, Minneapolis and Omaha, and the Northern Pacific. The names were always pronounced with great solemnity. Just looking at the tracks, it was impossible tell which ones led to which company. But ever since the Klar family had arrived in the Hollow, the sounds of the railroad, the smell of coal smoke, and the sight of steam streaking above the treetops whenever the Duluth train approached had formed a constant backdrop to their everyday activities. Later in life Elisabet would often say that she had a hard time sleeping at night when she could no longer hear the train going past, either close by or off in the distance. The smell of soot and grease and hot metal always clung to Gustaf's clothes when he came home in the evening. His handkerchief turned black when he blew his nose, and soot had settled deep inside his ear canals.

Gustaf hadn't talked much about his work after coming to the Hollow. He would set off early each morning, and sometimes he'd bring home a little money the same day. If he was lucky, he'd find an odd job that would last a couple of weeks. But he did say that when spring came he'd get back to building the porch.

On those days when he wasn't able to earn anything, it seemed as if he'd lost all gumption. One time he gathered his courage and walked all the way over to the bridge that spanned the river to find out if there was work at any of the big steam mills, which operated day and night. But so far no luck. On another day he'd headed for Wacouta Street beyond the railroad area, trying to talk his way into a job at one of the shoe factories. When he came back home, he said it was hopeless. It was just like in New York, except that here you had to speak either Polish or German even to get in the door.

Occasionally people who lived in the Hollow would bring Gustaf shoes that needed repair, and then a sense of calm would come over him as he got out his tools and a shoemaking last that he'd whittled from an old tree root. But there was no money in it because few people in the Hollow could pay cash. Instead, it was a matter of doing the repair as a favor and later receiving a favor in return.

One evening when he'd gone over to the Schulze shoe factory for the third time, Gustaf came home and sat down at the kitchen table. He didn't even bother to take off his gray work jacket before he started talking to Anna, who stood at the counter with her back turned. She could hear from his tone of voice that he'd been practicing what to say on his way home.

"This is leading nowhere," he said. "I've been thinking about the matter, and it's leading nowhere."

He didn't sound resigned or sad. Anna turned around and looked at her husband. He seemed perfectly calm as he sat there.

"You always have to know somebody," he went on. "Somebody you're related to or somebody who comes from the same place. Otherwise you never even get a chance to show what skills you have."

He paused for a moment and then said, "I talked to a man outside Schulze's today. He's German and works there as a cutter. He's been there for several years now. And he told me what he earns. A dollar a day."

Gustaf smiled as he said that, then looked down at his hands. "I can make that much working for the Great Northern," he added.

Anna didn't want to upset his strangely calm mood, yet she couldn't help saying, "But you've already done a lot of odd jobs for the Great Northern. The work isn't steady. Do you really think there will be more work when spring comes?"

He thought about this before replying. Then he said, "As I see it, I've never seriously *been there.* Not really."

Anna didn't understand. She sat down at the table across from him, tucked a strand of hair behind her ear, and waited for Gustaf to go on.

"The whole time I've been on my way someplace else," he said. "I wanted to work at a shoe factory, or at the Washburn Mill in Minneapolis. And I thought then we could have moved over there."

Anna ran her hands over her arms, which Gustaf knew was a sign of nervousness on her part. He raised his hand, as if to counter her uneasiness before it took hold.

"But nothing's ever going to come of that," he told her. "Do you know why?" She shook her head. Again he looked down as he gathered his thoughts.

"A dollar a day," he said. "You can't earn any more than that, no matter what you do. Even if I got work at Schulze's or Gotzian's and was allowed to make shoes, my wages wouldn't be any higher. *One dollar.* That's all I could possibly make. Do you understand?"

He laughed mirthlessly and went on, "I think the foremen at both the Great Northern and the Northern Pacific can tell, just by looking at me. They can see I'm just showing up temporarily, that I'm actually on my way someplace else. And if that's the case, I won't get steady work, because they know I may be gone next week. But if I decide to truly *be there,* to stay right where I am, then they'll get used to seeing me and they'll keep me working steadily. Sometimes you have to give the foreman an extra bribe several weeks in a row, but that could be worth it in the long run."

"Jonathan Lundgren got hired for a permanent job again," Anna said, noting how strong her voice sounded.

Gustaf nodded.

"And if that Hammerberg boy can get a job, in spite of his youth . . . Well, then."

He smiled.

"Now I know what I need to do," he said. He paused for a moment before adding in a completely different tone of voice, "So I think I'll see about doing something with the porch." Today he wasn't feeling worn out. He'd only gone as far as Schulze's and back, after all. He left the house, closing the door behind him. Anna heard him start to move the boards that had been lying outside in all kinds of weather during the winter and probably weren't in the best of shape anymore. She got up and went back over to the kitchen counter, not sure what it was she'd been doing. She sighed heavily and looked down at her hands, noticing how they were shaking. *I'm still young. I'm still here.* But she could feel a sense of calm spreading inside her. Now they knew what direction to take. When she looked out the window, she saw it was still light.

*Great Northern Railway, St. Paul*
April 1898

WALKING BETWEEN THE ENGINES on the tracks inside the Great Northern's repair shop was like making your way between two huge prehistoric beasts: they were tall and dark and at the moment silent. But in an instant they might come to life with a loud hissing sound. Gustaf noticed how tense he felt, as if the black iron monsters might suddenly turn on him. In the distance he heard shouts and the ring of metal on metal; the morning light filtered through the glass roof covered with frost. He shivered. Behind him came Jonathan Lundgren. He knew that for the time being this tall, monosyllabic neighbor of his was his ticket to a job.

Farther inside the repair shop, Foreman Lawson was standing on a stool underneath the ladder to the engineer's cab of one of the locomotives. Gustaf recognized the man from before. He was tall and dark, and he was always chewing tobacco, spitting out brown streams of saliva wherever it suited him. He spoke a rapid-fire English that was hard to follow. Right now Lawson was focused on what sounded like the lead-up to an argument with several shorter men standing around him. Every so often Lawson would shake the sledgehammer he was holding close to his chest. Gustaf and Jonathan moved nearer. Lawson peered down at them. When he caught sight of Jonathan, he said, "Hey, Lundgren, come over here, will you?"

They joined the other men clustered around Lawson, although still keeping a certain distance.

"Lundgren, can you talk some sense into these thick-skulled Irishmen? They're refusing to work today."

Jonathan moved closer, and Gustaf went with him, no longer keeping to the background as he would have done only a few days earlier. He recognized some of the men in the group, including the Gavin boy. Standing behind him was his pal O'Tierney, who still had his hand wrapped in a grimy bandage from the big fight the previous week. All the men stared impassively at Jonathan and Gustaf as they approached.

"What's the problem, Foreman?" asked Jonathan.

"It's that fool there." Lawson pointed at O'Tierney. "He can barely even lift a sledgehammer, because he's only got the use of one hand. The others say they won't work if I don't hire him too. So what do you Swedes say? Can you hold a sledgehammer in both hands today?"

Gustaf saw Lundgren's back stiffen. Then the tall Swede stepped over to Lawson, and the two men leaned close to exchange a few words. The foreman still pressed his sledgehammer to the front of his shirt as he listened. Then he looked up and spat off to the side. "Awright," he said. But he didn't look pleased.

Jonathan came back to Gustaf.

"What did you say to him?"

Lundgren glanced at the group of men, now in the process of dispersing.

"I just said that O'Tierney was a real idiot, but Gavin has a newborn son at home and he does good work as long as somebody keeps an eye on him. And if O'Tierney can only work at half- speed, then he can't expect more than half a day's wages. It looks like the men went for it. But Lawson wants me to go along with them today. To supervise."

Gustaf must have given him a surprised look, because Lundgren raised his voice a bit, and for once he seemed annoyed.

"You said you wanted a foot in the door. Well, that's what we've got. Lawson is counting on us."

*Or at least he's counting on you,* thought Gustaf. He offered no objections, but he was not looking forward to standing over O'Tierney and trying to get him to work harder. Gavin had never done him any wrong. On the contrary. Gustaf hadn't talked to him since arriving in the Hollow, but because they'd traveled on the same ship, they usually greeted each other whenever they met, though without speaking. The Irishman would merely shake his head briefly. Apparently that was how people said hello in Ireland.

"Coming?" said Lundgren. Gustaf lifted his sledgehammer to his shoulder and followed Jonathan outside where a slight wind was blowing. The temperature was still below freezing, but the day was bright, and it wasn't too slippery. They stayed about thirty feet behind the Irishmen, walking along the track down to the river. They were supposed to break off the coating of ice from the switches and track crossings, which was a significantly easier task at this time of year than even a few weeks earlier.

"Next week you're on your own," said Lundgren after a while. "I'm going with the train as far as Grand Forks and back, as a brakeman."

"All right," said Gustaf. "Do I dare ask what your pay will be?"

Lundgren smiled. "One dollar," he said. They laughed and kept on walking behind the dark figures of the Irishmen. The smell of thawing earth hovered in the air.

In the afternoon a squall blew in over the Mississippi. The men took shelter in a grove of alderwood trees but still got soaking wet. The freezing rain formed a coating on the metal, forcing them to go back the same way they'd come to recheck the work they'd already done.

The cold and the damp made all of them work more slowly and put them in a foul mood. Some of the Irishmen passed around a pocket flask, and after a while they grew more talkative. Gustaf couldn't understand a word they said.

As dusk began to set, he noticed O'Tierney a short distance away, looking like a small insect against the bluish snow as he listlessly bent over a switch and tapped at it with his sledgehammer. He looked like a child playing with grown-up tools, mostly just going through the motions. Gustaf went over and without a word took the sledgehammer from the man's good hand. Then he swung the hammer three times, hitting the ice so hard that a chunk slid off from the hinge. He handed the hammer back to O'Tierney, who silently accepted it. But the man's eyes gleamed with hatred from under the wide visor of his cap.

On their way back to the depot, the two Swedes walked side by side with the group of Irishmen ahead of them.

"Watch out for that O'Tierney," said Lundgren as they neared the barracks. Gustaf was already looking forward to warming his hands in front of the stove in the toolshed.

"What do you mean?" he asked. "I was just giving him a hand."

Lundgren grinned, black spittle dripping between his front teeth.

"I don't think that's how he viewed the matter. That man named Gavin told me O'Tierney thinks it's our fault he's getting only half a day's wages today."

"That's not true," Gustaf protested. But Lundgren merely pulled down his cap, too cold to do any more talking, and withdrew into himself.

This time Gustaf took the route through the tunnels, too worn out to take the trouble to go a different way. Lundgren had stayed behind to have a chat with the brakemen on the Fargo line, and Gustaf didn't feel like waiting for him.

The tunnels were short enough that you could hear if a train was approaching from the other side, so he stopped at the entrance to listen. Both vaults disappeared into the dark, and there wasn't a sound except for the drip of melting snow and voices up on Seventh Street. So he went in.

O'Tierney was standing just inside the opposite entrance. He jumped out from the wall as if he were a jack-in-the-box, stretching both hands out in front of him. In his good hand he held what looked like a rock from the embankment.

In some sense Gustaf had actually been prepared for this, even before Lundgren warned him. The threat had been building, and it could just as well have been someone else in some other situation: as long as you kept to yourself and stood at the back of the group of gray-clad men and didn't draw attention, no one would bother you. But if you stepped forward, you could feel everyone else's gaze stabbing you in the back.

Without a word, O'Tierney ran toward Gustaf. There was no one else around. At that moment he felt something snap inside his head, like when a switch shifts for an approaching train, and the old rage suddenly reappeared in a wave of heat. He stood his ground, and when the shorter man raised his hand holding the rock, he punched him in the face with all his might, sending him flying into the wall. Before O'Tierney could collect himself, Gustaf grabbed the collar of his jacket and slammed his head against the stone wall. Twice. That was enough. O'Tierney went limp in his arms. He lowered him down next to the tunnel wall until the Irishman was practically reclining at his feet. Then he turned on his heel and walked out of the tunnel on the side facing the Hollow.

When he stepped out into the twilight, he heard off in the distance the whistle of the Duluth train somewhere beyond the Hamm brewery. He spun around and dashed back into the dark.

O'Tierney was still out. Even though the man was lying a short distance away from the tracks, Gustaf pictured how he might regain consciousness and do something reckless at the very moment when the train passed through. And then all the old blackness would be stirred up again and descend once more on both him and his family.

Gustaf bent down, grabbed the smaller man under the armpits, and quickly dragged him toward the tunnel entrance. O'Tierney's boots bounced against the railroad ties, and the man struggled helplessly in his grasp as he began to come to.

Gustaf dropped him in the snowdrift next to the tunnel entrance. O'Tierney rolled over, muttering something into the black snow. Gustaf wondered if the Irishman was pretending to be more groggy than he really was in order to avoid a further beating. Then Gustaf straightened up and left.

The train passed by with its usual sudden burst of wind. The smoke was sucked down into the tunnel entrance, and for a brief time Gustaf was swathed in an eye-stinging haze. He looked up at the illuminated windows of the train cars, catching sight of people holding their suitcases and waiting to get off—gentlemen in dark suits and women wearing hats, all of them focused on their impending encounter with the new city. None of them looked out the window.

## *The Tragic Story of Agnes Karin, David, and Horrible Hans, As Found in the Court Records of the Blue Earth County Courthouse, Mankato, Minnesota*
## 1898–99

NOBODY KNEW WHAT HAD REALLY HAPPENED until the police came back and began asking questions. Nobody was even sure where David Lundgren had gone, only that he'd left for "work." Plenty of men did that, and a good deal of time might pass before they were heard from again.

If anyone in the Hollow had read the newspapers on a more regular basis, they might have found out much earlier what had happened. But only occasionally did they have access to any papers, and then only issues of the *Svenska Amerikanska Posten* that were several days old. And then the articles that were of greatest interest described events from back home in Sweden. It was mostly elderly people who bothered to read newspapers at all.

Then one morning the police arrived at the widow Lundgren's place, wanting to talk to both her and Jonathan, although he'd already left for work. Again it was Constable Olsson who was sent, and this time he sat down at the widow's kitchen table and took off his cap. After a while Mrs. Lundgren decided she wanted Inga to come over and join them. Not because she didn't understand what the constable was saying—he was born in Kalmar and still spoke good Swedish—but because she was feeling so upset.

When Inga arrived she found Olsson sitting at the table, sweating in his buttoned-up uniform, his hair plastered to his head. She realized at once that the constable was just as liable to tell them what had happened as he was to ask questions, so she kept quiet and let him carry on at his own pace.

Had David been in touch with his mother and brother? The widow shook her head, and Inga interjected that they hadn't heard a word from him since he'd left, but the constable could ask Jonathan if he knew anything. News traveled faster via the railroad. But Jonathan was somewhere along the line, maybe even as far away as Minot in North Dakota, and he wasn't expected back until Friday.

"David's in jail." That's what Mrs. Lundgren had said, looking gloomy and much older, when Inga came in.

"In custody," Constable Olsson corrected her, as if there were any real difference. She ignored him and exclaimed, "He's killed Horrible Hans!"

"We don't know that yet," replied Olsson, sitting up straighter and looking annoyed, before adding, "I'm the one doing the talking here."

The widow didn't seem to be paying much attention to him.

It took a while before Inga could piece together the whole story, based on Olsson's questions and Mrs. Lundgren's curt replies. Inga wished more than once that David's brother had been there to spread the great sense of calm that always pervaded him, although some people in the Hollow continued to insist it was nothing more than sluggishness. Again she recalled how David, without saying a word, yet unrelentingly, had compelled all of them to come to this place called Swede Hollow. He had done it so convincingly that they'd simply been caught up in his wake and could do nothing but follow along.

This is what happened. David had taken the train to Mankato, where his brother's acquaintance had claimed to have seen a man who resembled Horrible Hans. At first he could find no trace of either Hans or his family. So he stayed in town and found various odd jobs, in particular with the local blacksmith, while he continued to ask around. Eventually he heard about a "German" family who had settled on an abandoned farm out by Lake Crystal. Many people had left the area after the harsh winter and depression of 1893, so there were still a number of houses standing empty, sometimes with farming equipment and other items left behind. The family had moved into the farm where the creek curved toward the lake, and it took a while before anyone found out they were there. But it was said the family consisted of a middle-aged man, his wife, elderly father, and two young daughters.

David remained in town where he'd gradually gained a reputation for being reliable and hard-working. But he never took any jobs on the Sabbath, not because he was religious, as he explained, but because he wanted time to look for "a place of his own." Then he'd set off on long hikes through the area.

One day he came into the general store looking cheerful and said that he thought he'd found an abandoned house over toward Lake Crystal, but a bit farther out on the prairie. It was a windswept place, but he thought he'd be able to cultivate the fields even though they'd lain fallow for many years and needed to be reclaimed. He said there was an old plow that he might try to repair. He didn't yet have any horses, and the house needed to be fixed up before it was even habitable. With some reluctance the shopkeeper allowed David to buy on credit a number of things he needed. He also advised him to go to the courthouse to inquire whether any documents needed to be signed.

After that no one heard much from him except when he showed up in town to work enough to make some cash to pay for essentials.

Spring arrived late that year. But when all the ice had melted away, the body of a man was found washed ashore along the Blue Earth River. He'd been there a long time, but his clothing was still intact. And in his pocket was a note from a store in Mankato. It was an IOU. The signature could no longer be deciphered, but when the note was shown to the shopkeeper, he knew what goods it referred to. The note belonged to that surly and morose "German" named Hans Johnson who hailed from the region of Kinna in Västergötland. The man was also known as Horrible Hans, although nobody in his new place of residence had ever heard him called by that name.

When the sheriff's men went out to the remote location of his farm, they found Agnes Karin and her two girls living there. They said that Hans had left the farm one morning about a month earlier and had never come back. The fact that they hadn't asked anyone for help was due partly to the language barrier, explained Agnes Karin, whose older daughter assisted her in talking to the men. Also, her husband had left before, although he'd never been gone this long. Agnes Karin stated several times that it was not unusual for her husband to take off on long expeditions in order to find various ways to make money, and they never knew where he went or when he would return home. But as it says in the records of the hearing, it was clear that the two spouses were not on the best of terms.

What was strange, as the sheriff's deputy later stated at the hearing, was that the corpse was wearing only a waistcoat, shirt, and pants. And the man's winter coat was still hanging on a hook inside the big dilapidated parlor. When Agnes Karin was asked what her husband was wearing when he disappeared, she said she wasn't quite sure because he'd left early in the morning when she and the children were still asleep. When she was later asked whether he really could afford to have two winter coats, and in that case the river might have carried off one of them, she said that her husband didn't like her to "poke around in his things."

On that occasion the two men made do with a round of questioning. Before they headed back to town, one of them asked, a bit anxiously, how the woman and her daughters were going to manage way out there on the farm. Agnes Karin told them that for a time at least her elderly father-in-law would continue to be part of the household, and they also received a good deal of help from their new neighbor, who had recently moved into the abandoned farm a bit farther downriver. Luckily enough, the man was also from Sweden.

There are several photographs of Agnes Karin and also one of David Lundgren. Agnes Karin has a thin face with slightly bulging eyes. In the picture where she is not wearing a kerchief, her hair appears to be quite thin. She looks young and childish, yet she was already past thirty when the picture was taken.

The photo of David Lundgren is from the prison in Stillwater after he'd served nearly half of his sentence. He's looking down, at some spot below the camera lens. His gaze is dark, but there is a strangely affable look to his face. The droopy mustache gives him a melancholy air. He still had thirteen years left in his prison term.

After the suspects were arrested and transported to Mankato from Iowa, it didn't take long for the trial to begin. It lasted a whole week. Jonathan Lundgren had done his best to be present, getting there with the help of his fellow workers on the Great Northern. But it was hard for him to be away from work too long.

The person who ended up talking to the sheriff was Horrible Hans's old father. Previously, he hadn't said anything during the initial interviews, when Agnes Karin and David were already in custody. But when the authorities sat him down and questioned him with the aid of an interpreter, the old man had plenty to tell them. He said that everything had been fine until David Lundgren had again appeared in their lives. Both Hans and Agnes Karin had recognized him at once. One day he was simply standing out in the road, staring at their house. He never came to the door, just appeared occasionally and stood there looking at the house. This was a familiar situation. Horrible Hans's innate bad temper grew worse, turning as fierce as before. According to what Agnes Karin later testified, he'd started beating her and the children worse than he'd done in a long while, even though this time they didn't dare exchange a single word with David Lundgren. From the house they would see him appear off in the distance, and after a while he would leave. That was all. But his presence was constantly felt, even when they couldn't see him.

The statements and testimonies diverged widely as to what actually happened on the day that Hans died. The only thing about which everyone could agree was that he set out on the same morning when the big snow storm blew in. Agnes Karin noticed that he got up earlier than usual, and she heard the front door open and close. But that was all. As of that morning he was gone, never to be seen again. Outside, the snow was coming down so hard that it was impossible to see the road. It was impossible to see anything at all.

The prosecutor had his account ready, and he presented it to everyone in a loud voice. He agreed that it wasn't plausible that David would have stood outside in the storm, waiting for Hans to appear. But maybe he was simply on his way to town and happened to pass his neighbors' house at the very moment when Hans came down to the road. Possibly both men had caught sight of each other and started arguing. Maybe it was all a chance encounter, as was often the case in such situations. But the prosecutor did not want to rule out the possibility that David had been on the lookout or at least had been waiting for just such an opportunity and may have seen his chance in the bad weather. Hadn't he followed the family by moving here? Didn't that signify intention? Suddenly, no matter how it came about, he'd caught his enemy and rival alone, with no one else in sight.

The attorney for the defense had a completely different theory. He reminded the court that David Lundgren had never owned a gun. Everyone could testify to that. He'd never had one in town, and he couldn't have afforded to buy one after moving out to the country. It was true that the dead man had been gunned down, shot in the back. There was one individual, however, who did in fact own an old firearm—someone who had made a habit of carrying it with him wherever he went on his property. And that person was the deceased. He was also said to sleep with the gun propped against the headboard, which meant that at times Agnes Karin feared for her life and never dared fall asleep before her husband did. It might well be, said the attorney, that the honorable prosecutor was correct and the two men had assaulted each other in the storm. But wasn't it more credible that it was the deceased who had set off that morning with a loaded gun in order to get rid of his rival once and for all? Or maybe he had dashed outside in his shirtsleeves, holding the gun in his hand, when he saw Lundgren down on the road. Wasn't it more likely that a scuffle had ensued when the accused, in self-defense, struggled with the deceased for control of the weapon? And the gun may have fired spontaneously, since the weapon in question was an old and outdated model from Civil War days. And the attorney then triumphantly held up the old gun high over his head.

For his part, the prosecutor didn't hesitate to remind the court that the deceased had died from a shot to the back. And he mentioned again where the gun had been found.

A couple of weeks after the body had been discovered, both sheriff deputies went to pick up Agnes Karin to take her to Mankato for questioning. But she wasn't there, and no one knew where she'd gone. Horrible Hans's old father was still at the farm, but he spoke little English. The older daughter did speak English fairly well, and she was able to tell the men that her mother had set off a week ago, leaving the two girls behind with the elderly man.

When the deputies then went over to David Lundgren's house farther along the road, they found the place locked up. There was no sign that anyone had lived there for quite some time. The last snow from the storm ten days earlier had begun to melt, but there were no footprints or tracks left from wagon wheels in the yard.

The ticket seller at the train station was able to report that he'd sold tickets to a man and a woman who matched the description of Agnes Karin and David Lundgren. They'd bought tickets all the way to Sioux City, Iowa.

When the two deputies arrived in that city, they probably thought at first that they'd hit a dead end in their search. But at the station a gatekeeper told them that a couple who sounded like the pair they were looking for had gotten off the train a couple of days ago and asked about cheap lodgings. He'd advised them to inquire at the home of the widow Miller, right across the street.

The widow opened the door and told the deputies that was correct. A few days earlier a married couple named Bertha and Erik Swanson had rented a room facing the yard. They were tired and wanted to take to their bed at once. She hadn't seen them since.

The rented room was in a separate outbuilding. With their weapons drawn, the deputies warily approached the door, which turned out to be unlocked. One of the men gave the door a swift kick and shoved it wide open.

Stretched out on the rumpled bed were Agnes Karin and David Lundgren, fully dressed and seemingly sound asleep. At first the deputies thought they'd arrived too late and the pair was dead, but then David opened his eyes and looked at them. He didn't say a word. Between Agnes Karin and David lay the gun, but he made no attempt whatsoever to reach for it.

*Great Northern Railway, Somewhere along the Line between Fargo and Grand Forks, North Dakota*
June 1900

THE TRAIN HAD MORE THAN THIRTY CARS, and it had been traveling for an eternity. Leonard sat in the brakeman's cabin in the freight car in the middle of the train, having dozed off for a while. He'd covered his face with his jacket as protection from the gusts of wind blowing through the open apertures. When the car suddenly careened, he jolted awake. Far away, as if on the other side of a dream, came two blasts of the engine's steam whistle. Instantly he was on his feet, still so groggy with sleep that he swayed as he stood there, held upright only by the wooden boards on the walls of the cramped cubbyhole. Then he reached out through the open cabin door and grabbed hold of the ladder, which was still icy cold even though the sun had been up for an hour. His foot found the bottom rung, and all of a sudden he was hanging outside in the wind. He grabbed his cap and stuffed it in his pocket before starting to climb. He had only one minute until the next signal from the engine, which would be the second and last. He leaned over the brake control wheel on the roof of the freight car, taking a firm grip with both hands as he planted his feet to counter the swaying motion and began turning the wheel. Then came the second, longer signal. Now he was turning for dear life. From below he heard the sound of screeching brakes.

The entire length of the train slowed until it finally came to a halt. Leonard straightened up and scanned his surroundings. There was almost nothing on which to fix his gaze. Stretching out in every direction was a green expanse, with the morning sun hovering just above the horizon. A light breeze rippled through the prairie grass. He had no idea where they were. He stood there with sleep still clouding his peripheral vision. A slow and rhythmic hissing came from the engine's boiler, which was now at rest. There was not a soul as far as the eye could see, and no houses anywhere. Off in the distance the landscape seemed to fold into several low hills. Nothing more. He could have been all alone in the world.

Then he turned around and the illusion evaporated. Ten cars up ahead he saw Vitale the Sicilian smoking his ever-present pipe and staring at the nearby locomotive. Something was going on up there, but

Leonard didn't know what it was. Johnston the engineer had come out of his cab and seemed to be dragging something off the cowcatcher. Maybe some animal had been on the track. Leonard wasn't sure, nor could he tell whether it was anything important.

In the Hollow he was regularly reminded that being a brakeman was dangerous work. It was a job that a man took for a while in order to prove that he was capable; in the best case he would soon move on to something else. In the worst case he died. A brakeman could be crushed by a swiftly approaching tunnel entrance, or he might lose his footing while climbing the ladder and fall off onto the embankment or in between train cars. Leonard had personally helped to retrieve what was left of several brakemen who had died in that way. During the two years he'd worked for the Great Northern three men he knew had been killed, and one of them was from the Hollow. Yet he didn't let such things bother him. He wasn't afraid. If you died, you died; if you lived, then tomorrow was another day. He blinked his eyes and again surveyed the landscape.

He was no longer the youngest worker making a living at the Great Northern. Several boys who were barely out of their teens, just as he'd been a couple of years ago, had now started. They moved as if their bodies were a few sizes too big for them, and they were still intent on showing off. For his part, Leonard was becoming more like the other men, the ones who wore gray jackets and caps and spoke only when something needed to be said. After work they'd head back home, where they lived their other lives. He was starting to look more like those men, yet he was not one of them. And he didn't think he ever would be.

But there were still things he wanted to do and skills he wanted to acquire. One of the older Swedes who worked on the railroad was a man from Gästrikland named Larsson. He was the one who had taught Leonard how to couple the train cars—though not so much by telling him what to do, because Larsson was a man of few words. But he was an agile worker who could demonstrate how to lift up the link and at exactly the right moment drop it expertly into the coupler pocket. Then, with a swift turn of his body, he'd step out of the way as the train cars slid together with a deep sighing sound. Larsson had been on the job a long time without suffering any injury other than to his ring finger, which he could no longer bend. Leonard had wondered why the older man—who was well over forty—would choose to continue in the same job. Until, that is, he personally began to experience the giddy rush of heat to his temples every time the procedure went smoothly and at his command the train cars, weighing several tons each, would glide together with a dull thud. His pulse would race long afterward, steady and swift.

He'd also witnessed more of what Larsson could do. A short distance from the turnaround point in Fargo there was a side track leading nowhere. Occasionally, a freight train might be illegally pulling too many cars. That's when some of them would be shunted onto the side track to wait for another locomotive to take them into the freight depot. If the train was running late, the train master would sometimes let Larsson tend to the matter all on his own. As the train approached the switching station, the engine driver would signal with three short blasts of the steam whistle, the sound echoing across the plain, and then he'd decrease speed. Larsson would be ready. Carrying a sledgehammer, he would climb between the cars and swiftly knock off the link-and-pin. The coupling would separate and the rear cars would roll slower and slower without an engine to pull them until the gap to the rest of the train was seventy-five to ninety feet. After the forward cars, still pulled by the locomotive, had accelerated past, Larsson would throw the switch in the track as fast as he could. Then the ten cars in the rear would roll onto the side track, clacking over the ties with Larsson still at the front, as if the small man were singlehandedly driving this engineless train into safe harbor. The speed gradually decreased, much like a boat soundlessly gliding toward the dock when the sail has been reefed in good time. Larsson would wave his sledgehammer in greeting, and the engine driver would respond with a brief and almost merry blast of the steam whistle. Crouched in the brakeman's cabin in what was now the rearmost car, Leonard would feel a stab of envy, bordering on anger, toward the older man. He wished he was the one who sat in front on the coupling of a freight car that, without mishap, was coming to rest on this lonely side track surrounded by grass and silence.

Now, up ahead, Johnston the engine driver sounded two signals, which meant he was ready for departure; the train had probably been standing still for only five minutes. Wide awake at last, Leonard straightened up and released the brake with three swift turns. Slowly the train began to move, but he stayed up on the roof for a little longer. He ought to climb down before the train picked up speed, which would make it dangerous to hang on to the side of the careening freight car. Not that he couldn't handle it, but he might be reprimanded for carelessness. Yet he stayed where he was on the swaying roof, holding his arms out to keep his balance, and feeling the wind tug at his jacket as the morning sun slowly rose above the prairie landscape, so green and desolate. Without beginning, without end.

# II

OLA VÄRMLÄNNING WAS A YOUNG MAN who seemed to be all alone in the world. Those who had met him described him as tall with a mop of blond hair, broad shoulders, and a big, winning smile. As his name would indicate, he was from Värmland in Sweden. He had also explained where he came from to many of the older people in the Hollow who had actually known him. But if anyone asked these people for more details, they would give differing replies. They might say that Ola Värmlänning was a pastor's son from a village outside Karlstad; or that he was the son of a log driver who drowned in the Klar River, causing Ola's mother to die of grief, so that orphaned at a young age Ola had decided to try his luck in America. Ola was also said to be the illegitimate son of a nobleman, perhaps even of royal blood, who had stayed at the main hotel in Kristinehamn and there took a liking to one of the waitresses. It was also said that Ola had managed to graduate from the Karlstad secondary school, and a number of people claimed to have seen him wearing an old and dirty graduation cap. Ola may have even begun divinity studies at Uppsala University, though he was forced to leave town abruptly after getting mixed up in some sort of trouble.

No matter. Here in the States, he had no family and no possessions other than what seemed to be a boundlessly cheerful disposition and occasionally a goodly sum of money that would be gone the next day. He had apparently lived off and on in the Hollow, though never for very long at a time, yet folks were always talking about him as if he'd been there quite recently. He was big and strong and he'd get sudden bursts of energy that prompted him to do the work of three men in just one day. But he could also be sluggish, with hardly enough oomph to swat away a fly that had landed on his nose. It was said that he'd built at least three of the houses down in the Hollow, and they did look as if they'd been hastily slapped together. People also said that he had single-handedly built the stairs up to Seventh Street in a week. (But an elderly carpenter by the name of Jansson declared that wasn't true. He claimed, on the contrary, that all the men in the Hollow had joined forces after yet another wagon accident occurred in the Drewry Tunnel up toward Beaumont

Street. It had taken the men the greater part of the winter to build those stairs.)

Yet there was one thing on which everyone agreed. It was the fact that Ola enjoyed drinking. And that may have been the reason why he finally left the Hollow, because it was located so close to the big Hamm Brewery. As he supposedly said, "All it took was a glance in the window to make a man thirsty." No one knew for sure where Ola had gone. But if anyone talked to Swedes from other parts of the city or from Minneapolis, they all knew who Ola Värmlänning was. He seemed to have been everywhere.

One of the stories that was still told had to do with his unquenchable thirst. This was during the time when the police were still sending constables down to the Hollow on patrol. On several occasions they had found it necessary to take Ola Värmlänning to the station to sober him up. He always went along amiably, and no one could fault his cheerful temperament.

One night a constable whom Ola considered to be a personal acquaintance came down to the Hollow. He asked Ola a bit harshly if he'd "thought better of things" yet. Ola said that he had. He'd done his best to get hired for various jobs, since people had told him that a strong young man didn't need to be idle in this country. And now he'd managed to combine two things he needed most by getting a job at the Hamm Brewery up on the hill. Constable Johnson must have looked dubious. In order to convince him, Ola had invited the policeman to visit him on the job, though he only worked at night.

It's hard to say whether Ola Värmlänning had counted on Johnson actually taking him up on the offer, but the very next night the constable happened to come up from the Hollow, and sure enough he found Ola at the Hamm Brewery's loading dock just below Minnehaha Street. He was busily rolling barrels up a plank and into a wagon bed. Behind him the door to the brewery stood open with a big, rusty key sticking out of the lock. When Ola caught sight of the policeman, his face lit up and he offered a hearty greeting, saying it was good that the constable had arrived at that moment because he found himself in an awful fix. Johnson said it was good to see he'd got a real job and that he was working hard. Then Ola explained that he'd been hired on a trial basis, and if he didn't finish loading everything before they came to get the wagon, he couldn't expect to be taken on permanently. "So you're here alone?" said Johnson suspiciously. "Yes," said Ola. "The others disappeared and left me on my own. They're all German and they stick together. So I assume they're now putting me to the test, and if I don't get the job done, it will be just one more proof that we Swedes are as lazy as they say we are."

This last remark annoyed Johnson, who was born in the Swedish region of Skövde. He asked Ola whether he needed any help. "That's terribly kind of you, Constable," replied Ola in his broad Värmland dialect. "I wouldn't want to trouble you if you have something else to do, but a little help would be much appreciated."

Together they rolled the last barrels into the wagon bed. Ola thanked Johnson profusely. Then, just as the constable was about to continue on his way up toward the street, Ola said morosely, "Of course, now all I have to do is get the wagon over to the Drewry Tunnel, because they'll be bringing horses to get it at five in the morning."

"You mean you're going to roll the loaded wagon down the hill all by yourself?" asked Constable Johnson in disbelief.

"Yes," said Ola, scratching his head. "You see, I boasted about how strong I am. I think that's probably why I got the job." And then he added, "Though I'm not German, just a dumb Swede." That riled Johnson again, so he set his helmet and billy club down on the loading dock. Together, and with great difficulty, the two men pushed the wagon filled with clattering barrels down the hill. It was a strenuous task, but finally the wagon was in place on the little turnaround area right beside the brewery tunnel entrance. Ola set rocks under the wheels and shook the constable's hand so hard it felt as if Johnson's arm would come loose inside his sleeve. "That was unbelievably generous of you, Constable," said Ola. "And I wish I could offer you something to drink, but these are not my barrels."

"That's all right, Ola," said Johnson, now soaked with sweat. "I'll be happy as long as you behave yourself and hold on to your job."

Ola followed the constable back up to the loading dock and watched as the man put on his helmet and stuck his billy club in his belt. He waved his cap until the policeman disappeared up the street. Then he put the big key back under the rock where it had been placed by the German worker who was the last to leave for the day, hiding it a bit carelessly so the shaft stuck out. Ola left the key exactly as he'd found it. Then he walked down the hill to where they'd parked the wagon, not far from the low, sagging building of Lame Lotta's illicit saloon. From there it was an easy matter to roll the barrels the remaining distance to her back door. The old woman was waiting, and she gave Ola a considerable reward for his efforts. The wagon was left where it was. But Ola took one of the barrels with him to his simple home right next to Phalen Creek. He carried it on his back, since he was a big and strong young man. He was so happy that he whistled as he walked, although he did so quietly, because he really didn't wish to disturb anyone.

## ST. PAUL DAILY GLOBE

### MANY SORE THROATS

**Diphtheria, Typhoid and Scarlet Fever Are Prevalent Among Schoolchildren**

### IN FIRST AND FIFTH WARDS

**If Disease Spreads There Is Danger of Two Schools Being Closed—Mostly Mild Types.**

Between diphtheria, typhoid fever and scarlet fever, St. Paul is troubled with an epidemic that threatens, if continued, to close at least two of the city schools. Of diphtheria alone it is estimated that St. Paul is now harboring at least 150 full-fledged cases, while typhoid is a close second. Unless it is diphtheria, none of the cases is confined to any one particular district, being scattered all over the city. As for diphtheria, however, the First and Fifth wards seem to be the most seriously affected, fully one-half of the cases being confined to these two districts.

Fortunately, however, yet in a manner preventing what should be a complete quarantine, is the fact that the majority of the cases are of a mild type, a sore throat and a light fever, which passes away after a few days of home treatment, being the extent of the symptoms. As a rule, the family physician is not called in, and the children affected continue to go to school, with the result that the disease is given a chance to spread.

Of those afflicted with typhoid and scarlet fever, few fatalities have so far been reported. Like the epidemic of diphtheria, the cases are mild and yield readily to home treatment.

As a precautionary measure, strict watch is being kept by all the teachers on the schoolchildren, and the least symptom revealing the presence of any of these three diseases results in the sending of the children affected to their homes without delay. Weekly visits are also made by the health inspectors, and suspicious cases investigated.

*Swede Hollow*
April 1902

THE SNOW RETREATED FIRST from the higher areas. The ground between the trees on the slope was now almost completely brown and gray, covered with mud, trash, and last year's withered leaves. At the very top, between the bare branches, Anna could see the chimneys of the Hamm mansion. She'd never been up there, but everybody said it was a stately house made of brick. Because the watchdogs ran loose in the yard, no one dared get too close. Looking farther down toward the creek, she saw that the ground still gleamed white between the gray roofs of the houses. And in the very center of her view, the water was a brownish-black streak. The creek never froze completely in the wintertime; the current merely flowed tirelessly between wider or narrower borders of ice. In a month's time it would be hidden behind the leafy crowns of the trees.

Anna couldn't look down at the creek without thinking of death. She found herself turning away or avoiding even a glance at the water if possible, trying to pretend that it simply wasn't there. And yet the creek ran right through her world.

If anyone had asked her, she might have said that it was as if death had cut off a piece of her soul. That's how she thought of it, even though she realized that was a childish sort of image: her soul as a round loaf of bread from which someone had removed a big, wedge-shaped chunk. She thought about his death and felt nothing. It had all been cut off and there was nothing left to feel. Inga had patiently listened to her explanation and then said, "It will probably all come back to you sometime in the future. And then it will hurt. But maybe the present situation is actually merciful. People don't feel something until they're able to endure it. And right now you have other things to think about."

Anna thought Inga was right. A year had now passed. She still avoided looking at the water, even though he hadn't drowned. But that's how the illness was carried, from the brown water that stank so badly in the summertime. Various thoughts crept closer from the edges of her mind. Recently a memory that verged on a daydream had come back to her: she saw Carl come running down the slope through the trees, his cheeks rosy, on a spring day like this one, warm and happy. He'd been sitting on her lap while she untangled the laundry line. But after running, his cough had slowly come back until he curled up in agony.

A stab of pain. An ache as if from a never-healed wound. And she wrapped her arms tighter around her under the heavy black shawl she still wore. The widow Lundgren had said she looked like one of the Irish women from the low houses down by the viaduct, but Anna didn't care. It was the only black garment she owned. Maybe the elderly Irish women were still mourning the fact that they'd left their homeland behind. She didn't know why they dressed the way they did, but she'd never given it much thought. Whenever she draped her black shawl over her shoulders and pulled it tight, she was allowed to settle into her silence undisturbed.

Maybe this was how it would be for the rest of her life. On days like today, when she thought that she'd finally recovered, that she'd become reconciled to what had happened, he would again come running through the trees, warm and alive, and come over to sit on her lap in the evening sun. There they would sit together, sharing a brief moment of silence, and everything was as it should be until the autumn again arrived. Better then to keep her gaze averted from the sorrow, knowing that it was there, just beyond her field of vision.

The other image that sometimes appeared to her was the sight of Gustaf holding the coffin on his lap. They had gone by wagon to the Oakland Cemetery, since the Swedish Lutheran Church did not have its own graveyard. The whole way there, Anna and the girls had sat together on the seat across from Gustaf. He had made the coffin himself, and there was nowhere else to put it, so he held it on his lap. He wore the dark suit he had borrowed from Jonathan Lundgren. The coffin was so small. In Anna's memory, Carl had seemed much bigger. As if death caused a person to shrink. She recalled how her own mother, who had died when Anna was only eight, had seemed so much smaller as she lay in her coffin.

People had been saying for years that it was not a good idea for the privies to be situated over Phalen Creek. Someone who had read an article aloud from the Swedish newspaper had used words like *sanitary nuisance* and *disease-ridden gully* and added that people should not be dumping all manner of rubbish directly into the creek. Personally, they'd said it was worse for those who lived downstream, thinking especially of the Irish. But during the previous year, the spring floods ran high. For three days in a row, foaming brown water came rushing down through the valley, rising into torrential currents in the middle of the creek bed. And it was easy to see that it wasn't just the residents of the Hollow who had dumped their waste into the water; many of those living upstream had done the same thing. The force of the current carried off all the trash on that day—and even a few outhouses vanished during the night. Some boys were sent to find where the privies had gotten caught downstream and then carry them back, which they did, except for a smaller one that disappeared altogether, presumably ending up in the Mississippi River. At first Anna had thought this was good, as if the spring had done its own spring cleaning. But when the creek stopped rushing madly along, big pools were left behind in depressions between the houses, and the stagnant water soon began to smell. The first flies of the year hatched, hovering in clouds above the pools and swarming inside the homes. They were everywhere.

During one warm spring week, a terrible stench permeated the Hollow. Then it was gone. Anna wasn't sure that was where the illness had come from; in fact, she'd heard it could only be passed from one person to another.

There was no struggle, and when she thought back on that time, it seemed to have happened very fast. One evening Carl came in as usual, but he didn't want any food. She coaxed him to eat just a little. Mostly he was thirsty. In the middle of the night he woke up whimpering, and there was nothing she could say to soothe him. He was coughing and sweaty with fever. The next day and night he began breathing as if he had a grater stuck in his throat, and no one in the family slept much during the week his illness lasted. He refused to eat anything and kept saying his throat hurt. He would drink lots of water and then vomit it up.

A doctor actually came to see them, unsummoned. During the epidemic that was raging, he'd been tasked to visit homes in all parts of the city, neighborhood by neighborhood, and the last place he went to was the Hollow. The doctor was quite young, but his face was furrowed and there were big bags under his eyes. He quickly examined Carl, who lay very still, soaked with sweat. Then he had a brief chat with Gustaf in English, saying bluntly that things didn't look good, and that it was important to continue to get the boy to drink as much water as possible, even though he knew it was difficult now that the disease had progressed so far. He also said that the girls should be kept away from their brother, so they could move in with Inga for a few days. Then the doctor spoke of a vaccination against the sickness, and he said the girls might be able to get inoculated at their school. But Anna had read in the Swedish paper about the girls in Chicago who had died from lockjaw after getting the shot, so she refused to hear any more talk of the matter. Then came the night when she listened and listened in the dark to Carl breathing, with longer and longer gaps between breaths until at last there was only silence. And she screamed.

In the Hollow a lot of children got sick, but only two died—Carl and the youngest Gavin boy. The two families had never talked to each other about it, since they lived at opposite ends of the valley and their paths almost never crossed. Besides, they had no common language except for one word: death. In Swedish the word was *död.* From what Anna understood, the Irish word for it was *bas.* Death seemed to be a short word in all languages.

The first weeks and months after Carl died, the family had visited the Oakland Cemetery as often as they could, bringing flowers from the Hollow to lay next to the simple wooden cross on which a lead plaque with his name had been fastened. That was all. The Gavin boy's grave looked the same and happened to be quite close, so on one occasion they had run into his parents and mutely greeted each other. Anna noticed how Gustaf and Mr. Gavin silently exchanged looks of bleak despair.

Gradually their visits to the cemetery were less frequent. It was roughly nine miles there and back, and traveling was difficult in the winter. That's when Anna would wake up and worry that he was cold.

It was the annual community cleaning day. Last year it had been canceled due to the flooding and subsequent epidemic. But the "tradition" was one of Inga's many bright ideas, and she usually got most of the residents in the upper part of the Hollow to join in. On a Sunday in April they were going to try and clear away the worst of the trash before anything started to rot and the insects swarmed in. The Klar girls had been sent out with a group of younger children to help clear the wooded slope of old newspapers and rags, empty bottles, and rusty growlers. Inga had even persuaded carpenter Nilsson to bring along a few men to try and repair the broken steps leading up to Seventh Street. The older man wasn't keen on working on the Sabbath, but he did as she asked because, as Inga expressed it, you never knew when somebody might have an accident so it was best to repair the steps. Grudgingly he slouched off, carrying his work tools, with several pieces of board under one arm. Inga supervised the work herself, since her house stood at one of the highest spots on the slope, and from there she could see how the work was progressing and whether anyone was sluffing off. She had brought her rag rugs outside where she could scrub them, and now she and Anna were both knocking the bottoms out of some big crates, which they then placed between the houses on the hill. Gustaf had promised to whitewash the crates, which would be filled with soil and flower seeds. By the time May arrived, they would provide bright spots of color against the background of gray earth.

Most of the houses in the upper part of the Hollow had more space and stood on higher ground, with greater distance to their neighbors than the houses clustered lower down where the ground leveled off and the ravine narrowed. A number of the houses higher up also had small garden plots where people had tried to grow vegetables. But the soil was mostly clay and there were few hours of sunlight in the area, shadowed as it was beneath the hillside leading up to the Hamm mansion. Here and there people had carved little picket fences to put up between the houses. During spring cleaning, they would whitewash the pickets so that for a few days or weeks the fences gleamed white against the unpainted boards of the houses. Then came the first heavy spring rains, and everything returned to the same gray as before. But for a few days anyone looking through the bare branches of the trees on the Hollow's slopes saw an orderly and whitewashed scene. Then the leaves appeared and hid the view, both up toward the street and down toward the lower section of the Hollow and the railroad tunnels.

From where Inga and Anna now stood, they could see more and more people emerging from the houses, carrying rakes and shovels. The trash the children carried down from the hillside was thrown onto a big pile in the Hollow's open area where the two footpaths converged. Some of the older ladies, all of them wearing similar kerchiefs and gray dresses, sorted through the rubbish to see if anything could be reused. The children continued to bring more rags, tin cans, and broken bottles. A few growlers were worth cleaning to be sold back to the bars up on Bradley Street, but most of them were completely rusted after spending a winter out in the open. When the women finished their sorting, they dumped whatever was left into Phalen Creek, where the water now flowed brown and wide. But most of the trash ended up swirling around where the creek widened a bit, only to form a kind of rampart and go no farther.

"We can't let it stay like that," said Inga, frowning. "Pretty soon the whole creek will be plugged up."

Before she could do anything about it, however, young Leonard Hammerberg showed up. He had on a jacket and peaked cap, but his feet were bare and his pants legs were rolled up to the knee. He was carrying a piece of board. Without hesitation, he stepped down into the still icy-cold water. Grimacing slightly, he made his way over to the island of trash and rags, carefully setting down his feet, which must have been practically numb, as he traversed the rocky and slippery creek bed. Using the board, he began shoving the trash forward, bit by bit, until the whole pile was pushed over the edge and disappeared into the next small rapids of foaming brown water, on its way to the Irish territory and out of sight.

The children cheered for Leonard, who stood there in the rushing current. He pulled off his cap and bowed, which nearly made him lose his balance, but he caught himself just in time.

"Let's hope he doesn't catch cold and fall ill," said Inga, always so practical-minded. But Anna thought she also noticed a trace of derision in the younger woman's voice. She on the other hand felt the usual festering uneasiness when she noticed that among the little group of admirers standing on shore, Elisabet was the one who clapped the longest at Leonard's antics.

THAT SAME WEEK Gustaf came home later than usual in the evening. At first Anna didn't give it much thought, but when dark fell and yet another hour passed, she began to worry. She kept going over to the door to peer outside.

Finally she heard him walk up the steps and across the porch floorboards. The door opened and Gustaf stood on the threshold with a brown paper sack under one arm. He looked tired. The anxiety that had started to surge inside her now eased, close to the place in her chest that now languished empty, where nothing moved at all. Gustaf set the package down and asked Anna whether there was anything to eat.

He was still sitting at the table when the girls retreated to their beds, which stood next to each other along one wall. Gustaf had made the beds himself, using wood that was left over from building the porch. He had also begged a few more boards from carpenter Nilsson. Ellen had already grown too big for her bed. Anna could see how she restlessly squirmed to find room for her long legs. She's probably going to be taller than I am, thought Anna, who had to keep letting out Ellen's clothing. Lately the girl had stubbornly insisted on doing the sewing herself, though with only modest results, but she was a quick learner. Right now Elisabet was already asleep, breathing quietly, with her hair spread out on the pillow and her face turned to the wall.

Gustaf got up to get the package he'd brought home. Carefully he untied the string and took off the wrapping paper, which he smoothed flat. Then he picked up a folded shawl and came over to his wife and placed the shawl around her shoulders. Anna stroked the cloth, which felt thick and soft under her fingertips. Part of the shawl was draped over her arm, and she saw that it was finely woven with a lovely floral pattern in red and green. And she thought it must look quite beautiful in the daylight.

She looked up at Gustaf. He was standing behind her with his hands on her shoulders, on top of the new shawl. She could feel his hands shaking.

"This is for you," he said. "You need to stop wearing the black one now. It's time."

She looked down at the table, her whole being knotted into a silent but intractable *No.* The new shawl lay on her arm, drawing her eye as if the cloth had a will of its own. Dozens of tiny little flowers, red and green. They shimmered in the glow from the candle. Gustaf's hands were still on her shoulders, but he was no longer shaking.

"Thank you," she said, trying to keep her voice steady. "Where did you find it?"

Gustaf came around the table and sat down across from her. They were keeping their voices as low as possible. Yet Anna was almost certain that Ellen was listening to them as she lay quietly in bed, not stirring in her sleep as she usually did.

"I had to go up to Seventh Street," he said, "to the vendors' stalls up there. It was hard to find something I thought would be suitable because I realized that you wouldn't want to wear anything fancy. But it's time. Do you understand?"

The words were somewhere inside her, ready to be spoken. *But he's dead. Everything that had to do with him is over. He's gone, and we're here. We are living in the hole that he left behind when he simply disappeared.* And farther down were the words that she'd never been able or willing to say even to herself, much less to her husband: *It's our fault.* But when she tried to grasp the words, they seemed to slip away. And unconsciously her fingers stroked the thick cloth of the shawl, draped in soft folds around her shoulders and over her arms.

"He's gone," Anna said. Her voice was toneless, not agitated. She was merely stating what they were really talking about.

Gustaf nodded without looking at her; he didn't dare. But then he spoke. "We're here now," he said. "This is where we're supposed to be. I didn't think like that about New York. Nothing has turned out the way we thought it would, but this is where we are now. He's gone, but we're here. And that's how it will be. And I will continue to live this life that I have. There's nothing else to be done."

Then he fell silent after forcing himself to say what he'd intended. Anna realized that he'd lingered on the way home in order to ponder what he would say. It was unlikely that anyone else would have been able to make sense of his seemingly disconnected statements, but she understood. So many times he had asked her to forgive his temperament and that one occasion when he had lost his head and sent them in a long arc that had forced them to leave Sweden. She also knew that Gustaf had been turning the same thoughts over and over in his mind every single day during the past year: *If only I hadn't. Then maybe he'd be alive today.* She had never said a word about that, because anything she said would have torn an even bigger hole in their lives. She looked at him now. His face was more lined because of all the work he did outdoors on the railroad, and there were streaks of gray in his mustache. He met her eye, and she saw the dark foreboding in his gaze as he tried to decipher what she might be thinking. There was nothing more to add. And so he waited.

Then she said, "Thank you. I hope it wasn't too expensive."

"I've been putting a little money aside," he said. "Just a few coins now and then." He sighed with relief but kept his eyes fixed on her as he sat there, with his hands clasped on the table, as if in prayer.

She rubbed a fold of the shawl between her thumb and index finger. The flowers seems to dance across the lovely black cloth, which was so finely woven that in the faint candlelight the flowers seemed to be strewn over the dark, calm surface of water. But they did not sink.

"I think it will look even more beautiful in the daylight," she said. "Tomorrow I think I'll go over to show it to Inga."

"Well, I thought it was beautiful too," Gustaf said with a sigh. "It'll be nice to see you wearing it tomorrow."

As he watched, Anna turned to take the black, Irish shawl from where she'd draped it over the back of her chair. She folded it carefully. Then she stood up and went over to their biggest suitcase, which now served as the storage chest for their best clothes. She could feel her husband's eyes on her back as she leaned down, placed the shawl inside the suitcase, and firmly closed the lid. Then she wrapped the new shawl tighter around her shoulders, allowing him to see her wearing it as he'd imagined.

"Thank you," she said again. He raised one hand to rub his face. He could breathe again.

"It's late," he said.

"Yes, it is," she said. "And tomorrow's another day."

She leaned over his shoulder to blow out the candle. In the dark she felt a breath of warmth from him as he sat at the table. Slowly he stood up, placed his arm around her shoulders, and drew her close. All was quiet. For a long moment they stood there in the dark, as one body, without speaking.

## *ST. PAUL DAILY GLOBE*

### A CITY'S SAD CHARGE

*The Poor, Who Are Always Looking for Needed Relief—*

*Swede Hollow and the People Who Dwell Within It—*

### SIGHTS AND SCENES AS OBSERVED AMONG THE LOWLY OF LIFE.

The inhabitants of Swede Hollow are too often (as might be expected) of the lowest order of mental and moral intelligence. One room, or at most two, serves as both bedroom and kitchen, to say nothing of a drawing room, library and the accessories of the bath. There are on an average about five individuals to a family. But in many cases as many as fifteen men, women and children sleep, eat and live in a single room in this quarter. The moral result is obvious at a glance, while for sanitary reasons the effect on the general health is manifest.

A stroll about the quarter shows an enormous amount of hidden and concentrated vice. The faces of the children are here and there indelibly tainted with the surface manifestations of leprosy, which but too clearly evidences the indiscriminately guilty loves of their progenitors. The boys and girls of a more mature age lean idly against the fence and occasionally shake off the all-prevailing lethargy long enough to make a fruitless endeavor to hit a stray chicken or goose with a rock. A round hundred of nondescript cur dogs complete the scene of poverty and desolation, and conclusively prove that Swede Hollow is by no means a desirable place in which to live.

Many of the children are continually upon the streets of the city, and absorb vice and iniquity with each succeeding day. A large proportion of them are not sent to school, and their parents are too ignorant or too criminal to pay proper attention to their welfare. Instead they are, boys and girls alike, sent upon the streets to earn a living by their wits, at selling papers, picking rags, peddling, or even thieving when chance presents itself. Fortunately there are no saloons in the immediate vicinity of the Hollow, but it is but a short distance to either Seventh or Third Street, and many is the laborer who brings home but a muttered curse and an unsteady step on Saturday night as a means of subsistence for the ensuing week.

On certain springtime evenings, lights up on the hill at the Hamm mansion glittered between the branches of the leafy trees. They were signals from another world, mere glimpses that vanished at once. Occasionally, when the wind blew from up on Dayton's Bluff, strains of music would reach the houses nearest to the foot of the steep slope.

The children knew they were not allowed up there. But on weekend evenings like that, they would often make their way up the hill, sneaking among the trees, moving slowly, arriving a little closer each time they paused. At last they would reach the fence that separated that other world from their own.

The fence wasn't especially high, but it was topped with sharp, barbed spikes. It was said that a boy named Johan was once speared through when he illegally tried to climb over the fence. And Mr. Hamm had left his body to hang there for a day or two, as a warning to others. Nobody knew what the boy's last name was, or in which house he had lived, because his parents were supposedly so grief-stricken by his death that they left the Hollow and moved far, far away.

The first time Ellen heard this story, she thought it was both horrid and exciting, providing a dramatic backdrop to those evenings when they would sneak around outside to observe one of the Hamms' lavish dinner parties. The story was a reminder of the seriousness of the situation. Some of the older boys claimed they could point out the exact fence spike in question—though each time it seemed to be a different one. But all the children agreed that it was in the back corner, farthest away from the dog kennel. If the boys tried to tell the story to any of the younger children, Ellen would angrily tell them to shush. In her mind all dead boys looked like Carl, and she didn't want to think about that.

It was a Saturday evening, and dusk had long since fallen over the Hollow. Up on Dayton's Bluff, daylight still lingered between the trees like an afterthought. The children were standing among the last trees in front of the fence, staring at the house. Ellen and Elisabet were joined by Leonard, who was actually too old to spend time with such young children, but occasionally he would accompany Elisabet. The group also included the brothers Erland and Jakob Lindgren who lived at the bottom of the Hollow, near the Irish sector. Their mother was dead, so they lived with their maternal grandmother who was one of the oldest women in the whole ravine. The younger boy, Jakob, was special because he had no nose. He had only a small bump in the middle of his face with tiny nostrils that were constantly rimmed with snot that he would wipe off with a flick of his wrist. The boy was also blind in one eye, but his mind was as quick as anyone's. Everybody said he was like that because his mother had come down with the pox before she gave birth to Jakob, possibly infected by the man who was his father, though nobody knew where he was. But that was never mentioned whenever Erland was around, because he would instantly cause a ruckus. Leonard was among those who always did his best to see to it that Jakob was left in peace. This evening the group also had an Irish boy in tow, a ten-year-old named Fergus who often came along. He never spoke, so they let him be.

The Hamm mansion was three stories high with a peculiar looking tower. There was another story circulating about how brewer Hamm's sister lived up there and wasn't quite right in the head. In fact, there was no entrance to the tower from inside the house, so her meals were delivered through a hatch in the wall. But that story had lost credibility after Hamm installed electricity and the lamp in the ceiling was turned on and off several times each evening, making it possible to see various people inside.

Tonight most of the mansion's windows were dark, but lights burned in the big crystal chandelier in the large hall on the ground floor. Through the tall windows facing the garden, the children caught glimpses of festively clad people seated around a table. When someone opened a window to air out the room, the sound of a violin floated out into the springtime night, along with voices talking and laughing; apparently people chattered even when the music was playing.

Ellen found it impossible to tear her eyes away from the tall windows, as if a story were being recounted inside and in order to know what happened next she had to take in every detail. She saw men wearing black suits and meticulously knotted ties, their hair smooth and shiny. The women wore dresses of gleaming green or oxblood red, some of them with glittering necklaces that caught the light from the thousands of crystal facets on the chandelier. The guests leaned close to each other, one of them saying something and the other laughing. If only Ellen could have heard their words, maybe she would have been able to glean the story of this other world in which people participated with such ease, as if they were on the other side of a surface, like fish that seem to pause, motionless and effortless, in the middle of the current on a hot summer day.

Scattered across the lawn were wrought iron poles that had been stuck in the ground. Crowning the tops were candles burning inside glass globes. A short time ago the Hamm chauffeur had surreptitiously walked across the garden with his uniform cap tucked under one arm. As the children watched, he waved at the dark entry facing the road, and a blond girl with short hair emerged from the shadows to follow in his footsteps. The man took her arm and led her forward while she covered her mouth with her free hand, trying to stifle her giggles. They hurried past the illuminated windows and disappeared.

"Oh yeah, it's easy to see what those two are up to," whispered Leonard as he stood between the Klar sisters. Ellen hated him for saying that.

But soon she had other things to ponder. A pair of low shadows came gliding across the lawn, heading for the dark area under the trees. At first she thought they were dogs, but they seemed too thin and delicate. As the children watched, two small spotted deer materialized out of the night, one full-grown and one a fawn that crept after its mother, prepared to flee at any moment.

"The dogs must be locked up for the night," murmured Leonard, hardly moving his lips. "Otherwise the deer wouldn't dare show themselves."

The deer headed boldly for the flowerbeds and quietly began nibbling at the tulip buds that had already sprouted. The deer's shadows fluttered back and forth in the flickering light from the glass globes. At that moment Ellen caught sight of something gleaming in the flowerbed where the deer were grazing.

Mrs. Hamm's crystal balls. Ellen had seen them once before and was totally captivated. There were so many stories about the Hamms, and she had no idea which of them were true. But according to one story, Mrs. Hamm had become interested in spiritualism during one of the couple's trips to Europe, and she'd bought several glass balls from someone claiming to be a medium. They were supposed to summon the dead, who would understand that the spirit of the person who lived here was open to the afterlife. Leonard had said the balls were made of German crystal, though Ellen had no idea why that was significant. Previously they had been kept in a big bowl on the veranda, some as big as the head of a child, others as small as marbles. But now they lay scattered over the flowerbed in the semi-darkness, as if someone had been playing with them a short time ago and then grew tired and left them behind. Ellen counted at least two dozen. The deer carefully stepped over them, interested only in what they could eat. Behind the tall windows, now closed, the lively dinner party continued, without a sound seeping outside. But Ellen no longer found it as interesting because she couldn't take her eyes off those glass balls.

Leonard had started whispering amusing comments to Elisabet. Ellen moved away from them and went closer to the fence, not really caring whether someone might see her from inside the house. She began climbing up the wrought iron fence crossbars, which were so cold now that night had fallen. Inch by inch she climbed toward the menacing spikes, topped with barbs. Then she was straddling the fence, looking down in the direction of the flowerbed where the deer were still visible against the darker foliage of the rhododendron bushes. Ellen cautiously touched the nearest spike, which felt surprisingly blunt under her fingertip, and she wondered distractedly how anyone could end up getting pierced through by something like that. Then she pushed herself off and dropped down on the other side of the fence, nearly falling headlong.

In a flash the deer sped across the lawn to merge with the surrounding darkness under the trees. Now Ellen heard the other children whispering behind her. Leonard hissed her name, sounding perplexed, as if he thought she'd forgotten it herself. Quickly she ran over and snatched up some of the glass balls. They felt ice-cold in her hands and rougher than she'd imagined. She stuffed as many as she could carry in her apron pocket and then walked quietly back to the fence, expecting at any moment to feel a hand grab her shoulder or the back of her neck, but something inside her made it impossible to hurry. Then she was at the fence, preparing to climb.

Now all the children from the Hollow were standing next to the fence, stupidly cheering her on. They kept their voices low, but she wished they wouldn't make any noise at all. Leonard clasped his hands like a stirrup and stuck them through the fence so she could climb higher and get a better hold. The glass balls in her pocket rattled against the wrought iron as she clambered up. It seemed much harder going in this direction. Finally she was once again straddling the top crossbar. Again she abruptly dropped over the side, landing on her hands and knees with the glass balls clinking against each other. Without a word the children gathered around Ellen. She didn't move.

Then they heard the sound of a door opening. She looked up at the house. One of the tall windows turned out to be a door to the dining room. It had swung open, and a man wearing a black suit stood there, the light forming a halo behind him. She couldn't see the man's face, but judging by his rotund shape, it had to be Mr. Hamm himself. Silently he peered into the dark. Through the open door streamed the faint sound of violins playing. Then he turned around and spoke to someone the children couldn't see, but they heard him say the words "a doe." Then the door closed again.

Ellen stood up. Her hands hurt, but otherwise she seemed to be in one piece.

"That was the stupidest thing I've ever seen," said Leonard with admiration. "How many did you get?" He held out his hand as if he wanted her to give him the glass balls, but she merely shook her head without speaking.

"We need to go now," he then whispered. "Right now. They'll probably let out the dogs at any moment." The children slowly began making their way down the steep slope. Only a minute later they heard the sound of the big hunting dogs whimpering excitedly as they picked up the scent of the deer out on the lawn. Ellen walked behind Leonard and Elisabet, heading toward the bottom of the Hollow where only a few windows showed any light. She kept running her fingers over the glass balls in her apron pocket. She counted five. And nobody was ever going to be allowed to touch them.

OLA VÄRMLÄNNING was the name of a young man who was no longer so young. He was still big and strong, and few could match his capacity for work—that is, on those days when he wasn't overwhelmed by a lassitude that he personally, in a moment of weakness, had described as a form of homesickness. Although not the normal sort of homesickness. Everything that Ola Värmlänning did was on a grand scale, and that included these spells of gloominess. Whenever they overtook him, he would lean against a wall, shut his eyes, and snarl hostilely at anyone who came too close. He could stay like that for hours. If anybody asked him why his eyes were closed, he'd say he was using his inner vision. And if anybody ventured to ask what he was seeing, he would always reply at once, "The Klar River in the evenings, up near Forshaga."

On other days he was back to normal. And then there was nothing wrong with his capacity for work. Or his thirst. He could be found here and there in the Twin Cities, always recognizable from quite a distance, with his mop of blond hair sticking up a head higher than anyone else's. He was almost always in a good mood, but people said it was getting hard to keep pace with him in the beer halls. He drank three times faster than anyone else, which also meant that he often drank three times as much over the course of an evening. He could be found working at the big mills along the river, or in the rail yards. He never seemed to hold a job for very long, yet he always managed to find another one, big and strong as he was. And then he'd acquire new work pals who would gladly keep him company at the saloon table.

But there was a side to Ola that could make any newfound pal uneasy. For example, one night Ola got up and went out to the street. Many of the men seated at the table took this to mean he was answering the call of nature. But when someone went out to see what had become of him, he found Ola glowering at a wooden Indian with his nose only inches away from the statue's face. At that time it was still common for tobacco shops in the Twin Cities to have the carved statue of an Indian out front, to advertise their wares, and not every shopkeeper bothered to bring the statue inside at night.

The men tried to drag Ola away from the statue, but he stood his ground, even when more men joined in.

"That old devil is glaring at me" was all they could get out of him when they tried to coax him back inside the saloon. Finally he seemed to come to himself and relented. But for the rest of the night he said very little.

That could have been a one-time occurrence that might have been explained as the result of cheap beer on an empty stomach. But only a week later lots of people witnessed Ola walking down a street in the center of St. Paul, and as soon as he came close to a wooden Indian—and there were many in that part of town—he would throw a punch with his mighty fist and knock the statue to the ground so hard that it often cracked when it struck the pavement. The shopkeepers were furious but also afraid. It had been a long time since they'd seen a man as big as Ola. As he headed down the street, toppling wooden Indians, Ola shouted at the top of his lungs, "AWAY WITH THESE WOODEN DEVILS!!!"

No one dared stop him. But that same evening, one of his work pals at the Washburn Mill came upon Ola sitting at a rickety table and holding a mug of beer in an unsteady hand. He seemed once again calm and composed. After chatting about one thing and another for a while, the mill worker took a risk and asked Ola why he hated Indians. At first he seemed surprised by the question. Then he said that he had nothing against Indians; the few he'd met were pleasant enough folks. "Then why," his work pal stammered, "do you hate wooden Indians so much?" "That's altogether a different matter," replied Ola. "They glare so wickedly at anyone who walks past," he said and then added almost in a whisper, "I suppose when they stare at me so critically I'm reminded of my old man back home in Kristinehamn. And then I get so devilishly angry and aggrieved that I can hardly stand it."

They talked no more about that subject.

In the end, no tobacco sellers in the Twin Cities dared to leave any statues outside after closing, in case Ola should happen past in the night, drunk and raging. If they did, only wooden splinters would be left of the statues in the morning. Eventually wooden Indians became a rare sight. By the time that Ola himself, inevitably, passed away, it was no longer the custom to use wooden Indians for advertisement purposes, and nobody was inclined to resume the practice. Maybe the statues that survived his attacks are up in some attic, staring fiercely into the dark, on the lookout for Ola, who has now forever more escaped the judgmental and vacantly glaring eyes of his father.

IT WAS LATE ONE EVENING in May, and the view of the lower part of the Hollow was already hidden by the burgeoning leaves on the trees. At this time of year no one felt the need to heat their homes anymore, nor did they waste any candles. In the twilight a dog barked insistently somewhere down by the low houses clustered near the tunnels in the Irish sector.

The evening was beginning to turn to night when a woman's scream echoed up through the ravine. The cry rose and fell, almost like a song, but the woman kept on screaming until her voice broke into a hoarse scratching sound. Yet she still didn't stop. Doors opened all around the Klar family home, and footsteps could be heard crossing the gravel. Ellen's father got up from the table, stuck his feet in his boots, and went out to the porch in his shirtsleeves. Both of the girls joined him, peering across the Hollow.

The screams were coming from halfway down the slope, near the place where Horrible Hans and Agnes Karin had once lived. The sound seemed to be coming from the creek bed itself. The girls followed their father as he slowly and without a word headed down the footpath toward Phalen Creek. Ellen came last, keeping one hand wrapped around the two smallest glass balls that she always carried in her apron pocket. She had hidden the others under the porch where the sandy soil was loose.

More people came rushing out of their houses and out to the path; everyone was headed in the same direction. The whole time the screaming continued from the creek bed, the sound fading a bit but then starting up with renewed strength. A bunch of gray figures had already gathered near the single pier upstream from the outhouses where the women sometimes did their washing if the creek was running sufficiently high. Ellen tried to push her way forward, thinking at first that everybody was staring at something in the creek bed. Then she noticed that they had tilted their heads back to look up and she raised her eyes. Beside her Elisabet suddenly uttered a squeal, as if she'd been struck with something sharp, and then she covered her face with her hands. Ellen realized at once she should have done the same. Over the coming nights, what she now saw would come back to her without warning just as she was falling asleep, and the sight would recur at regular intervals for the rest of her life.

A man appeared to be hovering beneath the crown of the tree. That was what she saw first. He was spinning around in the air, with his hands at his sides. Then she understood. He wore a gray coat and pants, and he had wet himself. From his neck a rope rose up to the thickest branch above his head.

That wasn't all. That was not the worst of it. She now heard the train to Duluth and the two blasts of the steam whistle before it passed through the tunnel at the bottom of the Hollow. Then came the sharp white spotlight dancing between the trees, making its way through the branches. And lighting up the hanged man's face.

His tongue had been forced out farther than she'd ever imagined possible. And his eyes were literally popping out of their sockets, looking like two tiny bird's eggs clinging to his face. But it was still possible to recognize Patrick O'Tierney. And the woman who was now soundlessly screaming from down by the creek was Mrs. O'Tierney. When Ellen looked away from the dead man, she saw how the woman seemed to be clawing at the air, in an attempt to take down what had so recently been her husband. But she was too short to reach him.

The body continued to hang there for well over an hour before several men climbed the tree, equipped with knives and a saw. During that time, trains passed two more times up on the embankment, and the engine's headlight cast its harsh white glare on the body, making its swaying shadow stretch out over the walls of the surrounding houses and over all the bystanders. Ellen shut her eyes but she could feel the shadow passing over her face on a gust of chilly evening wind. Many of the Irish and Italians in the crowd repeatedly made the sign of the cross. None of them said much. She was freezing, and she kept close to her father. Gustaf made no effort to help take down the corpse, but neither did he turn to go back home, and as long as he stayed, Ellen would stay with him. She kept her hand wrapped around the glass balls in her pocket until they became slick with sweat and difficult to hold. She noticed how the same words kept reverberating inside her head, keeping time with the turning of the little glass balls: *Get me out of here. Get me out of here.* She didn't yet know what those words meant. They were like the refrain of a ballad. But she stayed where she was.

Some of the men were preparing to catch the body. They had waded out into Phalen Creek, holding taut a tattered old sheet between them. The other men up in the tree began motioning to them, and for some reason the men in the water started chanting, "Heave-ho, heave-ho," as if the sheet they were holding was a sail they were about to raise. Then one of the men in the tree gave a signal and the rope was cut. The body dropped toward the water, breaking right through the old sheet and landing in the creek with a sound like a sack of coal hitting pavement. Mrs. O'Tierney, now utterly silent, waded over to the heap in the middle of the current and tried to drag it ashore, but she couldn't budge it. Several of the men hurried over, now drenched and covered with mud. They picked up the dead man by the feet and under the arms. And while Ellen averted her eyes, scared that she might again catch sight of the face, she happened to notice Elisabet and Leonard Hammerberg. Her sister had collapsed into his arms, and judging by the way her back was shaking, she was crying. Flat-faced Leonard stood there, stroking her hair with what looked like a pleased smile. His eyes met Ellen's, and his smile got even bigger. As if he wanted to say, "See? I've won."

THE WEEKS TWINED TOGETHER into a thin gray rope of mornings and evenings, without beginning or end. Walking at dawn to various homes along Payne Avenue or on Seventh Street where spring cleaning waited to be done. Sometimes heading to cross streets like Minnehaha Street. That's where many families lived who went to the same church as carpenter Nilsson and his wife. Sometimes venturing even farther to neighborhoods where she didn't know the street names or recognize a single face among the crowds. Always with Inga leading the way like a commander. Ellen would follow with Elisabet and Lisbet, the Nilsson daughter who wasn't crazy. They didn't always know where they were headed on the days when Inga summoned them.

On a few occasions they'd gone all the way over to the big houses around Lafayette Park, where all the furnishings seemed to be made of dark, polished wood. Ellen knew that the wages they received were a little higher in those parts of town, but she wasn't fond of the days when they worked there. Those homes seemed so silent and stifling, as if the people who lived in them never spoke, neither English nor Swedish. And they were paid by a "housemaid," who wore a cap and a starched white apron that never seemed to bear the slightest trace of housework. The housemaid didn't speak either as she counted out the coins into Inga's reddened hand. Ellen thought there was something strange about hiring a servant woman, who in turn paid others to do her work. But she accepted her wages without a word.

On their way home in the twilight one summer evening, she happened to walk beside Inga instead of with her sister. The other two girls were larking about as they walked behind, and Ellen didn't want any part of it. Instead, she hurried to catch up with the older woman. At first they said nothing to each other as they walked along side by side. Silence never felt uncomfortable when she was with Inga. But after fifteen minutes or so, Inga said without looking at Ellen, "So I can see you want something else."

Ellen gave a start, as if Inga had said something dire, though she'd spoken calmly and kindly. But it was unsettling how the older woman had guessed at her thoughts. This was not the first time it had happened.

"I'm not ashamed to be cleaning houses, if that's what you're thinking," Ellen replied. Without looking at Inga, she then added, "But it does get to be a little monotonous."

She could hear how wrong this sounded, because she knew that Inga had largely supported herself with these types of jobs since coming to this country. And she'd been willing to share the work with them when they needed money. But Ellen also knew how hard it was to lie to Inga. If she tried, Inga would merely stare at her without speaking, but her expression would say, "You can do better than that." That's how it had been ever since she and Elisabet were children.

"I don't think you should be ashamed of doing a decent day's work," Inga said at last. "But I know what you mean. I've been thinking that it's time for you to try something new."

For a while they walked on in silence.

"Let me talk to some people I know," Inga said at last, as if she'd been pondering how to formulate her words properly. "I'll let you know what they say."

## *The Tragic Story about Agnes Karin, David, and Horrible Hans, As Recounted by David's Brother, Jonathan Lundgren*

FOR A WEEK autumn had hovered over the city like a lid. The colder air held down the coal smoke issuing from the chimneys, forming a gray veil above the higher rooftops on the other side of the Lafayette Bridge. And from the river, as gray and motionless as ever, could be heard the muffled steam whistles from the barges, shrouded in the cold that now rose from the gray water.

They were on their way back to the Hollow, mutely walking along, their thoughts roaming at random. Neither of them had said anything for a long time. Jonathan carried his empty knapsack over his shoulder. In the morning it had held the bread Inga had given him, which he'd shared with Gustaf when they had a break from their work. Jonathan's silence was of the burdensome kind, laden with words that he hadn't yet sorted out. Gustaf, equally silent, was waiting patiently as he walked along beside this big, stooped companion of his. They had known each other ever since the Klars had arrived in the Hollow, and by now they'd been working together for six years. But Jonathan still talked very little about himself or his concerns; more often he would speak of the job or what tasks needed to get done. He was like an ever-present, soothing shadow when it came to everyday matters. But now something was weighing on him, and he wanted to unburden himself.

Before they came to Seventh Street and the dark openings of the railroad tunnels, Jonathan began talking as he looked straight ahead. The words reached Gustaf through the evening's dim light. He kept his head down and simply listened.

Jonathan had tried to make it a habit, at least every other month, to go to the prison in Stillwater to see his brother. Gustaf no longer remembered much about David, other than that he was somewhat shorter, darker, and if possible even more taciturn than Jonathan. He also knew that Jonathan had gone there this past Sunday, traveling in the engine cab of one of the trains. At other times he would scrape together the money to take the streetcar all the way there. It got him closer but was more expensive. Now he was weighed down by something that had happened, and he needed to get it off his chest.

Things were better at the prison now, Jonathan explained. David had arrived as a condemned murderer and was ranked the lowest of the low. He had to wear striped prison garb, and it had taken almost a year before he was allowed any visitors. When Jonathan went there the first time, he'd found David with a black eye. His brother either would not or could not tell him what he'd been through. Gradually David had worked his way up through the ranks. There were three kinds of prisoners, and having passed through a complicated points system, he had now reached the highest group. He was assigned to the workshop, and he wore a gray prison uniform. He was also allowed visitors once a month, and he could keep the tobacco that Jonathan usually brought for him.

His most recent visits to the prison had all ended in the same way. David would ask about Agnes Karin and whether she would come to see him now that he could have visitors. Jonathan could only tell him the truth: that they had no idea where she was. She was no longer in contact with anybody in the Hollow, and no one had seen her or the children since the trial.

One day when Jonathan was at work, Pastor Sandstrom, the Swedish Lutheran pastor, came to the Hollow on one of his rare visits and headed straight for the home of the widow Lundgren. Once again the widow asked Inga to come over, this time because she was feeling nervous about talking to the pastor. What Sandstrom wanted to discuss was David and Agnes Karin's "civil status," as he called it. Inga explained that they had never managed to get engaged, either formally or informally. When they made the strange decision to flee to Sioux City, it was no doubt their intention to get married, but there wasn't time before the sheriff arrested both of them and took them back to Mankato.

Sandstrom listened carefully and then said that in the midst of this whole sad story, that was probably a good thing, because yesterday he'd received a letter from Agnes Karin. She was now living in Rochester, and she had asked the pastor for a certificate from the Swedish Lutheran Church, verifying that she was a widow and not a married woman. She and a man named Anton Carlberg were planning to have marriage banns posted, and after the wedding she and the children would move with her new husband to San Francisco. Now she was simply waiting for the certificate from the church, which she had joined when they first arrived in the United States. Carlberg was a member of a Methodist congregation, and he wanted everything to be in order.

When Sandstrom finished speaking, the widow Lundgren slapped her hands together and sighed heavily. She didn't say another word during the pastor's visit; instead, she let Inga carry the conversation.

Jonathan had been turning these thoughts over and over in his mind the whole way up to Stillwater, trying to figure out how much to tell David. At first he'd planned to say nothing, not because he didn't dare break the news, but because he had no answers to all the questions his brother was bound to ask. Nobody had known that Agnes Karin was living in Rochester, and nobody knew who this Carlberg was. But when the two brothers were sitting across from each other at the worn prison table, and David again asked after Agnes Karin, the words just spilled out of Jonathan's mouth.

David reacted the way he always did. He fell silent, and for a long time he merely stared down at the scratched tabletop. Jonathan thought that meant the visit was over, and he'd already taken out the packet of tobacco he'd brought along, turning to the guard for his nod of approval. Then, without looking up, David had begun to recount what had actually happened on that morning near the Blue Earth River.

He'd been awakened in his little house by the wind blowing through the timbered wall because he hadn't yet had time to seal the cracks. When he threw open the front door, he was met with a white world that struck him right in the face. No matter which direction he looked, he saw only stinging snow. He immediately began to worry about Agnes Karin and the girls. He didn't know whether Horrible Hans was home or off on one of his begging expeditions. In the worst case, they were alone in this storm. He put on all the clothes he owned and began making his way up to their farmhouse, which was only in slightly better condition than his own cabin. The country road had vanished, and he could see only a few feet ahead, but he followed a row of fence posts up the hill. As he came near the spot where the farm's barn supposedly stood, he saw a shadow appear up ahead in the snowstorm. It was Agnes Karin. When he reached her, she screamed in his ear, "You have to help me, David!" Then she turned on her heel and walked back the same way she'd come. He followed her, as he'd always done.

Just before they reached the house, he saw a dark shape on the white drift at the bottom of the steps. It was Horrible Hans, lying facedown in the snow. He was dead. Agnes Karin stood next to the dead man with her arms at her sides, waiting. At first David wanted to go inside the house to talk, but she stopped him. "The children and the old man are asleep," she shouted to him. "I don't want them to see this." And then she repeated, "You have to help me!"

There was nothing else to do but move the body away before the children woke up. First they dragged the corpse over to the sheltering wall of the barn, but when they got that far, Agnes Karin motioned for David to continue on. And he realized what she wanted. They should take the dead man all the way down to the bend in the river. But the snow was now knee-deep, and it was impossible to see the road. Agnes Karin kept on tugging at the corpse, though she could barely budge it on her own. So David went over and picked up the body of Horrible Hans, throwing it over his shoulder. And then they headed into all that whiteness, blindly following the slope down toward the spot where the river had to be. The wind was blowing in their faces, the snowflakes so sharp that their eyes filled with tears.

After they'd gone quite a ways, Agnes Karin abruptly stopped and stood motionless in the whiteness, just as she'd done before. When David went over to her, she shouted into his ear, "I have to go back to the children before they wake up." And then she began trudging back up the hill, and he was left there with the dead man lying at his feet.

It took him a good hour to get the body down to the river. There were no tracks visible in the snow behind him, and up ahead he could see hardly anything. And he began to weep. He wasn't ashamed to tell his brother that. It was cold and the storm tore at him, and the corpse got heavier for every step he took. He began to think he'd never make any progress at all. Instead, he'd be struggling forever in this swirling white darkness, with his dead rival as his only companion.

Then he sensed rather than heard a crunching beneath his feet. He realized he was treading on clumps of reeds, bent down and almost entirely covered by a snowdrift. In front of him the riverbank sloped steeply down to the ice. He toppled the dead man over the edge and watched him disappear. Then he slid down after the corpse. He didn't really care whether the ice held or not. He shoved Horrible Hans forward, little by little, until he caught sight of a stretch of open black water in the middle of the channel. The dark patch came and went in his field of vision. He lay down on his stomach and felt the icy cold seeping all the way through his shirt. Then he pushed the corpse forward, inch by inch, until he could feel the ice growing thinner underneath him. The next moment the dead man slid soundlessly into the water. Cautiously David backed away, using his hands to push himself toward shore until his foot struck a rock. Only then did he dare get up. He stood there in the wind, trembling.

When he turned around, he saw nothing. He couldn't even make out the open patch in the ice in the midst of all that emptiness. He realized he was soaked with sweat, and his whole body began shuddering with cold. Soon he too might fall victim to the cold if he didn't keep moving and turn his back to the wind. He headed back the same way he'd come, plodding for an eternity up the slope to the spot where he hoped to find the house. At last he caught sight of the gray timbered wall of the barn and realized the snow storm was finally subsiding.

He stumbled inside the home's biggest room, which was the kitchen, and slammed the door behind him. The house was quiet, with a small fire burning in the woodstove. All his attention was focused on getting warm, and with hands outstretched he dropped to his knees in front of the stove. After a while he turned his head and noticed Agnes Karin calmly sitting on the bench with an old gun leaning against the wall next to her. He saw no sign of the children or of Horrible Hans's deaf old father, so he assumed they were still asleep behind the wallboards. He had no idea what time it was, and it was impossible to guess. Outside the only window in the room, the wind was still gusting white. He got up and went over to Agnes Karin. Without a word she pulled down the front of her blouse and moved her hair aside so he could see the fiery red marks at her neck.

"This time he was going to kill me," she said. "When I woke up he was trying to strangle me. I got away and ran outside, but he came after me with the gun. I tore it out of his hands and shot him. And that was that. Then I set off to get you."

David merely shook his head without saying anything. But as he told Jonathan five years later while sitting at a table in the Minnesota State Prison in Stillwater, he'd always wondered how Horrible Hans had ended up getting shot in the back. If things had happened as she'd said, that is. But he and Agnes Karin had never discussed the matter. Not a word did they exchange about the events of that morning during the few short months that followed, when they lived together as man and wife. That was when, for the first time in his life, David felt happy.

All this Jonathan Lundgren, who was usually so taciturn, told Gustaf as they stood freezing next to the arched entrance to the railroad tunnel below Seventh Street. And Gustaf didn't need to ask whether the story was actually true, because he realized that no matter what, Jonathan believed his brother. When he asked whether they were going to tell anyone about this, Jonathan shook his head. "David doesn't want to," he said. He would tell Inga, and it was all right for Gustaf to tell Anna. But otherwise they would let it be. He wasn't planning on telling his mother, because it would only upset her. She had resigned herself to what had happened and merely hoped that she'd live long enough to see David released from Stillwater someday. And when they parted, David had made his brother promise not to do anything about what he'd heard. He said it would serve no purpose, and it would be best to leave well enough alone. If nothing else, for Agnes Karin's sake.

IT TOOK INGA SEVERAL MONTHS to come up with something for Ellen. They hadn't spoken of the matter since that late summer evening when they were walking home from Lafayette Park, and Ellen hadn't wanted to broach the subject. If Inga found out anything, she'd say so. Since then they'd had a number of cleaning jobs in the neighborhood around Minnehaha Street with no mention of the topic. But one evening at the end of September, Inga came over to the Klar family home and seemed to have a lot to tell them. The first thing she said was that she was going to buy her house.

She said she wanted Anna to be the first to know, because soon a lot of talk would be going on in the Hollow, where rumors always spread fast. The other day Inga had gone down to the Ramsey County courthouse to have a talk with the clerks. When they realized it wasn't going to be easy to get rid of her, they finally explained what she needed to do. It turned out that it was possible to register as the owner of a house in Phalen Creek if no one else was already listed as the owner.

That all sounded so strange. At first Anna couldn't figure out what Inga was talking about. Gustaf wasn't yet home from work, but the girls drew closer to listen.

"But isn't Waggoner the one who owns all the houses?" said Anna. "We pay him rent every month."

That was both true and not true, Inga explained. It was true that Sheriff Waggoner had registered the area as an "addition" when the city plan was drawn up. And he might well insist that the property was his. But back then a number of the houses were already in place. And the house in which Inga now lived alone was one of the oldest in the Hollow. It had undoubtedly been there long before Waggoner thought up a scheme for making some ready cash.

"So I asked to see the city plan and the map they have down there at the courthouse. At first they refused, but you know how stubborn I can be, Anna. Finally they gave in. And you can clearly see that when Waggoner registered the land twenty years ago, there were already four or five houses here. And one of them is mine. Or at least it will be mine. It's going to cost me twenty dollars, but when I get the papers, I'll be the official owner."

"And you have the money?" said Anna.

"It's almost everything I've managed to put aside. If there's trouble, I think Waggoner will have to give in, because he registered the land when people were already living here. And even though none of those people live in the Hollow anymore, the houses are still here. I asked the clerk at the courthouse how to go about things, and he showed me the papers, because otherwise he'd never have gotten rid of me. I have to go back next week and bring the money, and then they'll stamp the papers and the house will be mine. It's debatable who owns the actual ground the house stands on, of course, but when Waggoner registered the property, there was no mention of the houses that were already here. But you can see them on the map. And they've got the map down at the courthouse."

Anna and the girls thought this was very strange, but Inga sat there at the kitchen table, defiant and stubborn, looking delighted by her efforts.

"And by the way, other people have done this before," she added. "But I don't think they did it properly. They just requested a building permit, either before or after they put up their house. That's cheaper. Only a few dollars per house. Jonson, who lives over by the stairs, did that. I saw the papers, and when I asked him about it, he said he did it mostly so there would be no argument about who owned the house, in case more Italians moved in nearby. I doubt he was thinking about Waggoner. Or bothered to look at a map."

Anna was getting uneasy, and it showed. Ellen thought, as she often did, that she could guess what her mother was thinking without having to ask. And she could put her mother's concerns into words; it was easier for her to speak than her mother.

"But if you end up arguing with Waggoner," Ellen now said, "won't that be dangerous for all the rest of us who live here? What if he gets mad and decides to evict us?"

Inga stared at her across the table, as if to say, *Don't you think I've thought of that?*

"I'm not going to wave the papers under the nose of Mr. Sheriff," she then said. "And besides, I don't think he has much to complain about. His men come here to get the rent once a month, and over at the courthouse they probably know all about that. But I don't think he's ever bothered to sign any papers saying that he's the landlord renting out houses. He just registered the land, and there's nothing that says he owns any houses, because that would cost money. A few dollars for every shack here in the Hollow, and that could add up to a considerable sum. And if more people decided to do what Jonson did and get themselves a building permit, then the sheriff could run into trouble. There'd be a whole bunch of questions about who owned what, and I doubt he'd want to deal with that sort of mess.

"So I really think you should try to scrape together a few dollars for a building permit too," Inga went on. "That would make it harder for Waggoner to argue. I can help you with the papers if you want."

But when she saw that Anna was still looking uneasy, Inga laughed and said, "Well, talk to Gustaf when he comes home and see what he says."

Finally Anna spoke. "But why do you want papers for your house? You've never needed them before. And maybe this will just cause trouble."

Inga had clearly been waiting for this question, because now she gave a big smile and looked even more pleased.

"That, my dear Anna, was really the reason I came here to tell you about all this. It's because I'm going to get married. But before I take the big step, I want papers proving the house is mine."

No one said a word. Then Anna laughed. An involuntary and shrill laugh that echoed off the kitchen's bare walls. Inga looked insulted. Elisabet lowered her eyes, suddenly feeling embarrassed and anxious, which happened to her so often whenever things got too serious. Ellen sensed how her sister seemed to retreat into herself. She looked down at her own hands and saw how dry and chapped they were from scrubbing so many stairs, yet she always managed to keep them clean. Elisabet's fingernails were rimmed with black. Ellen stared at them and felt a sudden aversion to sitting next to her sister. She had that feeling once in a while. She couldn't help it.

"Forgive me, dear Inga. Please forgive me," said Anna now. "I didn't mean to laugh. But your news came as such a surprise. Let me put on some coffee while you tell us more."

None of them was prepared for what Inga told them, yet Ellen realized she wasn't particularly surprised. Especially when they heard the name of Inga's fiancé. It was Jonathan Lundgren, of course. Both Anna and Elisabet were excited to hear it was him. *Who else would it be?* thought Ellen. She pictured the way Jonathan had been shambling around Inga the past few months, like some big, timid dog, scared of being chased away. And how Inga had let him stay without protest.

There were no wedding plans yet, and they hadn't even told Mrs. Lundgren. But the widow was getting old and deaf, and she had a hard time getting around. She would probably be relieved to have another woman as part of her household, even though Inga already spent a good deal of time over there.

Ellen glanced at her sister. Elisabet was listening to Anna and Inga talk with a look in her eye that Ellen found increasingly unsettling. Elisabet seemed to be taking far too much interest in the news, as if she thought it would really change anything. But they would all go on exactly as before. The only difference would be that someone would be coming out a different door at dawn, on his way to work. But Elisabet looked elated as she intently followed what Inga and her mother were saying, though she didn't say anything herself. If they had been younger, Ellen might have kicked her sister under the table, or pinched her hard on the arm, to try and rouse her from this strange spell into which she seemed to be sinking deeper and deeper with every word that was spoken. But both girls were older now, and Ellen sat there quietly, with a peculiar anger simmering inside. She didn't know where it came from, but it was directed at her little sister's gullible cheerfulness.

As if sensing the dark mood growing in and around Ellen, Inga suddenly glanced at the girl and gave a start. Then she sat up straight.

"Oh, that's right," said Inga. "Ellen, there's something else I wanted to say. We shouldn't just be talking about me. I have a question for you. We talked about this some time ago, that you might try some other type of work, now that you're a big girl."

Elisabet looked disconcerted. She realized that the topic of conversation was about to change direction again, but she wasn't sure in what way. Ellen found Elisabet's discomfort just as annoying as her previous cheerfulness. But she pushed all that aside as she listened to Inga.

"There's an opening," said Inga now. "I talked to the pastor of the Baptist Church when I went there to clean on Thursday. Some of the girls in the congregation have found work at the Klinkenfuer factory up on Margaret Street. But now their family is moving to Superior, so three of them will be quitting all at once. If you go over there early tomorrow morning, there are three places to fill, no matter what the foreman may say. I know that for certain."

All of them sat in silence for a long moment, feeling that various changes were about to take place, perhaps too many and too fast. But that's what could happen whenever Inga got it into her head that something needed to be done.

Elisabet was smiling again, a big, trusting smile, now that whatever had threatened was gone. Inga was smiling too, that inward-turned smile of hers, the way a cat seems to smile. It was a look mostly seen on the faces of older women who wanted to hide the gap in their front teeth. Yet Inga was still in full possession of all of hers.

* * *

THE KLINKENFUER FACTORY was housed in the upper two floors of a three-story building made of brown sandstone, located a good distance up Margaret Street. There was no entrance to the factory from the street. Workers had to go through the wagon entrance to the back. When Ellen arrived at six in the morning on Monday, a group of young women was already waiting outside at the foot of the stairs for the wrought iron gate to be opened. They were talking to each other in loud voices, speaking Italian. Ellen thought she recognized from the Hollow a thin girl with a dark complexion and long curly hair. But she wasn't sure.

She went to stand a short distance from the others and waited. After a few minutes a dark-haired man wearing a waistcoat and striped shirt appeared to open the gate, not saying a word. The girls hurried up the stairs. Ellen gathered her courage and went over to the man, who studied her with a stern look as she stammered what she'd planned to say.

"Are you one of the Baptists?" he said at last. "The girls who quit were from Swede Hollow too. They were Baptists."

She didn't know what would be the right answer, so she simply stated the truth: she was not a Baptist, but her neighbors were. The man continued to stare at her without comment.

"You speak better English than they did," he said then. "But can you sew?"

"I made the dress I'm wearing," said Ellen, standing up straighter. She waited for the foreman, if that's what he was, to pluck at her sleeve and examine a seam. Instead, he headed up the stairs without looking back. Hesitantly she followed.

The foreman continued on to the top floor, where the air was filled with the clatter of sewing machines, the sound merging into something like a buzzing chorus of insects. Ten tables were scattered around beneath the ceiling rafters. Light came from two windows at floor level, and from a solitary electric lamp bulb hanging from the rough ceiling boards. Some of the girls she'd seen in the courtyard were already sitting at the row of tables closest to the windows. They were silent and focused, their eyes fixed on the work their hands were doing as they continuously slid the fabric under the double needles. They were sewing work pants from dark blue material. Moving quickly and efficiently, they set one pants leg after another onto the worktable and stitched the seams as the sewing machine needles pumped up and down. Ellen couldn't understand how their fingers could move so fast.

The foreman had gone over to an unoccupied table in the corner, farthest away from the windows. From a pallet on the floor, he picked up a bundle of fabric tied with string.

"Here," he said to Ellen. "Try sewing these shirts. The pieces have already been cut, so it shouldn't be hard. When you're done, come and show them to me. Okay?"

She nodded.

"Liz, here . . . Liz! She'll show you how to get started." He motioned to a woman sitting at a nearby table. "Liz, honey, will you come over here f'awhile?"

Then he turned on his heel and disappeared down the stairs.

Liz, who appeared to be in her forties, didn't bother with lengthy explanations as she showed the newcomer the ropes.

"You just do like this. Start pumping the pedal under the table and keep moving steadily so the fabric doesn't bunch up. Don't pedal faster than you can slide the seam along. Single needle. Double needle. Like this, up-down, right? Have you ever used a sewing machine before?"

Ellen lied and said yes, but she didn't think the woman believed her.

The bundle consisted of the back and front pieces of collarless work shirts and sleeve pieces with the cuffs already sewn on. Liz showed Ellen briefly how to place the pieces together and also gave her a soiled shirt as a sample, so she could see how the seams should look. Then she said simply, "You'll have to work on your own. Okay?" And she went back to her own table.

It took Ellen a while to figure out how the soiled sample shirt had been made. Her eyes welled with tears, whether from nervousness or the heat in the room, she wasn't sure. She blinked but stubbornly refused to raise her wrist to wipe her eyes because she didn't want anyone to see, though nobody was paying any attention to her. Everyone was bending over their work with the clattering needles. She blinked again. Then she started sewing. "Mind your fingers, honey. No blood on the garments," said Liz quietly from her table.

The first shirt was a disaster. Ellen could tell that at once. The fabric crinkled and tugged around the armholes, and the sleeves were sewn in crooked. She pretended not to notice and folded the shirt as neatly as she could. Then she started on the next one.

This time the hem of the shirt ended up crooked and sticking out.

"Careful with the needles," Liz told her from her workplace. "If they fall out or the machine breaks, they'll take the cost out of your wages."

She seemed to notice everything without even looking up from her own work or slowing her pace.

Ellen folded up the shirt and started on another. The needle and thread seemed to flicker before her eyes; she was sweating and scared that she might drop the fabric.

The next time she looked up, the room was cloaked in a dirty yellowish glow. Dust floated up and down through the light from the windows, and the bare bulb hanging from the ceiling had been switched off. Otherwise everything was exactly the same. The other women were bending over their tables. The clatter from ten feet pressing the sewing machine pedals, and the numbing, monotone rattle of twenty needles piercing the coarse cotton fabric formed an undercurrent for the whole world. No one had said a word all morning. Now Ellen was no longer sweating. Instead, she was cold. Lying on the bench next to her were the ten flannel shirts she had sewn. She stood up unsteadily.

When she went downstairs she found the foreman standing there with his back turned, bending over a belt-driven machine on which the drive wheel seemed to be jammed. As if he had eyes in the back of his head, he raised one hand to signal her to wait. For a long time she stood in the dim light near the stairs, holding her pile of folded shirts. Finally he came over, a shadowy figure between her and the daylight coming in the window, and took the shirts from her hands. One by one he held them up to the light and laughed.

"This one and this one we can't use. Or this one."

Ellen stood there without moving, her head bowed. After a few minutes of silence she looked up. The foreman was holding one of the shirts in his hand, running his finger along the seam, as if trying to pull out the thread. But he couldn't. Without looking at Ellen, he said, "Did Liz help you a lot with this one?"

She shook her head vigorously, not daring to speak because her voice would have quavered.

"You won't get any wages today. Not for these. But from now on you'll get five cents for every acceptable shirt. Understand?"

Ellen nodded.

"We start work at six, including Saturdays. Don't be late."

Then he turned away and left. Nobody paid her any mind. For a moment she didn't budge. Then she headed downstairs on wobbly legs and went out through the wagon entrance to the street.

It was already early afternoon. She stood still, not sure where to go.

Everything had changed. And yet everything around her looked exactly the same as before. From a great distance she heard the whistle of the Duluth train as it passed the Hollow, muffled by the leaves still crowning the trees.

A FEW YEARS EARLIER the Klar sisters had gone with Inga to pay a visit to a woman who lived somewhere along Seventh Street. Inga had merely intended to bring greetings from back home, since the woman's relatives in Sweden no longer had her address. But when they arrived at her simple rented room, the landlady told them that Inga's friend was still at her job, working in a basement factory sewing sacks for the big mills in Minneapolis. The girls followed Inga down the stairs to enter the premises, located well below street level. The place consisted of one long, dark room where women stood at big workbenches in front of rows of crude sewing machines. With swift, abrupt movements, they sewed together rough jute sacks that were stamped WASHBURN-CROSBY GOLD MEDAL. The dust from the jute hovered in the air of the big, low room, with no means of escape. Ellen had started coughing after only a few minutes, and Elisabet did too. When Inga found her friend, she followed them up the stairs and outside. She spoke with a nasal voice, as if she suffered from a chronic cold. Her eyes were red-rimmed, and the strands of gray hair that had come loose from the pins trying to hold them in place were plastered to her sweaty face. Ellen watched as the woman made use of this brief pause to re-pin her hair and then realized that she was actually the same age as Inga. All the gray in the woman's hair was from the dust.

So that's how Ellen had pictured her work as a seamstress. But the Klinkenfuer factory was different. The work was hard, and anyone who did not meet her quota would receive a stern reprimand. But the room was swept every evening, and the foreman kept the workplace and machines in good condition. It took Ellen a number of weeks before she could manage to produce an acceptable number of garments each day, which provoked several stinging reproofs from the foreman, Mangini. But as Liz rather acidly remarked after he'd left, Ellen was the one who suffered most when she lagged behind because she was being paid per shirt. The next few weeks had gone better, and she'd received a semi-promise from Mangini that she'd be allowed to sew overalls and pants as soon as she picked up her speed.

Life now assumed a different kind of rhythm. She got up very early, along with her father, and they ate whatever food there was and drank a cup of leftover coffee. They said very little to each other in the morning, mostly because they didn't want to wake Elisabet or Anna, who were usually still asleep. But Ellen noticed that her father appreciated her quiet companionship at the kitchen table. Then they would step outside into the morning, walking together over to the stairs and up to Seventh Street, where they would go their separate ways. Ellen would wrap her shawl around her head and walk as fast as she could, leaning into the wind and heading for Margaret Street. Her father, often along with Jonathan Lundgren, would join the group of muttering men moving in the opposite direction, down toward the train depots.

Ellen knew that Elisabet was jealous. Her sister continued to help with various cleaning jobs, "going off to work," as Inga liked to say. But on some days Elisabet would sit at home with no particular tasks to do other than helping her mother with the housecleaning or going over to Larson's or Palmqvist's or one of the smaller shops to buy whatever was needed. Anna had never liked doing the shopping. She was scared of walking through the long Drewry Tunnel, and she would take big detours whenever she had to go up to the street. In the shops she always felt uncertain and would fix her eyes on the floor, speaking so softly that the shopkeeper had to ask what she'd said. Yet the family always did their shopping on the Swedish street where everyone understood Swedish. Anna never ventured far from the Hollow unless it was absolutely necessary.

What felt like a safe place for their mother soon began to seem too small and confining for the two girls. Ellen had now gone much farther, and her domain suddenly extended quite a distance along Margaret Street. But Elisabet remained behind in the old world.

And then there was the money. Only after a few weeks did Ellen start earning wages that amounted to anything significant. Mangini had promised five cents per shirt, and that's what she got, although she knew girls who got seven or eight cents. They were slightly older, and Mangini favored them, maybe because they were Italian like him. Some of the girls were German. Liz was American. Ellen was the only Swede. After a couple of weeks she began to work faster, and Mangini praised her, saying that she was a "big girl now." She had mixed feelings about that.

On some days she managed to make a whole dollar. The cashier, sitting near the exit, would pay the seamstresses every Saturday afternoon from a small tin box. The first time Ellen made five dollars for the week, she handed the full amount to her mother, who was so happy she clapped her hands. Then she said, as if it were unimportant, that maybe they shouldn't tell Gustaf how much she'd made. At first Ellen didn't understand why, but after a while it sunk in. A dollar a day was about as much as her father ever earned for a week's hard labor.

After that Ellen was more cautious. She made sure never to bring home more than four dollars a week. She worked as hard as ever, and she became more deft at sewing, but she would keep back a few coins in her apron pocket. When no one was looking, she would put them in a metal box under the porch where she kept the Hamm glass balls. She still carried a couple of the little balls with her, and whenever she felt nervous or tired, she would rub them together in her pocket, without taking them out. With the constant whirring from the sewing machines, she couldn't hear the strangely captivating clicking of glass against glass, but she could feel it through her apron. And she found it soothing. Now the bigger glass balls in the box were joined by more and more coins, both big and small. There was a whole silver dollar and soon a couple of bills. She seldom counted the money, since what she saved was not the important thing.

The Klar girls had made extra money before, when Inga shared her cleaning jobs with them, but the income was irregular. Now Ellen had a steady influx of coins, which she could place on the worn kitchen table. One day Anna sent Elisabet up to Larson's grocery store to pay off what the family owed. That made Ellen mad. She felt stingy in a way that surprised her and almost brought her to despair. She didn't say a word all evening, letting her silence speak for itself, though her mother pretended not to notice. Ellen had wanted to be the one to set the money on the shop counter and watch the clerk strike the credit from the ledger with the blue pencil he always had tucked behind his ear.

Elisabet was given a little bag of polka mints for paying off the debt. With a big smile, she happily, and thoughtlessly, showed Ellen the mints. But when she saw her big sister's expression, she immediately gave her half. They sat in the corner, letting each candy melt in their mouths. Without saying anything they felt like children again, as they looked at each other and smiled.

On other days Elisabet would be cranky and peevish and act as if she were criticizing her sister for having a job to go to. Finally Ellen began asking at the Klinkenfuer factory whether any other seamstresses were needed, but so far there hadn't been any openings. Yet life was different.

Her father hadn't said anything about the money, and Ellen didn't want to mention it either. One day when they parted at the railroad viaduct, she glanced over her shoulder as she hurried along Seventh Street. Gustaf was still standing next to the stairs, and she couldn't see his eyes under the visor of his cap. But it occurred to her that he wore a proud expression, standing there so straight-backed as he watched her go. Then he turned on his heel and dashed after the other men on their way down to the Great Northern's rail yards.

ALMOST NO ONE WAS SURPRISED to hear that Jonathan Lundgren and Inga Norström were going to get married. When the news spread through the Hollow, most people reacted by saying they had expected this to happen, and it was good to hear that Jonathan had finally found himself a dependable woman. Everybody agreed that Jonathan was the one to be congratulated in this regard. After saying as much, some people would feel obliged to add that Jonathan himself was a decent man and a good worker, but that was the extent of their praise. It was as if behind Jonathan's calm presence they could always glimpse the shadowy figure of his brother, the Murderer.

The couple planned to move into Inga's house, since it was bigger, and besides, she now had papers naming her as the owner. The widow Lundgren would remain in her old house, which stood just across the path, so there would be no distance at all between them. Inga had already spoken to Jonathan, Gustaf, and carpenter Nilsson about a number of things that needed to be repaired in her house before she and Jonathan could live there together as a lawfully married couple. The roof leaked in a few places, and in the winter the wind seeped through the wallboards facing south. But the stone foundation was still solid.

Along with Anna, she had once again filled several old crates with soil and then planted bulbs that bloomed in the spring. She had gotten Gustaf and Jonathan to put up a low board fence around a little garden patch next to the steps, even though not much would grow in the hard clay. Gustaf had hurriedly put together a similar fence reaching down to his own family's house, but there was only enough whitewash for Inga's side, and half of theirs, so part of their fence remained unpainted over the winter and summer.

Many people shook their heads at these notions of Inga and Anna, saying they were trying to seem better than their neighbors. But the following spring several of the small houses farther down in the Hollow also had crates filled with soil, with Easter lilies blooming next to their doorsteps.

From the beginning Inga had made it clear that the wedding was not to be anything out of the ordinary, thereby making it sound as if the couple could have celebrated in grand style if they'd chosen to do so. The ceremony itself would take place in the Swedish Lutheran Church at Eighth Street and Maria Avenue immediately following the regular Sunday service. That seemed most suitable since no one had to go to work on Sunday, and there wouldn't be any additional expenses. Inga had already spoken to Pastor Sandstrom, who had agreed to marry them. Then the couple would host a reception with coffee and cake at their home. And that would be that.

Most people who lived in the Hollow were not big churchgoers. Carpenter Nilsson's family and a few others attended the First Swedish Baptist Church; an equal number of the Swedish families went to the Swedish Lutheran Church, although not every Sunday. The Italian families were more faithful about attending church, going to St. John's Catholic Church on Fifth Street. At first some of the Irish also went to St. John's, but later they preferred to walk all the way to Assumption Church on Seventh Street, where the congregation was predominantly Irish and the priest also spoke Irish.

Otherwise there was little sign of any church activities within the Hollow, except when members of the Scandinavian Salvation Army on Minnehaha Street would come to visit. Then people would gather to listen to the music. A group of little Irish boys, led by the younger Flaherty brother, would often show up to shout "Soupers!" at the Salvation Army representatives. The boys would throw stones and try to puncture the big bass drum that one of the male soldiers carried in front of his sizable stomach. Finally Leonard and some of the older boys would chase them away.

On this particular morning folks emerged from their houses well before the service was to begin at ten o'clock. The bells were ringing at the Swedish Lutheran Church, the sound clearly audible through the branches of the deciduous trees, bare of leaves now that autumn had arrived. In the summertime the groves of trees on the steep slope hid the view of the Hollow from the street above. Most of the people now headed in long lines for the stairs up to Seventh Street were wearing the best clothes they owned. Gone were the gray or dark-blue work jackets, gone were the faded aprons that made up their everyday attire. Today many of the men wore dark jackets and waistcoats. Those who didn't have any Sunday clothes had at least made the effort to put on a white shirt. Most of the women wore dark dresses and shawls. Walking with her family at the very back of the line, Ellen couldn't help thinking that it looked more like they were on their way to a funeral rather than a wedding. She tried over and over to erase this thought from her mind, the way she might swat at a pesky fly, but it kept coming back.

Pastor Sandstrom stood on the church steps to welcome everybody. Ellen wondered whether he did this every Sunday and whether the church was normally as full as it was today. Those who'd come from the Hollow ended up in the very back. Before Ellen sat down, she noticed the tall figure of Jonathan dressed in black and sitting next to stout Inga in the front pew. Like all the other women, Inga had on a black dress, but she wore a wreath with a white bridal veil on her head. Ellen had never seen anything like the veil in Inga's house, so she assumed it had been borrowed from the church.

It was clear that many people who had come for the wedding were not accustomed to attending church. The men muttered and whispered to each other, drawing reproving looks from a number of women seated closer to the front.

The congregation sang a hymn that Ellen hadn't heard before. Then Pastor Sandstrom stood in the pulpit and began preaching in Swedish, which made Ellen happy as she sat squeezed in between her mother and Elisabet. She wasn't used to hearing her own language used in that fashion, and the pastor's words rose up to the vaulted, white-painted, wooden ceiling high overhead. He welcomed everyone on this morning, offering a special greeting to those who had come to attend the wedding, which would take place immediately after the service. Then he began singing a hymn without opening his hymnal. It was "A Mighty Fortress Is Our God," one of the few hymns that Ellen knew. The whole congregation launched into singing the verses, and even though their voices were not especially beautiful, they sang with such vigor that the pew she was sitting in shook in time to the music. Then Ellen couldn't help thinking about Horrible Hans's old father. From what she'd heard, he had died and was now buried somewhere far out on the prairie, in a place where he could never have imagined he'd end up one day. And no one visited his grave. The thought made her mood turn gloomy again, until she glanced at Elisabet, who was singing with flushed cheeks and shining eyes. Then she had to laugh.

While the pastor gave his sermon, Ellen almost dozed off. The church was getting hot even though it was early October. As she sat there with her eyes half-closed, she noticed something odd. The church seemed to be divided into two sections. The people sitting up front near the tall windows wore lighter clothing. Those who sat toward the back, underneath the gallery where she was sitting with her family, wore dark clothes. There was also a faint smell of sweat, along with a lingering trace of booze on the men's breath from their Saturday night drinking. When several men sitting in the pew in front of Ellen began muttering to each other, they again received sharp glances from the women in the forward pews.

Suddenly she seemed to picture the entire scene, as if her soul had floated upward and turned a dreamlike somersault near the ceiling and was now observing from a great distance those congregants unaccustomed to attending church. They were crowded together under the gallery, enclosed in their own atmosphere of sweat-stained waistcoats and round collars, garments that exuded an air of boiled root vegetables, rotting wood, the previous day's quiet drunkenness, and the pinches of snuff that some of the men hadn't had the sense to spit out before climbing the church steps. It made her dizzy, and she felt the same slight nausea she'd sometimes experienced as a child when she went up the stairs to Seventh Street and then turned to look back and saw from above the treetops and patched roofs of the Hollow.

She had never observed herself or those she knew in this way before, as if from outside. Now she realized how they must look from up front: like a dark, shapeless mass crowded into the very back of the church. Their particular smell filled her nostrils so she could hardly breathe. She wanted to jump up and dash outside into the fresh air. But she sat in the middle of the pew, squeezed in, with people on both sides. And she didn't want to embarrass Inga. This was her day.

When the service was over and the notes of the last hymn died away, the wedding was to take place at once, with no pause in between. Yet some of the women in the front pew stood up and silently walked down the side aisles, their eyes fixed on the thick red carpet. They did not look at the people sitting in back as they passed.

Pastor Sandstrom cleared his throat a few times as he watched the women leave. Then the doors to the church closed once again with a quiet sigh and the marriage ceremony began. *Dearly beloved, we are gathered here today.* Ellen thought Sandstrom looked both pleased and happy, as if he truly meant every solemn word he said, and she thought it must be more enjoyable to marry people than to bury them. Everyone stood up and sang. Jonathan and Inga were standing at the front of the church. The bride's face was bright red under the white veil. In her hand she held a flower bouquet, and Ellen had to wonder where they'd found flowers at this time of year. Later Inga would tell her that it was a bridal bouquet that could be borrowed from the church, dried flowers that had been hand painted in various colors. Ellen could almost see the heat radiating off Inga, standing there in her dark dress, and it struck her with great force that Inga was beautiful, practically glowing. She had never thought of Inga in that way before.

Afterward they clustered together, standing in the wind blowing across the yard in front of the church. Everyone agreed that it was a lovely wedding. Jonathan and Inga were still inside with Sandstrom, because apparently a number of papers had to be signed when someone got married.

Elisabet was restless and anxious to get moving, just as she always was when they were children. She'd been sitting in one place for nearly two hours, after all. Finally, the two sisters headed arm in arm down Seventh Street while their parents lingered behind. Elisabet was still feeling elated, chattering on about the bouquet and what sort of cakes Inga might be serving. Ellen wanted to talk about something else entirely, and finally she hissed, "Did you see those women? The ones who left?" Elisabet hardly looked up as she replied, "I suppose they had to go home to make dinner."

As they walked along, Ellen caught a whiff of that same faint stink of hopelessness emanating from her sister's familiar, brown-patterned dress. Their mother had sewn an additional strip of fabric to the hem when it got to be too short for Elisabet. And Ellen wondered whether the smell would ever leave her.

OLA VÄRMLÄNNING WAS A MAN who had a hard time finding his place in the world. He was restless and quickly grew tired of being in the same place—or it could be that what had once seemed the right place for him now belonged to the past and he could no longer return there. He came and went. He could be found at various work sites in both St. Paul and Minneapolis, and then even farther afield, anywhere he could find a job that would last a couple of weeks, where he could earn a little money and then move on. Yet he was someone whom other people noticed. Big and tall, he towered over everyone else with his mop of blond hair, which was at first a buttery yellow, then gray, and prematurely turned completely white. His face continued to be round and boyish. No one knew exactly how old he was, and it really didn't matter as long as he could do the work of two or three men.

A year into the new century he became an increasingly rare sight on the city's streets and in the taverns, and people began to wonder where he'd gone. There was always someone who knew his whereabouts, not because he'd personally seen Ola, but because he knew somebody else who had seen him. Apparently he'd been working his way north, making it all the way to the iron mines of the Mesabi Range. Plenty of people had seen him there, in the expanding mine district around Hibbing,

Grand Rapids, and Virginia, Minnesota. He seemed to thrive among the Swedes and Finns up there; he'd said it was almost like being back home in the Finnmark area of Värmland. Others said they'd met him in the ore shipping ports of Duluth and Two Harbors. He seemed to be in so many places. But there was only one Ola Värmlänning, as demonstrated all too well by the story that began to circulate about the time he was working in the mining district—a story that was finally brought to the Twin Cities by the Swedes who returned after spending time in the north.

For several months Ola had been working for Union Mining outside Virginia. It was a mine that was growing rapidly, and great risks were taken to get at the ore as quickly as possible. Explosives were used extensively, and frequently there were workers who didn't understand the warnings, because a number of different languages were spoken in the mine. Anyone who joined one of the various unions was blacklisted and fired. So the workers simply had to accept the risks and keep going. Or move on. Ola Värmlänning hadn't planned to stay very long, but he enjoyed the camaraderie down in the mine shafts because there were lots of Swedes from the same part of Sweden where he came from. Virginia was a town on the rise, and soon there were so many taverns and gambling halls that on any free evening there was a new place to try. Ola said that he had everything he needed close at hand, including a spruce forest. He was happy to stay in Virginia for a while, though he had a hard time keeping his mouth shut whenever he thought the mine managers were driving him and the other workers too hard. There weren't many foremen who dared speak against Ola if he was within earshot, but they did keep an eye on him. Yet he worked harder than most.

Then came the big explosion. A blasting went wrong, which happened now and then, though it never slowed the pace of work. But this time a wall of rock shifted, causing a mine passage to collapse and shutting it off from the rest of the mine. It took hours to determine whether anyone was inside and who they were. It turned out that five men were missing. Ola Värmlänning was one of them.

They dug all night in the light from burning torches, not knowing whether they'd be able to pull anyone out alive from all the rubble. Just as the first light of dawn appeared over the tops of the pines on the ridge, there was movement amid the piles of rock. It seemed as if someone was shoving at it from inside. Now they renewed their efforts, using both shovels and their hands.

The man on the other side was Ola, of course. His face was black, but otherwise he seemed in one piece. When he caught sight of the men outside, he merely grunted and went back into the mine without saying a word. After a while he reappeared, seeming to stagger as he moved forward. When he emerged into the light of day, everybody understood why.

On his back Ola carried one of the mine ponies. The horse was alive but had an ugly wound on its back. As gently as possible, Ola lowered the animal to the ground. Then he straightened up, his spine audibly creaking, and again went back into the mine. Now several men followed him, carrying torches, and helped to bring out the four other mine workers who'd been trapped inside. Two had broken legs, and a third had a deep gash in his skull, but they were all alive. Small rocks were still falling from the ceiling of the mine shaft, and it could collapse at any moment. When everyone was out and Ola had been given a glass of weak beer, a foreman finally asked him, "Why did you bring the horse out first?"

"I did it for your sake," Ola replied, looking at the foreman who stood closest. "Wasn't that what you wanted?"

Everyone shook their heads and said they didn't understand. So Ola had to explain: "If one of us happened to die, nobody would be sad, because we're a dime a dozen, and there are plenty of others ready to take our place. But fine ponies like this one don't grow on trees. So I thought it was worth at least five workers."

He said this with a serious expression, but after a moment he couldn't keep a straight face any longer and he started laughing. And the laughter spread to the mine workers standing all around, until everybody was bellowing with mirth. Except the foremen and engineers, that is. The laughter was said to stem from a sense of relief that everyone, including the horse, had survived. But after that Ola fell into disfavor, and he developed a reputation as a troublemaker and a communist, although he wasn't a union member and had never hurt a fly. Suddenly he had a hard time finding any work at all, even though he was still big and strong. After a while he decided to move on, and he began working his way back south to his old haunts and neighborhoods in the Twin Cities.

And it was there that his story came to an end. Everyone agreed on that, even though no one who recounted the tale had been present when it happened.

In September 1903, a strike broke out among several of the big mills at St. Anthony's Falls in Minneapolis. Fifteen hundred workers rose up and walked off the job after being denied their demand for an eight-hour workday. Soon the strike spread to more of the mills, effectively shutting them down. And outside the Washburn Mill the striking workers gathered in great numbers, held back by rows of policemen wearing dark coats and armed with sturdy billy clubs. At first things were orderly. But after a few days barricades went up along Second Street—a palisade of boards that cut off the mills and the river from the city and the striking workers. A rumor soon began to spread about why the barricades were there—not to prevent the workers from getting in, but because the mills were bringing in students from the university as well as newly arrived immigrants who would be quartered in the warehouse buildings along the river and who would do the work behind the protection of the newly erected wooden planks. It was said that eight hundred strike breakers were already in place and more were on the way by boat. As the rumor spread, anger began surging through the ranks of the striking workers, and cries of "Scabs, scabs, scabs!" could be heard, at first only in occasional outbursts but growing steadily.

After being in the city for a few weeks, Ola Värmlänning had taken a job at the Washburn Mill, where he'd worked many times before. When the workers rose up and called a strike, he initially wasn't sure what to do, but rather than being left behind, he joined them. So that was the situation now. He had already been blacklisted up north in the mining district, and now it seemed as if things would be no better here, and the same might well happen to him in the Twin Cities.

No matter where he turned, he could see traces of his hard work. He'd worked at all the mills. He'd also helped to build the Stone Arch Bridge on which the train crossed the river. The bridge was said to have been built by Hill, the railroad king, but Ola had never seen him even once during all the years it took to finish the construction. Ola had also worked on many of the big stone warehouses nearby. And it seemed to him so wrong that he would no longer be allowed to find work among these streets and buildings he had helped construct. The more he thought about it, the more angry he became. All around him workers were chanting louder and louder: "Scabs, scabs, scabs!" The police were growing nervous, and they had closed ranks so they now stood with linked arms, their billy clubs drawn.

Then someone starting throwing bricks. There were bricks scattered around a vacant lot down the street, and several men ran over there and began lobbing bricks to those who stood closest to the lines of police. Several bricks flew over Ola's head and landed on the ground between the first rows of workers and the police, who retreated a few steps until they stood with their backs against the board fence. For a moment everyone fell silent, and that's when they could all hear the sound of hammering on the other side of the barricade. That made the demonstrators even angrier. But Ola didn't think they were especially good at throwing bricks. Without further ado, he grabbed a brick away from a thin, young millworker standing next to him and said, "This is how you should do it." And he assumed the stance of a baseball pitcher, spun halfway around, and then hurled the brick at breakneck speed.

It sailed over the policemen without touching even a hair on their heads before knocking a hole right through the board wall behind them and disappearing on the other side. No one made a sound. Ola turned around and said something to the younger strikers behind him, something like "That's how you throw a brick." But what he didn't see as he stood there, turned away, was the brick that came flying back from the other side of the fence, not at quite the same speed, but very nearly. As if seeking the exact spot where it had started its path, the brick fell in a wide arc toward Ola and struck him on the back of the head, making a sound like steel against iron. Ola broke off mid-sentence and dropped to the ground. Everyone standing close to him had to jump aside so as not to land under the falling giant, and everybody agreed that he was already dead before his wide forehead struck the pavement.

There he lay, big and broad and very dead. It was difficult to move him, but finally they managed to turn him over so that his wide-open blue eyes were looking up at the sky. They had to find a door to use as a stretcher, and it took eight men to lift it so they could take Ola away. There he lay on the door as the men carried him through the crowd. Afterward people said he looked calm, almost happy. And yet he was dead. All the striking workers removed their caps as his body was carried past—Swedes, Irish, Poles, and Italians alike. A great silence settled over Second Street.

A few days later the strike ended. In early October those who were allowed to go back to work did so, but most had to look around for other jobs. And the fence was torn down. Nobody knew where Ola's body had been taken, and it will do no good to try and find his headstone. No one knew what his real last name was, since he was always called simply Ola Värmlänning. Some thought his name was Johansson; others said his real name was Gustafsson. A small group of his former colleagues claimed he was called Bergstrom. But even if any of these names were correct, it would still be impossible to find him. Because there are so many gravestones with those sorts of names in the city's cemeteries.

### *The Story about Gustaf Klar, As He Personally Recounted It to David Lundgren in the Minnesota State Prison, Stillwater*

IT SO HAPPENED that Inga fell ill just when Jonathan was about to head out to visit his brother, David, in the prison in Stillwater. It was hard to know what was wrong with her. It was not because her cough had returned, but even though no one said anything aloud about the matter, it could be—at least Anna had mentioned as much to Ellen—that Inga was pregnant. Yet it was not at all clear whether that was the case, because lately she'd put on a good deal of weight. And Jonathan said nothing, of course.

But on the evening before he was due to leave, Jonathan came over to the Klar family's house and asked to speak to Gustaf. He didn't come inside but asked Gustaf to step out on the porch, where they talked for a while in the winter darkness. Gustaf was in shirtsleeves and waistcoat. Then he came back inside and sat down at the kitchen table.

"Jonathan can't go to Stillwater tomorrow," he said, "because he can't leave Inga on her own."

"I can look after Inga," Anna started to say, but then she fell silent because something in Gustaf's demeanor indicated he had already decided to go.

"The problem is that if nobody goes to visit David, he won't get any tobacco for the month," said Gustaf. "And things are hard enough for him in prison as it is."

They had all heard Jonathan say that David was nevertheless managing as best as any man could in a place like the Minnesota State Prison. At least he hadn't complained in such a way that Jonathan felt a need to share what his brother said.

"Jonathan will pay for my streetcar ticket," Gustaf went on. "And the tobacco, of course. There might even be a little extra for me. He's hoping I'll be willing to go."

Anna nodded her agreement.

The prison had its own stop on the Twin City Lines; it was the very last stop. Aside from the conductor and the driver, Gustaf was the only one onboard. He sat as close to the coal-burning heater as he could in order to absorb some of the heat. But soon he had to get off the streetcar. The driver barely paused before turning the streetcar around and heading back toward Stillwater, with the wires on the streetcar's roof crackling blue light that flashed across the snow.

For a moment Gustaf stood still, as if to take his bearings. A front of dove-gray clouds hovered over the hills to the west. Then he walked up the stone steps and proceeded to the main entrance of the prison. A thin layer of new fallen snow, as yet unmarked, stretched out before him.

The portal was tall enough to allow a freight train to pass beneath its vault. Beyond the metal bars he glimpsed what reminded him, strangely enough, of the tower and pinnacles of a castle. The guard, who stood in a sentry box made of brick, eyed Gustaf up and down before demanding to see his papers. Without a word, the guard then let him into a large paved inner courtyard where the snow was swirling around in peculiar, restless gusts. Another guard motioned mutely with his billy club toward an open doorway in the nearest building. Gustaf stepped inside a long and narrow room with yellow-painted walls. The man seated behind the counter asked for his name and address and then told him to empty his pockets. Gustaf placed the few coins in his possession on the counter and then slid toward the man the tobacco packets, which were wrapped in a red handkerchief. "You can give the tobacco to the prisoner," said the guard, "but not the handkerchief." Not once did he look Gustaf in the eye.

Then the guard opened the door that was bolted with two locks. The door opened to a hall with low wooden tables set in a row. Light slanted in through the barred windows high up near the ceiling. Sitting at one of the tables was a gray-clad figure with hunched shoulders. Gustaf had nearly reached the man before he could determine that this was in fact David Lundgren. He seemed to have shrunk during the ten years that had passed since Gustaf had last seen him. David's hair was still thick, but it had turned an iron-gray.

David looked up, his expression impassive, though there seemed to be a trace of a smile on his lips.

"So Jonathan couldn't come today," he said at last. "He's always been good about visiting me here."

Gustaf was relieved that David recognized him. He'd been worried that the years in prison might have clouded the man's mind, as he'd heard sometimes happened to those who couldn't endure their time inside. But the man sitting across from him seemed calm and matter-of-fact. He asked Gustaf about his family and then wanted to know what had prevented his brother from coming to Stillwater on this particular

February afternoon. The more he talked, the more he seemed like his younger self. When Gustaf mentioned that Inga was having health problems, David smiled in a strange way, which made Gustaf wonder again whether the man might be mentally unstable. But then David said, "I'd heard that Jonathan had finally found himself a woman, and I'm glad. It's about time. But it took a while before he told me it was Inga. She's a good, dependable person, that one." This last remark he said without even a hint of a smile, his expression deeply serious.

Gustaf slid the tobacco packets across the table. David picked them up and immediately stuffed them in the pockets of his gray prisoner's jacket. Then he cast a glance around, even though they were alone in the room. He seemed extremely wary.

"That's as much as they'll let us have," said David. "But sometimes it doesn't always last—if we're allowed to keep any of it at all, that is."

They sat in silence for a long moment, but neither of them was willing to end the visit. It had taken Gustaf the better part of a day to get here, and he didn't want it to be a wasted trip, though he wasn't sure exactly what was expected of him. Finally he pointed at the white stripe on David's sleeve and asked what it signified. David looked down and smiled.

"It means that I'm a 'number one,'" he said. "A first-class prisoner."

He spoke as if this were self-evident, as if someone had asked him for the time of day. But then he explained. The prisoners were divided into three groups. The most disorderly and dangerous men wore striped prison garb. Those classified as less troublesome wore gray. Those who were regarded as conscientious and were specifically assigned to the better prison jobs were given a white stripe.

"Sometimes it can be risky," David went on. "It riles some of the other men, who try their best to take you down a notch by picking fights and so on. Or by stealing your stuff." He patted his pockets where he'd stowed the tobacco.

"But mostly it's fine. The guards think I'm okay. In the best case, it means you might get out a year ahead of time." And then he added, "Not that I'm in any hurry."

But something seemed to have thawed inside David now, and he leaned back in his chair and began talking about his time in prison. He explained that if you landed in trouble and got on the bad side of one of the vicious guards or if you got into a serious brawl with another prisoner, then you could end up in the Hole. That had never happened to him, but he'd heard what it was like. The Hole was a narrow cell with double doors, the first made of wood, the second of iron bars. If you landed in the Hole, the guards fastened your handcuffs to the highest crossbar so that your feet could barely touch the floor. Then they closed the wooden door so it was right in front of your face, and that's all you had to look at. You had to hang there like that for half a day before they came to take you down. And you had to piss and shit right where you were. If you were a bad case, you might spend several weeks in the Hole. David had never seen any man come out of there untamed. One man had stopped talking afterward and hadn't uttered a word in years.

"But you've managed," said Gustaf, mostly just for something to say.

David nodded.

"They say it's not worth it to try and rile me, because I never get mad. Sometimes it helps to be a murderer." He smiled.

Gustaf realized the remark was meant to be a joke, but the words slowly began to set something in motion inside him, though at first he couldn't identify what it was.

David kept on talking. He said it also helped to stay on good terms with the Italians. For a long time he'd shared a cell with a Sicilian, who also happened to have relatives living in the Hollow, and they'd talked a bit. The Italians stuck together in the prison, and few men dared to harass them. David had made sure to stay in the shadow of his cellmate as long as possible. There were also plenty of Swedes and Norwegians in the prison, as well as a few Finns, but they mostly kept to themselves, so they didn't offer much help.

As Gustaf listened to David, entirely new thoughts arose in his mind. They were all centered around that one, bright-red word: *murderer.*

Finally David fell silent and looked at Gustaf expectantly. Gustaf was completely calm as he began to speak.

"Jonathan told me," he said. "He told me about what really happened when Horrible Hans died."

David looked at him without saying a word.

"I don't think you did it," Gustaf went on. David shrugged, as if to say, It no longer makes any difference.

"But there's something else I want to talk to you about," said Gustaf. "It has to do with me."

Then he started talking, though he had no idea how much David knew about his past, about what had happened, and where he and his family had come from. These were things that people learned about each other if they lived in the same place for a long time, although both David and Jonathan were men of few words. During the crossing from England so many years ago, Gustaf had tried to say as little as possible. All that was now so long ago that it might have been about someone else entirely, someone whose son was still alive. But what happened before that had suddenly come vividly alive inside Gustaf.

"This was before, when we had three children at home," he said. "That's why I decided to protest. I thought we deserved a little better."

As he spoke he stared down at his hands, which lay palm up on the table in front of him. Even his hands seemed to belong to somebody else.

"What happened," he went on, "is that there were eventually a lot of us employed by the shoemaking shop. Twelve of us worked together as a team in one of the buildings, and ten in the other. It was actually an old cowshed that had been fixed up. The boss had spent several years over here in the States, mostly in the area around New York, saving his money so he could make a fresh start back home. When he got back to Sweden, he started his own workshop, though now he wasn't interested in running just a shoemaking shop; instead he called it a 'factory.' And he appointed Jerk Ersa as foreman to supervise the work. That's when the trouble started. Jerk had never liked me or my brother, so he kept a close eye on us and was always ridiculing our work, even though it was just as good as anyone else's, if not better. And we had to keep increasing our speed. That was Jerk's assignment: to get us to work faster. Finally three or four of us said, 'If we're going to work faster, then we should get a krona more per week.' 'We'll have to see how it goes,' was all the boss said, and that was that. But Jerk had decided we were troublemakers, and he wanted to get rid of us. He was no longer satisfied with merely criticizing our work; now he began to sabotage us. On at least one occasion I personally saw him ripping apart the seams of shoes that I'd made."

Gustaf fell silent. David had still not spoken. Gustaf could feel that the man's brown eyes were fixed on his face, but he didn't look up as he went on.

"One day Jerk came over to my workbench when I was almost done with the upper leather of a shoe and said, 'Give me that.' I wanted to finish the work first, because I didn't want to give him a chance to complain, so I kept on sewing. He stayed where he was and raised his voice until he was practically shouting, 'Give me that!' I picked up a knife to cut off a piece of leather that was sticking out before giving him the shoe. But he leaned down and grabbed the shoe. I refused to let go, so we ended up standing there, tugging in opposite directions. It probably looked quite comical. Then I raised my hand holding the knife, and without thinking,

I stabbed him in the neck. I wasn't even especially mad. I just aimed for his neck because it was the softest spot. I still don't know why I did it, except that I wanted to shut him up. It's like what a lot of people say when they've done something awful—I've heard it so many times, and it sounds like they're trying to think up an excuse, but it's probably true. It was as if for a moment I was not myself; I was somebody else. All I remember is that I felt very calm. The foreman fell to the floor without a word and began kicking his legs. That's when I got scared and tossed the knife aside. I tried to stanch the bleeding by pressing on his neck. Some of the other men came over and pulled me away because they thought I wanted to strangle him, on top of stabbing him."

Gustaf paused for a moment.

"But when they pulled me away, the blood started pouring out again. I can still picture the scene if I close my eyes."

"What happened then?" asked David, his voice oddly calm.

"That's the strange part. I don't really know. Jerk Ersa ended up in the hospital in Örebro. He wasn't able to speak as they drove him over there. My brother had witnessed the whole incident, so he tried to explain that it wasn't my fault, that Jerk had provoked me. And that I was already holding the knife in my hand. I just sat there. I'd wiped off the knife and put it back in its place on the cutting bench. But the floor was still stained with blood. I sat at my place and didn't know what to do. They told me to go home. They didn't want me there. When I looked up, I realized they were afraid of me now, and nobody dared look me in the eye. That night I went over to my brother's house and slept up in the attic. When I got home, Anna said the police had come by, asking for me. So we left Sweden as soon as we could. We'd already talked about leaving, and we had all the necessary papers, but we'd been putting it off because we weren't sure about emigrating. Until that evening, that is."

The two men sat in silence across from each other. Gustaf realized visiting hours must be over soon. Outside the narrow windows up near the ceiling, the light had already turned gray, and he could hardly make out David's face. His mane of hair was silhouetted against the dirty yellow wall. David sat very still. Then he said, "So how did it go? For that man, Jerk Ersa?"

Gustaf hesitated before replying.

"I've wondered about that so many times. I don't know. He was alive when we left, but he was in bad shape. He couldn't talk anymore, only make hissing sounds. Somebody said that he didn't have long to live. That's what the police told my brother."

"So you don't know?" said David. "Whether he died or not, I mean."

Gustaf shook his head.

David paused before saying, "If only you knew the stories that I've heard in here. But I believe you. What you've told me sounds like the truth."

"I don't believe in God," said Gustaf, "but it struck me that things are not the way they should be."

And now he fixed his eyes on David, peering at him in the dim light. "Here you sit in prison for a murder you didn't commit, while I'm a free man, even though I might have killed someone. It seems completely backward."

"So," said David, still as calm as ever, "do you wish things were different in any way?"

Now Gustaf didn't know what to say, so he said nothing.

Then the guard opened the door behind him. He saw a strip of yellow electric light slide up the wall. The two men stood up.

"If that's how it is," said David quietly as they leaned toward each other, "and if that's what's bothering you, then you should know that I, for one, forgive you—in the absence of anyone else who could do that."

The words came out of nowhere and struck Gustaf with great force. He merely nodded mutely to David, who stood there with his face again in shadow. Then he followed the guard out. That was all.

When the gate closed behind Gustaf, he stood there motionless for a long moment, reorienting himself to the outside world. Then he looked for the nearest streetlamp and began walking back toward the streetcar turnaround spot. A few snowflakes drifted slantwise through the air. He was breathing hard, each breath like a stab of iron in his chest. It was as if something had been living inside him for far too long, and finally he had pulled his ribs apart and yanked it out, leaving behind an emptiness that was now slowly filling with all the sorrow he'd managed to hide from himself for so many years.

LIZ HAD ANOTHER JOB that she did after the workday was over at the Klinkenfuer factory. Mangini clearly knew about this, but he was willing to overlook it, as long as it didn't affect the speed of her work. Liz had worked at the factory longer than anyone else, and few seamstresses could keep up with her, so she was allowed certain liberties.

Ellen didn't know about this until she took on some extra tasks that paid her fifty cents more per week. She would stay behind to sweep up the fabric scraps, trash, and dust, sorting out the bigger fabric pieces and putting them in a box so they could be used sometime in the future. It took her an hour after the normal workday, and sometimes she was so tired that her eyes stung and she had a hard time raising her arms above shoulder height when she put on her coat. But she liked the feeling of being the last one there on certain evenings. She also had to lock up and then drop the key in the mail slot on her way out.

On some evenings Liz would also stay behind. She withdrew to her own corner and sat there sewing on something, mostly by hand. She used the sewing machine only on a few occasions, when Ellen would hear a sudden clatter behind her back as she swept the room. Liz never said much, just gave a nod in her direction. On those evenings when they were both there, she and Liz would leave together and part outside the wagon entrance after saying good night. On other evenings Liz would leave with the other women, and Ellen was left on her own. And that was actually what she preferred.

After a week when Liz had stayed late on several days, Ellen couldn't resist asking the other woman what she was working on. At first Liz offered only an annoyed look in reply. Then her expression seemed to soften, and she pulled out a cardboard box from under the worktable where she sat.

"I've kept careful accounts the whole time," she said. "I pay for every single piece of fabric. Mangini knows all about it, but the other girls might get jealous. And I'm not sure that old Mr. Klinkenfuer would be too pleased. So I hope you won't say anything, Ellen. All right?"

Ellen nodded.

In the box, folded as neatly as on the shelves in a shop, were a skirt, a blouse, and what looked like a woman's small jacket. The blouse was made of plain cotton, like the shirts Ellen sewed every day. But the skirt and jacket were made of heavier, dark material. She couldn't help reaching out her hand to run her fingers over the fabric. Liz gave her a warning look, though she knew that cleanliness was important to Ellen. It was one of the things they had in common, in spite of their age difference. Downstairs in the building was a sink and faucet, and the two of them went there often to rinse the chaff and sweat from their eyes and face. This took them away from their work for a short time, but otherwise, by the afternoon, it got hard for them to see what they were doing, and that's when most of the accidents occurred.

"I'm not sewing these things for myself, if that's what you're thinking," said Liz. "I've taken on some work on the side, sewing and altering clothes for some of the office ladies who live in the neighborhood but work downtown. I do a lot of the sewing at home. But one day I gathered my courage to ask Mangini if I could stitch some of the seams on the machine here, so the clothing would look like it was factory made. Only after work hours, of course. And he has always had a soft spot for me, so he gave me permission. I pay him a little money for the material I use. But I buy most of the fabric myself, because it has to be of a finer quality. I think the small payments I give him probably end up in his own pocket."

Liz smiled. Ellen wondered what she meant when she said that Mangini had a "soft spot" for her. As far as she knew, Mangini was married and had two children, while Liz was a spinster and lived by herself in a rented room in the area beyond Maria Avenue. But she didn't really want to know anything more.

Ellen could hardly take her eyes off the garments in the cardboard box. The seams were so even that it was impossible to see where Liz had used the sewing machine. And the black fabric draped in soft folds that were barely visible. That sort of clothing would keep you warm even during the coldest winter months in Minnesota, yet wouldn't make you sweat at work—though she wasn't sure how much a typist or secretary would sweat. She wondered how much Liz earned from this extra work, but she didn't ask. Liz, for her part, could see how impressed Ellen was, and she smiled with satisfaction. Then she placed tissue paper over the garments and pushed the box back under the table, out of sight.

On their way out to the street, Ellen couldn't help asking, "But shouldn't you really have your own seamstress shop? Since you're so talented?"

At first Liz didn't reply as she walked along with her head bowed.

"I did have my own shop once," she said at last. "But you're young. You don't realize how easy it is for a seamstress to acquire a bad reputation, especially a woman who isn't married. As soon as you sew even one garment for a man, the gossip starts to fly."

Then she shook her head and withdrew into herself again, saying only a brief good night before she turned away and disappeared up Margaret Street.

On other evenings Ellen would be all alone, and so tired that she could hardly see the trash in the corners, especially on the lower floor where most of the windows faced the courtyard. Mangini thought it was best if she didn't switch on the electric light in the ceiling because it could be seen from outside and might attract what he called the "wrong sort of people." But he also said, "I trust you, Ellen, so I'm going to lend you something." He went over to the small glassed-in office in the far corner. He unlocked the door and let her peek inside. She saw a desk, a locked roll-front cabinet, and several boxes of papers. This was where the cashier sat a couple of days a week. What Mangini wanted to show her was on top of the cabinet: a simple lantern with a candle inside and a lens that attracted the light so it became focused in a small cone.

"You can use this in the winter when it's dark," he said to Ellen. "The key to the office is hanging on a peg above my desk over in the corner. Just make sure nothing catches fire, and put the key back in the morning. All right?" He looked at her in a way that made her feel he was taking her measure; it was the same way she'd felt on that very first day when she came to ask for work. But mostly she thought about what she'd seen sitting on the desk: a typewriter under its cover with the letters UNDERWOOD in gold script. She'd never seen an actual typewriter before.

A few evenings passed before she dared take a closer look at the typewriter. She would sweep up as best she could in the existing light and then go to get the lantern. The first few times she merely walked past the typewriter. Then one evening she cautiously lifted off the cover, after running her fingers over it to make sure there was nothing that might indicate it had been removed. But she found no latches or hooks. With the cover gone, she let her fingertips glide over the shiny, round keys, which gleamed in the light from the lantern. They made her think of the buttons on a policeman's uniform. That was all she did before setting the cover back in place and putting out the lantern.

The next day Liz was there, sewing for as long as she could see what she was doing. But the following evening Ellen was once again alone, sweeping the floor and sorting remnants. Then she went inside the office. She took off the typewriter cover and set the lantern next to it on the desk. She took a crumpled piece of paper from the wastebasket and smoothed it out. It took a few tries before she figured out how to insert the paper in the roller. Her fingers grew sweaty at the thought she might break something in the typewriter, which seemed as fragile as an insect.

When the paper was in place, she pressed on the keys, one by one. At first, when the type bars struck the paper, the sound made her jump. But she kept on going. The first thing she typed was her name.

UNLIKE GUSTAF AND THE GIRLS, who continually sought to widen the circles in which they moved, Anna found it harder to leave the Hollow as time passed. This change in perspective came over her gradually. When the family first settled in, she still took an interest in looking around. But after a while she began to feel as if there were no longer any doors open to other places beyond where they lived. For a time she thought it might be pleasant to accompany Inga up to the Swedish shops on Payne Avenue when they had a little extra money. There was bound to be so much to see in the shop windows and vendors' stalls—maybe nothing that she could afford to buy, but she thought it would be amusing to daydream about all the things she'd see.

Yet she slowly began to realize that her world was below the street level, down in the Hollow. She couldn't say exactly when this happened, yet it didn't bother her, although she could see Gustaf and the girls were worried. It had something to do with Carl. When he died, the rest of the world seemed more and more colorless and washed out. Anna stayed where things were familiar, and she did the same things she'd always done after they'd arrived here. Nothing else seemed important anymore.

She would still go up to the street to shop for groceries, and she no longer took detours so she wouldn't have to walk through the Drewry Tunnel. It didn't frighten her anymore. But if possible, she avoided shopping at Larson's, though it was closest. The family was doing slightly better now that Ellen had found a job, and soon Elisabet would undoubtedly find work as well, maybe joining her sister at the Klinkenfuer factory if that could be arranged. Ellen had promised to keep her eyes open, and girls who worked there often left for other jobs. Lately Anna had been able to pay the family's grocery bills at the end of each month, but she didn't care for the way old man Larson would peer at her from behind his spectacles and under those bushy brows of his. He always gave her a look that seemed to be measuring and weighing her, just like the scales hanging above the counter. Anna preferred instead to go farther up the street. But after a while she stopped doing even that. She no longer went farther than Minnehaha Street. Beyond that neighborhood, there were too many people who spoke languages other than Swedish, which made her uneasy. Her circle got smaller and smaller, but she wasn't concerned. She had her own world. Yet she realized after a while that others saw this as a problem. Including Inga.

Anna didn't know whether the idea originated with Gustaf or Inga, but he was the one who suggested that on Sunday they should go on a little outing to Elliot Park in Minneapolis. It was the end of April and the weather was getting warmer. They would take the streetcar from Seventh Street and transfer downtown to the streetcar line that went all the way out to the park. Inga and the girls would come too. Elisabet had asked whether Leonard could come with them, but Gustaf said no, and she hadn't insisted. Anna offered no objections to the plan, but the closer it got to Sunday, the greater her apprehension, until she almost felt as if she were suffocating.

Elisabet was brimming with anticipation even though she wasn't allowed to bring Leonard along. Ellen said nothing, lost in her own thoughts, as always. Inga seemed to be looking forward to the day. "It'll be nice to see something different," she said, "and to meet some folks besides the same people sitting around here in the Hollow with us." Inga's good humor helped to ease Anna's fear somewhat, but her sense of dread returned during the long hours of Sunday morning.

In honor of the day, Gustaf had bought himself a paper collar, which he fastened to his whitest shirt. Anna wore her dark dress and wrapped the shawl with the tiny flowers around her shoulders. "Shall we go?" she said.

Gustaf had bought streetcar tokens, which he handed out with a solemn air, as if his daughters were still little girls. On the slope up to Dayton's Bluff, some of the shrubbery had already sprouted buds, which obscured the view of the Hamm mansion. They said very little to each other as they headed for the streetcar stop, but the girls ran on ahead and then waited for the others on the bridge. Inga came last, breathing heavily.

There was a hint of warmer weather in the air and scents of spring, with sun-warmed gravel and a misty gust from the river that lifted rubbish from the gutters and whirled it across the cobblestones, only to vanish as suddenly as it had come. Soon the yellow streetcar appeared over the hill and came to a halt with the ring of its bell. This was the first time Anna would take a streetcar. She sat down on the worn wooden bench and looked out the window. The city glided past with low, dark buildings and shops that were closed because it was Sunday. Along the river she saw trees, their branches still leafless, and telephone wires that undulated up and down. She dozed off.

Then they changed streetcars and rode across the Mississippi. Anna peered down at the frothing brown water. Feeling suddenly nervous, she grabbed Gustaf's arm. She had never been this far away from the Hollow since they'd arrived in the city.

"We're all the way over in Minneapolis now," said Inga with satisfaction. "We'll be there soon."

They got off at Washington Avenue. From there it was only a few blocks' walk to the park. Lots of people were out—men wearing suit jackets and straw hats, women in light-colored dresses. Many of them also seemed to be on their way to Elliot Park. The gates to the park were visible at the end of the long street, which was lined on both sides with brown, three-story buildings made of stone.

Inga and Anna lingered behind as Gustaf and the girls hurried on ahead.

"I didn't think there'd be so many people," said Anna, linking arms with her friend. "And I thought most of them would be Swedes."

"They probably are," said Inga. "It's called Swede Park, after all. But this is my first time here too."

Inside the park a swirl of delicate early spring greenery bordered the open area surrounding a trickling fountain.

"It's probably green because it's a little warmer here," Inga remarked. "The tall buildings offer a different kind of shelter from the wind. Almost like down in the Hollow."

They strolled through the shadows of the tall trees closest to the gate. The crowd of people had swelled now that it was afternoon, and even though everyone was conversing as they walked, a peculiar quiet seemed to hover over the park. Wherever Anna turned, she heard voices speaking Swedish. She closed her eyes and for a moment thought she was back home in Sweden. Then she opened her eyes and swiftly blinked away the illusion. She noticed, much to her own surprise, that the feeling of homesickness was gone from her body; in fact, she felt no sense of longing at all. She sat down on a bench, and Inga sat down beside her. Together they watched the sunlight play across the bright green of the lawn, where a few robins had appeared.

It was starting to get quite warm. The girls had gone off somewhere. Gustaf came over and stood in the shade near their bench. Then he said that he'd take a walk around the park to have a look at things and come back. They were in no hurry, after all.

Gustaf had often heard his workmates speak of the "Swedish park." The younger men went there to flirt with the Swedish housemaids who worked in the posher neighborhoods in Minneapolis. But the girls most often "had expensive taste" and usually "nothing ever came of it," as the men said. Yet some of them continued to go to the park on the weekends. That was where it was possible to meet the most Swedes in one place, and there was a lot to see. And it cost them nothing.

All around him Gustaf heard the calm murmur of Swedish voices. A little farther along the gravel path he saw a small kiosk surrounded by men in shirtsleeves. When he got closer, he noticed several familiar faces, including Johnson and Lundqvist from the Great Northern. There were others he recognized, though none of them lived in the Hollow.

Lundqvist was a foreman who demanded respect, but he was not the worst of the lot. The railroad men knew who Gustaf was and gave him a restrained greeting.

"Do you like ice cream, Klar?" asked Lundqvist as he stood there, rubbing his handkerchief over his red and sweaty bald pate.

"I don't know," Gustaf replied truthfully. "I've never tasted it."

"Then it's about time you did," said Lundqvist. "Here, it's my treat."

He placed a nickel on the wooden counter, and the girl scooped a white ball of ice cream into a cup made of biscuit.

"Here you are. You eat the whole cup too," said Lundqvist, handing it to Gustaf. The cup felt cold in his hand. He looked at the other men standing in a circle around him; some of them he knew, some of them he didn't. And he felt as if he were undergoing some sort of test, which made him suspicious. Especially the part about eating the cup as well as the ice cream, although it did feel fairly soft to the touch. He took a bite and his mouth turned ice cold. But the ice cream tasted sweet and good, reminding him of porridge with a lot of sugar.

The other men smiled at his expression, but he still couldn't determine whether they were merely being sociable and in a cheerful Sunday mood, or whether they were subjecting him to some kind of sly joke. Finally he bit into the biscuit cup. When he was done, he wiped his hands on his pants and thanked Lundqvist for the treat. For a moment no one spoke. Then Lundqvist said, "Are you here on your own, Klar?"

"No," said Gustaf. "My wife and children are here too."

"Then I think you ought to offer your wife and children some ice cream," said Lunqvist. "Since they've never tasted it before."

Gustaf searched his pockets for coins and finally found five cents, which he handed to the girl at the counter in exchange for another cup of ice cream.

"Best hurry off with that," said Lundqvist. "It melts fast."

Gustaf nodded to the group of men, then turned and left, feeling their eyes on his back. They had not been unfriendly, but he would never be one of them or have access to that mute sense of ease they shared.

He could feel rather than see the scoop of ice cream melting, so he walked faster, though he had to watch where he was going. Along the path, beneath the trees, he encountered more and more men and women who wore clothes in lighter colors. All of them moved out of his way, though without giving him so much as a glance—the way they might avoid a puddle of water or a patch of mud on the pavement, as their thoughts were on other matters. The men carried walking sticks with silver knobs and the women wore hats. They laughed as they headed in the opposite direction, and Gustaf had to weave his way through the crowd, holding the little, rapidly melting gift in his hand.

Elisabet was more eager, striding along the gravel path as if she had a clear goal in mind. At first Ellen stayed a few steps behind her sister and walked along with her eyes fixed on the hem of Elisabet's brown skirt. She wished they'd had nicer clothes to wear. She didn't want to look up and see everyone else's lavish Sunday outfits. Elisabet trotted onward until they came to a crossroad, where she stopped to wait for her sister. In the distance they could hear a band playing, though they couldn't see where the music was coming from. Elisabet stood in the shade, peering across the expanse of lawn.

"What are you looking for?" asked Ellen.

"I thought there would be more young people here," said Elisabet. "There's supposed to be a dance area somewhere, but I can't see it."

"That must be where the music is coming from," said Ellen. They looked across the lawn. In the distance they saw a row of five-story buildings towering above the newly budding treetops.

"Come on," said Elisabet, cutting across the wide, sunlit space. Ellen followed, wondering whether they were allowed to walk on the grass.

The music was coming from a small pavilion located on the far side of the park. Lots of people were sitting at the long, white-painted tables that belonged to a little restaurant. A band was playing on the pavilion stage, and below was a simple, eight-sided dance floor made of boards shiny with wear. The young people that Elisabet was hoping to see had gathered at the foot of the pavilion steps. For the moment the dance floor was empty. Now that Elisabet had found the place she was looking for, she suddenly looked shy. She stopped and seemed on the verge of turning around to leave.

"I have a little money," said Ellen. "We could buy something."

The restaurant served mostly coffee and cookies. They each ordered a glass of lemonade and sat down at the only unoccupied table, which stood in the full glare of the sun. Slowly they sipped their drinks through the red-and-white straws. The sun felt hot, even though it was only April. Ellen vaguely recognized several of the tunes the band played, tunes that her father used to play on his concertina before Carl died.

Then a few youths who had been hanging around in the pavilion's shadow came sauntering over to where the girls were sitting. Without asking, a blond boy sat down on the vacant chair. He wore a white shirt with a cheap collar and the sleeves rolled up, and a black waistcoat with a gold chain. He carried his jacket over his arm. His friends strolled around between the restaurant and the pavilion, as if unsure where to go. The boy smiled. He seemed to be about eighteen or nineteen.

"Samuel is my name," he said in Swedish. "I haven't seen you here before."

His tone was brusque, but he gave them a friendly smile. Ellen thought maybe that was the way people talked here in the park. She told him their names and then added, "This is the first Sunday we've come here." She cast a quick glance at Elisabet, silently telling her, "Don't say that we're here with our parents." But Elisabet had no intention of saying any such thing.

Samuel said he often came to the park with his friends. He worked for the Twin City Lines, in the streetcar repair shop, but he was soon going to be a conductor. He talked as if he owned the whole park as he sat there with one arm draped over the back of his chair. His friends still kept their distance, as if waiting for something. Ellen drank her lemonade.

"May I offer you another one?" he said suddenly. Ellen politely declined, but Elisabet nodded and smiled. Ellen glared at her sister, who avoided her eye.

Samuel came back a minute later with a glass for Elisabet and one for himself. He surreptitiously took out a little pocket flask and added a few drops to his lemonade. When he offered some to Elisabet, she demurely declined, much to Ellen's relief. He quickly slipped the flask back under the table.

There was something about the situation that Ellen didn't understand. Samuel seemed sincere enough, and he hadn't said or done anything rude. Yet he seemed to be fishing for something, and his friends kept casting glances in their direction.

She told him that she worked as a seamstress in St. Paul.

"So you're not from Bohemian Flats?" said Samuel, studying them through narrowed eyes.

She had no idea what that was.

"Is that someplace here in Minneapolis?" she asked.

He nodded.

"Under the bridge. The one you rode across on your way here, if you're from St. Paul. That's where a lot of Swedes live."

Ellen shook her head.

"We're from Swede Hollow," explained Elisabet, mostly to join in the conversation. "Although we're actually from Örebro."

For some reason this last remark sounded quite funny, and the three of them laughed.

"I think I've heard people talk about the Hollow in St. Paul," said

Samuel. “I suppose the streetcar line goes past it.” He narrowed his eyes again.

For a moment none of them spoke. The musicians had picked up their instruments, and the sun glinted off the brass, casting strange reflections across the ceiling inside the pavilion. Ellen wondered whether the chain on Samuel’s waistcoat was really attached to a pocket watch, or whether it was merely for show. She considered asking him for the time, just to tease him, but decided not to.

The band began playing again, this time a simpler waltz melody. Some of the couples sitting at the tables got up and somewhat hesitantly headed for the dance floor.

“Would one of you ladies care to dance?” asked Samuel, looking them in the eye. Ellen shook her head, but to her surprise Elisabet said yes. Samuel quickly stood up and offered her his arm, and together they stepped onto the dance floor.

Ellen looked up at the sky at the dazzling sun. Dark spots drifted across her field of vision, and for a moment she had the feeling that she was underwater. This was something that occasionally came over her, also at work. But right now she was neither tired nor hot.

Suddenly Elisabet was back, looking agitated, her cheeks bright red. She tugged at her sister’s arm. Samuel was nowhere to be seen.

“Come on, Ellen. I want to leave. Let’s go,” said Elisabet, dragging Ellen out of her chair. “Now.”

The two girls hurried along the gravel path toward the tree-lined lane. Out of the corner of her eye, Ellen saw that Samuel had rejoined his friends in the shade of the pavilion. They were all looking in their direction. Samuel smiled and pointed. All the boys seemed to be laughing.

When they entered the shade of the trees, Elisabet calmed down. They slowed their pace and strolled along like all the other Sunday visitors. Elisabet glanced nervously over her shoulder a couple of times.

“What happened?” asked Ellen at last. Elisabet was holding tightly to her arm, but she didn’t look at her.

“He grabbed me,” she said. “Several times, even though I told him to stop. And everybody could see what he was doing, but they just laughed. They laughed as if it was funny, even though I told him not to.”

Slowly they walked down the path toward the gates where they’d left Inga and their parents.

“That wouldn’t have happened if Leonard was allowed to come with us,” said Elisabet, wiping her nose. But her voice was once again calm. That was how Elisabet was—she never seemed to stay upset for long. It was one of the things that Ellen truly envied about her sister.

* * *

Anna had accepted the cup of ice cream, giving Gustaf a look that was half-amused, half-nervous.

"I've heard that ice cream can make you sick," she said, looking uncertainly at the melting white lump.

"No, that's not true," said Inga. "They were even starting to sell ice cream in Stockholm before we left, at the big Exhibition. I read about it in the newspaper."

Anna hesitantly lifted the ice cream to her lips and cautiously licked it. Then she took a bite and looked up at Gustaf with a smile. "It's good," she said. A tiny white streak colored her upper lip, as if she'd been drinking milk. She smiled again, and behind Anna, Inga gave him a big smile.

The girls approached, walking beneath the shady vault of the trees, two darker patches against all the light. He could tell from far away that they were his daughters, two short figures wearing shawls.

"Where have you been?" asked Anna, holding the empty biscuit cup in her hand. She didn't want to eat it.

"We went over to the dance pavilion," said Ellen. "But we didn't really care for it. We wondered whether you'd like to go home soon."

"I think we should take a walk around, now that we're here," replied Gustaf. Before Anna could say anything, Inga pulled her friend up from the bench and linked arms with her.

"I've heard there's supposed to be an area in the park with animals," she said. "Let's go and have a look at them."

Together they walked along the lane on the north side of the park. By now it was late afternoon, and most people were sitting on the benches or at tables that were set with picnic food.

In the northwest corner of the park they saw a small enclosed pasture with a waist-high fence. The smell of haystacks gusted toward them. Men in shirtsleeves were leaning forward with their elbows propped on a railing as they watched what was going on in the pasture. Three men wearing riding breeches were leading small, fat ponies around and around in a circle. Children sat astride the horses and held tightly to the reins, as if everything depended on maintaining control. Other children were waiting in a long line behind a crude turnstile. Everyone was speaking quietly in Swedish, as if not wanting to disturb the horses, though the animals were perfectly calm and seemed almost bored.

Inga and Anna stood there, arm in arm, and watched. Then came time for the riders to change. The horses were led forward, and the children were helped down. One of the children who was ready for a turn was a little blond boy about five years old. His father stepped forward to lift him into the saddle and put his feet in the stirrups. Then the ponies began making their rounds again in the pasture. They were tall enough that the children riding them were at eye level with the grown-ups who were watching. The blond boy sat up straight, and he too gripped the reins tightly. When he passed the Klar family, he looked at them with his clear blue eyes and smiled. It was a lovely smile, filled with anticipation.

Gustaf saw Anna turn pale and grip the wooden railing. The big hole in his own chest opened. There he stood, looking down at his hands and wondering how he could endure such an abyss inside him, day after day, through all the daily chores and tasks. An abyss without beginning or end.

"I think it's time we go home," said Anna, almost to herself.

"Yes," said Gustaf. "It's bound to get a bit chilly toward evening, so it's best we leave."

Inga merely nodded. Then they all headed for the park's tall gates. As they walked up to the streetcar stop on Washington, none of them said a word.

The next Sunday, for the first time, Anna went with carpenter Nilsson's family to the First Swedish Baptist Church on Payne Avenue. She did not make much of her decision to accompany them, nor was it something that had suddenly occurred to her. And she didn't go every Sunday. It was mostly to meet people and to listen to the music. And, as Inga said, it was good for her to get out a bit.

THE SCREAM RACED UP through the stairwell and pierced right through the eternal buzzing insect chorus of the sewing machines. The scream rose and fell in strength but it did not stop. Ellen was deeply immersed in her work, as if she were underwater, inside a warm and closed place where the light was yellow and she consisted of only hands and perfectly straight seams. She heard the scream from a distance through the wall of absence and concentration. Part of her understood at once what had happened but wanted to remain inside the simple world of straight lines stitched through coarse, sheet-white cotton fabric. She recognized all too well the voice that was screaming. And yet she continued to sew.

Liz poked at her shoulder. "Hey, Ellen, something's happened to your sister. Downstairs."

She got up, gathered up her skirts, and rushed down the stairs.

For the past week Elisabet had been sitting at the rows of sewing machines next to the window, sewing sleeves onto work jackets made of rough blue material. It was poorly paid work but, as Mangini said, it was a start. The sewing machines were a different type from those upstairs. The fabric was heavier so the machines were bigger and more cumbersome, with bigger needles. They ran on electricity, but if the fabric jammed, extra force could be applied by manually turning the drive wheel on the side. But you had to be careful not to look at the wheel instead of what you were sewing. That was a mistake you only made once, as the foreman said.

Ellen caught sight of her sister the instant she came downstairs. Elisabet's right hand was positioned under the needle bar. She was no longer screaming, but she was sobbing with her head cradled in her left arm. The needle had pierced through her hand, pinning it in place, and a dark splotch of blood was spreading through the wrinkled denim fabric. One of the Italian girls hurried over and tried to stop the blood flow with a scrap of white cotton material, which quickly turned red as well. Ellen looked around for Mangini, who now came calmly up the stairs; he too had been summoned by Elisabet's screams. He went over to stand beside her and said in a matter-of-fact tone of voice, "Okay, I'm going to pull the lever up now, okay? This is going to hurt a bit, but you'll soon be free." Elisabet nodded, keeping her head down on the crook of her arm. Only the knot of her hair was visible. She was crying quietly, her shoulders still shaking. "Ellen, hold your sister's hand while I do this," said Mangini. Ellen gripped Elisabet's fingers, thinking it had been a long time since they had walked hand in hand, the way little girls do. Elisabet held on so tight that it hurt. It occurred to Ellen that it would be best if her fingers didn't get injured too, because then neither of them would be earning any money. She dismissed the thought and tried to focus on her sister's pain. But she couldn't.

Mangini quickly raised the needle bar, and Elisabet screamed again. Her fingernails bit into the back of Ellen's hand, but she didn't flinch. The heavy-duty needle was now free of the fabric, but it was still impaled in Elisabet's hand, though the bleeding had stopped. Mangini swore. "Keep holding her hand while I go get a wrench, will you?" The cashier had emerged from his little glass cage, wearing a visor around his bald pate and protectors over his shirt sleeves. Mangini said to him, "Hey, Al, better call the doctor."

Elisabet was calmer now. Next to her stood some of the other girls, all of them Italian. They had no common language, but they made little cooing sounds, like doves, and stroked Elisabet's back as she sat there, bowed over the bloodstained workbench.

"What are they doing? I don't want to look," she said faintly as she cradled her head, still holding Ellen's hand.

"The foreman has gone to get some tools," said Ellen. "And they're calling a doctor to see to you."

When she heard the word *doctor,* Elisabet began crying again. "I didn't mean for this to happen," she said.

The comment almost made Ellen laugh, but she kept herself in check and quietly patted Elisabet on the back. "It'll be fast," she said.

Mangini came back, bringing pliers and a wrench. "Hold her still," he said brusquely to Ellen, a stern look on his face. Then he quickly unscrewed the whole needle bar as he snapped some words in Italian over his shoulder at the other girls. One by one they returned to their work. And the insect chorus resumed.

It took almost an hour before the doctor arrived. While they waited, Ellen sat with her arm linked through Elisabet's and held her hand in the air, as Mangini had told her to do. The big needle was still sticking straight through her hand, and Elisabet had turned away so she didn't have to see it. Ellen had plenty of time to study the shiny needle sticking through the back of her sister's hand. Around the steel a little mound of clotted blood had formed, and streaking her arm were lines that looked like rivers on a map. The whole scene exerted the same sort of enticement over Ellen as the drawings at the back of the newspaper—little puzzles that she had to strain to decipher. Yet she realized that the pain had not diminished in the slightest. She could feel Elisabet's pulse racing.

The doctor was an elderly man with white hair and a two-day stubble, equally white. He didn't introduce himself, nor did he ask their names, uttering only a brief "Oi-oi" as he shook his head. Then he opened his bag and took out some cotton wadding and a bottle of sharply smelling iodine, which he used to wipe off the blood. He motioned to Ellen to take hold of Elisabet's arm to keep her still. Elisabet turned her head away and shut her eyes tight. The doctor got out a pliers, pressed the girl's hand onto the table, and yanked on the needle. Elisabet's body tensed like a bow, but she didn't scream. Round drops of fresh blood spattered over the already stained surface of the table.

The doctor held up the needle to the light. "No bone," he said. "That's good." Then he cleaned the wound and efficiently bandaged Elisabet's hand. Yellow iodine seeped through the white bandage, but no blood.

The doctor told Ellen that the bandage should be kept on for at least two weeks. If Elisabet developed a high fever or if her arm swelled up, she should go to Bethesda Hospital, which treated emergency cases. Did they know where the hospital was?

Elisabet sat there with her eyes closed and didn't seem to be listening to what was said. Her pale face was covered with tiny beads of sweat, and her breathing was shallow. But Ellen nodded and said she understood. The doctor closed up his bag and motioned to Mangini that he was done. Then he disappeared down the stairs.

Mangini squatted down in front of Elisabet and in a calm and clear voice asked her whether she would be able to walk home. Elisabet nodded without opening her eyes. He told her to rest for a bit, and then he took Ellen by the arm and pulled her aside. "It would be best if you made sure she gets home all right. There will be pain after the shock wears off."

Ellen stood there, waiting, because Mangini clearly had more to say. He looked her in the eye. "It will take at least three weeks for her hand to heal. And depending on whether anything was damaged, she may not recover the full use of her hand. Do you understand what I'm saying?"

Ellen nodded.

"I can't keep her on. By tomorrow I'll have to hire someone else to take her place. Do you understand?"

Again she nodded.

Mangini sighed.

"Elisabet never was able to pick up her pace. But you're a good worker, Ellen," he said. "I wish I had more like you. You don't have any other sisters down there in the Hollow, do you?"

*No,* she thought of saying, *but I have a brother who's dead.* She merely shook her head.

"Well, I need to ask you to take your sister home. And maybe you can explain things to her when she's feeling better." At first it looked as if he was going to shake Ellen's hand, but then he simply turned on his heel and left.

As they headed down Margaret Street, Elisabet leaned heavily on her sister's arm. It felt strange to be outside in the warm spring weather in the middle of the day; a gentle breeze caressed their faces as they walked. When they came to Seventh Street, Elisabet let go of Ellen's arm and said, "I can walk on my own."

"How does your hand feel?" asked Ellen.

"It's throbbing. But it's better now. If only it doesn't start bleeding again."

As they approached the stairs leading down to the Hollow, Elisabet paused to look below at the rooftops and the crowns of the trees. Then she began talking, her face averted.

"I know I've made a mess of things," she said. "You don't need to tell me that. I heard everything the foreman said even though he was trying to speak quietly. And I know you were blamed for getting me hired."

"Unlucky hands," said Ellen. "You're not the first one to get a needle in her hand. And there are other jobs to be had."

Elisabet began unsteadily making her way down the stairs. She couldn't hold on to the railing, so Ellen took her arm. Silently they walked side by side down the narrow staircase alongside the ravine and beneath the steep shadow of the railroad viaduct. Even though Ellen tried to put it out of her mind, she couldn't help thinking about the dollar she would lose by being away from work for the remainder of the day.

AT NIGHT I WOULD WAKE UP with my hand throbbing. It didn't exactly hurt, but it felt like a little animal was living its own life inside my hand. At first I was scared and kept an eye out for what the doctor had said I should watch for, in case the wound swelled up or my arm got big or if red streaks appeared under my skin. But nothing like that happened. It just throbbed, sometimes hard, sometimes weaker, as if my heart had moved down into my hand. I lay in the dark and listened to the others sleeping and felt my pulse beating, and it was actually quite calm even though it kept me awake. Mother wanted to wash the bandage, because after a while it turned completely gray, but Ellen thought it was best to leave it be, at least for the first week, while new skin formed underneath. So Mother did as she said. I didn't really know what to do with myself, it no longer hurt to move my fingers, but I couldn't wash the dishes or cook. Ellen said it would take whatever amount of time it needed to take, at least a couple of weeks, that's what the doctor said. Ellen and Inga were away all day, and Mother had her own chores to do. It was lovely, warm weather, cooler than up on the street, because half the Hollow was always in shadow. Leonard kept me company whenever he could; he was working too, of course, but sometimes he'd have a day off in the middle of the week because he did shift work, which meant working for days in a row on the freight train to Fargo; he could do several trips in a week without getting off the train even once. I'd never been to Fargo, but he said the ride there was nice, even though there wasn't a lot to see; in fact, it was like traveling across an ocean although not with water but with grass in every direction, and I thought that sounded lovely. And he said there were antelopes. I didn't know what they were, but he said they were like deer only bigger and they could jump awfully high. Sometimes they got run over by the train, and then the birds would gather overhead to get themselves a good meal, and the next time you rode past there would be nothing left except maybe the horns. When Leonard was home we would go for a "promenade," as he said, even though we never left the Hollow but just kept to ourselves, walking among the trees below the Hamm mansion, or near the spring on the hill. At first we'd sit in the shade down by Phalen Creek, but after a week the water began to smell really bad, the way it always did in the spring and summer. If nobody was looking, he liked to hold my hand. The houses stood very close together up on the hill, because then the slope got suddenly steep, and when you walked from the spring down to the open space in front of Inga's house, there was a cranny between two houses that was always in shadow. That's where carpenter Nilsson used to leave his ladder and any boards he had left over. You could slip in there from the wooded side without anyone seeing you and stand in the shade in case it was too hot outside. Leonard wanted to go in there because he said it was so hot, and he tugged at my good hand. When we got inside the shade he started kissing me; he'd done that before, but now he kept at it for a long time. We leaned against the wall and stood still as he breathed down my neck and I got very hot. Then he began touching me, like that boy did in Elliot Park, but this was Leonard, after all, and I didn't have anything against it. Long ago I realized that one day he and I would end up together, but I wasn't in any hurry. But he was, and maybe that's because he was older. He touched me through my clothes, and we stood there and closed our eyes for a while. But when he began to fumble with my dress, I grabbed his hand and said I was scared somebody might come. Then he stopped. But I could see that he was mad even though he pretended not to be.

A few days later Inga came over, like she often did, but it was me she wanted to talk to, not Mother. She thought we should take a little walk up on the street, so I went with her. After a while she started talking. She said she didn't think it was good for a girl my age to just sit around at home. She thought I should start thinking about what I was going to do when my hand was healed instead of just waiting around for better days. So she wanted to show me a few places. We walked along Seventh Street, and she pointed out several laundries, really big places with heavy white smoke pouring out of pipes that stuck out of the wall in the alley next door. I could feel the heat, and it smelled of wet clothes. When Inga saw me wrinkle my nose, she said it was a good job, and you didn't have to be Chinese to handle things when it got a little hot and damp, because lots of Swedes worked there, and you could keep yourself clean and the pay wasn't much worse than at Klinkenfuer's. "We won't go inside today," said Inga, "because that ugly bandage on your hand might frighten them, but I want you to think about it, and then I can come back here with you later." On the way home, Inga said in a serious voice, "I know that Anna needs you girls to help out right now, but it's uncertain how long Ellen will be staying here. So you have to think about how the family will manage things then." It felt good to have Inga talking to me like that, because I realized she considered me to be a grown-up now, but I hadn't given much thought to the fact that Ellen might look for work someplace else. "But where would she go?" I asked Inga. "She has a good job at Klinkenfuer's, so why would she leave?" "You never know," said Inga a bit sharply. "All of a sudden folks are just gone." That's all she said, and I understood it was best not to ask any more questions at the moment, because I realized she was thinking about what happened in Sweden when her parents died and that was something she never wanted to talk about.

I didn't really want to work in a laundry. Getting a needle through my hand was one thing, and it was starting to heal, but I've always been afraid of burning myself. I've often had nightmares about that. After the fire on Ellis Island when I was little, I couldn't stop thinking about it, even though we were never truly in danger back then. For a while I thought of telling Inga when I had a chance, because she'd been there too. But then Leonard came back from Fargo and I talked to him instead, and he said that the laundries weren't especially dangerous places. Of course you sometimes read in the newspaper about someone who got scalded from the steam and died, but the same thing could happen working on a train; lots of things were dangerous, but a person had to work. "And have you ever thought about how many people go to work at a laundry here in town?" he asked. "There must be several hundred." And there were several thousand working on the railroad. It was true that from time to time the papers reported that someone had been killed by falling off a train or someone got badly burned in a laundry, but those incidents were only reported because they were especially bad cases. Most of the time nothing happened, but the papers didn't write about that. "Just think," he said, "what if it said Betsy Klar went to work and then she went home and nothing happened? There wouldn't be space to report anything else, and who would want to read about that?" Lately he'd started calling me Betsy. He was the only one who did that. We were sitting on the hill behind Inga's house, and he was chewing on a blade of grass when he said all this to me, and I gave him a sidelong glance and laughed a little, as if he was joking, but actually it all sounded very sensible. He talked about his job being dangerous, but things always went fine.

And just imagine if nobody wanted to work as a brakeman, he said, then things would be even more dangerous. Soon they'd think up other ways to brake the train cars than having someone do it manually, and they were already doing that on passenger trains because the cars weren't as heavy. But by the time that day arrived, he'd already be working as a fireman or even an engine driver. He talked for a while longer, and then he grabbed my good hand and wanted us to go in between the houses again, but this time I said no.

The fact that he'd talked so much about the newspapers made me sit down and page through a few that Ellen had brought home. She often picked up papers that others had left behind, copies of the *Svenska Amerikanska Posten* and sometimes papers in English. I thought those were hard to read, but I was looking through the Swedish paper when Ellen came home from work. The paper had started printing color pictures on Saturday, it was the only newspaper that did that. "You're reading the paper?" she asked me. "Yes," I said. "I have nothing else to do." But I thought it was annoying how a long article might end at the bottom of the page and then you had to search a while to find where it continued, sometimes on a different page. Ellen read the paper differently; she would choose a page at the beginning or at the end and read up and down each column, from start to finish. "What are you reading?" I asked her, and without looking up she told me it was the list of job openings. Then I felt a slight chill and thought about what Inga had said the other day. Later when Inga came over to have coffee with Mother, I told her that Leonard and I had talked about the laundry jobs, and he thought it might be worth a try too. "Did he really say that?" said Inga, giving me that look of hers that sometimes made you wonder whether she might need spectacles, because she would stare as if she wasn't quite sure what she was seeing. "Yes, he did," I said, and I almost felt annoyed with her, but it was hard to be mad at Inga. Some people were a little scared of her, but I wasn't. The next day I took off the bandage and the wound was practically healed. My hand was all yellow under the bandage, so at first I was afraid something was wrong, but then I realized the color was from the iodine the doctor had put on it. There was a big scab that tugged and itched, but I managed not to pick at it. Mother washed the bandage for me, and then hung it up to dry on the front stoop, and when I put it back on, it was still warm from the sun. When Leonard came over, he noticed at once that the bandage was clean, and he wanted to know how my hand was. "Almost as good as new," I said. "By next week I can probably leave off the bandage permanently." We took a walk up to the spring, and while we were sitting there, the Duluth train went past; you could barely see it above the rooftops, only the plume of smoke was visible, billowing between the tree branches. It was a fine, warm evening, and we sat there in silence until we could no longer hear the train. Then Leonard took me by the arm and quite firmly led me in between the houses to our little cranny that was empty except for the ladder and boards. The mud on the ground had dried and cracked so it was almost like a real floor. Leonard looked strangely serious, and he kissed me very hard, and it was hotter in there than usual, so I started to sweat. My hand throbbed under the bandage, but it didn't hurt. He put his arms around me and then ran his hand down my skirt so it slid up against the wall, moving up inch by inch, and the wall plank felt warm against my skin as I stood there. "You're not wearing anything underneath?" he said with a smile, and I told him that was probably something only posh ladies did, the kind that wore silk dresses, though I wasn't sure if that was true, but if I worked at the laundry, maybe I'd find out things like that and also how to take care of fancy clothes.

AT FIRST studying the job listings was merely a way of passing time. Ellen didn't take them seriously; they were more like a window to other lives than her own. She would fantasize about the meaning behind an announcement like: *Efficient and conscientious Swedish girl wanted to do housework for a traveling family. Travel experience necessary.* Others were easier to imagine: *A capable girl wanted to do cleaning at night for the Whitlock attorneys' office. References and English proficiency required.* But the job listings that truly caught Ellen's attention were those farther down that were formulated more tersely, even though the space they took up was about the same: *Unmarried women 18–20. Typist wanted. Must present work samples. Proficiency in English and Swedish. Apply to the Shelby law offices.* That announcement appeared at least once a week, and its recurrence seemed to indicate that they were having trouble finding the right girl, or that no one managed to keep the job for long.

Whenever Ellen brought a newspaper home, she would scan the columns of job listings in the evening. On her way home from work, she often found the morning edition of the Swedish paper left behind at a streetcar stop, stuffed into a wastebasket or tossed on the street. She was ashamed to admit that once in a while, early in the morning, she would snatch a paper from a doorstep she passed on Margaret Street on her way to Klinkenfuer's. After supper, she would sit down with the papers, mostly because she wanted some time to herself. But it was the classified ads that she read with the greatest interest, especially in the *Svenska Amerikanska Posten.* If she couldn't get hold of the Swedish paper, she would read the *St. Paul Daily Globe,* but the two papers were not equally captivating. It wasn't that the English was a problem, because after working for more than six months at Klinkenfuer's, Ellen could read and speak the language well. It was the style of the Swedish announcements that seemed more vivid and garrulous, as if wanting to shout something important to someone who was heading off on a train: *The Lindstrom home with two horses and shed in good condition offered for sale due to return journey.*

Ellen's hands had grown hard. On her wrist she had a callus that was just as thick as the kind you could get on the heel of your foot from wearing wet shoes too long. Her skin had adapted to the rough wood of the worktable and the needle's attempts to nibble at her fingertips. During the first weeks on the job, her wrist and fingers had stung from a white crisscrossing of tiny little scars. Now she hardly noticed if she stuck herself. She still sat next to Liz under the ceiling beams in the corner. It was hot there, but she appreciated the older woman's quiet companionship. And it was Liz she talked to during the breaks, when most of the Italian seamstresses resorted to their own language.

Everything had settled into place, yet she still read the columns of job announcements in the evening, mostly as a means of retreat. Maybe it was because Elisabet was always so eager to talk when Ellen came home, so she needed to withdraw. But she thought her life was bound to stay the same for the time being.

The following day everything changed. Ellen had actually noticed an odd mood in the room earlier in the morning. Some of the Italian girls had been whispering to each other, and now and then they would cast a glance in her direction. But nothing happened until the brief lunch break. Ellen and Liz had gone outside to the courtyard, as usual, and sat down in the shade of the entrance leading to the street. Suddenly they heard the sound of Italian shoes coming straight toward them. In front stood a dark-haired girl the others called Sophia, and behind her stood a shorter and slightly older girl named Maria. Ellen knew them only by their first names. They wanted to talk to her, so she stood up. Sophia said something in Italian, a long speech that Ellen didn't understand at all, though her tone of voice was friendly and almost apologetic. Maria stepped forward, and Ellen realized it was her job to act as translator.

"We've been thinking about your sister," she said. "The girl who, uh, was injured. Is she all right now?"

"She's better," said Ellen. "She's looking for a new job."

"But no job yet?"

Ellen shook her head.

Sophia handed her a little brown paper sack. "For her," she said. "*Prego.*"

Maria also took a step forward and said eagerly, "We have taken up a collection. We know that life is hard down in the Hollow. Many Italians live there."

Both girls curtsied, almost as if they were still in school. Ellen thanked them, not fully understanding. The two Italian seamstresses turned around and walked off, taking quick, resounding steps back to the other girls standing in the far corner of the courtyard. Liz had listened to the whole encounter with an amused smile. Holding her sandwich in one hand, she said, "What was that all about?"

The sack contained a handful of crumpled bills. Ellen counted eight dollars. She could feel heat quickly rise from the nape of her neck. The eyes of the Italian girls were fixed on her back. She turned to Liz and said, "I have to give this back. Right now." She'd already taken a step away when Liz called to her.

"Don't do that," she said quietly. "That would be stupid."

"But we're not beggars," said Ellen, and she could hear her voice quiver with indignation. "Father works. And I do too."

Liz placed her hand on Ellen's arm, which was unusual. Otherwise she never touched anyone and always managed to slip elegantly aside if there was a risk of bumping into someone while working. Now she gripped Ellen's arm with her long, strong seamstress fingers.

"Listen to me," she said in a low voice. "They always do this whenever anybody gets hurt. Usually it's just for other Italian girls, but this is an exception. They collected money for your sister, and that's something new. Accept what they've given you and take it home. The next time they collect money for someone, ask to be included. Okay? If you do something stupid right now, you'll ruin things for others in the future. Do you understand?"

Ellen swallowed hard. In her mind's eye she pictured herself striding across the courtyard and, with a determined motion, handing back the little crumpled sack to Sophia, who apparently would be insulted. But Liz was always right.

"Then I hope one of them gets hurt soon so I can give back some of the money," she said crossly, but she instantly heard for herself how stupid that sounded. Liz responded to her outburst with a snort and then went back to her sandwich, taking elegant little bites, like a raccoon.

For the rest of the day Ellen felt the paper sack burning in the pocket of her apron. Time after time she found herself thinking about the long dead Horrible Hans and how, during his last days in the Hollow, he'd gone from one tavern to another, wherever Swedes gathered to drink. Cap in hand, Horrible Hans would bow and scrape to get a coin or two, which the mill workers would toss to him. Sometimes the coins would land on the ground so he had to bend down to pick them up. He always took whatever he could get, but as he left, he would raise his fist at those who had humiliated him. The men merely laughed, and the next time he came by, the same scenario would play out again, down to the smallest detail. Ellen had never seen this herself, but Leonard had talked about what he'd witnessed. In his telling, it became a joke: "Have you heard about how that man acts?"

But she always remembered what her mother had recounted a few years earlier about Lieutenant Gustafsson, the Salvation Army lady in New York. Ellen had to promise not to tell her father that she knew anything about it. Her mother had saved the embroidered handkerchief, hiding it among the towels and sheets, and she took it out to show her daughter, as if it were a precious treasure. Without putting it into words, Ellen knew why her father must never hear about it, and why the handkerchief had been hidden away, at the very bottom of their biggest suitcase.

That night she took the sack home, as she'd promised Liz she would do. She didn't give it to Elisabet, but instead handed it to her mother, who accepted the money and the explanation with an impassive expression. But Ellen caught a glimpse of Anna's face as she turned away with the bills in her hand, and she thought she saw a look of pure relief. Then she thought to herself that by this time she had much more than eight dollars hidden in a tin box and buried in the sandy ground underneath the porch.

The next morning she went over to Sophia to thank her for helping her sister. She spoke in a loud, clear voice so that the others would hear. Then they shook hands. After that everything was back to normal. The Italians still kept to one corner during the lunch break, while Ellen and Liz sat in the other. But for the rest of the day Ellen felt as if she were under a glass dome in which the air was slowly seeping out.

That evening she did the cleaning as fast as she could. Liz had gone home, and Ellen was the only person on both floors of the factory. She went over to the cashier's glass cage, holding the lantern in her hand, and lifted off the typewriter cover, which she set on the floor. Without glancing around, she took a new and untouched piece of paper from the stack next to the typewriter. Then she took an already typed document from the steel basket marked “out.” It was a note of credit to one of the larger shops selling work clothes on Seventh Street. Ellen began copying the document, typing slowly and carefully, line after line, paragraph after paragraph. It took a while before she figured out how the indentation tabs worked.

AT THE FRONT of the Baptist church there was a painting of Jesus as the good shepherd, which showed him lifting a lamb out of the briar bushes and holding a staff under one arm. Above him arched a sky of the clearest blue, extending all the way up to the curved ceiling. High overhead were painted golden stars, but they didn’t look real; they were more like specks of dirt against the blue. Anna didn’t usually pay much attention to what was said from the pulpit, but her gaze always got lost in the blue, which was the same color as a summer sky. If she concentrated and looked straight ahead, she could almost shut out everything on either side—the big, broad-leaved plants on the pedestals, the wooden columns painted to look like marble, the paintings, and even the pastor himself as he sat on his chair on the dais while the choir sang. She looked straight ahead and everything was the same, pale, sky-blue, with nothing in the way. At that moment she wouldn’t be thinking of anything else; she merely listened to the song surging around her, though she did not sing. Occasionally she would silently mouth the words. Then someone would poke her in the side because it was time to pass around the collection box. Usually she had nothing to give and would simply send it on to the wife of carpenter Nilsson. On the other side of her sat the two grown daughters, and there was no mistaking that they were sisters. When they sat still like that, side by side, it was hard to see which girl was healthy and which girl was not. They stared straight ahead, their expressions blank. Both had the same high forehead and clear brown eyes. The sister who was ill was named Kristina. Anna hadn’t known her name until she started going to church with the Nilssons, because normally no one in that family felt compelled to speak unless spoken to directly. Anna realized they’d become accustomed to keeping to themselves—as if for a long time so much of their life had involved turning their backs to the surrounding world, which didn’t understand. Everything centered on Kristina, who was the very hub of the family. Sometimes she’d talk to herself, keeping her head bowed as she muttered sounds that were probably actual words, though they were not comprehensible. If anyone spoke to her, she would smile in a friendly way and then shake her head, as if to signal she didn’t speak the same language. But in the church she was always silent.

Whenever Anna's anxiety became too great, she would go to church with the family. On their way home, she would walk along as quietly as Mrs. Nilsson, maybe exchanging a few words about something they happened to see, though rarely was it anything important. Occasionally Anna thought she should stop attending church with the Nilssons. They didn't really need her company, and aside from the pastor she didn't know the name of anyone else in the congregation. But then a week or two would go by, and she'd begin to feel as if the very air was hard to breathe. She knew that something inside her would ease during that silent promenade up to the church at the corner of Payne Avenue and Sims Street, where she would listen to the music and stare intently at the summery blue. There she would feel at peace and for a time imagine herself outside of everything else.

Mrs. Nilsson and the girls never stayed afterward to have coffee in the church when it was served once a month. Instead, they would go straight home, and Anna was grateful for that. As they walked together back to the Hollow, she felt serene and would start thinking about her daily chores as she exchanged a few words with Mrs. Nilsson about the weather. They never spoke of God.

But one Sunday in early October something happened. Anna's thoughts wandered as she sat in the church. She kept trying to look straight ahead and focus her attention on the sky-blue backdrop of the painting that rose up to the vaulted ceiling. But after a while the wall was no longer blue. It was white. A completely opaque white. She blinked and rubbed her eyes. When she looked again, she saw the blue color, as well as the briar bushes, the injured lamb, and the Savior's thin hands. The pastor was sitting on his chair holding his Bible, and there were tiny beads of sweat on his brow. Even though the air had been frosty that morning, it was now quite warm in the big church where every single pew was occupied. Anna looked down at her hands resting on her lap, lightly clasped but not in prayer. Then she looked up at the painting and tried to relax.

Yet after a while the blue faded again and the white returned, enfolding everything. Her face was carried upward, into the white, as if toward a wall she had to go through, though that was impossible; the wall was hard and smooth, with no openings. In the distance she heard the pastor speaking, but she couldn't make out any of his words. She noticed all of a sudden that she'd completely forgotten to breathe, and she drew in a lungful of air with what must have sounded like a slight shriek. Mrs. Nilsson gave her a nervous look and then went back to staring straight ahead.

During the rest of the church service, Anna sat looking down at her hands, which were trembling, but she couldn't do anything to keep them still. She didn't dare look up. The whole time, at the edge of her vision, she sensed the whiteness was ready to flood her whole world if she so much as glanced at it.

When the service was over, everyone stood up, chatting to each other as they headed for the door. Anna stayed where she was. She noticed Mrs. Nilsson and the girls sweep past, Kristina with that faintly unclean odor about her that never seemed to go away. All three then paused in the aisle, looking uncertain. Mrs. Nilsson came over to Anna and touched her shoulder. "I'll have a word with the pastor," she said and went over to the dais. To Anna, sitting with her head bowed, Mrs. Nilsson's gray dress seemed like a blurry patch on the other side of the pew's dark wood. She didn't dare look up. The whiteness was there, hovering in her field of vision and ready to envelop her so she would no longer have a way out.

The man who sat down next to Anna was not Pastor Petersson, who had preached the sermon, but one of the assistant ministers. He was a very young man, with blond hair. He wore steel-rimmed spectacles, and he had on a dark suit. He introduced himself as Pastor Anderson, pronouncing his name the American way. For a while he didn't say another word. The church emptied out, but Anna was aware of the Nilssons over by the doors leading to the vestibule. Then the pastor asked her politely if she would like him to pray with her. She shook her head. Again the pastor fell silent. After a while he sighed and began fingering his leather-bound Bible. Then he spoke.

"We've had the pleasure of seeing you here with us from time to time, Mrs. Klar. If there is something weighing on you, I want you to know that we often speak with members of our congregation and other visitors about matters they may find difficult in life. The Lord can help."

Anna didn't look at him, thinking this was what he said every day to all sorts of different people. But something was rising into her throat, words over which she had no control. At first she thought she was going to say something about Carl. Since his death she hadn't talked about him to anyone other than Inga and Gustaf. Not even the girls. But those were not the words that now spilled from her lips.

"I'm frightened," she said. "I'm frightened for my younger daughter. I'm frightened all the time."

She heard that she was whispering, and the young man had to lean closer to hear what she said.

"You're frightened, Mrs. Klar? Has something happened? Is there illness in your family?"

She shook her head. Images of Carl passed through her mind, unsummoned, when she closed her eyes. That happened often. She didn't intend to say anything more; she had already said too much. Yet the words kept coming, as if being pulled by a fishing line and hauled into the close, stifling air inside the church.

"I'm so frightened," she said again. "I'm frightened about how things will go. It's hard enough as it is." Then she added, "I'm frightened of what Gustaf will say." And without saying the words aloud, she thought, *And what he will do.*

"Gustaf is your husband?" the pastor quietly asked. Anna nodded. She took a few breaths and thought, *I don't know him. I don't know who this young man is, except that his name is Anderson and he has a lovely Bible and he was probably born in the States.* Then she said quickly, all in one breath, "I think she's pregnant, she hasn't said anything yet, but I can tell, and soon other people will see it too."

Pastor Anderson sat in silence for a moment. Then he tilted his head to one side, and she was afraid he might smile, but he didn't.

"I assume that your daughter isn't yet married," he said calmly.

Anna shook her head.

"Is there any fiancé in the picture?" he asked, now looking up at the deserted dais.

She nodded and said, "He has a job working on the railroad."

The pastor sighed.

"You and your family live in the Hollow, isn't that right, Mrs. Klar? You're neighbors with the Nilssons?"

She nodded.

"How would you feel if I asked Deaconess Stromberg to come and have a talk with your daughter one day this week? When your husband is at work." And he added in a kindly tone of voice, "I want you to know this isn't the first time this has happened, Mrs. Klar."

Anna was afraid he might touch her, put his hand on her shoulder or take her hand, so she moved away a bit. She was thinking that she needed to get out of this big, suffocating room, out to the street where the Nilssons were undoubtedly waiting for her, though they wouldn't wait forever. She didn't want to think about how it would be to walk home alone through the unfamiliar streets where she didn't recognize a single face and all the words meant something else, even though she could probably find her way to the tunnel. The pastor sat there, young and silent, waiting for her to answer. She had to put an end to this.

"Yes," she said at last. "That would be good. That's very kind of you. Elisabet works at the Johnson laundry from Wednesday to Saturday, but otherwise she's home with me."

"And the Nilssons know where you live?" said Anderson. She nodded.

"Then I'll speak to the deaconess," said Anderson, getting to his feet. Anna also stood up and followed him into the center aisle. She still didn't dare look at him as she gave a brief curtsy. He merely smiled, nodded, and left.

The padded church doors closed behind her with a sigh. All three Nilsson women were waiting for her on the front steps. Mrs. Nilsson and Lisbet looked at Anna as she came out of the church, while Kristina stood off to one side, with her eyes fixed on the street. Her lips were moving silently.

"Was it good to speak to the pastor?" asked Mrs. Nilsson as they walked along Payne Avenue with her daughters following a few steps behind. Anna nodded and forced herself to say, "Yes, I suppose so." Then neither of them spoke again as they walked toward Beaumont Street and the tunnel to go home. It was a comfortable silence. The weather was cool without being chilly. But the sky was covered by a shapeless, whitish haze without beginning or end; it arched overhead, enveloping them from all directions, no matter where they went. Anna didn't dare look up but instead kept her gaze fixed on the pavement. She knew that when the pavement ended, they would soon be home.

THE OLD, ALL-TOO-FAMILIAR ANGER slid easily into place, the way a pane of glass fits into a finished window frame. Once again it separated Gustaf from the rest of the world. No matter where he turned, it was there. Everything looked the same, everything was familiar, yet there was a barrier between him and everyday life. He wanted to kill. He wanted Leonard Hammerberg to die. This was something messy and blurry that soiled everything around him—a blot, a smudge that prevented him from seeing clearly and that had to be rubbed away with a great deal of effort. Then maybe the world would return to the way it used to look. But he didn't know whether that was even possible anymore. Leonard had ruined everything. The minute Gustaf thought about the matter, his pulse would start hammering in his temples. And it didn't stop.

On his way back from work, he walked in silence beside Jonathan. Mechanically he clenched and unclenched his fists, no longer aware of the usual ache in his arms or the dull pain in his back.

During the past week it had snowed off and on, leaving a thin layer of snow on the slope down toward the Irish sector. The wind had blown snow into the corners of the brick wall below the viaduct up toward Seventh Street and formed a drift two feet high that was already coated with soot. Gustaf went over to the snowdrift and fell to his knees. He stuck his hands and arms as deep as he could into the crusty snow, feeling the icy surface tearing at his wrists as the cold seeped through his jacket and shirtsleeves. Then he screamed at the brick wall's contorted patterns of stone and soot until there was no air left in his lungs. He grabbed handfuls of snow to rub over his face, as if that might wash him clean. The snow was greasy and smelled of sulfur, but the cold woke him. Ice water dripped from his face, leaving dark streaks in the white snow he'd dug up. And all hope of anything else was sullied and dashed, broken and trickling away.

Suddenly Jonathan stood next to him, yanking him to his feet. "Gustaf Klar, goddamit!" Jonathan never swore. Gustaf stood there, motionless, pressing his face against the brick wall until he could be sure that he could hide all emotion. Then he turned around.

"I don't know what to do," he said. "Tell me what to do."

"You're not going to kill anybody," said Jonathan. "You're talking too much about that. Wasn't that how all your problems started in the past?"

Jonathan turned and disappeared into the darkness of the tunnel. He was tired of waiting. A moment later Gustaf followed. They walked in silence, listening to the echo of their own footsteps and the dripping water from the tunnel ceiling. Gustaf held out his hand to catch a few drops. Black water. When they emerged on the other side, he took a few steps away from the embankment and picked up from the ground a handful of cleaner snow to rub over his face until he had left only a tiny lump of ice, which he then pressed to the back of his neck in order to prevent the anger from drawing him into its white darkness. Ice water ran down his back.

"It's bad enough having one person to visit up in Stillwater," said Jonathan as they stepped away from the tunnel into the twilight. "Have you thought about that? What would Anna and the girls do?"

Gustaf felt another stab of pain when Lundgren mentioned the "girls," and he turned his face away, trying not to cry. Jonathan went on, speaking in a low voice that nonetheless reverberated off the stone walls.

"As I see it, Klar, whenever anything happens, you seem to think it's the first time that anyone in the whole world has ever landed in trouble. Maybe you should consider this instead: no matter what, there's going to be another mouth to feed. Either you take on the responsibility yourself, or else you crack down on Hammerberg and find out whether he's man enough or not. But if you kill him, then not just one but two people who are responsible for supporting your family will disappear. You'd realize that if you weren't behaving like such a damn fool."

Gustaf listened to Jonathan as he walked along with his head bowed, and he thought, *If there was more space in the world, then there'd be room for that sort of wisdom.* But at the moment the world felt so closed in that he could hardly breathe, and something simply had to be *eliminated.* His anger was like a living beast inside him, twisting and turning and refusing to ease up until it was released out into the world and could do what it was demanding to do. After that happened, he'd see what was left.

"I have something else to say," Jonathan went on as they walked along on either side of the railroad tracks. "Inga is also going to have a baby," he said. "You can't tell from looking at her yet, but she's due about the same time as Elisabet. Or maybe a little later."

They stopped as Jonathan continued talking.

"And soon every single one of us is going to be needed. You have your family, and we have ours, but if we're all going to stay afloat, we can't have any more disasters. And everyone has to do their part. Do you understand what I'm saying?"

Gustaf nodded, mostly just to reassure his friend. They started walking again. He knew he ought to say something, offer his congratulations, say something soothing about how it was bound to turn out all right. But he couldn't muster those sorts of words. He found only an empty space when he searched for what to say. Again he was clenching and unclenching his fists as he walked along, hunched forward, as if preparing to run. And everywhere he looked he saw a smudge of dirt at the edge of his vision; it was something he'd never be able escape if he didn't rub it away once and for all, the way he might use the sleeve of his jacket to wipe off the spot left by a smashed fly on the windowpane.

Leonard was clearly keeping his distance. No one had seen him in the Hollow for several weeks, though he apparently was still going to work. Jonathan had reluctantly made inquiries of the other brakemen at the railroad yard, and they had all seen Leonard. He'd worked his normal shifts to North Dakota and back, but whenever he came in, he'd ask for other available assignments and then leave on the next train, without taking any time off. Leonard's mother was dead, and their house at the very bottom of the Hollow now remained dark at night. Leonard was not there, even though he wouldn't be stupid enough to turn on a light if he did venture home. All indications were that he was constantly on the move, seen only during those brief times when he came into the rail yard before leaving again. If anyone wanted to get hold of him, they would keep an eye out for his train—provided they knew which train he was on—and then grab him before he hopped on the next one. "He'll probably get worn out eventually," said Gustaf. "And then I'll grab him." Jonathan merely gave him a long, disapproving look.

A lot of the workers at the rail yard knew full well why Gustaf was after Leonard, and they were unwilling to intervene. But it became almost a sport, trying to guess where Leonard had gone. One day he was onboard a freight train headed for Sioux Falls; the next day he was traveling to Ellendale. What no one dared say out loud was that one day he might not come back. Elisabet knew as little of his whereabouts as anyone else. She avoided her father as much as she could, and at home they never spoke. She would leave for her shifts at the Johnson laundry on Seventh Street and come back with her face flushed bright red. It was impossible to tell whether this was because she'd been crying or because of the damp and heat in the stifling room where she worked all day with twenty other girls. As Inga said, she probably wouldn't be able to continue until "full term." The deaconess from the First Swedish Baptist Church had come to visit several times, speaking at great length while Elisabet mostly sat in silence with her head bowed. The deaconess persistently urged her to ask Leonard to join them next time, "to see if the whole situation might be worked out." But Leonard was still nowhere to be found.

"You're the one he's scared of," Jonathan told Gustaf, who took this to mean that his friend thought he was making matters worse. But even if he'd been able to rein himself in, that wouldn't make Leonard come back. And there was no chance of talking to him when he kept traveling in wide arcs across half the Midwest.

Finally Inga asked Jonathan to speak to his work colleagues at the Great Northern, but without telling Gustaf. They would send a message to Leonard via the railroad workers who were headed in the same direction. The message would then move like an echo from train to train and station to station, even to the remote locations of wooden train platforms next to grain elevators way out on the prairie, manned only by a single laborer or station worker. Eventually somebody would get hold of Leonard. The message was simply this: they wanted to talk to him, and Elisabet was doing well. That was all.

No one knew where the message ended up reaching him, but at long last Leonard came home. He appeared one evening in early December, coming down the stairs from Seventh Street with his usual sailcloth bag slung over his shoulder. He made no attempt to hide. First he dropped off his bag at the little shack belonging to his deceased mother. Then he slowly walked up the hill, and everybody saw him coming even though it was pitch-dark outside. He might have been on his way to Inga's house, but as he passed the Klar home on the slope, Gustaf came rushing out the door in his shirtsleeves and took up position in the middle of the path. There the two men stood, eyeing each other without saying a word. Elisabet also came dashing out of the house and ran barefoot through the snow up to Inga's place, where she pounded her fist on the front door. By the time Jonathan ran down the path, Gustaf had already shoved Leonard against the wall of the house and had a hand around the man's neck, though not in a stranglehold. Leonard's arms hung limply at his sides, with his palms open. They stood there motionless, both of them breathing hard, as if it took an inordinate amount of effort just to keep still. After determining that neither of them had a knife, Jonathan put a hand on each man's chest and forced them apart. All three stood silently in the moonlight. Gustaf and Leonard were both shivering. Then Jonathan prodded them up the path to his house, where they all went inside, closing the door behind them.

For the next hour everyone far and wide could hear men's voices bellowing, and at least once something slammed against a wall, making the faint light in the window disappear for a moment, as if the candle had been knocked over and had to be relit. After that, calm was restored. Finally Gustaf Klar came out and trudged home. For safety's sake, Leonard spent the night with Inga and Jonathan.

Inga freely told anyone who would listen that it was good for Leonard to keep away until "things" calmed down. Other people in the Hollow didn't hesitate to call him cowardly, though not to his face. But later in the week Inga went with Leonard to the Swedish Lutheran Church to have a talk with Pastor Sandstrom. That was the church where Leonard was registered, and they wanted to find out how the pastor felt about marrying a couple when the bride was already in her fifth month. As Inga said, without a trace of irony, maybe he ought to consider that it was better late than never.

For his part, Sandstrom explained that naturally there were certain rules regarding such a situation. A conversation to determine penance was required, along with assurances of one sort and another. Leonard, and Elisabet as well, would have to beg forgiveness from the congregation, though he hurried to add that this could be done before him alone, as he was the pastor of the church. He did expect them do so on their knees, and he tried to stress that all of this was customary and reasonable, yet he found it hard to be stern and authoritative while Inga had her eyes fixed on him.

THE DECISION HAD BEEN GROWING so slowly that Ellen wasn't sure when it went from daydream to an actual plan, until she realized that she'd marked the date in her mind when she would take a little outing in town. Every evening she continued to read carefully all the job announcements in both the Swedish and English-language newspapers that she was able to find. But now she'd also taken note of where the various workplaces were located and how to get there.

On a Monday at the end of January, a small fire broke out at the Klinkenfuer factory. The second floor filled with gray smoke that poured up the stairwell, and they all rushed out to the courtyard, blindly coughing. There they stood for an hour, shivering in the cold, while Mangini and several other men ran up and down the stairs with fire extinguishers and buckets. The men spoke to each other in brusque, agitated voices, but they didn't seem particularly worried. "It wasn't anything serious," said Mangini. He explained that a bearing in one of the big, belt-driven sewing machines had snapped and sprayed sparks into all the textile dust and chaff that were lying around. Then he went back inside. Liz stood apart from the others, holding her white cardboard box under one arm. The first thing she'd grabbed was the sewing she did after work hours, and now she stood there in silence. Without saying a word, she made it clear that she didn't want to talk to anybody, presumably to keep her little secret to herself. Ellen thought she was being standoffish for no reason, since it wasn't as if she didn't know. But Liz was and always would be careful about keeping to herself.

Finally Mangini returned. He smelled of smoke, and his shirtsleeves were covered with soot. At first he spoke for a long time in Italian, and Ellen saw how the other girls began protesting at what he was saying, but one by one they gave in. Slowly they moved away, heading for the street. Then he came over to Liz and Ellen.

"Tomorrow we'll be closed," he said in English. "Maybe Wednesday too, but be here in the morning. We'll have to wait and see. The old belt-driven machine burned up, and we'll also have to replace part of the floor."

Liz nodded and got ready to leave. Ellen lingered for a moment.

"So there's no work tomorrow?" she said to the foreman. "And maybe not on Wednesday either? What about later in the week?"

"How would I know?" he said, throwing out his arms. His black hair was standing on end. "At least things didn't get any worse. I heard that last year in a sewing factory in New York folks died from smoke inhalation." This he said in a curt tone of voice, signaling that the conversation was over. Then he went back through the soot-darkened entrance and up the stairs.

In her apron pocket Ellen had two of the little glass balls and a few coins. Without taking out the money she counted a dollar and twenty-five cents. Then she headed for Margaret Street. Instead of turning off toward the Hollow, she walked along Seventh Street in the opposite direction, toward the streetcar stop.

The Shelby law offices were in a seven-story building on Fourth Street in downtown Minneapolis. Since Ellen wasn't sure about where the streetcar lines went, she'd ended up transferring twice before she found the address. At first she thought the whole building was all one office, but when she got closer to the big entryway she saw the row of brass plates that stated that the Shelby law offices were on floors four, five, and six. There was also a sign for the NORTH AMERICAN TELEGRAPH COMPANY and for the H. W. WHITE INVESTMENT CO. Above the door it said in gold letters a foot and a half tall, PHOENIX BUILDING. She walked past, reading the signs without stopping. None of them was in Swedish. Then she paused on the other side of the street without knowing what to do next. She walked past again, this time venturing up to the big doors. She opened them and went inside.

The lobby was lit with electric bulbs inside lamps that looked like flowers. Farther in she saw a stairwell and tall doors with glass panes. Just inside the front door an elderly man wearing a uniform sat in a wooden cage. He looked up from his newspaper when she came in, eyeing her up and down before he said, "May I help you, Miss?"

"I came here to hear about a cleaning job," she managed to say. "At the Shelby law offices."

"I haven't heard anything about that," the man said. "In any case, it's too late in the day. If you want to get ahead, you need to show up early. So, off you go."

He sat there giving her a stern look as she backed her way out the door.

She took up position farther down Fourth Street, not yet willing to give up. The wind was blowing from the north, and the street slowly filled with people hurrying along with their heads down, many carrying paper parcels as they went home from work. The tall double doors of the Phoenix Building opened and a group of young women came out. They were chatting and laughing and holding on to their hats in the wintry gusts before they went their separate ways. Three of them paused to exchange a few words in the shelter of the doorway before setting off into the wind. Ellen couldn't hear what they said as they stood with their heads close together, but the hatred that surged without warning inside her, heated and fierce, sharpened her awareness of every detail of their clothing. Short jackets with white blouses underneath. Dark skirts that reached to their ankles, proper winter coats, and modern high-button shoes made for winter weather. Two of them wore identical round hats that were clearly held in place with hat pins or the wind would have taken them at once. Their too-red lips moved soundlessly as they filled the air with superfluous words that were dispersed long before they reached Ellen. No one paid her any attention as she stood there, motionless, in the doorway and out of reach of the snowy gusts, rubbing together the glass balls in her pocket. She felt rather than heard how the clinking of glass traveled up her hand and arm. And yet it soon drowned out all the sounds from the street.

When she got off the streetcar at the intersection of Seventh Street and Maria Avenue, she thought at first she'd go home on this winter evening. But she remained standing all alone on the platform long after the streetcar disappeared down the hill in one last shower of blue sparks. In her mind there wasn't a sound to be heard. Then she started off in the opposite direction, the way Liz usually went at the end of the workday.

She knew that Liz rented a room not far from the factory, and she knew it was somewhere on Maria Avenue, but she didn't have the address. The neighborhood consisted of two-story wooden buildings. In some of the windows electric lights were on behind the curtains, but others were dark. The street was nearly deserted. The wind had subsided, and calm had returned, but by now most people were probably sitting down to supper.

Ellen had come around a corner near Maple Street and was on her way toward Seventh Street to head for home when off in the distance she caught sight of a familiar figure coming out the front door of a building and down the steps. It was Mangini. He headed along the street without looking back, rounded a corner, and was gone. She was certain it was him, even though she knew he lived farther up toward Minnehaha. She walked around the block again, wanting to make sure that he wasn't coming back. Then she quickly walked up the steps and knocked as hard as she dared on the frosted pane of the front door.

The door opened a crack and an older woman with gray hair pinned up stared at her without saying a word.

"I'm looking for Liz," said Ellen briskly. "Is she home?"

The woman shook her head.

"I've told her she can't be receiving her customers here at all hours," said the woman in a thin, rasping voice that made Ellen think of a crow. "There's too much running in and out as it is."

"This'll only take a minute. I'll be quick about it," she said.

The landlady opened the door enough for Ellen to slip inside the stairwell. The foyer was paneled in dark wood, and a thick, oxblood red carpet covered the floor. The only light came from a sconce at the very end of the hall; otherwise it was very dark. Ellen couldn't see the woman's face.

"Her last customer just left," said the landlady. "I've told her it's too late for visitors. It doesn't look good."

"Is Liz here?" Ellen asked.

"She went out to get something. You can't stay here, Miss. You'll have to wait in her room. But there has to be an end to all this coming and going."

She turned and nodded toward the closest wooden door on the other side of the threshold. Ellen went in, hearing the door close behind her.

The atmosphere in the small room told her she'd found the right place. It had the same air of acerbic cleanliness that she associated with Liz, yet it was also stuffy and closed in. A faint white light from a lamppost on the other side of the street slanted in through the only window.

She stood stock still in the middle of the room as her eyes got used to the dim light. She gave a start when her gaze fell on what she at first thought was a human shape in the corner, as if someone was crouched down, observing her. But when she looked closer, it turned out to be a mannequin without legs sitting on the floor. Overhead came the sound of someone walking across creaking floorboards.

Then Ellen caught sight of the white cardboard box. It was on a big round table next to the window, in the midst of measuring tapes and spools of thread. She went over, cautiously lifted the lid, and stuck her hand inside to stroke the dark cloth of the short, folded jacket.

"Leave that alone," said Liz from the door. She spoke quietly, but in a sharp and commanding tone of voice. Embarrassed, Ellen took a step back from the table and clasped her hands in front of her.

They stared at each other through the dim light without speaking. Then Liz, still wearing her coat, struck a match and lit the oil lamp next to the unmade bed. Her shadow climbed the wall and then shrank as she turned up the wick.

"You'll have to tell me what you're doing here, Ellen," said Liz in that same curt, rapid-fire tone. "I don't like people sneaking around me."

"I came here to talk to you," replied Ellen, ashamed to hear how her voice quavered. "About that." She pointed at the box on the table.

They sat down. Ellen took a seat on the room's only chair, while Liz perched on the edge of the bed. At work they had their prescribed way of talking and they knew what few words were needed. Right now they were in uncharted territory.

"I've always thought you're so talented, Liz. It must be nice to be able to do such fine stitching that it looks machine-made. And to be able to cut out the patterns yourself."

She saw the older woman smile, though with no sign of joy. It was merely a slight tug at the corners of her mouth.

"Yes, it helps a bit," said Liz. "But it's not going to make me rich." She was breathing shallowly as she sat there, weighing each word she said, apparently uncertain how to go on. All of a sudden—and in an entirely different tone of voice from what Ellen would have ever associated with Liz at the Klinkenfuer factory—she began talking about her sister who was in a tuberculosis sanatorium in St. Peter, way out on the prairie. And how the two sisters were the only ones left in the family, and it was expensive.

"She's living with people who aren't quite right in the head," Liz said. "But there's nothing wrong with her. Except for her lungs."

Ellen didn't know why Liz had chosen to tell her all this. But she heard herself talking about Carl, about his cough and how he'd withered away in a matter of weeks. This was the first time she'd talked to anybody about his death. And yet he'd died three years ago.

They sat there for a while, wrapped in the yellow glow of the lamp, without speaking.

"Is there something you want from me?" asked Liz at last, her voice now completely steady.

Ellen took out the page she'd ripped from the English-language newspaper, placed it on the table, and smoothed it out. Liz picked up the page and held it to the light. In the glow of the lamp she looked much older, with lines etched around her mouth and at the corners of her eyes. Her lips moved silently as she read the announcement Ellen had pointed out: *Unmarried women 18–20 years old. Typist wanted. Proficiency in English and Swedish. Apply in person to the Shelby law offices.*

"How clever of them," said Liz. "They want folks who speak Swedish, but they put the job announcement in the American paper so they know that anyone who applies will speak both languages properly."

Liz handed the page back to Ellen.

"I know what you've been up to at the factory in the evenings," she said. Before Ellen could say anything, Liz waved her hand dismissively, as if to say, *You don't have to say anything.*

"You've been keeping an eye on me, and I've done the same with you. And sometimes those black smudges on your hands have made me a little worried about the cloth."

"Mangini?" said Ellen.

"He doesn't know. I would have heard if he did. And old Al doesn't see too good anymore, so he doesn't notice everything going on around him. But the question is whether your typing is good enough."

"I've gotten real fast on the typewriter," Ellen said. "It's like a competition I've been having with myself. And I hardly make any mistakes anymore."

Liz gave her a long look.

"I know you learn fast when you want to," she said. "But there are other things you need to be able to handle. You have to have good posture and hold your fingers correctly when you're typing. You can't answer back. You have to sit on your chair, obedient as a dog, all day long, with your back perfectly straight. I've heard the typist girls complain, and I happen to know what sort of temperament you have. Could you do all that? And manage to stay calm?"

"That's not the problem," Ellen said. "You can't know whether you're any good at something until you try. It was the same with starting at Klinkenfuer's. But at least you have to try."

She turned to look behind her and pointed at the box on the table.

Liz nodded.

"I've gone over there and seen those girls," said Ellen. "They pay a lot of attention to how they look." She paused for a moment and then added all in one breath, "I have a little money put aside. Not much. But I can pay you if you'll let me borrow that suit. Just for a day. While I make a try. You'll get it back the very same evening."

"And what am I supposed to tell the girl who asked me to sew those clothes?"

Ellen couldn't see Liz's expression but she could tell by her tone of voice that she found the idea amusing.

"Maybe you could tell her you need a little more time. Or that the fire at the factory has delayed things."

"So, just for tomorrow?"

Ellen nodded without replying, her eyes lowered. Liz got up and stepped behind her. Without raising her head, Ellen watched the white cardboard box land on her lap. Cautiously she wrapped her hands around the edges. Her heart was beating very fast.

"I think you may need better shoes on your feet too," said Liz, as she poked her head inside a cupboard. "In this kind of weather."

When Ellen looked up, Liz was holding a pair of sturdy women's shoes in her hand. She handed them over with a wide smile on her thin lips. Ellen felt the flush of embarrassment on her face, and she hoped it wasn't visible in the lamp light. When she'd stood alone in this room, her first impulse had been to grab the box and leave before Liz came back from her errands.

She'd discovered that she needed to change streetcars only once, at the post office, so she sat drowsily near the streetcar's heater for the second, longer part of the trip. Then she awoke with a start and stumbled off at the corner of Fourth and Marquette. It was almost seven o'clock and lights were already on in the windows of the Phoenix Building that belonged to the Shelby law offices.

She was about to step through the door when she remembered the stern watchman in the foyer. She paused and looked down at the coat she was wearing over the clothes she'd borrowed from Liz. It was the same threadbare, washed-out brown coat she'd had on yesterday. Hesitantly she stepped into the alleyway next to the building. In the dark she could only make out a pile of boards that had been left over from some construction job. She took off her coat and folded it into a parcel. Then she lifted up the top pieces of wood and wedged her coat underneath where it felt dryer. Shivering, with only the short jacket offering any protection against the cold, she went back to Fourth Street, stepping into the January wind. The high-button shoes Liz had given her were too big. She had on two pairs of socks, but she was still a bit unsteady on her feet and afraid it would show.

The watchman hardly gave her a glance when she came in. She started to say something about Shelby's, but he merely grunted and motioned her toward the stairwell without a word. After climbing a few steps she started to get some warmth back in her fingers, which was the important thing. But her stomach was still icy with apprehension.

She almost turned around to leave the minute she entered what looked like an outer waiting room. At least fifteen girls were sitting there in a row against the wall. Most of them were older than she was. The room felt hot and the air had a faintly unpleasant smell. What made her decide to go inside and take one of the last remaining chairs was the silence. No one looked at anyone else. *So I guess I'm as invisible as all the others,* thought Ellen.

She noticed that several of the girls had brought along a newspaper they were leafing through, and she regretted not having anything to read. But then she looked at the girl sitting across from her, who was probably in her early twenties, and she saw that her hand was shaking and she seemed to be reading the same page over and over. Others kept their eyes fixed on their laps or stared vacantly straight ahead, as if the room were empty. After a while Ellen began studying the clothes the others were wearing, noting that some of them wore skirts and blouses that fit much better. Others had on jackets that were worn shiny at the elbows and had frayed sleeves. The girl across from her with the trembling hands had ink stains on her fingers that she hadn't managed to scrub clean. Ellen told herself that she didn't stick out—she was neither the finest nor the worst dressed of the lot.

The waiting room got hotter, and she was worried about soiling Liz's outfit. The clothes didn't really belong to Liz either. They belonged to some nameless girl in an office somewhere downtown. She felt a solitary drop of sweat run down her back, and she leaned forward so it wouldn't soak into her blouse. She whispered in Swedish to the girl sitting next to her, wanting to know how long they would have to wait. The girl, blond and slender with her hair pulled back in a knot so tightly that it seemed to stretch the skin as thin as paper over her shiny forehead, merely looked at Ellen with big, frightened, pale eyes and hissed, "Shhh!" And once again they all sat in silence.

Suddenly a door opened to the inner office. A man wearing a dark suit appeared in the doorway and scanned the waiting room. He didn't speak, merely pointed at the two girls sitting closest. They got up and followed him inside. Then the door closed. Ellen sat on her chair, her back straight, and tried through sheer force of will to stop herself from sweating. Gradually she lost all sense of time.

At regular intervals the door would open and the girls would be ushered in, two by two. In the distance Ellen could hear the clatter of typewriters, but it was impossible to know whether she was hearing the other girls taking typing tests or whether that was the usual sound in an office like Shelby's. The thin, nervous girl sitting next to her was motioned inside. She got up and, hunching forward, silently moved toward the door. She looked like an animal that swiftly vanishes in the grass beyond the light from a doorway that suddenly opens at night. The girl's fear made Ellen feel calm.

Finally she was the only girl left. The door opened one last time, and the man in the suit appeared, tall and dark, with a mustache, round spectacles, and a center part in his hair. He motioned to Ellen to follow him. She stood up and went into the next room, which was long and narrow. At the far end was a single window that showed a uniformly gray winter sky and the nearby rooftops with gray smoke rising straight up like cats' tails from the chimneys. She realized it must have gotten even colder outside, but she had no idea what time it was. She was clearly the last girl to be interviewed today.

Sitting on a swivel chair was a younger man with unruly brown hair. He wore a light-colored suit. He got up and came over to them. Ellen noticed that his complexion looked unhealthy, with deep pits that were visible when he turned toward the light from the window.

"Your name, Miss?" he said in English. She introduced herself as Ellen Klar from St. Paul and then curtsied.

The tall, dark man said behind her in Swedish, "And how long have you been working as a typist, Miss Klar?"

She turned around and replied in Swedish, "A year and a half. My father has a shoemaker shop, and I take care of the paperwork."

"Does he have any employees?" asked the younger man, continuing in English.

"Three," she said in the same language. "But they come and go."

She realized they were testing her ability to jump from one language to the other, but she wasn't nervous yet.

The young man with the pitted face came closer. He smelled strongly of aftershave. He pointed at the other, Swedish-speaking man who was still standing at the door with an impassive expression.

"This is Mr. Lundquist," he said. "Lundquist takes care of our Swedish-speaking clients, and he needs more girls to handle his correspondence. Why don't you have a seat here, Miss Klar, and show us what you can do."

He pointed at a low desk with a typewriter that was bigger than any she'd ever seen before. It was a wide machine with big keys that made her think of some sort of musical instrument. The younger man set a sheet of paper next to her and said curtly, "Copy that."

It was an invoice addressed to the Anderson furniture company in Minneapolis. She did as requested.

“So,” said Lundquist when she was finished. “Type it again, but this time in Swedish.”

It was now that she got scared. Some of the words in the invoice seemed impenetrable to her, words she had seldom or never encountered in the newspapers. She typed as fast as she could, hoping she’d guessed at the correct Swedish words, without looking up from the page. Now she was truly sweating, but she no longer cared.

After a moment she thought it was all over and they’d show her the door. She didn’t remember any of the other girls spending this long in the room. But they kept giving her more papers to copy and translate. A short business letter about the transfer of a vacant lot, and an order on company letterhead from a printing press in St. Paul. She was starting to feel a little dizzy.

Then the paper flow stopped. She sat on the chair without turning around, but she could tell that both men had gone over to the window and were conferring in voices so low that she grasped only a few words. She swallowed and swallowed, longing for a glass of water. Soon they’d tell her to leave. That was what she wished for most at the moment, to get out of this stifling, narrow room, out into the wintry air. In her mind she went over what she would say to Liz when she dropped off the sweat-soaked garments. Maybe she could get Elisabet to take them over to the laundry, though she didn’t know whether she dared entrust her sister with such an important task. Then the men came back and stood behind her.

“I see that Miss Klar is self-taught,” said the younger man in English.

She stood up, since it felt impolite to sit there with her back turned, but she wasn’t sure that was the right thing to do. She stood ramrod straight next to the chair, not looking at him.

“Yes,” she said. “That’s true. But I’ve had many chances to study others typing.”

“No coursework? No certificate to show us?”

She shook her head.

Now Lundquist stepped forward. This time he too spoke in English.

“You’re quite young, Miss. Some of your word choices were a bit . . . original,” he said with a brief laugh, as if he were genuinely amused by what he’d said. “But I’ve never seen anyone type so fast. And correctly. Both in Swedish and in English.”

She didn’t know what to say. She curtsied, still without looking up, and Lundquist went on. “English is the language we use here in the office, of course. But I need at least two girls who can take care of our growing

Swedish clientele. Not many people can make themselves understood in any language but their own. Were you born here, Miss Klar?"

She shook her head. "No, Mr. Lundquist. But I was very young when we came here."

"Well, there's certainly nothing wrong with your English," he said. She sensed rather than saw the two men exchange looks. Then the man with the pitted face said, "What do you think, Miss? Can your father do without your help starting on Monday next week?"

She looked up and saw that his eyes were green. There was something about one of the pupils; it was irregular and made it hard to meet his eye. But he was smiling.

"I'm sure that will be fine, Mr. Shelby," Ellen said as calmly as she could.

She was back in the alleyway, standing next to the pile of boards with one hand pressed against the brick wall, noticing suddenly that she needed to pee so badly it hurt. She didn't know what to do. So she squatted down behind the boards and hitched up her skirt. After that it took a while to find where she'd hidden her coat. It had frozen into a solid lump during the hours she'd been inside the Phoenix Building, and she realized she wouldn't be able to put it on the whole way home. The temperature was still falling, and it would soon be evening. For a moment she thought she might throw up, but then she realized the ache in her stomach was because she hadn't eaten anything all day.

As she waited for the streetcar, the streetlights came on, block by block. It was so cold she was shaking, but she watched with delight as the light gradually spread along Fourth Street. She wondered whether someone was sitting in a room somewhere, pressing big light buttons and slowly illuminating the city each evening. The streetcar stopped almost without a sound in front of her as she stood there, looking the other way. Shivering, she climbed onboard with her token in one hand and her frozen coat in the other. As the streetlights floated past on the other side of the frost-covered windows, she sank into the rhythm of the wheels rolling along the tracks and of all the languages that were being spoken, gently and quietly, around her. She tried as best she could to stay awake.

JONATHAN LUNDGREN SAID that the worst of it was not, in fact, that everything had become more dangerous. It was that greater risks had to be taken for no good reason. That was the hardest thing to accept. He could understand that the younger men were the first to be let go when times were bad, since they had no family to support. But there were too few workers left, and eventually something was bound to happen. In the long run they couldn't carry on with so few men. He thought they really needed at least a third more in order to keep the trains and tracks in good condition. Yet nearly a third of the men living in the Hollow had no work or were only able to pick up odd jobs here and there. He said it couldn't go on like that. They needed to have more men working, and there were far too many without jobs. It just couldn't last.

Lundgren, who had formerly been so taciturn, had begun unburdening his heart about one thing or another. Gustaf Klar thought this was probably because Jonathan now lived with Inga, who had an opinion about almost everything. No doubt she was filling her husband's head with all manner of ideas, which he then brought with him to work. But it was actually wrong to blame Inga. Jonathan had become a little more talkative after he had told Gustaf about his brother, David.

"I suppose it's because there's no money," ventured Gustaf. "Prices are high everywhere."

Lundgren merely snorted at this attempt to explain the world. "They're stuffing their money into stocks in New York," he said. "That's where it's all going. If we kept the money here in the Twin Cities, there'd be enough to build the railroad all the way to the West Coast and back, like that man Hill wants to do. But right now every dollar is disappearing in other directions—places where the money does nobody any good."

Then he said no more about the subject.

There was work for those who had a family to support, including the newly married Leonard Hammerberg, though he gave his father-in-law as wide a berth as possible while on the job. But they'd all been forced to accept lower wages, so that for every dollar they used to get, they now received only seventy-five cents. Next month their wages might sink to sixty-five. No one knew for sure. Yet there was more and more work to do.

The men would head off as usual in the wintry dawn, but when they reached the rail yards, they were now met with a desolation that sapped from their bodies all desire to work even before they picked up their tools. The area in front of the loading dock used to be a bustling commotion in the mornings, with crowds of men of all sorts—Finns, Swedes, Italians, and Irishmen—looking for odd jobs. But now it was deserted. There was no work for day laborers. At the end of the week Gustaf would come home with barely even five dollars. He would jam the coins in his pocket, and the whole way home he'd think angrily that he'd worked an entire day for free for the Great Northern. But, as another voice in his head told him, it was either that or no work at all.

If not for Ellen's fancy new job in Minneapolis, the Klar family would have had a hard time making ends meet. She had to get up at the crack of dawn, almost an hour earlier than Gustaf. She would wash with green soap and then a special lavender soap that no one else was allowed to touch, scrubbing herself so vigorously that she woke everyone else. Then she'd take her fine clothes from the hanger up in the loft, quickly get dressed, and disappear into the dark night to make her way to the streetcar stop. She didn't get back home until a good hour after her father. By then she was so tired that it was hard to get a word out of her about her day before she climbed into bed and instantly fell asleep. No one was allowed to touch her clothes, not even Elisabet when she came over to sleep at home on those nights when Leonard was away for a few days for work. On the other hand, Elisabet was so big now that she couldn't climb the ladder Gustaf had made for the girls when they were old enough to sleep up in the loft. Now she had to sleep in her old bed next to the stove.

Life went on. On some nights when Gustaf awoke feeling anxious, and if both girls were home, he'd imagine that things were back the way they used to be. But whenever such thoughts arose, his mind would drift perilously close to the images of Carl that would keep popping up if he wasn't careful. Then he would go mute inside until he could make himself think about something else and try to fall asleep again. The family was getting by. It was a matter of taking one week at a time.

In the morning Gustaf would set off like a sleepwalker with Jonathan Lundgren at his side. He heard his friend saying they were approaching some sort of limit as far as what was needed just to survive, and that the situation could get dangerous if things went on like this. Gustaf would merely grunt a few phrases like, "Yes, that's probably true," but he wasn't really listening.

Until, that is, one day in early March. The first hints of spring were appearing and the icicles, as tall as a man, outside the windows of the train repair shop began dripping in the midday thaw. Jonathan Lundgren came in, stomped the snow off his boots, and shouted so loud his words echoed in the huge, vault-like room, "Everyone outside, right now!" Gustaf realized the foreman must have sent him. He put down his tools and followed everyone else out to the slush and mud in the yard. About fifty men wearing gray jackets and caps stood there, and Gustaf again noted how few workers were left. He looked for Lundgren's broad back and then went over to stand beside him as Foreman Lawson called for everyone's attention from the loading dock. Gustaf heard him say,

"Off the tracks," and he knew what that meant. He went back to the shop to get sledgehammers and crowbars, and Lundgren followed him. This had happened before. One or more train cars would drive through a frozen switch and jump off the track. Then all the men and horses were needed to push the cars back in place. But Lundgren stared at Gustaf from under the visor of his cap and said, "Take the crowbar. It'll probably be needed. This time I think it's something much worse."

It turned out to be no ordinary accident. As many men as could crowd onboard climbed into an open boxcar, which they hitched to the old steam locomotive called the Mule. Usually it never left the rail yard. Those who hadn't found room trotted behind. The engine chugged very slowly along the southbound track, down to the track closest to the river. They didn't have to go far. At the curve near the still frozen Pig's Eye Lake they found one of the bigger locomotives turned on its side with the front end over the embankment so that its forward wheels were hanging in the air. The tender and a boxcar were also lying on their side. Gustaf heard the other men around him swearing quietly. The scene scared them all. The engine must have entered the curve at too high a speed, and the switch had frozen solid in the open air. These kinds of disasters occurred only when at least two things went wrong. There must have been a horrendous bang, though they hadn't heard anything.

Several men were already standing around the wrecked engine, but they seemed bewildered, their shovels and picks hanging from their hands. Then Gustaf caught sight of a covered ambulance wagon on the far side of the engine. A hospital medic was sitting on the driver's seat with his head in his hands, apparently incapable of doing anything at all. The closer they got, the clearer it became that Jonathan Lundgren had been right. Something terrible had happened.

The boxcar stopped with an abrupt screech a short distance behind the overturned freight car. When Gustaf and the other men jumped to the ground, he saw that the boards of the wall lying on the track had shattered into splinters. Pieces of red-painted boards with fresh wood showing at the broken edges lay scattered across the snow-covered embankment in a peculiar zigzag pattern. He realized the car must have been dragged on its side for quite a ways. Off in the distance he heard shouts, but the Mule stood hissing loudly between them and the wrecked freight car, so they couldn't hear what anyone was saying. Through the smoke Gustaf saw Foreman Lawson motioning the men forward, toward the engine, and he followed the others.

They stood clustered next to the side of the locomotive facing away from the water. Lying on its side, the engine looked unnaturally big, as if it could never fit beneath the high-vaulted ceiling of the repair workshop. Lawson raised his hands and everyone fell silent.

"Men," he said, "a terrible thing has happened. Engine driver Rossi is dead. He's stuck inside the engine cab, and we have to pull him out. He was with fireman Nelson, who managed to escape mostly unscathed when he fell out. He ended up bruised a bit from rolling down the embankment, but he's going to be all right. I've sent him home. We can't do anything more for Rossi, other than take his body home to his wife and children. But before we can pull him out, we have to get the engine more or less upright again. We have a few hours left before dark. Will you keep working until we get the job done—for Rossi's sake?"

Scattered shouts of "Aye" echoed through the wintry air. Some of the men had removed their caps when they heard the news, but now they put them back on. Then they picked up their crowbars and walked in single file over to the engine.

Gustaf ended up with Jonathan very close to the engine driver's cab. It was slow work. Whenever they managed to raise the locomotive an inch or so, several men would run over and shove loose railroad ties between the chassis and the embankment. It was dangerous work, and there was a great creaking every time they let go. It was a matter of raising the engine enough so they could wrap chains around the entire body of the locomotive and then hitch them to the Mule. But it would take many hours of hard work before they could do that.

Later in the afternoon, when they'd managed to raise the locomotive a few feet into the proper position, Gustaf got a good look inside the engine cab through the side vent. Shock rippled through his body when he realized he could glimpse Rossi inside. The engine driver was a man in his sixties, with a big gray mustache and a bald pate. The dead man was slumped forward with his head hanging and his eyes closed. He looked like he was asleep. But the angle was odd, as if he were hanging from the far wall.

Then they heard Lawson shouting another order, and the entire, huge metal carcass of the engine shuddered as a hundred hands gripped their crowbars and pressed down with all their might. Gustaf was already drenched with sweat and freezing. He didn't want to look up and see more of Rossi's gray, slumbering face above them, but he couldn't stop himself from looking. At first he couldn't understand how the man's body could stay seated in the same position while the whole engine was shaking as it was slowly forced upward.

Then he realized what must have happened, and he felt an icy shiver that had nothing to do with his sweat-soaked shirt. A big hole gaped in the side of the engine cab, cutting right through the metal. In the opening he could now see more of Rossi's body. The metal had been ripped open by the eccentric rod from the engine's forward wheels. It had come loose and probably struck the tracks full force. Then it was hurled straight up toward the cab, stabbing Rossi through the chest and nailing him to the far wall, where he now hung with a strangely peaceful look on his gray face. Gustaf hoped it had happened as fast as he imagined. He cast a glance at Jonathan, who nodded. He too had pictured the chain of events.

When it was close to four o'clock, a light snowfall began. The men took a short break and a wagon arrived with hot coffee and wheat rolls that were plain and dry. They stood in groups of three or four, exchanging a few words in low voices as they stamped their feet and drank their coffee. Everyone kept their back turned to the engine cab. Somebody said they'd also found a dead hobo inside the freight car. No one knew who he was, but that was not unusual. Several newly arrived men had now begun putting up a winch of block and tackle on the far side of the locomotive.

After about ten minutes they all went back to work, without Lawson or any of the other foremen having to summon them. Everybody wanted to get out of there, but they knew they weren't going anywhere until the Mule could be hitched to the chains around the wrecked engine and Rossi could be pulled free and placed on a stretcher. When they resumed the same positions and leaned on their crowbars on command, Gustaf tried not to look inside the cab, but his gaze was drawn there so swiftly that he forgot to keep his eyes fixed on the black steel of the steam boiler. Rossi's face was as peaceful as before, but his skull was now covered with a thin layer of new snow. Gustaf looked away.

They didn't get home until after eleven at night. The snow had moved on, and the moon was shining through the drifting haze of clouds, illuminating the route through the Hollow, where all the houses were now dark. The men walked along saying only a few words in English, which each had mastered to a varying degree. A group of men accompanied Gustaf and Jonathan, who usually left work alone, but all day long they had worked together with the same goal in mind: to free their dead coworker. And besides, all of them had to go through the railroad tunnels. The Irishmen disappeared first, heading for their homes near the bridge abutment while the Italians continued a little farther up the hill. Then they too turned off, muttering "Good night" before they were gone. That was something new. Normally they didn't say a word.

All was quiet as Gustaf and Jonathan walked the last part of the way up to their own homes. The only sound was the wind in the trees on the slope up toward Dayton's Bluff and a faint trickling that they heard as they passed the creek, invisible in the dark.

The windows were dark in Gustaf's house, but in spite of his weariness, he noticed that something was different. He opened the door and went in.

Anna and Elisabet were sitting at the table in the dark. He didn't see Ellen and assumed she was already asleep up in the loft. The two women sat in silence, waiting for him, and he realized they'd heard the news. The train wreck had probably been the big topic of conversation in the neighborhood all day. The Rossi family had never lived in the Hollow, but they had relatives among some of the Italian newcomers farther down the hill.

Anna looked up when Gustaf came in and took off his boots. His eyes weren't yet accustomed to the dim light indoors, so he couldn't make out her expression, but her eyes were shiny in the faint moonlight coming through the window. Even though he was exhausted, he sat down at the table across from his wife and daughter. They were saving on candles and also didn't want to disturb Ellen. But clearly there was something they wanted to say. The very air in the room felt as if it had already absorbed far too many words.

"How did it go?" asked Anna at last. She leaned forward and whispered the words.

"We got him out. A Catholic priest came over instead of the family and took Rossi away. We couldn't finish taking care of the engine tonight. That'll have to wait until tomorrow."

He didn't say any more about the subject, but he was thinking about what Jonathan Lundgren had muttered as they put their tools back in the shop. He said that a couple of days' interruption of service on the train line wasn't going to help matters for the Great Northern, and the men could probably count on yet another wage cut before the month was out. But right now Gustaf didn't want to brood over that or even mention it to his wife and daughter.

"Would you like to tell your father what we've been talking about?" said Anna quietly as she placed her hand on Elisabet's arm. Her daughter swallowed hard. Up in the loft, Ellen turned over, annoyed but only half-awake, prompting loud creaks from her bed, which had been made for a much smaller girl.

"There's been so much death," said Elisabet, speaking in a voice that suddenly sounded more grown up than Gustaf had previously noticed.

Her voice seemed stronger. He thought maybe that had happened because she was pregnant, but he didn't really know.

Elisabet went on: "I think the baby is a boy. I'm almost positive about that. And I thought—if Father doesn't think it's terribly stupid of me—that I'd like to name him Carl. Leonard says he's happy with the name."

Then she fell silent, waiting for Gustaf to reply. He felt her nervousness streaming toward him in the dark. She inhaled deeply, stifling a sob. For a moment he wasn't sure what he thought. Anger surged to the surface, swerving like a fish. *It's not possible to replace somebody like that.* But then he felt a sense of calm settle over him, maybe because he was so tired. The image of his own son sped past, as if Carl had silently run by, little more than a swift movement seen out of the corner of his eye. Like a gust of wind blowing through the room, though he knew he'd only imagined it because he was half-asleep. But there was no pain afterward. He waited for it, but he continued to feel calm.

"Let's wait till he's here," Gustaf said then. "Let's see if he looks anything the same. If he does, that'll be fine."

None of them wanted to be the first to get up. They sat at the table for a while longer without speaking. Up in the loft, Ellen was now breathing quietly, sound asleep. It must have been close to midnight, and everything was about to start over again, exactly where it had all once ended.

ELLEN DIDN'T LIKE HER WORKMATES. She sat in the same room with five other girls. Three of them were Swedes, and as soon as the door closed to the bigger office, they would begin chatting with each other, whispering from behind their typewriters. Even though they spoke Swedish, Ellen rarely heard what they said. Once again she was the new person, and she knew from her experience at the Klinkenfuer factory that it meant she had to start at the very bottom. The other girls didn't pay much attention to her. Sometimes but not always they would give her a slight nod when she arrived in the morning. During the first weeks she didn't know anyone's name, and they didn't bother to introduce themselves. Gradually she learned their names from the papers she typed and from hearing them talking to each other. The Swedes were Cecilia Clara, Hilda Maria, and Karolina. The American girls answered to the names of Pearl and Mabel and mostly kept to themselves.

In the beginning Ellen didn't have time to wonder what the other girls thought of her, the newcomer. She was dealing with her own fear, until eventually it resolved into something else. She began each day feeling so scared that she shook all over, although she didn't think anyone else noticed. It took a couple of weeks before her fear was transformed into an all-absorbing focus on the task at hand. Sometimes she would get so immersed in her work that she saw only what was right in front of her on the worn wooden surface of the desk.

She loved the double-page documents on certificate-size paper with deckle edges and the way they sounded when she unwrapped them. Sometimes they were tied with violet cloth ribbons when they arrived. It was much more satisfying to translate and type a contract written on that sort of paper than to take pages of lined writing paper from a pad on which Mr. Lundquist—his first name turned out to be Ferdinand, but no one in the office called him anything but Fred—had scribbled various notes while speaking with a client. It was her job to bring order to his notes.

On certain days it would get quite stuffy in the long and narrow typing room if the door was kept closed, and the other girls always reeked of perfume. Ellen felt a sorrow mixed with panic when she realized she could no longer compete with the cleanliness of her workmates. When she got her first wages, she went out at lunchtime to the slightly nicer drugstore on the other side of Fourth Street and bought three bars of expensive lavender soap wrapped in crepe paper. She left the little parcel on her desk all afternoon, hoping the strong scent would mask any other odors she might have brought with her from the Hollow or the streetcar. Or, in the worst-case scenario, the smells streaming from her own pores, impossible to stop.

Nobody said anything. Nobody offered a single critical remark about her clothes or her person. But what scared her and formed a muted backdrop to her whole day was that someone might notice how she smelled. And she was fairly certain that it was not something she could get rid of entirely, no matter how much she scrubbed her skin and washed her clothes. She counted her coins and went to see Liz to buy another secondhand blouse so she would have one to wear and one to wash.

Those first weeks Ellen sat as far away from everyone else as she could, which was no doubt perceived as embarrassment on her part. Gradually she realized that the three other Swedish girls, who shared a rented room in Minneapolis, used their perfume as a way of masking any other odors. They all smelled the same every day and could probably get away with not changing their blouses for several weeks in a row.

After a while they began talking to her, offering casual remarks, as if it were the most natural thing in the world: "Have you seen the paper from Lundstrom's, Ellen? Do you have any envelopes left, Ellen? Ugh, what awful weather today, and I didn't bring my umbrella—could I borrow yours, Ellen, when I run across the street with a letter?" Although she had no umbrella to lend, of course.

After a month or so, everybody took her presence for granted. The three other Swedes stuck together, arriving and leaving at the same time. But they still hadn't seen through her. She no longer hated them, but she avoided them as best she could. Ellen sat at her place in the corner, spoke only if necessary, and nobody sniffed knowingly at the air whenever they passed her. When asked where she lived, she merely replied, "St. Paul." The address she listed on the employment contract was for Larson's grocery store. Nobody would ask any questions if a letter arrived for her there, since no one in the Hollow had a proper address. They all went to Larson's to get any mail that came for them. Mr. Larson didn't like it, even though it caused him no trouble, and it did force people to go to his store.

In general, little was said in the office other than a few polite comments to Mr. Lundquist and brief exchanges with the other girls. It was always late by the time Ellen got home. For her, Minneapolis was still nothing more than a long, low tunnel of darkness and slush. And the Hollow was always dark when she got back.

On certain nights Elisabet didn't want to sleep alone in Leonard's house. Ellen knew she was scared because Leonard's mother had died there when Leonard was out working on the line. Elisabet didn't need to say it out loud, because Ellen knew what was going on in her sister's mind. She also knew that on those evenings Elisabet would sit and wait for her, longing to chat. She wanted to talk about the baby she was expecting and what it would be like. But when Ellen got home, she didn't have the energy to talk for more than a short time. A wall seemed to come down inside her, and she saw her sister's face, but she couldn't take in what she was saying. She excused herself by explaining she was tired, but Elisabet wouldn't always let her get away with that.

One evening Elisabet grabbed Ellen's arm so hard that her fingernails sank into her skin as she hissed, "It feels like you don't even live here anymore, so why don't you just move out?"

Ellen couldn't think of anything to say, but the remark followed her into her dreams. *But where?* Where was she supposed to go?

She was neither here nor there. It felt as if she spent most of her spare time sitting on the hard bench in the streetcar, enveloped in the smell of damp wool, tobacco smoke, and melting snow. Her sole task was to follow the slow procession of the streetlamps on the other side of the windowpane that was coated with ice and the steam created by the breathing of hundreds of strangers. Sometimes Ellen would fall asleep, but she always awoke with a jolt, terrified that she might have missed her stop. After Maria Avenue, where she had to get off, the streetcar continued on, heading for the great unknown, and it wouldn't stop until it reached faraway Wildwood. She spent the entire year and some months afterward wrapped in a glass globe of silence, typing other people's words.

Ellen felt a certain peace in not belonging here or there but in between. At home in the Hollow she was always on her way to work, and once she arrived at the office, she was invisible, or nearly so. That was not where she belonged. The seat in the streetcar was hers, along with the darkness outside. That was all. Until one evening when she came home and found Elisabet sitting on the front steps wrapped in the worn red quilt their mother had brought from her parents' home. Ellen saw her sister from far away, as she came up the slope. A hunched figure in the shadow of the covered porch. She realized Elisabet was waiting for her, so she walked a little slower, uncertain what to expect. Finally she reached the house. Elisabet looked up, her eyes swollen from crying, which was so often the case these days. Her whole body was swollen from the pregnancy, and she cried easily. But right now she had something on her mind.

Elisabet got up and stood as erect as a statue as Ellen came toward her. When they met on the steps, Elisabet took her big sister's hand and said quietly, "Promise me you won't move away until after the baby is born and everything has settled down. Promise me."

Elisabet's hand was ice-cold. She must have been sitting there for a long time. Ellen got worried, thinking she needed to get her indoors before anything happened to her. She put her arm around her sister's shoulders and tried to turn her around toward the door, but Elisabet refused to budge. "Promise me," she said again. Ellen thought to herself, *Where do you think I would go?* Aloud she said, "I promise." Elisabet nodded and sighed with relief. Then they both went inside.

Spring was late in coming. Down in the Hollow it was usually somewhat warmer than up on the street, and the hazel trees along the creek began sprouting buds while the trees on Seventh Street were still completely bare. Elisabet's due date was getting closer, though Ellen wasn't sure exactly when it was supposed to be. They didn't talk about such things. Yet she knew that Elisabet did talk to Inga about all those kinds of matters, as if Inga knew everything, as usual, even though she was also expecting her first child shortly after Elisabet.

When the last of the snow drifts disappeared, Ellen's shoes were dry when she got off the streetcar on Fourth Street in Minneapolis. Only in the alleyway, where the sun never reached, did a dirty yellow layer of snow linger next to the brick wall. The first fly to appear in the bay window made her look up from her work as if awakened from a dream. She watched the buzzing insect for a long time as it kept flying against the glass, as if it were carrying out some urgent task. In the mornings she began worrying about where to get different shoes. When it got too warm for Liz's worn high-button shoes, they would attract the attention, and ridicule, of the other girls.

She typed. The papers passed more quickly across her desk than anyone else's. She didn't care about the occasional sharp comment from the other girls, like the day when Mabel walked past and behind her back snapped, "By all means, don't wait for us." At first Ellen didn't realize that the American girl was speaking to her. She glanced up and smiled, but Mabel looked away.

When Ellen was focusing on her typing, she was able to leave everything else behind. *With reference to the verbal agreement as of the 17th of this month, it is hereby incumbent upon Johannes Nilsson, farmer in Scandia, to hand over to the new owner before the end of the month the aforementioned property, including all inventory.*

Toward the end of the month Mr. Shelby Jr. began appearing more often in the typing room. Now that winter was over, the door to the office frequently stood open. At any moment, and without warning, he might show up with more papers that were a priority, and he'd usually turn to Ellen. "Miss Klar, when you're finished," he'd say. She could almost cry when she saw that the stack of papers, which had been gradually diminishing, would suddenly be just as big as when she'd started in the morning. Yet he'd stand there, chatting, as if she had all the time in the world. Maybe he did, but she did not. Yet she said, "Yes, Mr. Shelby. No, Mr. Shelby." And tried to smile. Until one day when he said, "Why don't you call me Sol? That's short for Solomon."

He was still young, though maybe ten years older than Ellen.

He was not unpleasant. It was just that he took up too much of her time. Often he gave her so much to type that she had to stay a half-hour after the others had left for the day. She didn't really mind staying for a while longer to work. It was wonderful to have the whole room to herself, and by now it was light enough in the evenings that her trip home wasn't as unnerving as before. But Mr. Shelby talked so much. About nothing. For instance, about some amusing Swedish client they had. And when he tried to imitate the man's way of talking, he sounded as if his mouth was full of porridge. Ellen laughed, even though it wasn't especially funny.

One day he came in carrying a ball that he tossed from one hand to the other. It was new and white and clearly had never been used before. He might have bought it at a shop that very day. "Do you like baseball, Miss Klar?" he asked. She merely shook her head and kept typing. He stood there holding the ball in his hand. She shook her head again, keeping her eyes fixed on the typewriter. Finally he nodded, set the ball on her desk, and silently left the room. She thought he must have forgotten the ball and would come back to get it, maybe after she'd left for the day. He often worked after hours behind the closed door to his office. But the baseball was still on her desk when she got to work the next morning. She didn't touch it.

Ellen got used to seeing Mr. Shelby appear in the typing room. He talked to the other girls as well, teasing them in the same way. But he always ended up coming over to where she sat, and as the spring progressed, a too-bright ray of sun would land on her desk from the only window in the room.

"I didn't know you had red hair, Miss Klar," he said.

She looked up in surprise.

"I don't, Mr. Shelby," she replied. "It must be because of the sunlight."

"Ah," he said with a smile. "Well, it looked reddish against the light. By the way, I said you could call me Sol, Miss Klar. All the others do. Sol. 'Mr. Shelby' is my father."

She nodded. She still couldn't bring herself to say his first name.

"I'd like to ask you a favor, Miss Klar," he went on. "If you have time for it, that is. Although it's on Sunday."

She didn't know what to say, so she merely nodded.

"We usually sponsor an outing for the office every year," he told her. "Perhaps you didn't know that since you haven't been with us very long."

She shook her head.

"Well, on Sunday I was thinking of going to look at some locations for this year's outing. And I thought I'd ask you to accompany me, Miss Klar. As the representative for the girls who work here. Someone usually goes along."

She looked down, not knowing how to reply.

"It's not an order. You may do as you please, Miss Klar."

Then she found herself nodding.

At home she told her family honestly that the boss had asked her to accompany him in order to make plans for an office outing. By now they were used to Ellen going off on her own, and her mother also admitted that she had no idea how things functioned in an office, though she did think it was a shame her daughter would have to work on a Sunday. Ellen replied that it wasn't so much work as an excursion. And in the middle of the day.

"But you'll be home before dark, won't you?" asked her mother, sitting in partial shadow on the other side of the table. At that time of year nobody in the Hollow lit candles or lamps.

"Yes, Mother," said Ellen, her voice sounding strangely meek, as if she were a child again.

Solomon Shelby Jr. had said they should meet outside the Phoenix Building at ten o'clock on Sunday morning. Ellen took the streetcar through a different Minneapolis than she was used to seeing. People dressed in their Sunday best were on their way to church, and the sun shone through the trees with barely sprouted yet luminous leaves. The city and the world seemed new. For a few moments she watched a family strolling along the sidewalk—first the father, wearing a dark suit and carrying a Bible, then the mother, followed by two little girls in white dresses with light blue sashes and rosettes. They held each other by the hand, and they couldn't help skipping a bit behind their solemn-looking parents. Then the family passed from Ellen's field of vision and was gone.

She didn't recognize Mr. Shelby at first because he'd dressed for the outing in a light, cream-colored suit with a straw hat on his head. He looked younger as he stood there in the shadow of the tall building, and she wondered again how old he might be. Twenty-eight? Twenty-nine? His pitted complexion made it hard to determine his age. Then he caught sight of her and stepped forward into the sunshine.

"Miss Klar," he greeted her calmly. He smiled and looked her in the eye. She felt awkward and wondered where the others were. But he was the only one there.

"I thought more people would be coming along," she said.

"No. I'm sorry if I gave you that impression. That was not my intention. But the two of us will manage, don't you think?"

He smiled again, and his good humor was infectious, as usual. She found herself smiling back.

"Where exactly are we going, Mr. Shelby?"

He shrugged casually, choosing to ignore the fact that she was clearly suspicious.

"There are several places we might choose. And you needn't worry, Miss Klar. The firm will pay all expenses, of course. We usually offer the employees an outing to some pleasant place. Last year we took an excursion on the river, but the weather was bad, and I don't think we'll do that again. It was not a success."

They stood in the middle of the sidewalk in the sunshine, which was rapidly getting hotter. People passed them on both sides, as if they were a sandbank in a stream, but Ellen had no intention of budging from the spot until she knew more.

"I was thinking we might have a look at Elliot Park," he said then. "I've heard it's supposed to be nice. They have new carousels."

"No," said Ellen in a firm voice that surprised even her. "Not Elliot Park."

For a moment Mr. Shelby looked a bit worried.

"No? I thought you might like going to the park, Miss Klar, since so many people seem to enjoy it. I've heard that from a number of our clients."

"No, not the park." She looked up, for a moment dazzled by the sun as she peered at him. "I've been there, you see. But you need to realize, Mr. Shelby, that all manner of reprobates go there too. It can get quite unpleasant at times. Especially a little later in the day."

"I wasn't aware of that, of course," he said. "I'm very glad that you're here, Miss Klar. You know about certain things, while I do not. Like that park, for example. Which might have led to unfortunate events."

All around them church bells had now begun chiming, and Ellen had to lean closer to hear what he said.

"I was saying that we might have a look at Como Park instead. It's a little farther away, but it's bigger and more country-like. If you have time, that is, Miss Klar."

She nodded. He smiled delightedly with his lips pressed together and then cast a glance over his shoulder.

"Here comes the streetcar," he said. "And it's headed in the right direction. Just in time. Shall we go?"

He offered Ellen his arm. She hesitated briefly but then linked her arm with his.

The streetcar was the same line she usually took. They sat up front, side by side, not talking much. Ellen noticed she was feeling more and more nervous with each stop they passed and as the neighborhoods became more familiar. She worried most that someone she knew might get onboard and she'd be forced to say hello. And then he'd ask her questions. But as they approached Snelling Avenue, Mr. Shelby got up and said it was time to change streetcars.

"So, you've never been out to Como Park before, Miss Klar?" he said after a while, presumably just for something to say. She shook her head.

"No, we usually stay at home on the weekends," she said. "Once we went to Elliot Park on a Sunday, but as Mr. Shelby knows, we didn't really care for the place."

"For God's sake," he said, sighing deeply, "call me Sol. It makes me nervous to hear you say 'Mr. Shelby.' My father is over fifty, and he wears spats on his shoes even on workdays. I hope that's not how you view me, Miss Klar."

He looked almost angry. Ellen swallowed hard and looked down. They had barely set out, and it already looked like it might be a long day.

He noticed he'd spoken too crossly and said, "Please forgive me. I realize it's proper to address each other more formally at work. You're right about that, Miss Klar. But now it's my day off. So tell me about Elliot Park."

"There's not much to tell," she replied. "It was pleasant enough. There's a restaurant with a dance floor and a fountain. But it got a bit rowdy toward evening."

*And pony rides for children who are still alive,* she thought.

"I've heard, of course, that common folks also go there," he said.

She gave him a sidelong glance. No doubt he meant to agree with her by saying that. She let it pass and looked out the window. The streetcar was now traveling through an unfamiliar neighborhood, with stone buildings that were two or three stories tall, and all the shop signs were in English.

Como Park turned out to be a big open space where gravel paths had been laid, meandering among the groves of trees. The park already had its own streetcar stop, but at first Ellen didn't think there was much to see. Sol Shelby Jr. seemed to know where he was going as they headed along a path that led to a small restaurant in the shade of a cluster of oak trees.

"There's not a lot to see here yet," he told her apologetically, as if he owned the park and ought to have made better preparations. "But there are big plans for it. It's going to have a zoo, and maybe a large greenhouse with exotic plants. And next Sunday, which is when we might come here, a band from Chicago will be playing."

They sat down, and he asked Ellen if she was hungry. She wasn't but the spring sun was getting quite hot, and she worried about sweat stains appearing under her arms, although Liz had showed her how to remove the stains with baking powder. She asked if she might have a glass of cold lemonade.

He came back with two tall glasses.

"In this heat I would have preferred a glass of beer," he said, "if you don't might my saying so, Miss Klar. But then I realized that it's Sunday."

Slowly they sipped their lemonade. He was testing her. She knew she was being subjected to some sort of examination, as if he wanted to see what her limits were. He peered at her over the rim of his glass.

"I was thinking we could set up a long table here in the shade next Sunday for a picnic. If the weather is good, that is. And maybe we could play baseball, if we can put together two teams of the male employees, although a number of them are getting on in years. Don't you think that might be nice, Miss Klar?"

He kept on talking as she sat there in the shade, gazing at the lawn. She felt as if she were being drawn, with eyes open, into some sort of waking dream. It was hot, and the lemonade tasted good, sweet and cold instead of sour. He had a pleasant voice that rose and fell rhythmically like music. She didn't catch everything he said, but that didn't matter. She nodded and smiled, and that seemed to be sufficient to please him. For Ellen, it was enough to sit under the trees among people who had never seen her before, where no one knew who she was.

Sol Shelby Jr. didn't want to go back immediately. He said that first he wanted to take a walk. There was a great deal to see, the park was big, and this was the first lovely spring day. If she had time, that is.

Again he offered his arm, and together they stepped into the sunshine as they set off along the gravel path. After a while he stopped to take from his pocket a cigarette case that looked to be made of nickel silver. He opened the case and offered Ellen one. He seemed pleased when she declined. Then he lit a cigarette for himself and nonchalantly tossed the used match over his shoulder. Again she had the feeling he was taking her measure. Presumably it would have been a mistake to accept a cigarette.

"So you've never smoked, Miss Klar?"

She shook her head.

"A wise decision," he said. "I don't think it looks very elegant for women to smoke. And they get bad teeth easier than men."

Ellen said she didn't know about that, but she thought it was unnecessary to adopt a bad habit that was also expensive.

"Swedes don't smoke much," he said. "From what I understand."

"At home"—she very nearly said *in the Hollow* but managed to hold back the words—"at home some of the men smoke pipes. But most of them use snuff."

"Ugh, yes," he said. "They can keep that habit for themselves. That must be why they smell."

They were walking toward the lake. An icy-cold breeze blowing off the water reminded them it was still early in the year. Ellen shivered. He offered her his jacket, but she declined. They chatted easily, and she almost forgot he was her boss. Nor did she mind if they walked for a while in silence. That didn't seem to bother him either. They continued to the bridge that spanned the water lily pond and paused in the middle to look down at the enormous leaves floating on the surface below. They looked like gigantic green cakes. He explained how heated water was piped into the pond so the plants would grow big. Otherwise they grew only in South America.

Then he said abruptly, "You haven't said anything about my face, Miss Klar."

She paused, looking distressed. He was squinting at her in the sunlight, and all of a sudden his expression seemed unpleasantly calculating as he regarded her through narrowed eyes.

"No, why should I?" she said.

"Most people wonder about it," he said curtly and then continued walking. "I'm certain that all of you talk about it at work."

She searched her memory and then was able to shake her head without stretching the truth. He stopped and looked at her.

"Really?" he said incredulously and then smiled.

"I don't talk much with the other girls. But I can't recall anyone ever saying anything. Not to me."

"Perhaps I'm exaggerating," he said, gazing at the water. "But sometimes I sense that's what people are thinking about when they look at me. Occasionally I forget about it, but not for long."

She gathered her courage and said, "It's not that bad. I think you pay more attention to it than other people do."

"Well, I have to look at myself in the mirror every day," he said.

He told her that years ago his father, Solomon Shelby Sr., had traveled to Cuba with the intention of investing in a sugarcane plantation.

Nothing came of the plan, but when he came home he was suffering from smallpox. His father did not become deathly ill, but he infected his son.

"I was ten years old," he said. "I developed the most dangerous form of the illness, and everyone thought I would die. My parents thought so too. I remember getting a vaccine shot, but then there's a gap in my memory of several weeks when I had a very high fever. Mother still thinks the vaccine made it worse, while Father usually says it's what saved my life. Sometimes they still argue about it. What I remember most is that it itched like hell, and I couldn't help scratching in my sleep. Finally they had to wrap my hands in bandages so I wouldn't scratch my skin to shreds. But I recovered."

Ellen realized that she was expected to say something, but it took her a while to find the right words.

"It's very common," she said. "And almost nobody pays it much attention anymore. At least not on a man. I noticed the first time we met, but since then I haven't given it a thought. I mean it."

He stopped and looked at her. "Would you dare to touch my face, Miss Klar? Or is it too repulsive?"

She now understood that this was the real test, the moment the entire day had been leading toward. What she'd perceived as him taking her measure really had just as much to do with himself. Without hesitation she reached out and gently stroked his cheek. The skin was rougher than she'd imagined, but he didn't have much stubble. When her fingertips touched his face, he closed his eyes. Then he heaved a big sigh, as if he'd been holding his breath for a very long time.

They ate a late lunch at a little stall that sold pancakes. It was starting to feel chilly, so they moved their chairs and the small table several times so they could keep sitting in the sunshine. They didn't talk much. Mostly he tried to entertain her by recounting anecdotes about clients he'd had. They weren't especially amusing, but he tried to make the most of them. She no longer laughed as politely as before. She merely smiled as she sat there, pondering how to put her clothes in order for the next day.

"You must forgive me, Miss Klar," he said at last, now giving her a big, relaxed smile instead of the strained smile from earlier in the day. "Here I am, talking about myself. I assume you'll be going home to your parents. Maybe they're wondering where you are. And could I possibly call you Ellen? Now that we're not at work?"

She smiled and said that would be fine.

He paid for the food and they walked arm in arm toward the waiting room in the streetcar station. It was close to four o'clock, and there were still several hours of daylight left. The air was chillier and a light breeze was blowing. Ellen wished she could afford to buy herself a hat like the other girls in the office had.

For the first few stations, they were alone onboard the streetcar. Just the two of them and the conductor, who soon started up a conversation with the driver and turned his back to them. They were sitting alone, toward the back of the streetcar.

With a sudden, sharp jolt of alarm, Ellen felt Sol Shelby Jr. put his hand on her thigh and give it a squeeze. He sat motionless, staring straight ahead and pretending nothing was happening, but the warmth from his hand penetrated right through the thick fabric of her skirt. Panic tightened her throat. Then she cautiously took his hand and lifted it away. But she didn't let go. His fingers intertwined with hers, and they sat there, not moving, not speaking, as the streetcar clattered on, getting closer to the city. Buildings appeared on either side and obscured the sky. The streetcar filled with more voices and the silhouettes of other passengers. But the two of them sat there without saying a word until they had to get off and go their separate ways on Snelling Avenue.

## *Swede Hollow / Duluth Line*

June 1904

ELISABET WAS A WEEK PAST DUE. She had calculated the date with Inga's help, and now she was growing more anxious for each day that passed. She said the baby was moving about as it should, but she was frightened of the birth itself; the baby was getting bigger and bigger. Most often she would go to stay with her mother or Inga rather than sit alone in the small house where she and Leonard lived among the Italians. She didn't dare be alone for extended periods of time, and she no longer had the energy to walk all the way up and down the hill several times a day. Leonard would sometimes come to get her when he was back from work, but on some evenings she didn't want to follow him home. He would eat supper with his in-laws and his young wife and then go back down the hill, while Elisabet would stay behind and sleep in the bed next to the door.

Leonard was still working the long trips to North Dakota and Montana. His foreman said nobody knew the route as well as he did, since he was aware of every curve and every difficult incline. There were no other job opportunities to be found, so he had to stay on.

Sometimes he felt as if he were looking at himself from the outside as he walked to work through the railroad tunnels down in the low, gray shantytown sector belonging to the Irish. It was almost as if he were observing himself from Seventh Street, far above on the viaduct. Things had turned out the way he'd once imagined they might—with him wearing a gray jacket and cap and joining the flood of other men pouring out of the Hollow each dawn. He no longer looked any different, and maybe that had never been a possibility. He was merely one gray figure among hundreds of others.

Leonard was good at his job and he knew what he was doing. Like his older workmates, he might soon lose a finger or two, but that didn't really scare him. It would be worse to lose a leg or a hand, which happened to workers at regular intervals. And there were other dangers that were more difficult to avoid.

He saw how his father-in-law, Gustaf, was beginning to look more and more like a shadow of himself with every passing day. He seemed hardened and hounded by an anger that lacked any release after they had "worked out" everything regarding Elisabet and the baby. He and Gustaf rarely spoke to each other, and even then only tersely and about ordinary matters. Sometimes the older man—increasingly rigid in both body and mind, unyielding and resigned—would walk along next to Leonard. Gustaf was one of the men who always did as he was told, for sixty-five cents a day. Just one more married man, with mouths to feed and tools to heft on someone else's orders. Yet unlike most of the other men who worked for the railroad, Gustaf didn't drink. He'd stopped drinking even before leaving Sweden.

His father-in-law's hair was still quite thick, but gray streaks had begun to appear. Leonard could remember when Gustaf's hair was entirely brown, though with a hue very like his own. But this man, who was twenty years older, had never interested him except in his role as Elisabet's father. He thought it wise to avoid Gustaf, and yet he always tried to humor him as best he could.

It now struck Leonard that a passing observer up on the viaduct would probably not be able to distinguish him from Gustaf as they walked along surrounded by many other men on their way to the rail yards. Two gray jackets, two married men, two pairs of interchangeable hands. And soon he too would be a father.

These sorts of thoughts preoccupied Leonard on his way to work and sometimes crept into his mind as he walked home, frequently alone and in the middle of the night if he'd been on the late train from the Fargo depot. But when he was out on the line, he never thought about such things. Out there, as one of the few railroad brakemen, he was entirely on his own, enveloped in his personal silence with only the wind in his ears. Out there he seldom thought of anything at all. He stayed as warm as he could, always on the alert and ready for those moments that depended on him using his hands, while he watched the desolate land extend out from the tracks. That was when he felt completely present.

Sometimes he wondered why the whole world couldn't be like that. He would prop his boots against the wall planks of the train car, hook his arm around the iron bar at the opening, and lean back into the wind. Out of the corner of his eye he would see the rails rushing past. Then he'd tilt his head back and look straight up into the red-streaked evening sky and the deepening blue-black darkness. If he let go, it would be all over. But that was not how he wanted to die. On the contrary, he wanted things to continue just as they were at that moment, with his eyes filling with tears from the fierce wind and with the sun setting over the gray, petrified sea of the prairie. It was his other life that might suddenly come to an end.

* * *

Leonard awoke because the train had slowed to a standstill. The sun was shining in his eyes, and he'd fallen asleep slumped against the wall of the brakeman's car. His legs were stiff and cold, but not frozen through. He had on the heavy blue sweater that Elisabet had knitted for him. He rolled out of the car and landed feet first on the embankment, tottering a bit on his numb toes. He leaned against the train and took a long piss. The sun was just rising above the edge of the prairie, big and yellow, and all was quiet. It had to be close to five o'clock. Then he hobbled toward the engine, hoping to find some hot coffee. He'd finished the last dregs from his own bottle long ago, and the sandwiches were all gone.

The fireman was an Irishman by the name of Mahoney. After exchanging morning greetings, the fireman, without being asked, handed Leonard an enamel mug of hot, bitter coffee. It was no doubt left over from the night before and had now been heated up on the boiler for the third or fourth time. But he drank it without complaint. At regular intervals, little puffs of white steam issued from the engine's smokestack overhead. When the two men spoke, their words also came out in tiny clouds of condensation in the morning air. Only now did Leonard notice how cold it was.

He handed back the mug and thanked the man.

"Why are we stopped here?" he asked. Mahoney nodded toward several freight cars back along the tracks.

"Riley noticed that somebody had broken into one of the boxcars again. It was supposed to be locked and bolted when we left, but apparently the door slid open in the wind. He's checking it now. Didn't want to go back to the depot until he knew what had happened."

Leonard shivered as he walked back along the embankment, the taste of burnt coffee still lingering in his mouth. Then he came to the boxcar and looked up to see the legs of Riley and the engine driver through the open doorway. He set his hands on the edge and heaved himself inside.

The two men were not alone in the dim light. Next to the wall lay the body of a man stretched out full length, but they didn't seem concerned with the corpse as they stood there talking with their backs turned to it. They nodded good morning to Leonard as he stood up and brushed off his knees.

The boxcar was filled with chaff because it had been used for transporting grain. Underneath and next to the dead man lay several sacks that he'd evidently used to cover himself in the cold night. The sacks were labeled WASHBURN-CROSBY GOLD MEDAL. Leonard nodded at the body.

“So who’s that?” he asked, mostly just for something to say.

Riley spat through the open doorway. He worked for the railroad police, and pinned to the breast pocket of his jacket was a silver badge with the Great Northern emblem. He also carried a revolver on his belt. He would show up at the rail yards whenever the thefts got too numerous, or someone was suspected of sabotage or labor organizers had made another appearance. Lots of men found it amusing to go behind Riley’s back and transact crooked dealings with stolen goods. He was well aware of this. Every time he talked to somebody he seemed to be considering how that person might be trying to dupe him. Leonard didn’t know why Riley was on board the train at all; it certainly wasn’t to deal with some dead tramp.

“Who knows?” said Riley. “Just another dead guy. The second this week. But this one’s a little older.”

Leonard cast a glance at the man lying on the sacks and then stepped closer. He was very thin, dressed in a nondescript, worn black suit with holes at the shoulders and knees. He lay on his back with his eyes closed, his hands clasped on his chest, as if he’d readied himself for his own burial. His face was dirty, and his gray hair was matted. But he looked calm as he lay there.

Leonard went back to join Riley and the engine driver. They were cutting a piece off a twist of tobacco and didn’t seem in a hurry.

“What did he die from?” asked Leonard. Riley looked as if it was beneath his dignity to answer so many questions, especially at this hour of the morning, but finally he said, “There are some empty bottles rolling around over there. My guess is he drank himself to death. Maybe on purpose, for all I know. That must be why he looks so content.”

“We need to get moving,” said the engine driver, spitting into the morning. But he gave no sign of going anywhere.

Leonard went back over to the corpse. Something gray was sticking up between the fingers of his clasped hands. It looked like a scrap of paper from a notebook. Rigor mortis had set in, but Leonard managed to wriggle out the paper without touching the dead man’s skin. It turned out to be a grubby, printed membership card with a name written in faded ink:

*Card of membership American Railway Union:*
*GUST. JOHANSON, employed as R.R. brakeman*

Leonard took the scrap of paper over to the light and handed it to Riley, who gave it only a cursory glance, though he did raise one eyebrow.

"So somebody must have let him onboard back in St. Paul," he said. "Those old membership cards went out of use after the Pullman strike, and no doubt he hasn't been able to find work ever since. You're probably too young to remember all that. But a number of men still travel free, and wherever they like, by showing their old union cards. Provided they can find some workmate we haven't managed to get rid of, that is."

He dropped the card through the open doorway where it fell onto the embankment.

"Shall we get going now?" asked the engine driver. Riley nodded.

"Give me a hand," he said as he took a pair of leather gloves out of his pocket. The engine driver and Riley picked up the corpse under the armpits, leaving the feet to Leonard. The body was rigid but strangely lightweight; it was like lifting a bunch of boards. They moved over to the open doorway and heaved the dead man as far as they could. The body struck the gravel on the embankment and then rolled down the slope until it disappeared in the thicket where the prairie grass started.

"It's easier this way," said Riley. "No fuss or ruckus, and the wild animals will take care of the rest." Then he turned to the engine driver. "Now we can go."

The two older men headed for the locomotive. Leonard turned to go back to his car at the end of the train, but then he stopped and backed up a few steps. He bent down and picked up the card from the gravel. Out of the corner of his eye he glimpsed the soles of the dead man's shoes sticking out of the bushes. He stuck the card in his pocket. Two quick blasts of the engine whistle signaled that he needed to hurry or he too might be left here in the middle of nowhere.

The news reached him as soon as he climbed off the train at the switchyard. One of the stokers who also lived in the Hollow came over to Leonard and said in a solemn voice, "I hear the baby arrived." At first he didn't understand; then it sank in. He suddenly felt his weight double as he stood there with his sailcloth sack flung over his shoulder.

"Do you know if it's a boy or a girl?" he said at last. The stoker shook his head.

"Jonathan Lundgren was here, looking for you. I'm supposed to tell you to hurry home. That's all I know."

*But the baby is already born,* thought Leonard. *Why all the hurry?* He began climbing over the rail yard's extensive tangle of tracks as he headed for Viaduct Street.

* * *

Leonard noticed that he had slowed his pace as he walked home. It was a mild spring evening, and he wanted to savor the moment before everything took shape and became forever set in stone. The sound of his dawdling footsteps echoed off the walls of the railroad tunnel. He passed the Irish shanties, hearing in the distance the muted cries of children and then the dogs began barking, as they always did whenever anyone went past. These were sounds he otherwise hardly noticed.

Leonard slowly plodded up the hill, passing his own small house, which stood in darkness. He didn't give it even a glance. Then he saw the Klars' home farther up, and he stopped to lean his back against the big elm tree at the foot of the slope leading to the Hamm mansion. It was very late, and all around him the Hollow was quiet. But in the house up the hill, a faint light could be seen in the window. He didn't know how long he stood like that, staring upward with his sack on the ground at his feet. He was waiting for some sound or movement, but there was only silence.

Far away he heard an entirely different and familiar sound: the short whistle blasts from the last train of the night to Duluth as it approached. Two quick blasts before the tunnels and the Connemara Patch; two more would come as the engine passed and made its way up the incline. Then Leonard began walking toward the embankment, taking the path to the Drewry Tunnel, past rows of darkened hovels. When he heard the next whistle blasts, he started to run.

He climbed up the embankment just as the headlight of the locomotive appeared through the branches farther down in the Hollow and lit up the brick walls of the Hamm Brewery. He stood a few feet from the track when the engine rushed past, wrapping him in smoke. He waited for the passenger cars to go by, watching the illuminated windows pass high overhead. Then came the three covered boxcars that were always last. He left his sack where it lay and trotted alongside the train until out of the corner of his eye he saw the ladder on the side of the last freight car. He stuck out his hand and grabbed hold as he pushed off with his feet against the gravel of the embankment and jumped, wrapping his other hand around a ladder rung. Then he pulled himself up and began climbing.

He reached the roof of the boxcar the same moment the locomotive entered the curve beyond the Hamm Brewery. He crouched down for the tunnel under Minnehaha Street and held his breath, enveloped in coal smoke. When the train passed Phalen Boulevard and began accelerating along the straightaway, he was able to stand up again. He looked back at the city lights behind him and then turned around to face forward. He stood there on the boxcar roof, his legs apart, as he stretched out his arms and closed his eyes, sailing blindly into the nighttime darkness, with the wind blowing against him and threading like a chilly mask across his face.

# III

*Minnesota State Reformatory for Men,*
*St. Cloud / Duluth, Minnesota*
1920–22

MY NAME WAS CARL JOHAN ALFRED HAMMERBERG. It was late in the afternoon when Carlson came to get me. He was the youngest of the guards, and sometimes it was easy to start talking to him as if he was a friend. He didn't really mind as long as no one else was listening. This time he was alone, but I was too tired to chat.

"Varshey wants to see you," was all he said. I was sitting on the bunk, having just returned from the workshop. My hands were covered with glue, and I had on the rough jacket that was stained all down the front. My eyes were stinging from sawdust.

"He doesn't have all day," said Carlson.

I was so beat that I found it hard to get up from the bottom bunk where I was sitting, but I did as I was told and followed him out to the corridor. It was summer and a little muggy, so the window facing the exercise yard stood open slightly. From the workshop down below came the sound of hammering on wood. I paused to look through the bars at the yellow evening sun while Carlson rattled his bunch of keys and opened all the locks on the steel door. In a moment he was ready.

"Don't just stand there daydreaming, Hammerberg," he said. Then I had to wait again while he relocked the door behind us.

Even though it was summer, a cold wind was blowing as we crossed the exercise yard. It was almost always like that. Pitkey, in the workshop, said it had something to do with the tower and the high walls catching the gusts in a certain way. The flag, which hadn't yet been lowered, snapped in the wind. We walked over to the main building. I hadn't been inside there since I was admitted to the prison, and I had to wait while Carlson unlocked the door with his big bunch of keys. Then we went in.

It was like entering the hull of an unfinished ship. That's what I thought the first time too. There were stairs and banisters like gunwales, but everything seemed to be turned inside out. And high overhead, the big glass ceiling was so dirty it gave the impression that the sky was always cloudy. Now it caught the evening light, creating a strange, unreal glow inside the vast hall. Murmuring voices came from every direction, though I couldn't see anyone except the guards on each level. We went up the big staircase and entered a green-painted corridor. "Wait here," said Carlson. He knocked on the big oak door and a voice called, "Come in." He stuck his head in the doorway and muttered a few words before coming back to me. Then he practically shoved me inside the office.

Prison Superintendent Varshey was sitting behind his big, dark desk. I hadn't seen him since I arrived, and he looked smaller than I remembered. But his voice was just as sharp. "Sit down, Hammerberg," he said. Carlson took up position next to the door.

I sat down on the very edge of the chair. I was trying to seem alert, though I was careful not to look him in the eye. I didn't want him to think I was disrespectful, like last time. So I sat there as he dealt with the papers on his desk. The dried glue was tugging at the skin on the backs of my hands, but I didn't dare scratch. I was worried that sawdust would fall out of my hair onto the rug. I sat as still as I could.

"So, Hammerberg. You've been here at St. Cloud for almost two years now. Am I right?" he said. I peered up at him from under the lock of hair falling over my forehead. He was looking right at me, with his hands clasped on his desk. I assumed I needed to reply, even though he knew the answer, of course.

"Yes, sir, Superintendent," I said.

He looked down at the papers in front of him.

"You've never given us any trouble, Hammerberg," he said then, looking up. "That's what it says here. You're a bit slow, but you do what you're told. No incidents."

I considered saying, "No, sir," but I thought he might think I was contradicting him, so I simply nodded.

He sat there in silence, as if waiting for something, but then he said, "That's good, Hammerberg. Is there anything you'd like to say for yourself, Hammerberg?"

I thought I needed to come up with something, so I said, "I think it's better in the workshop than at the quarry. I've had a job in a workshop before."

He didn't seem to be listening but went on, "And you've turned eighteen now. Right, Hammerberg?"

I thought it probably said as much on the papers, so I merely replied, "Yes, sir."

For a moment he didn't speak. He was holding a slip of paper that was smaller than the others.

"We've received a letter," he said finally. "It has something to do with you, Hammerberg, although my Swedish isn't that good. So I was thinking you could tell us what it says."

He held out the paper to me. I had to stand up to take it, and Carlson took a step closer from the doorway, as if to show he was paying attention. I didn't think it was necessary. Then I recognized the handwriting on the paper. It was my mother's big, printed script.

I read the note a couple of times. I noticed I was blinking my eyes.

"Well, Hammerberg," said Varshey. "What does it say?"

When I didn't reply at once, he said in an unexpectedly kind tone of voice, "Take your time."

It took me a few moments before I could read the note aloud in English:

> Dulut, 24 June 1922
>
> Esteemed Mr Vashy,
> Excuse me for this request. Please send home my son Charl Hammerberg. I can take care of him. I can get him a job.
>
> Sincerly
> Mrs Betsy Hammerberg

I thought it was too bad my mother hadn't spelled the superintendent's name correctly, because that much he could see for himself even if he couldn't read the rest of the words. I handed the letter back to him. He hadn't told me to sit down again, so I didn't.

"And as I understand it, Betsy is your mother," Varshey said as he absent-mindedly folded up the piece of paper and placed it with the other papers on his desk. He took off his glasses and squinted at me for a moment. "So tell me this," he went on. "Is Mrs. Hammerberg a widow?"

I didn't know what to tell him, so I just said, "I don't know."

I could hear how stupid that sounded, so I added, "I've never met my father."

After that neither of us spoke for a while.

Mother almost never wrote anything. She would quickly jot down her name in the ledger lying on the counter at Spencer's grocery store, leaning close to the page. When she did that, she always looked older than she was. Actually, she wasn't very old at all. Lots of people were surprised that I had such a young mother.

But whenever it was necessary to write something down, she would almost always get help from Mrs. Janson, the neighbor lady who lived on the first floor of the yellow-painted building. She was also from St. Paul and Swede Hollow. I didn't like it when she came over, because she talked so much. But Mother seemed to enjoy her visits. After Mrs. Janson left, I would ask my mother what they'd talked about, and she said it was nothing, mostly about what things were like in the Hollow in the old days. Once I asked her about my father, and at first she didn't reply, just busied herself with something with her back turned, probably waiting for me to leave. I usually didn't ask about him, so I don't know why I did that time. Mother had never said he was dead, but if others assumed he was, she didn't deny it. So when I asked her what he'd done, she didn't answer. When she got quiet like that, my only choice was to go out, even though Mother disapproved.

Every morning I'd walk down the hill. During the winter of the year when the circus came to Duluth, I would walk all the way out to the shipyard if there wasn't too much snow. It was always hard going back up the hill on the way home, but Mother said we were lucky to be living so close to town.

I never had any reason to go up to the heights on a daily basis. The higher you climbed, the quieter it got, with fewer houses and fewer people. When I was out on my own, I would come to the intersection of Grand and Central and sometimes go as far as Highland. There was a big, flat rock far from the nearest lit window, and that's where I used to stop for a while. From there everything looked different. The lake gleamed in the moonlight, and the aerial lift bridge in the harbor looked like the skeleton of a horse against the water with the lights from Superior glittering on the other side of the sound. The late-night streetcar going to Proctor would clatter past down below with flickering spotlights, like a little electric toy. I don't know why I went up there. Then it was a matter of returning home and going to bed until I was awakened by all the noise and voices of the Tamminen family just before dawn. They had once owned a farm and still acted as if they had animals to care for.

When I was an apprentice at the Radford & Wright carpentry shop, I didn't have far to go. Only a few blocks. I would go up to Grand and walk along until I had to turn off a few blocks before the high school's tower. The city was different in the morning. Quiet and subdued if it was still dark, but in motion. I walked along the street with the others, surrounded by dark-clad people and the sound of wooden soles scraping on ice and pavement. Some might exchange a few words, but mostly we were silent until the factory whistles blew. That's when we had to wake up. Then we entered the big hall that always smelled of newly sawn wood and varnish. But when times got bad after the war, I had to start working at the Riverside shipyard. I was lucky they still had jobs there, but it was like starting over again for me. And Riverside was farther away. It took me forty-five minutes to walk there. I would take Grand, though in the opposite direction. There were lots of others who also walked all the way there, though two or three streetcars would occasionally clatter past. Sometimes I considered hopping onboard, but then I wouldn't have had enough money to pay for a ticket into town when Saturday rolled around.

During that winter and spring we built two barges. When you're standing at the bottom of a ship's hull you can imagine yourself indoors, even though you're not. I started out as a rivet catcher, which takes skill, even though it may not sound like it. You had to be ready when Jonson the "cook" (or stoker) yelled, "Rivet!" and tossed it from the hearth. Then you had to catch it in a bucket and swiftly lift it out with a pair of tongs before it got cold and take it over to the riveter. At first I was really slow, and everybody got mad at me, but in the end I got to be real good at it. You end up not thinking about what you're doing and just do it.

I turned sixteen while I was working there. Almost everybody out at Riverside was older. Everyone on my work crew was married except me. But there were a few guys my age on another crew, and we used to meet up on our way home. George and Lester were eighteen, but Larry was twenty. They lived a bit closer to town, and sometimes I'd go with them for a short way, before I almost always headed for home. Larry liked to play dice, and he used to go to some speakeasy, but I never did. Then he used to brag about how much he'd won the night before. I would go home and eat supper with my mother and leaf through the Swedish newspaper, which she got when the Jansons were done with it. Sometimes they'd clip out a section, and you had to guess what might have been there. Mother would sit with her mending on the other side of the table, and sometimes she'd stare at me so hard it felt like I couldn't breathe. Then I'd tell her I was going out for a while. "You be a good boy, now," she used to say as I went out the door. That was a habit of hers.

In the spring it got easier to walk to and from the shipyard. In the morning it was often foggy, but in the evening we'd linger a bit on the way home, especially when it started to stay light and there was no wind blowing off the lake. We might stand at the intersection of Grand and Ramsey, chatting for an hour or so, until we got hungry. Lester had a harmonica, and he used to get it out and play a quick little tune whenever any girls from the high school walked past, but they never paid any attention to us.

On that Monday in June we knew that Robinson's circus had come to town. Everybody was talking about it, but they had set up their tents in the field out by Vernon Street, and I thought it was too far to go. When the circus parade passed through town, we'd been at work, so none of us had seen it. George and Lester wanted to go out there, but Larry thought it was childish to get so excited about a circus. It wasn't like they had elephants or anything. But George wanted to see the woman snake charmer. I realized that Larry hadn't been having much luck with the dice lately, but later I found out he'd gone out there after all, because if there was a circus, there were bound to be dice.

I was allowed to borrow Lester's harmonica overnight, and I sat out in the yard trying to play tunes until it started getting dark and Mr. Tamminen told me to stop. Then I went inside. I didn't hear anything about the rape until I went to work on Tuesday morning. By then it was all anyone was talking about.

The other men on my work crew were furious and kept shouting to each other above the din of the compressor. Things like, *Have they caught them yet?* and *Those bastards!* I didn't know what they were talking about until break time. They were angry but also indignant. Apparently the news hadn't appeared in the papers yet, or maybe no one dared write about it, which is what stoker Jonson said. But he also said that folks would still hear all about it. Apparently it had happened the night before. The victim was a girl from the west part of town. They said she lived on Seventh Street, and "she's only a few years older than you." That's when I felt cold with fear, because it meant I might know her. It could be one of the girls who used to walk past when we stood and talked on the street corner.

The girl and her fiancé had gone to the circus and then strolled among the tents to be on their own for a while. That's when they happened upon a bunch of Negroes who worked for the circus, and an argument had ensued. It ended with six of the Negroes rushing at the couple and knocking down the fiancé. One of them had threatened the pair with a gun. Then they attacked the girl.

When the older men at the shipyard got this far in the story, they stopped talking. The break would soon be over, so I asked them what happened to the girl. When no one answered, I repeated the question. "So what happened to the girl?" "Well, what do you think?" replied Jonson, looking scornful. "What the hell do you think? There were six of them. It's not certain she'll make it through the night."

The men got up even before the whistle blew, as if they didn't want to say any more about the subject. But for the rest of the afternoon they worked harder than usual, and they were much quieter. During the supper break some of the older men went off to a corner of the yard. I asked

Larson what was going on, but he told me curtly to mind my own business, because this was a matter for grown men. But I was stubborn and kept asking questions. From what I gathered, after hearing a few remarks here and there, the police had stopped the circus train, which was about to leave town, and arrested some of the Negro circus workers. Now they sat in jail over on Superior Street.

"But they'll soon be out of there, just wait and see," said Larson.

The fact that the other men stood there talking with their backs turned made me feel stupid. I tried not to let on, but I kept thinking about it, and that slowed me down so much that Larson yelled at me and called me an idiot. That usually made me feel bad, but this time I hardly noticed.

We talked about the incident on the way home, wondering if it could be one of the girls from the high school. Larry said he knew who it was, but she wasn't anybody we knew. She was a little older, nineteen, almost as old as him, and she didn't go to school anymore but had a job in town. But when we urged him to tell us her name, he got mad and told us to shut up, he didn't want to say. "She might die," he said, and then we didn't talk for a while. Nothing was the same. It was hot for that time of the evening, and all the men were clustered together in small groups, keeping their voices low as they walked along. That wasn't normal. And most of the men didn't turn off at their streets but continued on into town, still in groups.

We stopped at the street corner as usual, though none of us said a word. I thought, a bit stupidly, that I should have brought Lester's harmonica to give back to him, but he didn't mention it. Larry stood there, punching at the nearest fence post, which was made of old, worn wood. He kept muttering to himself through clenched teeth, "Damn, damn, damn." Then he got a splinter in his knuckle, but he pulled it out with his teeth. He glared angrily at the rest of us. When he lowered his hand, there was blood on his palm, but it didn't seem to be hurting him. "Who wants to go with me into town?" The others nodded and set off. At first I followed close, but eventually I started to lag behind so they ended up a good distance down the hill. Then Larry turned around and shouted, "Are you coming or aren't you, Hammerberg?" That was near the old maple tree at the widow Lindstrom's place. I stood at the fence, not sure what to do, so I said, "I don't have any money for the streetcar. Not on me." "Go home and get some money," said George. "We'll wait here." So there was nothing to do but go home. I had hoped that Mother would be over at Mrs. Janson's, but she was sitting at the kitchen table, and I realized she had already heard that something was going on, because she looked worried. I went over to my bed and pulled out the tin box from underneath. That's where I kept my money. She said, "You're not going out again, are you?" And I said, "It's nothing special, Mother. Lester and George and Larry and I are just going into town for a while to see what happens." She threw out her hand, as if to say what a dumb idea that was, but she didn't say anything as she looked out the window. I stuffed the coins in my pocket, grabbed my cap from the table, and left. She was still sitting there. "Don't do anything stupid, Carl," she called after me. "Of course not, Mother," I said without turning around.

The others were waiting under the maple tree, all three of them, exactly where I'd left them. Then we went up to Grand to catch the next streetcar. I think it was ten minutes before we heard it coming down the hill. No one said a word.

The conductor wouldn't take our money. "Not today, boys," he said. "Not today." Then he turned away.

The closer we got to town, the more people we saw on the streets, and everyone seemed to be heading in the same direction. When we reached Twenty-second West, a big crowd filled the middle of the street, and the streetcar made only slow progress as the driver clanged the bell, and Larry said, "Let's get off here. It'll be faster to walk." So that's what we did. Lots of other folks got off too, so we weren't the only ones.

It seemed like people didn't really know what to do. Some of them stayed up on the sidewalk while others gathered in groups in the middle of the street, standing there and talking without paying any attention to the cars and streetcars. The whole time more and more people kept showing up. Then we heard the sound of a car engine, and someone honked. The crowd parted to let the vehicle through. It was a Ford truck with an open bed, and a sign on the side said *Dondinos* in white letters. It drove real slow and kept on honking, but people didn't get mad. They just moved aside to let it pass and then regrouped.

When the truck drew even with us, I saw something trailing behind. It was a rope with a big loop at the end, as if the truck was pulling some invisible load. The man in back was big. He wore a suit and had a thick black mustache. He caught sight of us and motioned us over. We walked along the side of the truck for a few minutes until he leaned down and asked, "You boys want to come along?" Larry said yes, and the man in the back of the truck leaned down and held out his hand to him. The rest of us ran after and jumped in too. We sat down on the wheel housings and looked at the crowds lining the street. Larry stood with his arms draped along the side, talking to the man with the mustache. I'd never seen him before, but afterward they said his name was Lindberg. He smiled and laughed and offered Larry some tobacco, but he didn't talk to the rest of us. It was nice sitting there, with the sun peeking out and people looking at us as we rode along Grand, though we were going awful slow. I sat and looked down at the rope and the loop hopping over the cobblestones behind us, and it looked a little like when you skip stones across the water. I wasn't tired at all.

Finally the truck stopped. We were really near the police station now. We jumped out, and I remember how the friend of the man with the mustache got out of the driver's seat and rolled up his sleeves. Then he began winding up the rope in coils around his elbow and shoulder, and I thought he looked really strong. When I glanced around I realized I was about to lose sight of Larry and Lester and George, so I dashed after them. They were making their way through the crowd toward the police station, and the only reason I could see them was that Larry was taller and he was wearing his cap. We couldn't get all the way up to the police station because there were too many people. George and I jumped up and tried to hold on as long as we could to the arm of one of the streetlamps in front of the station. I managed to hang on for a few minutes, but then I had to let go and rest before jumping up again. The old guys standing around me got annoyed, but then one of them said, "Can you see anything, boys?" And we could, although not much. There were three or four policemen lined up outside the front entrance, and I saw more through the window. None of them seemed to be carrying a gun, but the ones outside were holding billy clubs. The officer in the middle was taller than the others and bareheaded. He had thick blond hair, and I thought I recognized him. He looked angry, and his face was red, but the men standing at the front of the crowd almost seemed to be joking with him, saying something like, "Oh, come on, Oskar." He raised his billy club, but not to hit anyone. It was like he wanted to warn off the nearest men, who then stepped back, forcing the crowd behind them closer together. I asked George if he knew who the blond guy was, and he said it was Sergeant Oskarsson, who lived a few blocks away from him. The men in front shouted to Oskarsson, "We want to talk to Murphy, Oskar. Ask him to come out." Oskarsson shouted something back, but we couldn't hear what he said. "Give us the Negroes," yelled a man next to me, over and over again. Then I saw Larry backing away from the group in front of the door. He didn't stop, just yelled at us to get down from the lamppost, so we followed him, wondering what he wanted. He said it was impossible to see anything there, so he and Lester were thinking of trying to go around back.

There weren't as many people in the alley, and when we got around to the back we saw that the parking lot behind the police station was empty. Not a single vehicle. And only about twenty or twenty-five men standing below the loading dock, where two policemen holding billy clubs stood blocking the big steel doors. I saw big dents in the metal, so somebody must have tried to get in. The officers seemed less tense than their colleagues out front, though they didn't answer when anyone tried to talk to them. Lester asked some of the men where the police cars were and they said that Chief Murphy and the others had left early in the morning to bring back more of the Negro circus workers who had continued on to Virginia, because it was clear that more of them were involved. So the constables were the only policemen left at the station. Then the man added, "Along with the ones they already arrested."

At that point there was a commotion in the alley and someone shouted, "The fire engine is coming!" Almost everyone ran back to the front of the building. The crowd had parted and farther up Superior Street the big fire truck was slowly approaching, but I saw only two firemen. The truck stopped a short distance away, and the firemen jumped out and began working to attach the fire hose to a hydrant on the corner. The people who stood closest got nervous and backed away, clearing a space so we could see what was going on. The firemen finished attaching the nozzle to the hydrant and then rolled the hose toward the police station. The crowd let them through. Then the man standing next to the fire truck turned on the water, and the hose came to life. Now folks realized what was about to happen, and they quickly backed away, so that a wall of people came toward me, and nobody looked where they were going. I almost fell over, but I grabbed the lamppost and regained my balance.

While everyone started running in different directions, I saw Sergeant Oskarsson grab the hose and hold it the way you're supposed to, tucking it firmly under his arm. Then he twisted the nozzle and water came spraying out, glittering in the evening sun. He moved the hose from side to side and cleared the space in front of the police station, and nobody dared go any closer. Oskarsson was already soaking wet, with his hair hanging in his eyes, but he couldn't let go of the hose to push his hair back. He shouted over his shoulder for his men to do something, but they looked uneasy and they stayed where they were on the steps, holding their billy clubs.

For a while it looked like folks would back away even farther. The street in front of the station was now almost deserted because everyone had fled from the spraying water to the side streets. Then some of the men got mad. Suddenly a rock flew through the air, right over my head, and landed at Oskarsson's feet. He ignored it, but the two other policemen took a step back. Then more rocks were thrown. They struck the brick wall above the policemen, doing no damage. But the next one hit an officer, making him yell. He stood still for moment, grimacing as he rubbed his elbow. Then he seemed to go crazy. He ran at the nearest group of men, hitting them again and again with the billy club he was holding in his uninjured hand. His other arm hung limply at his side, and I realized it was probably broken and it must have hurt like hell. More rocks flew through the air, but none seemed to hit their targets.

Then one of the men from the truck came over to us—I think his name was Olsson—and he said, "Give me a hand, boys." We followed him over to the fire hydrant, where men were in the process of unrolling another hose they'd taken out of the fire engine. They handed us one end of the new hose and told us to carry it, and I think at least one of the men standing there was from the fire brigade, but I didn't know who the others were. So we picked up the hose and carried it a short distance away until others in the group came to help and we lifted it over the heads of the nearest bystanders. That's all we did. I tried to grab the arm of the lamppost again to see what was going on, but that was harder to do now that people were coming back from the side streets. Oskarsson must have figured out what was happening, because he said something to his men, and they ran forward, swinging their billy clubs at the arms of the men carrying the new hose so they dropped it just as the water started spraying out. For a while there was a lot of commotion, with people backing away from the entrance to the police station, so I let go of the lamppost again. Even though water was spraying everywhere, I didn't really get wet.

After that something changed. It was like the men standing in front decided not to be scared of the hose Oskarsson was holding. Instead, they banded together. The crowd surged forward and somebody screamed loudly, not from pain but from anger. Maybe it was Oskarsson, because then somebody else was holding the hose, and I saw it was turned in a different direction, toward the front entrance, and water was spraying over the brick façade and splashing over the closed doors. Somebody shouted, "Get the windows!" and when the water was aimed at the big window with the words DULUTH POLICE in gold letters, the glass broke almost instantly. Then they sprayed the other windows until all of them were broken. Now everybody pushed forward in order to see better. We did too. And when we reached the entrance, the door was already open, and water was running down the steps to the street. Water was still spraying from the hose, splashing through the broken windowpanes and doorway, and people were shouting angrily. I wanted to see what was happening, so I went inside with the others. It would have been impossible to turn around because of everyone shoving us from behind. When we got inside, there was water all over the black-and-white checked floor, and through an open door I saw that two soaked constables had put Oskarsson in a chair and were pressing a bloodstained handkerchief to his face. Water kept pouring in until somebody outside must have turned off the hydrant, and when it stopped, everything got so quiet that you could hear water dripping from the ceiling and stairwell. For a moment I wondered why the police were only using billy clubs when they had pistols and even shotguns at the station, but then I didn't give it any more thought. I didn't know where Lester and the others had gone. At first I thought they were with me, but when I looked around, I couldn't see them, and I couldn't go back down the steps because there were too many people. I told myself that I'd never been inside a jail before, so I wanted to have a look at the cells.

For a while there was a lot of noise on the second floor, where one of the constables was still swinging his billy club, until some of the bigger men in front were able to push him down the steps. He landed with his back against all the people crowding onto the stairs. They parted to let him through, shoving him all the way to the bottom. It looked almost comical, as if he were some sort of toy that could climb down ladders. Then he was gone. Somebody shouted after him, because the wooden doors to the cells on the left were locked and the keys were probably still in the policeman's pocket. Someone started pounding on the door panel with a rock, while several young guys that I didn't know caught sight of a fire alarm box farther down the hall, and they ran over and kicked it in. They came back with a sturdy axe, and somebody cheered. Soon they'd broken a hole in the door, and they kept hacking off big pieces of wood. But they still couldn't open the door.

At that point I got bored with the whole situation. I was standing so far in the back that I couldn't see much, and things almost seemed to be returning to normal. So I went over to the opposite end of the corridor, where a door was ajar.

The room inside was only dimly lit, and it smelled of piss. The bars of the cells gleamed in the light from the doorway. I heard what sounded like someone whimpering, so I went in.

The bunks in the first cell were empty. I thought the other one was empty too, until I noticed something move in the far corner. It was real dark, but I stared hard until I was able to see a colored man huddled on the bunk, rocking back and forth. I hadn't seen him at first because he was holding his hands in front of his face and sitting in shadow. He was the one making that whimpering sound. I just stood there, not saying anything. When I turned I saw he wasn't alone. On the other bunk sat an equally dark-skinned boy, a little older than me. He didn't move as he sat there, leaning forward with his hands between his knees, the palms pressed tight together. He was looking at me with wide, red-rimmed eyes, and the acrid smell of sweat was suddenly very strong. He didn't say a word as he stared at me.

All I did was shake my head and back out of there. He kept looking at me until I was out in the corridor. Then I closed the door behind me.

At the other end of the hallway they'd made a big enough hole in the door panel that they could lift up a small man wearing a white shirt and help him through. I knew who he was because he worked at the shipyard. His name was Lundstrom, but he was always called Shorty. By the time I rejoined the crowd, he was already inside. He peeked out and said there was no key there either. The whole stairway was packed with people, and there was no way to get out, so I stayed where I was, wanting to see what would happen when they broke down the door. They began hacking at the panel again, taking turns, and before long only a splinter of wood was left hanging from the hinges, and the rest of the door was in pieces on the floor. Now everyone poured inside to the cell area. It looked about the same as the one at the other end of the corridor, but there were more cells. I couldn't get any closer. Somebody screamed. I couldn't tell whether it was one of the prisoners or someone outside, but I thought it was one of the Negroes. Then I heard some sort of ruckus on the stairs and somebody yelled, "Let us through, goddamnit!" A couple of men appeared, carrying sledgehammers and hoes they'd found somewhere, and the others actually let them through. Then the crowd closed in front of me again, but I heard them hammering at the mortar on the wall, not on the locks to the cell doors. It took a while, and for a time everyone was pretty quiet as they watched the men slowly make a hole in the wall. Somebody threw chunks of concrete into the hallway, right in front of where I was standing. Above the pounding and hammering only one voice could be heard. It must have been one of the Negroes in the cells, and at first I thought he was singing. But then I recognized the words and realized he was saying the Lord's Prayer.

After a long time everyone around me began cheering, and I realized the men were now inside the cell. No matter how I craned my neck, I couldn't see a thing, but I heard the men inside the cell shouting, long and loud. Then the crowd parted in front of me, and three men came forward, dragging one of the colored circus workers between them. He was twisting and turning in their grasp, but when they got to the stairwell and he saw all those people gathered there, the fight went out of him. No one spoke. Then someone on the steps shouted, "They've got them!" and everybody started talking at once. A gap opened up along the wall so the men could take the circus worker down. Leading the way was a big, fat man wearing a hat. I knew his name was Anderson. He kept telling everybody blocking the way to let them through. The men standing closest kicked at the thin prisoner, and several landed punches on his back. I hurried to follow along with everyone else to see what would happen next.

The floor in the foyer of the police station was wet and muddy, with broken window frames and shattered glass everywhere, so you had to watch where you stepped. It felt good to get out into the fresh air again. At the lamppost I ran into Lester, who seemed surprised to see me. "Were you inside?" he said. I asked about the others, and he said they'd gone to see what they were going to do with the prisoner. So we hurried up the street after them.

The whole mob, and now there were several hundred men, had stopped at the corner of Second Avenue. I don't know why they'd chosen that spot, but there was an open space between the buildings and a tall lamppost. When we got there, a boy had already climbed up the post. He was my age, and afterward a lot of folks said I was the one up there, but it wasn't me. I was with Lester the whole time, and we soon found George and Larry too. The boy was straddling the lamp, waving and laughing, as if he'd come to perform some kind of strange circus trick. Somebody shouted to him, "Here, grab this!" and tossed him a rope with a loop. I think it was the same rope I'd seen from the truck, but I'm not sure. The boy grabbed it, but then he hesitated and just sat there. The men standing underneath yelled at him to hurry up and wrap the rope around the section below the lamp, where an ornamental iron piece was meant to look like flower stalks. Then the boy made up his mind and pulled the rope through. After that he slid down from the lamppost and disappeared, and I don't know where he went.

As we were standing there, someone grabbed my shoulder. When I looked up, I saw a priest wearing a black coat and white collar. I realized he was from the Catholic church, because Lester had taken off his cap and said, "Good evening, Father Powers." The priest didn't return the greeting. Instead, he said quickly, sounding out of breath, "Come on, boys. Help me before something terrible happens. Give me a boost up!" Lester knew at once what he meant and bent down with his hands clasped to form a stirrup, and the priest put his foot on his hands. Then I did the same, and George came over and squatted down next to us. Then we lifted the priest up. He wasn't standing steady but rocked back and forth, and it must have looked funny because a bunch of men started laughing.

But Father Powers shouted at the top of his lungs, "Think what you're doing! This is murder, this is a crime, it's forbidden by the laws of God and man!"

He kept on like that, but no one paid any attention. Most people simply turned away. A few shouted, "Shut up!" over their shoulders. A young man wearing blue overalls said calmly, almost politely, "This has nothing to do with the law." Then he turned his back.

Now something was happening up ahead, and no one was looking at us anymore. We put Father Powers down. He said nothing at all, just stood there for a moment, white in the face, before pushing his way through the crowd to try and reach the lamppost from another direction. But I saw how he was shoved aside.

At first I couldn't see what was going on until there were screams and shouts over by the lamppost. A forest of hands rose up in the air, and after a moment I realized they were all reaching for the end of the rope, trying to pull on it. Then the black boy came into view. They had ripped his shirt so it hung down his back, and they'd used it to tie his hands at his waist. Several men dragged him into the open space, and those standing closest kicked at him, striking his stomach and head until Anderson hauled him to his feet again and placed the rope around his neck. The boy's face was bloody, and he kicked his legs wildly. Slowly he was hoisted into the air, but he kept on kicking as he hung there. I couldn't see his face, which was tilted straight up by the noose. I don't think his neck broke, I think he was strangled, because he kicked for a very long time. I heard some people cheering, and more were laughing than when the priest spoke. Then the boy stopped kicking and hung there, motionless. There was just a slight twitching in one leg. When his body went limp, they pulled on the rope and lowered him down until his feet dangled just a short way off the ground. Then they tied the rope tight again.

It was starting to get dark and there was a chill in the air even though it had been a summery temperature just a short time ago. I backed away, thinking I'd seen enough and didn't want to be there any longer. But Lester said, "Where are you going?" "I was thinking of going home," I told him. "But that was only the first one," he said. "There are more. You can't leave now."

As I stood there, not knowing what to do, they brought the second Negro from the circus. A big man wearing a sailor's uniform walked behind him, holding him by the shoulders and pushing him on ahead.

The Negro was struggling and screaming, "No no no no," trying the whole time to look around, but the sailor just smiled and kept shoving him forward. They passed us as we stood there, and then the crowd around the lamppost parted to let them through, and when the boy saw the other Negro who had already been hanged, he seemed to go limp and sagged forward, not saying another word. I think he might have fainted. Then the wall of people closed again and I saw nothing until I heard a scream and the second Negro was hanging there, kicking his legs, just like the first one, but I think this time it took longer before he was hanged and stopped moving. Some people cheered, but not as many as the first time.

I moved a short distance away because I really didn't want to see any more. I made my way around the edge of the crowd, looking for my pals. I didn't see when they brought over the third Negro, but I heard it. After fifteen minutes or so I found Larry down on First Avenue, and then Lester and George showed up. I wanted to go home, but the others wanted to look at the bodies one more time, so we went back and pushed our way forward. More and more people had started to leave, so we managed to get almost all the way up to the lamppost. When we stood there looking at the dead boys, the man from the newspaper came over and took pictures. That was how they knew we'd been there. More people were walking away. The three colored boys hung very still, high up in the light from the streetlamp, with their feet dangling off the ground. Finally we headed down to Third Avenue West and waited for the streetcar. It arrived on schedule, and I still had money in my pocket, so I could afford to take it all the way home. We didn't say anything more to each other before I got off at my stop.

It took several days before the police came to get me. They showed up at work, and then I sat in jail for a week before the trial. But I told them over and over, just like I'm doing now, what happened. And I never held on to any rope.

I don't know how much the letter from my mother had to do with the matter, but several days passed and then Varshey told me he was going to talk to the lawyer. After a week Carlson came back, and this time he was decent and laughed as he unlocked the door. He said, "Congratulations, Hammerberg, you get to go home." They gave me my things wrapped up in brown paper and tied with a string and enough money for the train with a little left over. Onboard the train I sat next to the window and looked at all the snow while I kept on trying to untie the knot but without any luck. Then I walked all the way from the train station because I wanted to try and save a few cents so I wouldn't arrive home empty-handed.

Somebody else had taken my job, and it was hard to find another one. Nobody talked about where I'd been, but once you've been in prison, you can't hide the fact, even if it's a place like St. Cloud. One of my first days home, I ran into Lester and talked to him for a while. He said he was in a hurry, but he stopped and we stood on the street corner, talking like we used to do. George and Larry had moved away and found some sort of work in St. Paul, while Lester was still employed at Riverside. He didn't ask me about how I'd been or where I'd gone, though I assumed he knew. But he did tell me one thing. He'd met that girl who people said had been attacked by the circus workers. She was married now and lived in Superior, and there was nothing wrong with her, as far as Lester could tell. So the people who claimed she'd almost died had made up that story. I thought a lot about that later on, even though I tried not to, but I couldn't help it. Those thoughts kept creeping into my mind. When I asked Lester whether there were any jobs out at the shipyard, he didn't want to talk to me anymore. But he promised to let me know if any came open.

My mother continued to take in sewing jobs, and sometimes she worked at one of the laundries down by the harbor, but it hardly paid anything. And there were plenty of people who wanted those jobs too. Lots of the Negroes in town decided to move away, and then we thought there'd be more work, but it hardly made any difference when they were gone. Finally Mother wrote to Aunt Ellen and told her the situation, and how we couldn't keep on like this, and she asked her whether she could help. Ellen came to visit, but she was in a really bad mood the whole time she was here. She had a little money, and she paid our bills at Spencer's, but she kept on talking about how she had to go back home to her husband and children. And I didn't like the fact that Mother and Aunt Ellen wouldn't let me go out when I wanted to. I said that if I didn't get out and talk to folks, I'd never find a new job, but they insisted that I should stay home as much as possible, especially in the evening. And I didn't feel like arguing all the time. But there was one thing I figured out from what Mother and Aunt Ellen said: we had ended up in Duluth because that's where they thought my father had gone. So he was the one my mother had been looking for, and then we just stayed on. No one knew whether he was alive or not, and I thought it would have been simpler just to say he was dead.

I started going out in the daytime, whenever Mother wasn't home. Then I'd try to stay away for as long as possible. At first I tried to find a job, and I talked to practically everybody I met. But after a while there was nobody left to ask, and I realized I'd have to leave town. Going to Superior wasn't far enough away. I thought I'd have to go to St. Paul or Minneapolis. I'd become friends with Clarence, who couldn't find work either. I'd met him down at the harbor, where I kept running into him day after day. He called himself a stevedore, but he almost never got hired because they thought he was too small, and there was almost no work anyway because it was such a cold winter, with ice covering parts of the lake. He was the one who started talking about going to the Twin Cities. He said there were more jobs to be had, and no one would question who you were. I liked the sound of that last part, but I didn't have any money. Clarence said he didn't either, but his uncle worked for the railroad and he might be able to help us.

On the day we were going to leave, I didn't say anything to Mother, but Aunt Ellen saw that something was going on, and she stopped me at the door. I told her the truth, that I was sick and tired of having nothing to do, and I needed to find work, and if I got a job I'd be able to help my mother instead of her supporting me. We stood in the doorway and talked for a while, and that felt good, like a conversation between grown-ups, and finally she let me go.

Clarence's uncle was big and fat. He chewed tobacco nonstop, and he said almost nothing. We followed him along the tracks at the harbor while he struck the rails with a sledgehammer and listened and spat out streams of tobacco. I thought he'd forgotten that he'd promised to help us, or maybe Clarence had made up the whole story. But Clarence merely grinned and told me to be patient. Then his uncle told us to wait there, and he left. When he came back to get us, we followed him along the tracks until we came to several brown freight cars that smelled of coke. He pointed at one of them and said, "Over there." Clarence climbed in first and held out his hand to pull me inside. Then his uncle shoved the door closed. At first it was pitch-dark, but then I noticed daylight seeping in through the gaps in the walls, and after a while I could make out Clarence sitting in the corner on a pile of sacks. He said we should hide under the sacks in case the railroad police showed up, but I didn't want to do that. I felt heavy-headed from the smell inside the boxcar, but it was a drafty space, so once the train got moving I felt all right. After a while it got real cold, and Clarence showed me how to slip my legs into a sack and then pull a couple more sacks over me. That was a good way to sit, and I didn't feel as cold. It was so noisy that we couldn't really talk much, but after a couple of hours that I mostly spent dozing, Clarence shouted in my ear that I had to get ready to jump. At first I didn't know what he meant, but when the train slowed down Clarence told me to help him shove open the door partway. I saw a bunch of low wooden buildings outside, with snow on the roofs. As the train drove over a small bridge, it decreased speed. When we reached the other side, Clarence yelled, "Now!" and then he jumped. I followed. I scraped the palms of my hands on the frozen gravel because I lost my balance, but otherwise it went fine.

Clarence knew where to go. He said it was just a matter of heading for the smokestack, so that's what we did. The Washburn Mill stood down by the river in the middle of town. It was more like a castle and three times as big as any factory back in Duluth. We followed the high fence around the whole area until we came to a sentry box next to the gate. Sitting inside was a man with white hair and a white mustache. He saw us coming and put down his newspaper. Clarence explained that we'd come from the north looking for work, and the man was as polite and pleasant as could be. But he shook his head and said if there was one thing that was in short supply, it was jobs. Clarence tried to reason with the guard, but then he just stopped talking and picked up his newspaper again.

We'd turned around to go when he called us back. I was the one he wanted to talk to, and at first it didn't occur to me that he was speaking Swedish. When I went back to the sentry box, the guard asked me my name. I said it was Carl and I was from Sweden, or at least my mother was. He asked where she'd come from, and I told him Närke and Örebro, where she was born. He thought about that for a moment and then told me he was from Kumla, which wasn't that far from Örebro. Then he said he really shouldn't be saying this, but if we came back in exactly one week, he'd have a talk with some people he knew, though he couldn't promise anything.

When we left, Clarence looked a little suspicious and asked me several times whether the man really said that, and I told him he did. Then he said we should try and find the freight yard and the Duluth train. It took us several hours to get there, and I was freezing the whole time. We stopped at places along the way, at shops and a smithy, to ask for work. But nobody really had time to talk to us. It was dark by the time we reached the freight yard, and we had to climb over a fence to get to the tracks. I was tired and hungry, but we hadn't brought along anything to eat, so the only thing to do was try and think about something else. I followed Clarence as he walked among the freight cars, and we kept to the far side of them so no one would see us. He read the chalk marks on the doors and shook his head. I'd almost given up when he said, "This one is going in the right direction." It was a big green car with sturdy walls and a sign that said GREAT NORTHERN, with icicles painted underneath. The doors were locked and bolted, but Clarence found a ladder on one side, and he quickly climbed up onto the roof. He wasn't as tired as I was. Then he told me to come up. The roof was made of metal and seemed to give a little as I crawled over it. There was a hatch in the middle, and it was slightly ajar. When both of us grabbed hold and swung it open, warm air gusted up from inside. It was dark and smelled sort of musty down there.

"It's a refrigerator car," said Clarence. "That's good, because they don't open these cars very often."

I was a little scared of going inside, but it seemed to be warm enough, even though it was a refrigerator car. Clarence ran his hand over the roof cornice and then swung himself down so he was hanging by his hands from the edge while he tried to find a foothold. Then he let go and jumped. I heard a thud when he landed and then he yelled from below, "Hurry up before somebody sees you." I tried to do the same thing he'd done, and it wasn't that hard. It was darker inside this boxcar. The only light came from the grill of a coal stove attached to the wall. I didn't understand how this could be a refrigerator car, so I asked Clarence to explain, because he seemed to know about such things. He said that sometimes he'd get hired at the harbor to fill up the tank on the roof with ice from the lake, but this one seemed to be empty at the moment. In fact, it was possible the crates were filled with something that shouldn't be kept cold, and that's why it was warm inside, which was lucky for us. I thought maybe there might be something to eat in the packing cases, but he said we shouldn't open anything, because that was stealing, and it would mean a jail sentence instead of just a reprimand, and this time around it probably wouldn't be St. Cloud. "You'll just have to hold out a little longer," said Clarence, looking up at the hatch. "How can we get that thing closed?" I wondered whether that was a good idea, because it was open when we arrived, but Clarence said that if anyone saw it open, they might get suspicious. We shoved one of the crates to the middle of the floor and then I stood on top of it and Clarence climbed onto my shoulders and was able to pull the hatch shut. Then it was almost pitch-dark, with only a slight glow from the stove.

We sat down in a corner and kept quiet because now we could hear people outside. Someone came over and tried the door to make sure it was properly locked. Then they left. It was nice and warm, and I started to get sleepy, and I must have dozed off for a while. I woke up when the car began moving. Gradually the steady rhythm made me drowsy and I dozed off again.

When I finally woke up, it was completely dark. The fire in the stove had gone out, and I had an awful headache. My mouth was dry, and I could hardly move. I couldn't see anything, but I felt Clarence lying across me, and he wasn't moving at all.

The freight car was thundering along at high speed, and I tried to shout, but no sound came out. Or maybe I just couldn't hear myself. I couldn't breathe, and the darkness was getting blacker, and I didn't really know where I was.

My name was Carl Johan Alfred Hammerberg.

I had nothing to do with hanging the first boy.

I didn't hold the rope, and I didn't do anything else to help.

I don't remember who I saw there. A man wearing a sailor's uniform was there, but I don't know who he was. He was holding the second colored man by the shoulders and laughing.

Then they brought the third one and they hanged him too. I took no part in any of that.

I never held the rope. I never met my father.

*Willard, Minneapolis / Duluth*
November 1922

ELLEN HAD JUST ARRIVED BACK HOME to Sol and the children, hung up her clothes in the wardrobe, and was starting to plan a simple dinner when the telephone rang. Minna, their maid, picked up the telephone out in the hall, and Ellen could hear at once from the girl's tone of voice that something was wrong—wrong in a way that made her grab hold of the kitchen table as she sat there with her grocery list only half-finished.

Minna silently appeared in the doorway. When Sol was present they always spoke English. Sometimes if they were alone in the house, Minna might let slip a word in Swedish. Ellen always made it clear that this was not entirely acceptable by hesitating before she answered or by saying a few phrases in English. But Ellen realized that the girl didn't yet have a full grasp of the new language, and she wanted to offer whatever help she could. So she'd make do with a brief remark, and then she too would switch to Swedish.

Now Minna was standing there, saying in pure Västgötska Swedish, "That was a call from your sister in Duluth, Mrs. Shelby. Or rather from the neighbor lady, because your sister couldn't come to the telephone. Something terrible has happened. You should probably call her back, Mrs. Shelby."

The girl's voice quavered. Ellen looked up and noticed distractedly that Minna's eyes were red-rimmed. It felt as if the floor wouldn't bear her weight as she slowly, with one hand touching the wallpaper, groped her way to the new telephone, the latest Bell model, which hung on the wall.

Then Ellen was back in Duluth, the city of coal smoke and icy winds, only a few days after she'd returned to the Twin Cities. It felt as if she hadn't even left. During the whole train ride north, the same thoughts kept running through her mind: *But I just talked to him last week, right before I went back home. I talked to him. He was there. He stood in the doorway and smiled. Then he left.* She pictured him like that, over and over again, the way he'd smiled and turned around and left. And the way the doorway where he'd just stood was then empty.

The Duluth depot was in the center of town. It was late by the time Ellen got off the train, and naturally she looked around for a cab. But the street outside the station's dark brick façade was deserted. She decided it didn't matter because she couldn't very well take a cab to her sister's lowly rented rooms on Fifty-first Street, far to the south. In her mind's eye she saw how people would stare as she paid the fare and then went into the small courtyard where all the buildings were made of unpainted, silvery-gray wood, and how the Finnish families would turn away after saying a few words in a language she didn't understand. Hunching forward into the wind and carrying her small suitcase, Ellen plodded up the hill to First Street, where she knew she would find a streetcar stop.

No one seemed to be around when she arrived. All the windows were dark, but the front door to the stairwell stood open. She went into the hall, automatically breathing through her mouth. Then she cautiously knocked on Elisabet's door.

It took a moment before someone opened. It wasn't Elisabet but instead the tall, Finnish man that Elisabet always referred to as Matt. He recognized her at once and stepped out into the hallway, quietly closing the door behind him. There they stood in the dim light without saying a word. As Matt looked at Ellen, she noticed he smelled faintly of newly sawn wood. She wondered briefly whether he was a carpenter, and it occurred to her that they'd never discussed what sort of work he did. She was under the impression that he didn't speak either Swedish or English very well.

"She is sleeping," he said now in English. "She has not slept since it happened. We will let her sleep."

"I'm here to help out," said Ellen without looking him in the eye as they stood there in the cramped space of the hall. He was much taller than she was. "I want to help with anything that needs to be done."

"Tomorrow," said Matt. "Go in if you like. But let her sleep."

He put on his cap and headed for the front door of the building. He turned around before stepping outside.

"Tomorrow," he repeated. "Have to work now. Let her sleep."

He gave Ellen a nod and left. She pushed open the door as quietly as she could. The curtains were drawn and the room was dark, but she knew instinctively where every piece of furniture stood. She went over to the kitchen table, set her suitcase on the floor, and cautiously pulled out one of the unpainted chairs. Then she sat down and closed her eyes. She pictured Carl again, smiling that crooked smile of his, as if he were thanking her for allowing him to go. Then he was gone.

When she opened her eyes again, it was still dark, and all she heard was her sister's steady, tranquil breathing from the bedroom alcove.

Elisabet was surprisingly calm when she awoke. But it was not the right sort of calm. She wouldn't look directly at Ellen, nor did she greet her. At first she didn't seem to realize that her sister had been away for several days and had now returned. Elisabet didn't seem to be fully present. That lasted until Ellen heated up some water and poured it into a basin so Elisabet could wash herself. When she went to get the green soap from the sink, she heard behind her back a low scream issue from Elisabet's throat. When she went over to her sister, she found her standing there, wearing only her shift, and crying as she bent her face over the steaming water. At first it was ordinary crying, but then she started sobbing loudly until the sound coming from her mouth was more like the howl of a wounded animal. Ellen quickly reminded herself that the neighbors knew what had happened. She noticed fleetingly that Elisabet seemed to have gotten quite plump around the middle. Then she stepped forward and put her arms around her sister's waist, intending to make her stand up. But Elisabet refused to budge. She held on tight to the countertop as she kept on sobbing with her mouth open and her face turned away. Ellen leaned forward and laid her cheek on Elisabet's back, hearing how horror and shock strained at her sister's lungs and airways. They stood there like that, leaning on each other, for a long time, until Elisabet's sobs became a soundless shuddering that went on and on. Ellen didn't let go until she grew calm.

Early in the morning Mrs. Janson came over. She was a short, thin woman in her forties who was prematurely gray and wore clothes the same color as her hair. She seemed almost to fade into the unpainted, weather-beaten wood of the walls behind her. She spoke Swedish with a heavy Finnish accent.

"We received a message," she said now to Ellen. "It is from your mother. She wants you to call a telephone number in St. Paul. They are waiting for you to call back."

She had jotted down the number on a little piece of cardboard, but Ellen already knew it by heart.

She followed Mrs. Janson into their small kitchen, which didn't seem to have been aired out since the summer. There she saw the telephone on the wall, shiny and black like a big, fat insect. She was reluctant to touch the receiver, but she didn't want to wipe if off while Mrs. Janson was watching. So she picked it up and quickly asked for the number to Larson's grocery store.

Anna instantly came on the line. They didn't waste words. Her mother spoke quickly and a little out of breath, the way people sound if they're not used to talking on the telephone, and especially if it's long distance.

"We can't come," Anna said. "The tickets. We can't afford them. Not the whole way there."

"I'll wire you money," said Ellen. "Do you hear me, Mother? I'll send the money. Go to the railway depot and talk to them at the ticket booth. Do you hear me? I'll wire the money."

"Your father," said the insect-like voice on the other end. "Your father will be mad."

For a moment neither spoke, and Ellen heard only the wind tugging at the telephone wires through the miles and miles of forest.

"You have to come," she said then, keeping her voice matter-of-fact but implacable. It was the same voice she used with Sol whenever he was unreasonable. "You have to think of Elisabet, Mother. Let Father be mad. He'll calm down on the train trip north."

Again silence.

"We'll pay you back," said Anna from a great distance. Ellen pictured her standing in the grocery store with her back to the row of big glass jars filled with candy. That was actually the only thing she remembered about Larson's store: the way the jars gleamed from up on the shelf, beyond the reach of a child's hands. It occurred to her only now that during the entire telephone conversation, her mother had been crying steadily.

"I'll tell Elisabet that you'll be here tonight," she said calmly. "On the nine o'clock train. Say hello to Father for me."

Then she tried to put the receiver back on its hook, but she was shaking so hard she almost dropped it. The whole time she could feel Mrs. Janson staring at her back. She paused for a moment before turning around. In a firm voice she asked whether there was anywhere for Elisabet's parents to stay the night.

Ellen had never really understood what sort of town Duluth was. It didn't seem to have any open spaces or parks, and the streets were laid out along the hillsides like terraces, all of them on their way somewhere else. The whole town seemed to her to be built on slopes. No one went down to the shore of Lake Superior, because that's where the railroad tracks were, as well as warehouses that extended as far as the eye could see. It was impossible to get any overview of the town, and the wind blew constantly through the long, straight streets. But she found her way down to the train station.

Her parents were standing outside the waiting room door, and her father was holding an all-too-familiar worn suitcase. It was the one they'd brought from Sweden so long ago. From a distance they looked small and stooped, and Ellen hurried forward, as if afraid the wind might blow them away. But when she got closer and they looked up, she saw the steely look in her father's eyes.

"Where's Elisabet?" he asked.

Anna nodded and managed a thin smile.

"She's at home," Ellen told them. "She's not very strong. It comes and goes."

When she said that, her mother gave a start and stepped forward as if to hurry on, but she had no idea which way to go.

"She's waiting for us," said Ellen. "We'll take the streetcar."

She turned to lead the way, but her father stood still, with one hand resting on his wife's shoulder, as if to hold her back.

"You're not to pay for anything else," he said. "We'll walk."

"But it's a long way. And the streetcar isn't expensive."

He simply stood there, and at first Ellen thought they were going to have a big argument over this. But then Anna simply took her by the arm, and the two of them began walking up the hill. Ellen didn't look back, yet she knew her father was following, staying a few steps behind them, as if to signal his disapproval.

They sat across from each other at the very back of the streetcar, which shook so much as it climbed the hill that it was hard to talk. Finally her father said something, and she leaned forward to catch his words when he repeated them. She tucked a strand of hair behind her ear to indicate she was listening. He recognized the gesture and smiled briefly, a warm smile that for a moment took her back to another time and place. Then it passed.

"I asked you whether Sol is here."

Ellen shook her head.

"Somebody had to stay home and see to the children," she said apologetically.

"So they're not coming either."

It was not a question, but she shook her head.

"They didn't know Carl," she said quietly, as if to herself.

"We didn't either," said Anna without taking her eyes off the window. "Not anymore."

There was nothing to see out there except the winter darkness and an occasional streetlight. After a while they were the only passengers in the streetcar.

"Why didn't he come to us?" said her father.

That wasn't meant to be a question either, and Ellen realized it was something he'd been repeating to himself, sometimes out loud, but most often silently: *Why didn't he come to us?*

None of them spoke again until it was time to get off the streetcar.

When they came into the kitchen, they found Elisabet sitting there, waiting for them. On the table was a single, lit candle. Otherwise the room was dark. She got up and stood there, motionless. In the dim light she suddenly looked so small and girlish.

"Mother," she said. "Father."

She curtsied. They were standing in the doorway. Gustaf was still holding the suitcase, as if he didn't dare set it down, afraid of shattering the fragile peace that had now closed so mercilessly around them. Anna stepped forward and took Elisabet's hands. They stood there for a moment, looking at each other without saying a word. Then Elisabet collapsed into her mother's arms. She started crying again, soundlessly, her back shaking. And Ellen thought, *How small Mother has suddenly become.*

She hadn't personally viewed Carl's body, which someone else had washed and dressed, probably Mrs. Janson. But Elisabet had seen him and, in a lucid moment, she said that he was unmarked and looked as if he were simply asleep. Now a coffin newly made of unpainted light pine rested in the middle of the wagon bed. It was the only bright spot in the yard; everything around them was gray. The wagon was headed for Oneota Cemetery, which wasn't far, so the mourners could walk. It had been decided that Elisabet and her father should sit next to the wagon driver, and everyone else would follow on foot.

A group of people had gathered to make their way to the cemetery in the gray morning light—so many dark-clad figures. They were already standing in the cramped inner courtyard when the family stepped outside into the cold. It was overcast with a chance of snow.

Slowly the wagon set off. Ellen watched anxiously as the coffin began to clatter when they reached the uneven surface of the uphill slope. She reminded herself that the lid had been screwed down tight, but then she felt ashamed at the thought and lowered her eyes. Anna was clinging to her arm, looking so small and fragile. With her other hand she clutched the ends of her black shawl, which she had wound twice around her head because of the wintry cold. But she wore no gloves.

The wagon soon pulled away from the mourners, but the others in the group knew the way. Ellen didn't recognize any of them except for Mrs. Janson and the tall man named Matt, who was silently walking at the very back. She had no idea who the others were. Neighbors, she thought, or maybe fellow workers. She had thought people would stay away because Carl had been in prison, even though it was for something he hadn't done. But she saw fifteen mourners, not counting Matt and Mrs. Janson. The road continued uphill, the way every road seemed to do in this town.

Later Ellen would not remember what the pastor had said. She could recall the faces of those standing nearest, but her own gaze was swallowed up by the grave. The pale winter light was such that the freshly dug grave opened to an impenetrable, steep black shadow. It was impossible to look down into the hole without speculating on how deep it must be. Six feet. It might as well have been a door open to the night. The coffin stood next to it, with the ropes at the ready. But not yet. And she noticed that her sister, who stood beside her, was also feeling dizzy from the darkness at their feet, yet she too kept looking down into the grave. Neither of them sang along with the simple hymn, and only a few days later Ellen tried in vain to remember whether the words had been in Swedish or not.

Then the moment arrived. Four men stepped forward and placed the ropes around their shoulders. They were familiar with the procedure; they'd done this before. The pine coffin looked so lightweight as it slowly sank into the darkness. The men didn't seem to strain at all; they looked calm and composed. Then it disappeared forever. The ropes came back up into the light.

That was when Elisabet fell to her knees on the frost-covered grass. At first Ellen thought her sister wanted to follow the coffin into the grave, so she stepped forward and placed her hands on Elisabet's shoulders, but through the thick wool of her coat, her body felt as hard as stone. At first she refused to budge. She did not move closer to the edge of the grave, nor did she get to her feet. She stayed where she was, unyielding and withdrawn.

Gustaf had also taken a step forward, but Ellen met his eye and shook her head. They looked at each other, as he stood very close to his daughters.

As if from a great distance the pastor again began to speak. He said a few brief remarks in English, and Ellen heard the sound of frozen gravel falling onto the lid of the coffin down below, but her eyes were fixed on Elisabet's blonde head. She had to remain alert; anything could happen. But her sister didn't move as she knelt there, and that's where she stayed for the rest of the graveside service.

Afterward everyone hurried away in small groups, as if to leave the family in peace. The pastor came over and said a few words in English to Gustaf, who shook his head as if he didn't understand, though Ellen knew he did. Then her father put on his cap and they both squatted down next to Elisabet. Speaking in a gentle voice that Ellen hadn't heard since they were children, he said it was time to go. Then they each took Elisabet by the arm and lifted her up. She seemed to weigh so little, and her feet hardly touched the grass. She was still staring down at the black opening of the grave, and she didn't say a word. The three of them then walked arm in arm toward the cemetery gate, with Anna following two steps behind, until all of them were out on the cobblestone street.

Elisabet looked around as if just awaking, and now she was able to stand on her own. They chatted with her for a good while, as if they wanted to make sure she was really there. She seemed to be herself again and responded lucidly. They talked about whether to go back to the apartment building, where Mrs. Janson was no doubt waiting to serve coffee. Then Elisabet gave a bland smile, seemingly out of habit. As her family hunched their shoulders against the cold wind blowing off Lake Superior, she said, "I suppose it's time to go home."

"Yes," Ellen heard herself say without looking at her parents, who were standing off to one side, like a couple of shadows at the edge of her vision. "Yes. Let's go home."

*Swede Hollow*
May 1928

Gustaf had always been fascinated by the way the big wheels of the locomotives turned, the way the eccentric shaft started up and then, moving back and forth, actually shoved the wheels around and set the whole enormous engine in motion, along with all the train cars. He'd been thinking about it ever since that accident happened so many years ago, the one that had cost engine driver Rossi his life. The way the eccentric rod had shot straight through the steel wall and speared his body, presumably before he had time to notice anything. It must have shot through with tremendous force. And yet, what pressure, depending on a single little nut and bolt that had to carry all the force that was needed, not just once but for years. If folks knew that, Gustaf sometimes said, they'd never dare travel by train.

Ever since he'd started working inside at the locomotive repair shop, he'd pondered these sorts of things, sitting in the evening with pen and paper and trying to figure out how the various mechanisms functioned. Not that he was personally responsible for such matters—that was the job of the foremen, who told the men what had to get done. But Gustaf lived in dread of making a mistake. Somebody had made a mistake and that had cost Rossi his life. A cracked nut or a loose screw, and everything could literally be transformed into a hell of twisted metal and hissing steam.

Anna told him not to brood about it so much. After all, he knew what he was supposed to do when asked, and he was very handy.

These days they had the evenings to themselves. In spite of everything that had happened, Elisabet was still living up in Duluth with Matt, her new Finnish beau whom they'd hardly seen except at the funeral. And Ellen and her mysterious Solomon, whom they'd met only at the wedding and on a few occasions afterward, lived far away on the other side of Minneapolis. So Gustaf and Anna had plenty of time to talk and pay attention to other things. But he tired more easily now, and that was one reason Foreman Lawson had finally found him a job indoors. Yet Gustaf couldn't get thoughts of the mechanism out of his head. Especially the part about the circular disk.

Lately Gustaf had been dwelling more and more on matters like the "eccentric," which was often talked about at the shop. He picked up words and associations during the course of his work, without really thinking about it. One evening he sat down and cut up pieces of cardboard from a box he'd found behind Larson's grocery store and brought home. He asked Anna for some thread and needles. Then he sat with his carpenter's pencil and her sewing box in front of him on the table and tried to put together wheels and axles so they would move. He hadn't worked with needle and thread since he stopped making shoes, and his fingers quickly faltered. But finally he got the model put together.

"All right," he said, showing Anna the model, which he'd placed on the table. "The piston goes down here and shoves the rod that way. And then the wheels turn. What's so ingenious is that first you get movement that goes around like a wheel, and then it changes to an up-and-down motion—which is transformed again into a turning motion, without losing too much power. That's the part that's so strange."

He tugged at the cardboard pieces to show her what he meant, and she politely pretended to be interested.

It was one thing to figure out how things functioned so that he wouldn't seem like a Swedish idiot on the job, but in fact he was utterly fascinated with the mechanisms. For decades he had worked alongside train engines, observing their movement out of the corner of his eye, and over time he'd become more and more hypnotized by the motion. The wheels turned, the eccentric rod moved back and forth, but then there was the circular disk, the *eccentric* itself, which drove the whole locomotive by virtue of being offset. It rotated *poorly,* as he said to himself; the disk was the misfit detail, the one thing that didn't function like all the other parts. But without it, the train could not be driven forward. It moved out of sync with the rest of the machinery, as if it actually was loose and risked coming off. But that's how it was supposed to be. Otherwise nothing would function.

Gustaf tried to explain to Jonathan Lundgren what he was thinking, because there weren't many others he could talk to about these matters. But Jonathan gave him an odd look and finally said, "You probably shouldn't talk so much about the *eccentric* when anyone is listening, or pretty soon they'll be making that your nickname at work."

And of course Jonathan was right. Yet there was something about it that meant Gustaf couldn't let go. It was the most important part of the machinery, the one thing on which everything depended because it did *not* move in a balanced and harmonic way. It was purposely different, and it was indispensable. This signified a truth that he couldn't put into words. He was unable to explain what he was thinking either to his wife or to his best friend and workmate.

But there was a deeper reason why he was having such a hard time letting these thoughts go. It was because he had the same sort of movement going on inside him. All of a sudden something would swerve inside his chest, catching him in midstride so he almost blacked out and for a moment his pulse would quicken. Then everything would return to normal. At first this didn't happen very often, but gradually it began occurring almost once a week, on his way to work as he walked up the stairs to Seventh Street, or on the steep slope while going through the tunnel toward Beaumont Street. Whenever it happened, he would pause for a moment and lean against the stair railing or tunnel wall as he thought, *It's the* eccentric*—the part that has been rotating so asymmetrically and yet prompted forward motion so that you got where you were supposed to go. It was that specific, unbalanced part that was always necessary for a functioning machine.* Then the sensation would pass.

Yet Gustaf knew that wasn't really the crux of the matter.

"Eighteen ninety-four and the Pullman strike," said Jonathan Lundgren. "You weren't here at the time. And the workshop strike of 1922. Those were the worst years. In '94 and '95, I ended up working as a lumberjack for a while, but then I was able to come back here. A lot of men couldn't. I was so young back then, and I had no idea what was really going on."

Lately Lundgren's hair had begun to turn white; it started with his beard stubble and then worked its way up to his head. Gustaf thought this seemed strange because his friend's face still looked young, with only a few wrinkles; or maybe it was because he was so used to seeing Jonathan on a daily basis that he simply didn't notice the changes creeping in. In Gustaf's mind, Jonathan looked the way he'd always looked. And he still moved like a young man; time didn't seem to have slowed him down any. That was not the case with Inga. After giving birth to two children, she found it increasingly difficult to get around. She never complained, but it was evident that she was in pain whenever she was forced to walk any distance.

Inga kept bringing over newspapers and brochures from Chicago that she'd subscribed to, both in Swedish and English. These publications wrote about such things as the execution of the Italians Sacco and Vanzetti over in Massachusetts. Gustaf didn't care for the fact that his friends Jonathan and Inga talked so much about things that took place far away in other states, incidents that would only provoke anxiety if you let yourself get too immersed in them. Every day Gustaf was forced to listen to Jonathan's opinions about one thing or another. Although he found it interesting to know that Sacco had apparently also started out as a shoemaker.

Personally, he'd always been more inclined to take one day at a time. He didn't know how anyone could do any different; you had to deal with whatever was right in front of you, otherwise you'd never make it to the next problem that needed to be solved. If you raised your eyes too far off what you were dealing with at the moment, you'd fall over and not be able to get up again.

Gustaf didn't understand what was at the heart of it all, but everything led back to David, who had now been in prison for more than twenty-five years. The thought that his brother had apparently not committed the actual murder had been gnawing at Jonathan ever since the first time he'd told Gustaf about it. This was a matter of *justice,* and Lundgren gradually got more and more obsessed with the issue. He couldn't make peace with the situation the way David seemed to have done. The more it gnawed at him, the bigger the hole became where *justice* ought to be. But it often got to be too much for Gustaf when Lundgren started ranting about the subject. He would simply give up trying to follow his arguments, even though he walked along beside him every day, listening to him say things like, "Sacco and Vanzetti were innocent, just like Joe Hill was." But when Lundgren tried to drag Carl, Elisabet's Carl, into the discussion and repeat Inga's claim that the boy had been unjustly sent to St. Cloud, Gustaf could no longer keep silent. "Leave Carl out of it!" he said.

That was one of the things he couldn't bear to think about too much, or it would reopen the same sort of hole inside him that he sensed inside Jonathan. Behind Elisabet's Carl was his own son Carl, an increasingly hazy and yet still moving shadow. Both had disappeared into a darkness, and it did no good to look at that for long. There were no words for such things. He had no words.

Now it was specific dates that Jonathan Lundgren was rambling on about. *Eighteen hundred ninety-four* was long before Gustaf and Anna had even thought about going to the United States. A year so far back in time that it was impossible to imagine, even though Lundgren had already been here in Minnesota. But it was worse trying to make peace with *1922.* That was when he and Lundgren were still working out on the line, doing repairs and maintenance, sometimes together with one of the Gavin "boys," whom they'd begun to understand better, even though the Irishman's English was still difficult to figure out. Gustaf remembered everything, but as if through a fog. It was right at the time when they'd heard that Elisabet's Carl had died in a refrigerator boxcar that might have actually passed where they were working, though they couldn't have known or done anything about it. Gustaf and Anna had hardly seen anything of the boy after he turned three. That was when Elisabet had made the crazy decision to move to Duluth. Suddenly Carl was dead, and they tried to scrape together the money for train tickets to Duluth. Gustaf could have undoubtedly traveled in the fireman's cabin, but in order for Anna to overcome her reluctance to leave the Hollow for a few days, they'd been forced to travel in an ordinary third-class compartment. Finally Anna had gone behind his back and borrowed the money from Ellen, which he hadn't liked. Afterward he'd paid back every penny.

As for the funeral up there in the north, Gustaf remembered that it was cold but with less snow than at home, although everything had been heavily coated with frost—the ground and trees, the lampposts and roadways. At night a thick, new layer of freezing fog had drifted in from Lake Superior. The shape of the harbor's aerial lift bridge resembled a frozen cloud statue. When they tossed earth onto the coffin, the hard clumps pounded on the wood like a minor avalanche. Elisabet silently fell to her knees on the frozen grass, and they practically had to carry her away from there, but she was no longer crying. Maybe she was already pregnant with her daughter at the time. There were moments during those days when she was ripped apart by grief and sorrow, and then she would suddenly recover and appear calm and withdrawn, as if she'd found something completely different to think about. That was when Gustaf had occasionally feared for her sanity, but afterward he thought he understood. The Finnish man—Matthew? Matt?—was already there in the background, though he said little and was never introduced as her fiancé.

Personally, Gustaf could never connect the dead boy they'd left behind with the blond three-year-old he remembered, in certain ways a bit like his own Carl, and yet so different.

That whole spring of 1922 seemed unreal to him. He noticed the agitated atmosphere around him when he was on the job, but he was wrapped up in his own thoughts, as was so often the case. At issue were the working conditions of the mechanics and repair shop workers, the men who labored inside the long, high-ceilinged train repair shops. He didn't really know any of them and only went inside to pick up tools. In the late spring the linemen held a meeting outdoors, out of sight of the supervisors and foremen. Everyone agreed that the latest wage cut for shop workers was so unreasonable, as they said, that soon it would spill over onto workers further down in the system, the way it always did.

They solemnly and unanimously promised each other not to take on any work that would break the strike called by the repair shop workers, when and if that occurred. But nobody thought they would have to walk off the job themselves; they assumed they could continue working outside the repair shops as usual. And that's what happened when the shop workers went on strike in July. Word was relayed to the various work crews not to take over any of the positions that were left vacant within the repair shops. But, as Jonathan Lundgren said, that would have been difficult anyway because all the men who walked off the job had taken their tools home with them, so there wasn't so much as a screwdriver left in the whole place.

A strange quiet settled in. The engine drivers, who were not part of the strike, backed the train cars in need of service into the big rail yard, which was soon so crowded that it was practically impassable. Gustaf had never seen so many cars in one place. In the Twin Cities there were maybe seven or eight thousand strikers who gathered for a meeting downtown. The streets were again blocked with crowds of men wearing work clothes, evidently on their way to workplaces where the gates were now closed. The strike spread from coast to coast and lasted a long time during that remarkably dry, hot summer when everything continued on as usual, though with fewer trains on the line and consequently fewer accidents. As the men went about their daily tasks, it was eerily calm.

This time the strike was not broken but instead faded slowly away. More and more of the repair shop workers simply found other jobs. There was work to be had up north in the mining district or across the border in Winnipeg. Both the Great Northern and the Northern Pacific were viewed as fully justified in hiring new men to fill the jobs left open. In September, the U.S. Supreme Court issued a ban on demonstrations and picket lines, and soon after that the strike was over.

Rumors began circulating about a secret list of troublemakers and socialists, and eventually there were few workers left in the shops of the Great Northern. Word was that there were no jobs, or not enough jobs to rehire those who came back after the strike. Yet trains were still parked because they hadn't been serviced on schedule, and there were no new engines ready to put into use. And more and more men headed north.

It was in late October that Foreman Lawson sought out Gustaf. He put his arm around him in a friendly manner and said, "It seems to me that you've been working out in the cold for too many years, Klar. Maybe we should try and find you a job inside the shop now that we're in need of more men. Let me talk to the supervisor."

Gustaf thanked him, and they shook hands on it. By the following week he was already starting his new job indoors. And right after that a job came open for Jonathan Lundgren as well.

Now Jonathan wanted to drag all of that up again with his talk of 1922. It was as if he felt a need to harp on something that was bothering his conscience.

"It wasn't handled fairly," he said, but Gustaf defended himself. They hadn't taken those jobs away from anyone else. Nobody had stepped in to fill the positions left vacant while the strike was going on, but by October the strike was over. Men had left the railroad behind and found work elsewhere, so there was a need for more workers.

Lundgren didn't react to his objections as they kept walking. Not until Gustaf brought up his one remaining argument: "This is the only kind of work I can do, now that I can't make shoes anymore." Then his friend grunted, nodded, and for the moment at least he let the subject drop.

Spring was on its way into summer. Gustaf walked along with a trace of fatigue and listlessness in his blood, which always seemed to happen around this time. But so far it hadn't let go of him, even though the end of May was fast approaching. He had a hard time getting out of bed in the morning, in spite of the fact that it was light outside, he could smell coffee brewing on the stove, and there was fresh cornbread. Previously, he'd always boasted of being an early riser, but this spring the weariness and torpor refused to leave his body.

On this morning Jonathan was waiting for him on the hill, even though he was a few minutes late. They set off immediately at their usual pace, but then Gustaf noticed he was out of breath, so he suggested to Jonathan that today they should take the route through the railroad tunnels instead of climbing the stairs. Jonathan nodded, and they turned off to take the little footbridge over Phalen Creek. The creek already stank, and they breathed through their mouths as they walked across the planks.

Jonathan didn't start in on his usual topics of conversation until they'd passed the Irish sector and had gone through the tunnels. Then he said, in a lower voice and sounding more serious than normal, "There's a meeting tonight, and it's important. We should stay after work for a while. I've talked to Inga, so at least she knows I might be late."

Gustaf felt an instant aversion rise up all the way from his feet. Yet another meeting, yet another plan about how to prepare again for a threatened "adjustment" to their wages. He merely nodded.

* * *

At first Gustaf had planned to stay after work too, if for no other reason than his loyalty to Jonathan. But after lunch they had to dismantle the outer casing of the steam boiler on one of the older locomotives that was now used only within the rail yard itself. There was nothing unusual about the task. They fastened chains around the loosened metal and pulled, first with four men lifting, and then the chain was rolled onto a reel, which one person could handle on his own. Gustaf was part of the crew, helping with the lifting maneuver until they'd raised the big metal piece up in the air and all the chains were where they were supposed to be. Then Gustaf let go and took a step back, listening to the steady, almost pleasant clatter as the chains were wound up. But something was still moving inside him. When he closed his eyes, things started spinning and he couldn't tell which way was up or down. And the big wheel inside him was turning; he could do nothing to stop it. He leaned his back against the wall and waited for the dizzy feeling to subside. It didn't.

One of the other men in the crew, a short Italian by the name of Davini, turned to Gustaf and shouted something over the noise. He couldn't make out what the man said, but he thought it might be, "Are you all right?" He nodded and turned away as nausea suddenly seized hold of him. He needed fresh air or he might throw up.

But he didn't feel any better outdoors. He looked up at the sky and then decided to go home. He had to leave. He went back inside to get his jacket and put it on. His pulse was pounding in his temples, and he felt a headache coming on. Out of the corner of his eye he saw Jonathan Lundgren walking toward him through the machine shop, and he was just about to say to him, "I don't feel like talking about your damn meeting right now," but he merely held up his hand with his fingers splayed, in a gesture halfway between "Stop" and a goodbye wave. Lundgren paused and looked at him in surprise. Then Gustaf backed out the half-open door.

He had taken this same route both morning and evening for more than twenty-five years, but today it seemed to him hopelessly long. Finally he reached the railroad tunnels, which even in the afternoon light seemed to wind their way into their own darkness. This was where he'd fought one night with O'Tierney, now long dead, back when he was still young.

At the spot where the slope headed up past the Italians' shanties, right next to the house where Horrible Hans and Agnes Karin once lived, Gustaf paused to catch his breath. He didn't know how he was going to make it all the way up. Then he leaned toward one of the elms and held on to the tree with both hands. Nausea overtook him, and he threw up on the trunk, first yellow and then white vomit. He didn't care whether anyone saw him; maybe they would think he was drunk. Then he stood still, sweating. After a while the shivering diminished and he thought he felt better. He tried to picture how the lack of balance inside him was actually what would drive him up the hill. Then he let go of the tree and walked home.

Anna looked up with alarm when her husband came in. She was folding sheets and putting them away in the linen cabinet that Gustaf had built the previous summer. He stood in the doorway, leaning on the frame, and said simply, "I got so tired. I'm not feeling well." She took him by the arm and drew him inside, where she sat him down on a chair at the kitchen table. Then she helped him undress, found him a clean nightshirt, and tucked him into bed. The sheets were clean, and the pillowcase smelled of starch. He wasn't feeling so bad anymore, but he dozed off.

When he woke up, it was evening. Anna was sitting on a chair next to the bed, and she'd lit a candle on the table.

"Jonathan was here, asking how you were," she said. "I told him you were sleeping."

Gustaf nodded as he lay there in bed. She asked whether he was hungry, and he said no. Then neither of them spoke for a while. It was nice just lying there without having to think of anything in particular. He stuck one arm out from under the blanket and took his wife's hand. It was dry and cool, but after a while he felt her skin warm up. He was scared, but he didn't want to frighten her. Yet she knew that something serious was about to happen to them.

He dozed off again, and when he awoke it was pitch-dark outside. Anna was still sitting there, holding his hand in both of hers, when there was a light knock on the door. She didn't get up but simply said quietly, "Come in." Jonathan stuck his head in and took off his cap.

"Inga says if you're not better by tomorrow, she'll call the doctor for you. She also says," he added with some embarrassment, "that you can't say no." Then he nodded and pulled the door closed after him.

"The doctor," said Gustaf, trying to laugh. He was sweating and the nausea had returned. Anna noticed and asked if he wanted something to drink. He said no, although the thought passed through his head that he wouldn't mind a dram, though he'd hardly touched strong liquor since they'd arrived in this new country of theirs.

"Inga's right," said Anna. "Tomorrow we'll call a doctor for you."

"Inga is always right," he said a bit spitefully. "But it costs money."

"Ellen can pay for it," said Anna. "I'm sure she will if we ask her. I'll call her tomorrow."

At first he wanted to refuse. Then he thought about how they'd met Ellen and her son and daughter in Elliot Park the last time they'd seen her. It was always like that. They'd meet in a park somewhere, never at her home or here in the Hollow. Solomon hadn't been with them. The children had politely greeted their grandparents in English and then run off to the swing sets. The grown-ups sat in the sun for a while, talking about nothing. Then they'd gone their separate ways. That was back in early autumn. Since then they'd had only a Christmas card from her, which they'd picked up at Larson's grocery.

Now Gustaf thought, *I'd like to see them again, and if she pays for the doctor, maybe she'll come over.* Then he realized he'd said this aloud.

"I'm sure she will," said Anna. "Would you like to rest for a while now?"

"But what about you?" he said. "Aren't you tired? Shouldn't you go to bed?"

"I'll sit here for the time being," she said. "And watch over you while you sleep."

Then she stroked his forehead and hair again and again, much the same way someone might pet a cat. It felt lovely, and he fell asleep.

When he awoke, he again felt like vomiting, so he sat up and pushed aside the blanket. He was soaked with sweat. The gray light of dawn was coming through the window. Something was already dripping down his chin, and he tried to wipe it away with his hand. In the faint glow from the candle, which was close to burning out, he saw that his hand was black with blood. Trembling, he stood up, covering his mouth with his hand. Anna had fallen asleep in her chair, but now she sat up with a jolt and said, "What is it?"

"I need to go out," he told her. His voice gurgled so it was hard to make out his words. "Otherwise I'll bleed all over everything."

"Lie down," she said, putting her hands on his shoulders. His whole body was now shaking with cold, and he had no strength to resist. She gently pushed him back down onto the bed.

Then he looked up at her in a panic, unable to utter a word. Something burst inside him, and a river of blood poured down his chin and over the sheet and blanket. She held both of his hands in a tight grip, watching every movement as his head tilted back; she leaned over him and looked into his eyes. He looked back at her and then he was gone.

* * *

She sat beside him for a while, holding his hand and crying quietly. Then she abruptly stopped, loosened his still warm fingers, and clasped his hands on his chest. She looked around for something to tie around his jaw. She set a new candle next to him and lit it. Then she stood there for a moment, looking down at the bed, which he'd built shortly after they moved into the house. He did not look peaceful. There were sharp lines around his mouth, and his lips were drawn back, as if he were about to say something. But his eyes were closed, and he looked like he was sleeping. She rattled off the Lord's Prayer a few times. Then she went outside to the porch. That was also something he had built. In a minute she would walk up to Inga and Jonathan's house and wake them, and they would realize at once what had happened. She stood still and looked out across the Hollow and thought, *Let them sleep a little longer. There's nothing they can do.*

All was quiet in the Hollow. It looked the way it would if all the people had left. She searched her memory, thinking the trees seemed taller and more numerous than when they first arrived. But it had been winter back then, with snow, and the tree branches were bare, allowing them to see all the way down to the railroad tunnel. In an hour the day would awake and everything would be the same as always. The sun wasn't yet visible through the trees up on Dayton's Bluff, but somewhere below, down among the bushes around Phalen Creek, a thrush was singing, faint and muted in the foliage.

*It's just me now,* she realized, and the thought settled inside her as if, in spite of everything, she'd been prepared for this. *For a short time yet, it's just me.* And, oddly enough, she found that she wasn't scared. Soon she'd go back inside to him and make sure he was laid out properly. She would wipe away the blood and change the bedclothes, and for the last time they would be alone together.

*Duluth / Swede Hollow*
June 1928

WE WERE ALL ABOUT TO GATHER for one last time, including Father, whom we would leave behind in the ground. Ellen called and left a message for me with Mrs. Janson. It's strange how everything has to be in such a hurry even though it's already too late. I remember the previous time when we were all together, that was also for a funeral, and it was my Carl who was going to be laid to rest, and I screamed inside for a week without managing to utter a sound. Except to Matti, who didn't say much either, but he was there the whole time, and he made the coffin for Carl; he worked on it for two nights, hammering and planing the wood without me asking him to do that, and he refused to take even a nickel in payment. But I didn't tell anyone about that because Ellen might have got it into her head to pay him, and then everything would have been ripped open and turned into words again. The worst moment in my life was when we had to leave the gravesite; I couldn't do it, I no longer knew what to do, and yet in a strange way part of me was thinking about what would happen the next day and the next, and even the next month. It was like I'd been turned inside out, with everything painful on the outside and everything you could have faith in hidden away and beyond reach. I don't know how else to describe it.

When I heard that Father was dead, I wasn't surprised, even though he'd looked healthy and fit the last time I saw him, but something sank inside of me for good, a weight that I'd never be able to get rid of again. I pictured it like the elevator counterweight I'd seen in an office building that I was cleaning down at the harbor. The weight was like a big black shadow that slid past inside the shaft, moving in the opposite direction before the elevator appeared—a heavy and inaccessible piece of darkness. And I said to Matt, "Matti, I can't stay in Duluth, even though this is where Carl is buried, and you live here, but little Elsa and I have to go back to the Twin Cities," and he just nodded and said he understood that's how things were. And then he said, "Let's just wait and see." I was never afraid of what he would say; it might take a while but after he'd thought things through, he would always have something sensible to say. I was worried about how it would be for little Elsa, so I talked to Mrs. Janson, who said she'd look after the girl, and in the evening Matti said he'd take care of Elsa if Mrs. Janson couldn't do it, at least in the evenings, since she was his daughter after all. And that was reassuring, even though I knew the child would be anxious while I was away. Then Matt said he and Elsa would come down to St. Paul after everything had been settled, and then we'd see what would happen next. And that made me feel happy and reassured.

The train trip was the worst part because I'd put on the black clothes I still had from Carl's funeral, and they fit me more or less, though I had to alter them a little. Mrs. Janson helped me with that. But when people see that you're in mourning, they act in a certain way, and that creates an uncomfortable atmosphere. I sat next to the window and looked out, thinking about Father, and I had the strange feeling that he would still be there when I arrived, even though the reason I was on that train at all was because he was gone, and then I cried.

When I got to Union Depot, Ellen was waiting for me, and I hadn't seen her since Carl's funeral. Her hair was cut short now, and she was wearing a dress that was much too light in color, and she looked at me and said, "The funeral isn't until the day after tomorrow." "I know that," I told her, "but these are the black garments I had, so I decided to wear them." And in a strange way it felt good to bicker with her, because then things seemed normal.

Father was going to be laid to rest in the Oakland Cemetery next to little Carl. The cross had long since vanished from Carl's grave, but we knew where he was buried, and when we asked Pastor Sandstrom whether it could be arranged, he said he'd take care of things, and the very next day he told us it would be fine. So much time had now passed that the gravesites there were once again available for use. I don't remember the whole funeral, because by then everything had become dark and prickly, and it was something we just had to get through; they say you're supposed to say goodbye, and that's right, you do, but at that moment you can't bear to pause long enough to remember things very well. Ellen and I had to take care of Mother, who was withdrawn and silent and kept looking down at her hands, and it was almost like she wasn't really there. I remembered how it had been at Carl's funeral and left her in peace. But back then it was winter and horribly cold. Out at the Oakland Cemetery, on the other hand, it was a beautiful summer afternoon. The grave itself was in the shade of a hedge, but the sun shone down on the rest of us as we stood in a circle. Mother repeated the words of the blessing, but I saw that Ellen did not; she stood there staring straight ahead as Pastor Sandstrom prayed in his quavering old-man's voice. I thought he'd gotten awfully stooped and gray, yet I was still a little afraid of him.

Afterward we were supposed to take taxis back, even though it wasn't very far, and Ellen was going to pay the cab fares, and the whole thing seemed so odd. But when we were sitting next to each other in the back of the open automobile, I told Ellen that I was glad that at least Father would be lying next to little Carl. I didn't mean that I was actually "glad," and Ellen gave me a strange look, but then she said she'd been thinking the same thing, that now they'd be together somehow, and she was going to see about getting a real headstone put up this time, and she'd make sure that Carl's name was on it too, because he couldn't be very far from where Father was buried. I got a little worried that she'd start talking about money again, but she didn't. It was strange to see that just as we were leaving the cemetery, the next funeral procession was arriving with a coffin on an open cart and with black-clad mourners following behind. There was no end to such things.

The funeral reception was going to be held at the home of Inga and Jonathan, who'd taken over the arrangements because Mother just couldn't do it, and besides, there was no room at her house. Pastor Sandstrom came with us to the Hollow and stayed fifteen minutes or so in Inga's kitchen before he thanked us and left. I thought that was nice of him; he was one person who didn't hesitate to come down to the Hollow when needed, but I didn't want to talk to him because he might remember me and then he might ask whether I'd heard anything about what had happened to Leonard, and I hadn't, so it was just as well not to say anything at all. After the pastor left, it was easier to talk. The strange thing about grief is that it comes and goes; you can be talking as usual with people and then it comes back and you stop in the middle of a sentence and can hardly breathe and you can't speak at all. But after Pastor Sandstrom left, only folks from the Hollow were there; everybody knew each other, and if someone started to cry or looked down at the table and didn't say anything for a long while, nobody got upset, because they all knew how it was. Some of Father's Irish and Italian coworkers were there too; we didn't talk much to them, but when they were about to leave, they came over and squeezed hands and looked us in the eye. I've always thought the Irish are good at dealing with death; they know how to behave in the face of grief. The Italians also knew what was the correct thing to do, even though they'd probably never been to a Swedish funeral before. Maybe Catholics are better at things like that.

Jonathan thanked them in English and shook their hands when they left. The whole time Mother sat with her hands on her lap and stared straight ahead; lots of people tried to talk to her, but she would just nod and say only a word or two in reply. Finally it got to be too much, and Inga took Mother by the arm and walked with her back to our house. I followed them a few minutes later, but then Inga came out and told me, "She's sleeping, she was completely exhausted, the poor thing. And I don't know what's to become of Anna now."

When she said that, I went to find Ellen and then the three of us sat on the porch of Jonathan and Inga's house, with a view across the Hollow. Someone was singing in the twilight; it sounded like the song was coming from where the Italians lived, and it was a tune I had never heard sung in the Hollow, although Inga didn't seem surprised, so she must have been used to hearing it. "That's Old Man Sanchelli," she said. "He sings the same stanza every evening when he comes home from work, at precisely eight o'clock. You could set your watch by him."

*America, America,*
*God shed his grace on thee,*
*And crown thy good*
*With brotherhood*
*From sea to shining sea*

When the singing stopped, I said what I'd been thinking: that I could come back to the Hollow for a while and live with Mother, to make sure she was doing all right, and maybe Inga knew of someplace I might find work, either cleaning or laundry washing. Times were bad up in Duluth. And Inga said they were bad down here too, but she could probably find me something if she took some time to look around. "What about little Elsa?" asked Ellen, and I said that she and Matt would come down on the train after I'd arranged things and we had somewhere to live. "And you two are still not married," said Ellen brusquely, but I didn't get mad. I just said that we'd talked about getting married, but it wouldn't work because nobody knew where Leonard was, and if we couldn't get hold of him and it was impossible to prove that he was dead, then I couldn't remarry because that would be *bigamy.* That made her laugh a little, for the first time in a long while, and she said that of course she didn't want her sister to be a *bigamist.* Matt had nothing against trying to find work in the Twin Cities. His family had come over after the civil war in Finland, and he'd worked in the forests. Then he ended up in Duluth after he got blacklisted by the sawmills farther north, and he was forced to move in with his parents across the courtyard. "I know he's a good man," said

Ellen without looking me in the eye, and Inga nodded silently as she sat there in the shadow, even though she hadn't met Matt. After Inga had been sitting there without speaking for a while, she mentioned something else that she'd clearly wanted to tell us, but she'd been waiting for the right time to bring it up. Next month David Lundgren was going to be released from Stillwater prison after serving out his sentence, and he would be coming to live with them.

There was another matter I wanted to talk to Ellen about, but not while Inga was there. I could tell my sister was getting ready to head back home to her husband and children because she'd started fumbling with her handbag, so I said I'd like us to take a little walk first, and then I'd accompany her part way up to the streetcar stop. She looked a little surprised, but she couldn't very well say no. First we went down to Phalen Creek, but she said it smelled so bad this time of year and she was afraid the smell would settle in her clothes. So instead we went over to the Drewry Tunnel and then up to the open space below the Hamm Brewery, at the top of the Hollow. We didn't talk much; I suppose we were both thinking about Father. Ellen told me about the times she and Father used to walk up to Seventh Street together, back when she was still working as a seamstress at the factory on Margaret Street, and then they would go their separate ways at the top of the stairs. I wondered whether she held it against me that I hadn't been able to do the work as well as she did, but there was no trace of reproach in her voice; she just wanted to talk about Father, the way she remembered him, and so I listened. But finally she said, "What was it you wanted to talk to me about, without Inga?"

"Mother has gotten so small," I said. "Have you noticed that?" Ellen nodded and just looked at me. "She won't be able to take care of herself much longer," I went on. "Without Father, she's going to get smaller for every day that goes by."

"She has Inga," said Ellen, and she had that set look on her face, but I knew she understood what I meant. "Inga. Yes, well," I said. "I can see that things are getting worse for her now, even though she pretends everything is fine. But Inga doesn't get out much anymore. She still keeps an eye on what's going on, but the question is how long she'll be able to do that. She has her girls and Jonathan." And then I decided to be blunt. "But I don't know how long her strength will hold out. Haven't you noticed all the worried looks Jonathan keeps giving her?"

Ellen looked as if I'd hit her. It wasn't pleasant thinking that Inga might not be there forever, but I thought Ellen knew what I was getting at.

Finally I said what was on my mind. "I'm going to come home and make sure they can all manage. I'll bring Matt with me, and he's a reliable sort. We'll take care of things. I just want you to know that everything will be all right, and I'll stay with Mother until we find our own place."

Ellen stood still for moment, without replying. Then she said, "So you're saying you want to come back here? To the Hollow?" It sounded like she didn't believe me.

"Yes," I said. "This is where I'm from, and I know how things are in the Hollow. So why shouldn't I live here? Somebody has to take charge, and it might as well be me, since I know how things work."

Ellen looked relieved, as if she'd been expecting to hear something else.

"You'll do that?" she said. "Will you really do that?"

I nodded, and it was as if she stood up straighter in her expensive black suit with the mourning veil on the hat and her shiny shoes. Then she took my hand in both of hers and held it for a moment. In the distance we heard the two signals from the Duluth train as it approached the railroad tunnels down by Connemara, and as we stood there I thought I was going to have trouble getting used to that sound again.

"I'll come and visit all of you," said Ellen.

"Yes, do that," I said.

"To see if there's anything you need," she said.

"Yes," I said. "I know you'll do that."

Then she squeezed my hand and let go and headed for the Drewry Tunnel. She turned around right before entering the vaulted arch to go up to the street, and maybe she was thinking of saying something, but at that moment the train gave the two warning signals, so she just shook her head and left. Then she was gone. Maybe you could say it was then and there that we parted for good, but I think both she and I knew that even if she showed up again on a few occasions, she had long ago put the Hollow behind her forever.

## *Swede Hollow*
## June 1935

THEY WERE WHISPERING to Anna from the edge of the woods; they were in there somewhere, in the dim light beneath the trees on the slope up toward Dayton's Bluff, those familiar, comforting voices. Inga was there, and Gustaf, her mother, and Carl, her own Carl, still seven years old; he never said anything, but sometimes she might catch a glimpse of him running between the trees. She liked to sit there on the bench in the evening, and suddenly she'd hear a few words, part of a sentence carried toward her on a gust of wind or simply echoing among the tree trunks, which were still lit by the sun. What they said was rarely important; it was the sound of the familiar voices that made her feel calm. She thought they probably had a lot of other things to talk about now, things she couldn't even comprehend. About that other place, and what went on up there beyond the cliff. She imagined it as a grand celebration, but with serene and somber people. Yet it was all very hazy, even in her own mind.

Lately she'd been feeling oddly fragile. She blamed herself for that; she ought to be able to muster her strength and attempt to climb the slope a short distance, to follow the sound of their voices upward through the trees. Maybe they were actually standing there waiting for her, and if she didn't hurry up, they might grow tired and disappear one day, and there would be only silence even when the wind blew. Then it wouldn't matter how hard she strained to listen as she sat on the bench in the evening, because there would no longer be any echoes to hear.

They would probably stay for a while longer, but she couldn't climb that high anymore. She'd never been good at such things, and it had been a long time since she'd ventured out of the Hollow. One day she'd pull herself together and make another attempt—before it was too late.

But sometimes she could hear them when the wind blew from that direction, though only a word here and there. She could only make out the tone of voice, which was always so soothing. They were there, and they seemed to be talking about wondrous things, though using perfectly ordinary phrases. And she could no longer follow.

"Golden," said Gustaf. She thought that's what he said. "Yes," said

Inga. That much she was convinced she'd heard. Then she'd stop listening so closely for a while, and when she tried again, they were silent. But then she caught a glimpse of Carl's shirt, just a flash of white between the tree trunks; it was the soft shirt he'd liked so much, and for that reason it had been hard to keep clean. The shirt was a little too big for him, and it actually still existed, carefully washed and ironed and lying at the bottom of the big suitcase at home. But she hadn't looked at it for a very long time.

Then Anna thought about the fact that when she was gone, no one would be able to hear them anymore. And that made her sad.

She was sitting there on the bench, lost in her own thoughts, when one of the younger girls came and took her by the arm. It was warm, and the sun shone in her face, so she couldn't really tell who it was. Maybe Elisabet's oldest daughter. Or maybe Inga's. They were so big now, and so alike. The girl smiled and helped her off the bench so she stood upright. "They're here, Mother Anna," said the girl. "And they're going to sing now. We thought you'd like to come and listen. We know it's something you like."

She could have said, *I want to stay here and listen to the ones up on the hill.* But she decided to go along. "Can I go dressed like this?" she asked, smoothing down her black skirt. "It's fine," said the girl, who then held her arm as they walked down the path. The Hollow was green in the warmth of early summer. There were more bushes and vegetation than she remembered from before; otherwise everything looked the same.

Members of the Swedish Salvation Army had taken up position on the open space below Inga's house. There were five of them, both men and women, with a trumpet, guitars, and a drum. People had begun to gather, curious, circling around, hovering a short distance away—Swedes and Italians and Poles. More were coming up the path from the bottom of the Hollow.

Then they began to play, singing in Swedish. *Säg känner du det underbara namnet* and *O Store Gud.* The girl sat down next to her on the bench outside Inga's house where a young Polish couple with four children now lived. Sometimes Anna wondered whether they knew that Inga was the actual owner of the house. She had papers to prove it. But there was no use making a fuss. At least that family let them sit here. She closed her eyes for a while and let the sun play over her eyelids. Red and black. Then she looked up again and her gaze fell on the young soldiers who were singing with open, smiling faces. One of the girls seemed to her strangely familiar, and she raised her hand to shade her eyes as she squinted. The young woman felt Anna's eyes on her, so she turned toward her and smiled as she kept singing and strummed her guitar. When their eyes met, Anna knew.

It was definitely Lieutenant Gustafsson. But what she couldn't understand was how the girl could still look so young and unmarked, with a childishly plump face, rosy cheeks, and curly hair sticking out from under her bonnet. Anna pondered this for a while and then grew tired again. She closed her eyes and allowed the music to carry her as Elisabet's or Inga's daughter held her hand. It was warm, and yet she was freezing. She was there and yet she wasn't. *This is me. Anna.* It was time to go now. She had lingered too long, but now it was time. *I'll enter, Lord, to dwell in peace with thee.*

*Swede Hollow*
December 1956

IT WAS NOT A REAL WINTER. Snow lay in scattered patches on the withered-yellow lawns in the neighborhood. All November and December the temperature had hovered around the thirty degree mark. Snow fell and melted away, then lingered when the sun didn't shine. Yet Ellen could tell that she wasn't dressed warmly enough; her long poplin coat wasn't sufficient to keep out the cold entirely. She'd parked the car up on Margaret Street and then walked the rest of the way toward what remained of the Hamm mansion. The site was no longer cordoned off, and she thought it would be safe to go in. Most of the structure still stood there, and if you drove past in the evening—which she'd done more times than she was willing to admit, even to herself—you might convince yourself it was still intact. Until, that is, you saw the evening sky between the splayed and charred beams of what had once been the peculiar tower. Now, in full daylight, Ellen saw how the windows had shattered and the brick walls were covered with soot. For several decades the house had been a home for invalids, and when the last inhabitants were moved out, the place had stood empty for a year. Then a teenage arsonist had done his best to level the building to the ground, using a can of gasoline and a cigarette lighter. Rumor had it that when the fire engines arrived, he was standing in front of the burning house and singing hymns at the top of his lungs.

Ellen climbed over what was left of the collapsed fence and stepped onto the lawn, which was now a meadow that no one had bothered to mow in years. The grass stood three feet high in frost-covered clumps that brushed against her legs. When she was a child, she was deathly afraid of venturing onto this very lawn, and she'd kept an eye out for the Hamm watchdogs. Her eyes automatically settled on the flowerbed where her enchanting glass balls had once lain, but there was now no trace of either plants or ornaments. Nothing but grass and piles of charred wood below the gaping window frames. An acrid smell of smoke and rotting wood still hung in the air.

The stench instantly carried her back to Ellis Island and memories of the fire that had haunted her through so many nights, when she would wake up and think she could smell smoke from the burning wood. When that happened, the only thing that would help was to get up and light a cigarette until the smell went away. She didn't have to actually smoke the cigarette; she could simply let it burn out in the ashtray. Then she'd be able to go back to bed.

The big wrought iron fence facing the slope was gone, replaced by a lower one made of wood, which was leaning precariously. She went as close as she could and looked down at the Hollow.

The view was better than she'd dared hope: the trees on the slope were wintertime bare, allowing her an unobstructed view across the Hollow, even down to the open space in front of the Drewry Tunnel. Through the trees she glimpsed their own house way down, on the left, with its sunken tar paper roof. Inga's house stood where it had always stood, a little farther up, towering over the other shanties on its stone foundation. The only thing she didn't recognize was the small white trailer off to the side and behind Inga's house; it had been hauled there and adorned with a whitewashed crucifix on the roof. She realized it must be some sort of simple chapel. The widow Lundgren's old house, where Elisabet and Matt had lived during the years they spent in the Hollow before finally returning north, was already gone. She could see no trace of it at the spot where it had once stood, right across from Inga's house. A lot had happened in the fifteen years since she'd last paid a visit down there.

She hadn't heard from her sister in a year, but she knew they still lived just north of Two Harbors, where Matt had opened a carpentry shop, which he still ran even though he was getting on in years. They had never wanted to go back to Duluth.

Below, the fire department was on the scene. Men in protective dark overalls were moving insect-like among the houses. She could see a pair of big hoses winding their way out of the opening to the Drewry Tunnel; they were no doubt hooked up to the only fire hydrant up on Beaumont Street. She knew exactly where it stood. But at the moment the firemen were walking around with small spray canisters, drenching the house walls with what was presumably gasoline or some other flammable substance, although she couldn't yet smell it from where she stood.

A crowd had gathered on the small ledge above the Drewry Tunnel on the other side of the Hollow. When she looked around, she saw that she was the only one on this side. She wondered whether any of the people over there were among the Hollow's last inhabitants who had now come to watch their houses go up in flame and smoke. No, they were probably just curiosity seekers from the neighborhood up on Railroad Island. Nobody would want to see their own home burn.

And yet she was here. According to yesterday's *Minneapolis Tribune,* the last residents had been fifty or so Mexican seasonal workers who had since moved into what the paper described as "decent housing." She assumed it was their little chapel she saw behind Inga's house; it too was about to go up in smoke. The *Tribune* had reported that the city's health department had "discovered" that people were still living in the Hollow, and that Phalen Creek was "contaminated" with E. coli. The words had filled Ellen with a fury she couldn't put into words. Nor could she explain how she felt to Sol, who had thought her anger over a newspaper article so comical that he'd laughed until his mirth dissolved into another, menacing coughing fit.

Down below, the firemen were moving back and forth, seemingly at random. Some of them even climbed up the slope to the open space below the Hamm Brewery, where they stopped to have a smoke, and she found herself sadistically hoping they'd catch fire and melt like tin soldiers.

She had clearly arrived much too early and briefly pondered whether she really wanted to wait around in the cold. But she stayed where she was. Sol had told her he'd be fine on his own, gesturing toward the living room. He had the TV and his *Sports Illustrated,* and the respirator was within reach. If he wanted a beer, he could manage to drag himself to the kitchen. When Ellen closed the front door behind her and went out to the car, she could practically feel his sense of contentment reaching her through the wall of the house. He enjoyed his time alone, even though he would never admit it. "We didn't get married so you could be my nurse," he'd sputtered one evening when they were having one of their arguments, which were rare these days.

It was December, and darkness had started to fall over the houses on the other side when the firemen finally decided it was time. Maybe they'd been waiting for dark. One of them held what looked to be a tar-covered torch, which he now lit with a cigarette lighter. Then he walked from house to house and made sure the fire caught hold on the paneling's crosscut timber. When he got to Inga's house, Ellen felt her pulse quicken as her throat constricted. At first she thought the whole thing was going to be a failure, since it took time for the fire to seize hold of the old wood. She thought about how damp the wood must be from decades of persistent autumn rains, which always managed to seep through the loose tar paper and fall in steady streams onto the cast-iron stove.

Then the first big flames appeared, licking around the corner of Inga's house far below. When Ellen turned her head, she could see how the fire had already reached the roof ridge of their own house. Suddenly she heard inside herself the sound of melting spring snow dripping from the eaves at daybreak, a sound that had often awakened her and Elisabet as they lay freezing in their too-short beds. (And she recalled, in a sudden flash of memory, the way her sister would wedge her cold feet between her own warm ones, which always made her give Elisabet a punch on the shoulder, though that never woke her.)

At first the fire moved slowly. But then it was as if the flames had worked their way through the winter-damp exterior of the wooden façade and reached the dry core. She stood and watched as the roof of their own house abruptly fell in, and new, yellow flames shot out through the remaining beams. Then the walls collapsed in a cloud of sparks and white smoke. *That was that,* she thought.

The firemen had gone over to the water-filled hoses and stood ready in case they might need to limit the spread of the fire. But from what Ellen understood, there was nothing in the Hollow that would be spared: even the *contamination* would be burned away, and the last shameful area of the city would be cleansed through fire.

As she stood there, she wished she'd had her grown children here to show them the spectacle. Not because she wanted their company, but so she could say vengefully, *Now it's too late.* They had never visited the Hollow. In the beginning she was the one who had kept them away, as she now acknowledged. Later, when she had in fact wanted to show them some of the area, they hadn't displayed the slightest interest. And by then everyone they might have known was gone. She didn't really blame them.

Carl might have come with her if she'd asked him; he was nice and was willing to humor her impulses if he was in the mood. But he now lived in Phoenix, for the sake of the climate. She had many times greatly regretted continuing the name, sullied as it was with death. Sol hadn't objected, though he insisted the boy should be given the double name of Carl Abraham, and that was what happened. But nobody called him anything but Carl. Not her, not Sol. His classmates had made a valiant attempt to nickname him Charlie, but it never caught on. He'd continued to be called simply Carl. If only she'd known how alike he would look as a child to her dead little brother, so alike that she sometimes feared what she'd done by giving him the same name. In 1942, when he'd disappeared in the Pacific, she was certain that she'd given him a curse that would be the death of him. When she found out that he'd been wounded in some strange place called Guadalcanal, she'd sat up all night in the dark living room, silently begging him for forgiveness. But he came back home with a Purple Heart, his arm in a sling, and a wound that never properly healed. It continued to torment him through several long Minnesota winters until his wife, Ruth, convinced him that they should move to dry, hot Arizona. After that they met mostly for Thanksgiving and sometimes Christmas. But these days Sol had a hard time handling long car rides.

Ellen had never managed to get AnnaBeth to come to the Hollow, no matter how hard she'd tried. The very idea of her mother's foreign origins frightened her.

Now the cluster of houses below was in flames, and the sound of the fire reached all the way up to where she was standing. A hot wind gusted up the slope, making the bare tree branches sway; all around her the frost on the grass was slowly melting. As she watched, the roof of Inga's house silently fell in and the walls began to lean. The small white trailer chapel was also burning, with a thicker black smoke that swirled up to her, making her eyes fill with tears.

All of a sudden she wondered what she was doing there, so she turned on her heel and left. As she fumbled for the car keys in her pocket, she saw the light from the fire flicker over the soot-covered brick façade of what had once been the Hamm mansion. When she got beyond the hot fiery wind coming from the Hollow, she realized how cold she was and began hurrying toward Margaret Street and into the white glow of the streetlights.

Yet she sat in her car for a long time, watching the light from the fire in her rearview mirror.

She was pondering one thing that she couldn't forget, something that slowly worked its way forward through all those years until it was no longer hidden away but emerged as a truth about her life. If a diffident and unassuming man by the name of David Lundgren, more than seventy years ago, hadn't become insanely obsessed with the equally reserved Agnes Karin, none of them might have ended up where they did and lived the lives they had. Those were the circumstances she'd pieced together from what people told her; it was the letter from Jonathan Lundgren to his mother back in Sweden that had set everything in motion toward this particular spot on the map. She no longer really remembered how any of them looked. They weren't even related. But there was no getting around the fact that it was because of them that she now sat here in a freezing car on a dark backstreet, waiting for that idea to once again settle in her mind, the way a cat curls up and falls asleep on the living room sofa.

Finally she turned the key in the ignition and pulled away from the curb, heading down Seventh Street toward University Avenue, which would take her into Minneapolis and across the river at Hennepin to Lyndale and toward their home in Edina on the other side of the city. She could no longer remember where the glass balls had ended up. But in the back of her mind, and at any time, she could still hear the soothing, dry, squeaking sound they used to make.

## *Swede Hollow*
## June 2007

DURING LUNCH BREAK he went to get his bicycle parked outside the university building and put on his helmet, lemon yellow and brand new. It was a present from Judy, and he'd promised her that he'd wear it from now on. A cloud-free sky and a light breeze from the river. He took Midway down toward Como Park, pedaling fast on his Trek Domane bike with the graphite-gray aluminum frame. Today he wanted to feel the speed.

He took a short cut through the park's open, grassy areas until he reached the bike path, which he usually took all the way around the lake. When he came out on Como Boulevard again, he was starting to sweat, and the tracks on the railroad crossing made the thin, hard tires of his bike rattle so much that his whole body vibrated and he laughed out loud. A few workshops and low wooden houses flew past on both sides.

He'd calculated it would take him about half an hour in each direction, but now he realized that had been optimistic. He wouldn't make it back in time for the afternoon meeting. But he kept on pedaling through the early summer heat. They'd probably be annoyed whether he came in late and sweaty or didn't show up at all; it was too nice a day to sit inside, and he'd given himself a specific task to carry out.

He biked along the sidewalk of Phalen Boulevard for quite a ways; it was almost one o'clock and the heat was starting to feel unbearable. He hadn't brought any water with him. He looked around for a neighborhood store but didn't see any nearby, so he decided to keep going.

Then he turned onto the Bruce Vento Trail, leaving the traffic behind. The bike path veered away from the street, taking him down a steep hill and through the greenery. He passed the old railroad viaduct below Phalen Boulevard and suddenly everything fell quiet. The road now followed what was previously the Duluth train embankment, and unpruned foliage and bushes reached out over the pavement. He slowed down and kept to the shady side. From Minnehaha Avenue high overhead came the sound of traffic, muted and faraway, as if he were underwater.

Now it was downhill the whole way. Farther down the hill he saw what had been the Hamm Brewery, long since shut down, with its enormous smokestack. He released the brakes and let the bike carry him until he came to the open space where the path split. That's where he stopped, unsure which way to go.

He hadn't set foot in the Hollow since he was a child. This morning he'd prepared for the excursion by studying a bike map, and he was still thinking it would be easy to find his way. But he hadn't remembered how big the Hollow was, and he had no idea where his family's house had once stood. He recalled his great-aunt holding his hand and pointing urgently, *There.* But it had been winter back then, and he'd seen only trees.

It didn't matter now. Nowhere in the Hollow was there any remaining trace of human habitation. The place looked the way you might picture an area of untamed nature.

He biked a little farther until he heard from below the murmur of Phalen Creek, where the water, almost invisible, flowed between the shrubbery covering the slopes. Sweat ran down into his eyes, and he was very thirsty. He unfastened his bike helmet and wiped his forehead.

For a second he felt discouraged, as if the whole expedition had been a mistake, some sort of half-baked idea. Yet even this morning he'd pictured it all so clearly: this was an important task for him. He didn't know why, and it was probably just for his own sake, but he'd made the decision, and now here he was. He looked around. He seemed to be all alone in the Hollow; the sun was blazing down on him from its zenith. Then he cleared his throat and shouted as loud as he could, "Ancestors of mine!"

The sound of his own voice echoed across the slope.

"I'm here to tell you something important: I want you to know that Judy and I are going to have our first child in September . . ."

He looked around. The Hollow was still quiet.

"And we want you to know . . ."

Silence.

"That without you, we wouldn't be here."

That was what he'd spent all day preparing to say. Then he stood there without moving, as if actually expecting some sort of reply. A gust of wind suddenly blew through the tall trees along the slope up toward Dayton's Bluff. Did that count? When did he get so superstitious?

No one came. Everything remained quiet. Not even the sound of traffic penetrated through the dense foliage. He stood there with his solemn words, no longer certain of their purpose.

Then he put the sweaty helmet back on and got on his bike. Without really knowing why, he raised his hand in a formal greeting toward the bushes and woods, released the brake, and continued rolling down the hill, into the shade of the leafy tunnel. Halfway down, he decided to pick up speed, and he pedaled as hard as he could until he saw the two big railroad tunnels open before him at the end of the Hollow. He raced inside their cellar-like darkness and cold, shouting a loud, *AHHhhhhhh*!!! just to hear the echo fill the air around him. Then he rode up the small incline on the other side, reached the sunshine on Seventh Street, and disappeared into the traffic.

# Author's Note

Swede Hollow is a glacial ravine barely two-thirds of a mile long in St. Paul's old northeastern district; it was literally a hole in the ground. Today this East Side neighborhood is wonderfully diverse, including many Hmong and Somali immigrants, and surrounds the Hollow with small shops and restaurants. There are also plenty of traces of the Italian inhabitants, such as the classic Yarusso-Bros. Italian Restaurant. But few visible signs remain of the earlier strong Swedish presence other than the place name of Swede Hollow.

The American census records, as well as Swedish church records, show that well into the twentieth century about a thousand people lived in the Hollow, and most of them listed Sweden as their birthplace. The area around Payne Avenue and Railroad Island also had a large Swedish population. There is only one Swedish written account from Swede Hollow, authored by Nels Hokanson and published in the winter 1969 issue of the Minnesota Historical Society's magazine.

The situation is much the same regarding the Swedes who landed in New York during the late nineteenth century. By 1900, there were approximately fifty thousand immigrants from Sweden in New York, including a group living on the Lower East Side. We know very little about them other than the fact that they existed.

In St. Paul the descendants of Italian immigrants were significantly better at documenting their history. In the archives of the Minnesota Historical Society (MNHS) the memoirs of Mike Sanchelli (1915–2003) make for fascinating reading. He too grew up in Swede Hollow. But when it comes to the poorest of the Swedish immigrants, there is a great gap in the research and historical accounts. I am very grateful to all the researchers and archivists who helped us to locate nearly all the facts available about life in the Hollow. The three newspaper articles about Swede Hollow from the *St. Paul Daily Globe* that appear in this book are actual articles, reprinted here close to their original form with only a few deletions and changes.

First and foremost, I thank Dag Blanck at the Swedish Institute for North American Studies at Uppsala University for guiding me so kindly and patiently through the available research about the Swedish presence in Minnesota. Along with his colleague Phil Anderson, Dag has published the excellent anthology *Swedes in the Twin Cities* (2001), which features many essays about "those at the bottom." Karna Anderson has ancestors who lived in the Hollow, and the Anderson family (Phil, Karna, Erik, and Kajsa) generously gave me access to their family photographs and to their genealogical research.

One of the few scholars to take an interest in Swede Hollow is David Lanegran, professor emeritus in geography at Macalester College in St. Paul. In the 1960s, he interviewed several people of Swedish heritage who had grown up in the Hollow, and he allowed me to make use of their accounts.

Another scholar who has dug into the often dark and suppressed aspects of the Swedish migration to Minnesota is the historian Roger McKnight, professor emeritus at Gustavus Adolphus College in St. Peter, Minnesota. In his book *Severed Ties and Silenced Voices* (2009), he writes about prisoners and crime among Swedish immigrants. The book provided background for my story about David and Agnes Karin, and Roger drew my attention to the stories about Ola Värmlänning.

The prominent composer Ann Millikan has written an entire opera about the different ethnic groups that once called Swede Hollow their home.

Joy K. Lintelman, historian and professor at Concordia College in Moorhead, Minnesota, has conducted research on Swedish female workers who emigrated to the United States. In her notable book *I Go to America* (2012), Lintelman writes about Minna Anderson, one of the sources for Vilhelm Moberg's acclaimed series *The Emigrants.* For my description of work at Klinkenfuer's (one of the better clothing factories in St. Paul) and other workplaces for women in the late nineteenth and early twentieth centuries, I made use of an excellent article by Mary C. Bader in the spring 2006 issue of the Minnesota Historical Society magazine. Bader also discusses labor unions and the way that unions in Minnesota were fought and more or less crushed—a story that is recounted in detail in *A Union against Unions* by William Millikan (2003). The involvement of Swedes in the union struggles is further discussed in historian Jimmy Engren's *Railroading and Labor Migration* (2007). In her autobiographical essay "Amerika-minnen" (1930), immigrant Evelina Månsson writes about workplaces like the Phoenix Building in Minneapolis and describes how an employee might use a typewriter at night.

The horrifying story about the murders that occurred in Duluth on June 15, 1920, when several Swedes took part in the lynching of Isaac

McGhie, Elias Clayton, and Elmer Jackson, is described in detail on the Minnesota Historical Society website (www.mnhs.org), which includes all the documentation, court records, and police interrogations. I tried to relate the course of events as accurately as possible. More background can be found in Warren Read's book *The Lyncher in Me* (2008).

I would not have been able to write this novel without the help of people who live in Minnesota. The author Larry Millett, an expert on the history of St. Paul, took time to guide us through the city's historic district and answer many questions from a novice. Bruce Karstadt, head of the American Swedish Institute (ASI) in Minneapolis, helped us to find access to the lesser known parts of the history of Swedish migration and put the ASI archives at our disposal. ASI board member William Beyer provided us with additional details.

A big thank you to the Swedish Academy, whose financial support made it possible for me to do on-site research.

The Minnesota Historical Society in St. Paul is in many ways a model for general education and publicly available archives. The staff at MNHS and at the Gale Family Library answered many strange questions, including how to do impossible searches in various census records. (The people who lived in the Hollow had no addresses, so how could they be located?) I offer special thanks to Debbie Miller, the patient librarian who knows everything.

We also received great help from kind archivists at the Bethesda Hospital in St. Paul, which was founded to provide care to the city's poorest citizens, including those living in the Hollow; and from Trinity Baptist Church (formerly the First Swedish Baptist Church) and the First Lutheran Church (formerly the First Evangelical Lutheran Swedish Church), both in St. Paul.

We have been treated to the greatest hospitality. I especially thank Karen and Doug McElrath. Doug managed to do the impossible and actually got me interested in baseball.

Melba Gustafson passed away in 2014, but it was when we met her in 2006 that I encountered the first traces of Swede Hollow in a small exhibition at the American Swedish Institute.

When I say *we* and *our,* I am referring, of course, to my wife, Rita, who with her knowledge and contacts in Minnesota helped me all along the way to dig up what facts could be found. Without her, this book would never have come into being, since it was due to her that we landed in the Twin Cities at all.

Finally, I don't think I need to point out that this is a novel. The Klar family, Inga Norström, David and Jonathan Lundgren, and the others never existed. Many aspects of this story about life in Swede Hollow are fiction, but the experiences are real, and real people lived there.

As I write this, a debate is under way in St. Paul about whether to lay new streetcar tracks on the old Duluth line that passes through the Hollow (today it is a bike path). This would bring more life and people back to the Hollow, yet it would burst the invisible bubble surrounding the area that now seems to exist outside time. Today, Swede Hollow is a strange, overgrown park with no trace of human habitation, a place that humans seem to have left behind. I'm not the only one to be fascinated by the peculiar silence in the Hollow. But the silence there is stretched taut over a chorus of voices from the past. I have tried my best, and with great respect, to summon a few of them.

*Ola Larsmo*
*Uppsala–St. Paul*
*2012–16*

OLA LARSMO is a Swedish novelist, critic, and journalist. He has written more than twenty books, including *En glänta i skogen* (A Glen in the Forest) and *Förrädare* (Traitors). He has been editor of *Bonnier's Literary Magazine* and a columnist for Sweden's largest newspaper, *Dagens Nyheter,* and he served as president of PEN in Sweden from 2009 until 2017. He received the Bjørnson Prize from the Norwegian Academy of Literature and Freedom of Expression, and in 2018 he was awarded the Kulturpris from Natur & Kultur, one of Sweden's most prestigious cultural awards.

TIINA NUNNALLY is an award-winning translator of Swedish, Norwegian, and Danish. Her numerous translations include works by Tove Ditlevsen, Jens Peter Jacobsen, Per Olov Enquist, and Dag Solstad. Her translation of *Kristin Lavransdatter III: The Cross* by Sigrid Undset won the PEN/Book-of-the-Month Club Translation Prize. She is the translator of Vidar Sundstøl's Minnesota Trilogy and his novel, *The Devil's Wedding Ring,* as well as Sigrid Undset's *Marta Oulie,* all published by the University of Minnesota Press.

COLLINS ST.
NORTH
HOPKINS
BRUND ST.
PARTRIDGE
WOODWARD
GROVE
WESTMINSTER ST.
ARKWRIGHT
RIVOLI
AVE.
BRIDGE
LAFAYETTE
DE SOTO
BURR
BRADLEY
MADISON
MONROE
ST.
LOCUST
TENTH
NINTH
EIGHTH
SEVENTH
SIXTH
JOHN
OLIVE
PINE
WILLIUS
NEILL
KITTSON
BROOK
6TH ST.
LAFAYETTE PARK
HOME FOR THE FRIENDLESS
COLLINS SUB.
LINCOLN SCHOOL
DAWSONS SUB.
J.W. BASS SUB.
J.W. BASS ADD. OF OUT LOTS
BOHRERS ADD.
GRAY & COBBS SUB
SCHURMEIERS SUB
BASS SUB
GREAT NORTHERN
NORTHERN PACIFIC R.R.
ST. PRES. CHURCH
WASHINGTON SCHOOL
STEAM LAUNDRY
ST. PAUL GAS LIGHT CO.
NOYES BROS. AND CUTLER WAREHOUSE
ST. PAUL WHITE LEAD OIL CO.
WILD BLOCK
SWED. LUTH. CHURCH
STE. MARIE R.R.